MW00761410

BLEEDING HEARTS

Happy Reading,
Marge!!
♡ Ash K

BLEEDING HEARTS

BOOK ONE OF THE DEMIMONDE

ASH KRAFTON

PINK NARCISSUS
PRESS

This is a work of fiction. All the characters and events portrayed in this book are fictitious or are used fictitiously.

BLEEDING HEARTS

Design by Duncan Eagleson
Cover photo © 2010 Moira Ashleigh

Published by Pink Narcissus Press
P.O. Box 303
Auburn, MA 01501
www.pinknarc.com

Library of Congress Control Number: 2011960011

ISBN: 978-0-9829913-6-7

First trade paperback edition: March 2012.

Dear Sophie,

From the moment I first read your column,
I knew you were special. Other columnists
just do a job but you put your heart into
every letter. I could tell you truly care for
your readers.

That's why it hurts so much to realize you
let me down. You knew I wasn't strong enough
to face my own fear. All you had to do was
reach out, grab my hand, pull me back from
that ledge.

But you didn't. You let me fall.
Why did I deserve to be abandoned by the
one person who could have helped me?

Signed,
Forever Lost in Balaton

Lifestyle

Dear Sophie

Bouquet Blues

Dear Sophie;

I was delighted to be asked to be a bridesmaid
at my BFF's wedding, and even more delighted
when I caught the bride's bouquet. But after
the reception, the bride's mother came and
demanded it back. She said they had paid for
it, and my friend wanted it as a keepsake.

Is this normal? I always assumed if you
caught the bouquet, you kept it.

Confused

PART I

"Well, Sophie, you've been busy." My editor placed the typed sheets on her desk and pushed her reading glasses to the top of her head, smiling in a way that suggested she wasn't simply commenting on my productivity.

Barbara Evans was definitely fiftyish but her exact age remained a secret closely guarded by her mother and the clerk at the Department of Motor Vehicles. No gray, no dye. No kidding. The wrinkles around her eyes were laugh lines; gravity had yet to wage war on the softer parts of her body.

I made a noncommittal noise as I fooled around at the coffee station in her office at *The Mag*. I swore I kept this job just so I could drink her coffee. An invitation to Barbara's office for coffee was like receiving royal honors.

"Unfortunately, I felt really inspired this week." I took a shallow sip of the coffee so I didn't scald my tongue. Carrying the mug over to her desk, I flopped into the big red leather chair across from her.

"I'll say. These letters make, what..." She shuffled through the perpetual piles on her desk until she found what she wanted. Barbara was old school, preferring paper to electronic files. "Seven. You made the regular issue as well as the summer bonus. I'm impressed."

Nodding, I reached for my cup. The summer bonus was a pain, if anyone asked me. However, I got paid to do it. Money was nice, so I kept my opinion to myself. I had yet to master a passable poker face and Barbara was a champion player.

"But you don't look like someone who's free and clear until next issue," she said. "You look more like you expect someone to jump out at you."

"I just... eh, it's nothing." I tried to downplay it but her assessment was dead-on, hopefully no pun intended. Her slight frown insisted she wanted a better answer and I grimaced, knowing she wouldn't like the answer. "I've been thinking about Patrick."

"Him again?" She clucked her tongue and walked around the desk. Perching on the edge, she softened her firm tone with a sympathetic look. "He needed professional help and you told him so. You did what you could."

"I don't feel like I did."

"Enough. You're not a psychiatrist. Let it go."

Barbara was right. I was an advice columnist. People sought me out because they wanted my help. Didn't help matters that, before joining The Mag, I'd spent more than a decade in nursing. I was driven to help, to care, to make things all better.

Didn't I have an obligation to help them? "But—"

"But nothing," she said. "I know you like to dwell. At least dwell on something cheerful. Think about those you help."

I scowled into my cup. She was right—I did get too hung up on people and their problems. It was just the way I was wired.

"What brought him up, anyway?"

"I got a letter from him yesterday," I said.

She gave me a careful look as if she were determining whether or not our friendship would survive a phone call to Crisis Intervention. "You mean from someone who sounds like him."

"No, him. His handwriting, his signature."

"I thought you said—"

"I did." I scooted on the slippery cushion so I could look up at her. "You saw the obituary."

"Dead is dead, Sophie." Barbara flipped through the stack in her inbox before selecting several pages from the middle. She tugged a paperclip free and dropped it into a tray as she reclaimed her seat. "They don't come back. Maybe he sent it before he—you know."

I cradled the cup, feeling the sting of heat through the ceramic. The warmth failed to travel past my palms and I tucked my arms to my chest. "It was postmarked this week."

"Do you want the column mail screened?"

"Wouldn't help. It was mailed to my apartment."

Now I had her attention.

She sat back in her chair, papers forgotten. "How could anyone have gotten your home address?"

"Beats me. The column mail comes here and I use a post office box for freelance subs."

"Anything else? Phone calls? Hang ups?"

"No. Just the letter." After a brief deliberation, I added more. Might as well spill all the beans and not just the ones she'd believe. "And the feeling someone's... waiting for me."

Barbara's expression said *Okay, I think you finally cracked* but her mouth issued more diplomatic words. "Seriously? Maybe you're being stalked."

"No, I don't think so. Just a vague feeling, like someone's waiting for me to... I don't know, open my eyes. See them." I didn't ask if she ever had that feeling. Most people didn't get impressions the way I did. I'd stopped asking that question a long time ago.

However, this was the first time a simple impression worried me. It was a solid, hovering kind of expectancy that killed my concentration and made me look over my shoulder wherever I went.

"That's probably because the letter came to your apartment." The phone rang and Barbara poked the voice mail button. "You feel vulnerable. Keep your eyes open and try to ignore it."

I half-agreed with her, raising the cup and hiding my mouth behind it. I couldn't shake the distinct feeling something awful loomed. The sense of foreboding was like wearing a turtleneck—a constant, constricting pressure. "Maybe I'll take self-defense classes."

"Never a bad idea for a woman living alone in the city. Then again, you might not need them. Your witticisms are sharp enough to draw blood."

I grinned. "Eh, it's a defense mechanism I developed from working with Donna. I used to be such a nice person."

"Speaking of her, she's looking for you."

I slid down in my chair so my head wasn't visible from the door. "Maybe I'll just stay in here while I finish my coffee. Wouldn't do to be caught out in the open."

Barbara removed her glasses and tossed them onto her desk. "What did you do now?"

"Nothing," I protested. "Just--that Expo thing. She's in charge."

She pressed her lips into a stern line. "Haven't you signed up yet?"

"Heck, no. I have stuff to do. Me stuff."

"Your *job* is me stuff."

"Easy for you to say. You're salaried. Saturday is my day off."

"Well, I won't blow your cover." She glanced over my head toward the door before she waved her pen warningly.

"But she'll get her claws into you. One way or another."

I scowled and took a double mouthful of coffee so I wouldn't have to respond. Claws, Expo, anything Donna— they all topped the list of *Things I Wanted Least.*

I stayed long enough to complete my hedonistic coffee experience before slinking back to my desk. This was work, after all; I wouldn't remain a staff writer if I didn't act like one.

I lived in Balaton, a harbor-dependent city halfway between Philadelphia and Wilmington. *Halfway* was an apt description in more ways than one. Big enough for a downtown but lacking the sprawl of a mega-city. Too small for a subway but wide enough for several bus routes. Taxes weren't as high as Philly but we didn't get a free ride on sales tax like glorious Delaware, either.

We weren't a major tourist destination, just another city people passed through on the way to somewhere else. I guessed that was why I never left. Balaton was midway between point A and point B—just like me.

This job was the closest fit I'd felt in a long time, even if the inseam wasn't quite right. I had a leg up in the game, at least. My inner voice. My gut instinct. My compassion.

The job was easy. All I had to do was tell people what they probably already knew. Nine times out of ten it was what they wanted to hear anyway, but they didn't trust themselves enough to follow their own advice. If people were brave enough to listen to the spark of wisdom that lived in each of us, I'd be out of a job.

Thank God for that one out of ten who actually needed my advice; they went a long way to validate me. Only problem was, they were the ones who kept me awake at night.

I sighed and plucked my mail from the basket hanging outside my cubicle before dropping into my chair. My position at *The Mag* was a haven for me. At least, it had been until Patrick's needy letters arrived. Damn those depressed men who get attached to the first sympathetic person they encounter. Damn the way they kill themselves and leave the rest of us to feel like it was our failure, not theirs.

Damn them for coming back.

I knew it couldn't be him. I knew dead was dead. Plenty of dead had happened around me in the past and never once had it been undone. Patrick could be no exception.

Question was: Who? Who now? Who was going to yank my heartstrings, get me completely tied up in their emotional plight, and bail on me at the end? Who would be the death of me?

I didn't want to find out.

A block away from my bus stop, an unkempt man with a gravelly voice and a coat that had seen better days crouched against the wall of a pawnshop. He raised a pleading palm when I passed. "Scuze, miss. Gotta quarter?"

No matter what I wished, I couldn't fix the homeless problem. I still had a long way to go in learning how to choose my battles. So I compromised: half the time, I walked by. The other half, I stopped. I left it up to fate to decide. Well, fate and how much change I had.

Sounded shallow when it was all laid out like that, but hey. Even a deep chick like me needed to have a shallow spot somewhere inside. Wasn't that what made us human?

"Yeah, sure." Digging into the front pocket of my cords, I pulled out some coins and surveyed the findings. I picked out two quarters and a bus token and dropped them into his outstretched hand. "Here you go."

"Whaz this?" He squinted at the token. "Canadian?"

"No, a bus token. If you take the Green Line to Fifteenth Street, there's a church-run shelter nearby. Food's decent."

His scrutiny turned doubtful. I thought he might give it back but he shoved his fist under his coat. He gathered himself and tore away from the cold grip of the sidewalk, shuffling off with an uneven gait. "Thanks."

After a sweeping glance to make sure no one was nearby, I dug around my purse for another token. The pizza shop on the corner sent out enticing aromatic invitations of tart tomato and garlicky goodness and I suddenly had half a mind to turn right around and have a slice or three, regardless of the fact I was full of coffee and not the least bit hungry.

Reminding myself of the trouble I'd had getting my hand into my front pocket, I pushed the nagging temptation clean out of my head.

"What a waste of money." A hard voice startled me and snapped my spine taut. It was hard to misinterpret that particular tone.

I counted to five before turning around. "Sorry? Did you say something?"

A hefty mountain of olive drab, mirrored Oakleys, and black work boots leaned against the wall of the pizza joint where the awning cast the deepest shadow. His black knit cap, the kind I imagined muggers favored, enhanced my perception of a threat. Strong. Harsh. Dangerous. Funny I didn't see him the first time I looked—he was sort of hard to miss.

"Of course I did." Caustic words dripped like acid as he snapped the collar of his canvas coat up around his ears. "You're delusional if you think he'll go to your little soup kitchen. He's a drunk. You gave him rum money."

"How do you know? Just because he's a bum doesn't mean he's..." I floundered, flustered, fishing for words and not finding them fast enough. "A bum."

He laughed, Brillo-Pad-on-skinned-knees mean.

"Of course he is. It's his nature. Why do you think he's on the street? Kiss your charity goodbye." He jammed his hands into his pockets, hunching his shoulders and looking, if it were at all possible, even more menacing. "You won't survive in this city if you don't stop being so naïve."

"I am not naïve!" My retort drew alarmed looks from a lady who clutched her bag and quickened her pace as she passed me. I should have followed her. "I just don't think the worst of everyone I meet. Unlike some people, apparently."

"So when a bum asks for a quarter, you offer to feed him for a lifetime? This is the city, lady. Learn the rules."

"Good advice. First rule is, don't talk to strangers." I never wanted a medal for being nice but I didn't need to be criticized, either. Turning on my heel, I stomped away.

Mr. Tall Dark And Pushy didn't seem to get the hint. His low voice grated across my nerves, sounding uncomfortably close behind. "I'm not finished."

"Oh yes, you are." I spun around, but when I saw he still hadn't moved, I faltered. I guessed arrogance made a voice carry.

Remembering the focus of my irritation, I jabbed my hands onto my hips, fighting the overwhelming urge to march over to him and do something foolish. Usually I'm more flight than fight. I should have been running, but my smart mouth had taken over. "I don't know who you think you are but you're messing with the wrong lady."

"No, I don't think I am." He straightened and shrugged his jacket into place.

I backed up a step, as if the distance between us were inches instead of feet. It was his reach that worried me. "You don't think, period. Who even talks to people like that?"

Even his chuckle was arrogant. "You've got spirit."

"You've got nerve. And no, I'm not coming any closer so quit telling me what to do."

"I didn't say a thing."

"Well—" I sputtered. Didn't I hear him say it? "Stop—thinking it, then."

He laughed, sounding delighted to have irked me to the point of incoherence. Dismissing me with a wave, his tone became more condescending. "Forget I said anything and go home."

I fisted my hands, wanting nothing more than to leave, but I had a historic need to have the last word. When sufficient words failed me I stamped my foot.

He leaned at the waist, looking over the tops of his sunglasses. His bright green eyes flashed, much brighter than if they'd simply captured a glint of sun. "I said, go on home."

I snapped an about-face and marched all the way to my stop without pausing. His sardonic laughter taunted me, scalding my cheeks long after I caught the bus. By the time I got home, I'd forgotten every odd detail, including the brief realization I hadn't seen his mouth move when he told me to leave. The weird occurrences had been swept from my mind, leaving behind a diluted version of a generic encounter.

I'd forgotten everything except being angry. What can I say? I could hold a grudge with both hands tied.

"He had a point, you know," Barbara said as we rode the elevator the next morning. "You are naïve sometimes."

"Oh, not you, too. Please, forget I said anything. I don't need another lecture."

"Don't worry. I'm not going to give one. I just think the bus token was excessive." The elevator dinged and spilled us into *The Mag*'s foyer. "What's got you so hot, anyway? Maybe this guy hit too close to the truth, hmm?"

"I'm over that. There was something else, something I can't remember. Something—not *right* about the whole thing."

"Let it go. It's in your blood to be nice. The fact you

didn't put the poor guy up in a room for the night speaks volumes for how far you've progressed. Good morning, ladies," she called to a group near the copier, who turned and waved back.

"Sophie, wait a minute, please." A voice not unlike the dragging of talons on a chalkboard cut through the cheerful hum of friendly chatter. Donna. I closed my eyes so nobody could see them roll and I dragged to a stop.

"See you later." Barbara maintained her course for her office, abandoning me. I sighed, plastered on a smile, and spun to face Donna, the office monster. Sorry, I meant *manager.*

Only Donna Slate could turn a nice word like *please* into a bitchy demand. Her sour expression matched her tone. Why not? Donna coordinated everything, from accessories to attitude.

"I noticed you still haven't signed up." The words marched out of her mouth with a prim and reprimanding cadence. In her manicured fingers, Donna held the sign-up sheet to work at the Annual Citywide Expo.

I suppressed a groan. Each year *The Mag* gave a presentation and set up a table, which we worked in shifts. *It's voluntary,* the supervisors said, but normally volunteers were not rounded up and hairy-eyeballed into compliance.

I'd hoped to avoid it this year. Last year I spent an hour and a half deflecting half-assed pick-up attempts from my fellow volunteer, some guy who worked in Marketing. Besides, who needed to waste a perfectly good Saturday with a woman who looked at me as if she were imagining ways to execute me?

"Oh. I've been meaning to take care of it..." I popped a light slap on my forehead in feigned forgetfulness. Maybe if I acted incompetent, I'd satisfy her apparent need to be the only one around here who did anything right.

"Right. You've been too busy. Well, you're not busy

now." With a hand on her hip and a smug smirk ruining her precisely lip-sticked mouth, she held out the paper.

I took the sheet and scoured the remaining slots. All the daytime shifts were full. This should teach me: either sign up first to get the least crappy job or stay out of the office until the whole mess blew over. I smiled with an effort to thaw her out as I scribbled my name next to one of the few remaining shifts. "Can't I just make a donation?"

Her tone dropped several degrees. "You are. Your time. You've got more than anyone else does, apparently."

My patience leaked away with every breath. "I don't see your name on here anywhere."

Donna plucked the page out of my fingers and brushed it off. "That's because I have the worst job of all. I have to hunt down people who think they're too good for things like this."

Holding out her pen, I smiled. It was venomous but hey, it was still a smile. Snatching the pen, she clicked off. Even her footsteps sounded bitchy, as if she had nails in her heels.

"You're welcome," I called. She didn't even acknowledge it.

As the sound of her footsteps disappeared, I frowned with annoyance. How ironic. Maybe that stranger had been right when he criticized me for being nice. Maybe I wouldn't survive in this city if I didn't learn the rules.

But one thing he didn't realize—some days, I actually did deserve a medal.

3

The sky wore a low ceiling of iron gray with a wispy under-layer of near-black that skulked slowly by. A curtain of cool drizzle had been falling since I'd rolled out of bed and showed no indication of letting up.

Production was well ahead of schedule, so I quit early, skipping lunch and leaving as soon as the payroll clerk made his rounds. After I finished at the office, I decided to visit one of my favorite haunts. It was Friday and my paycheck, tucked away in my purse, spared me another week's worrying about the rent.

One sodden and crowded bus ride later, I found myself in University Heights, standing in the courtyard of a stately building. Rain darkened the red brick walls, making them look awash with old blood. The edifice had the same style as the others on campus: old brick and modern tinted window, lines and squares and angles. Ivy League. Traditional.

Sheltered under my umbrella, I gazed through the rain at the great front windows of the University Museum of

Archeology and Anthropology and shivered. My mood was perfect for visiting the dead.

The wind shifted, blowing the rain sideways and reminding me to go inside before I got drenched. I avoided what puddles I could as I crossed the bricked courtyard before hurrying inside.

The admissions clerk was chatting on the phone but she smiled and covered the receiver with her free hand. "New exhibit this week. Biblical scholars, missing texts. Right up your alley."

I grinned. "Sounds interesting."

"Presentation, too. Islamic Dome, three o'clock." She slid a flyer across the counter. "Watch the time. It fills up fast."

I waved my thanks and she resumed her phone call. Shrugging out of my soggy jacket, I hung it on the rack in the main lobby. I slipped through the arches leading into the atrium of the museum. A brief glance at my watch showed it was already after two o'clock so I headed down the corridor toward the Middle Eastern regional exhibits.

Halfway down the corridor I paused, reconsidering my plan. As much as I wanted to hear the lecture, I retraced my steps to the atrium and climbed a staircase on the other side of the museum.

I had a sudden, inexplicable craving to visit Old Egypt.

In the great hall housing the Egyptian exhibitions, I immediately noted the change in the atmosphere. The room was cool and dry, its climate controlled to mimic the conditions in which the relics had existed in their native land.

The entire room had been designed to resemble an Old Kingdom temple. The main lights were dimmed while strategically-placed spotlights emphasized massive columns and magnificent wall carvings like sunbeams through temple windows.

I scanned the room. No other tourists. Even better. I meandered, enjoying the rare opportunity to linger.

Craning my neck, I ran my gaze up each of the columns, reading the images, admiring the palm leaves carved at the tops like great stone trees. Eyes toward the ceilings, I turned slowly around, admiring the handiwork of the ancient artists.

What was it like to live in those lands and those times? Could an ancient version of my spirit have been there, stepping barefoot and silently through a sandy temple like this one?

Lost in contemplation, I was completely unprepared for the shock of smacking into someone, bumping him hard enough to lose my balance. I'd have fallen had he not caught my arm. Wide-eyed with consternation, I stammered an apology to the handsome but serious-faced gentleman.

"You are not hurt, I hope?" His voice, deep and smooth, sent shivers marching down my neck, between my shoulders, down my spine.

"I'm okay." I shook my head, too shy to make direct eye contact, wishing I'd checked my hair and lipstick before coming in. "I'm far too adept at being inept."

He flashed a grin and I caught a glimpse of nice white teeth. "Temples are places for spiritual reflection. It is forgivable if your vision was turned inward, rather than toward where you were walking."

His expression softened by amusement, he tilted his head toward the pillars. "Majestic, aren't they?"

I stole another glance at him—black hair smoothed back into a discreet tail, clear light skin framed by long sideburns, strong jaw culminating in a square, cleft chin. Like the other items in the museum, something about him made me want to look closer, inspect each detail.

A subtle flush warmed my cheeks and ears so I quickly

turned back to the heights of the exhibition. Murmuring a sound of agreement, I circled the column, stepping a few feet away so I could see both him and the stone. "Do you visit this museum often?"

Furtive glances allowed me to take in more of his appearance a tiny section at a time. Clothing dark as his hair. Long blazer, something in between a suit coat and an over-coat. In one hand he carried a bound book and fountain pen, as if he'd been making notes.

His gaze was calm and steady and entirely on me. Taking a deep breath I permitted the contact of the direct look. My boldness was well-rewarded. His Paul Newman lips brought to mind the sculptured busts on display in the Greco-Roman Quarters and he wore a stern expression that cast a veil of hardness upon his features, enhancing the impression he'd been carved from marble.

Except for his eyes. The Roman busts bore eyes that were blank and white but this man's eyes were alive with bright green color. Like gemstones, they glittered and drew my gaze.

"No, actually," he said. "My first time here. Although, I admit, I'm drawn to places like this." His voice made music of the words—deep bass notes and soothing rhythm.

"Ah!" I said. "A man after my own heart." His left eyebrow arched so sharply I thought it might disappear into his hairline and I hurriedly continued. "Are you a professor?"

"No, nothing like that. I do studying of my own, it's not a living. It's more of a hobby. Personal research, of sorts."

"Studying past times is one of my pastimes. It's my preferred form of entertainment."

"Mmm." Eyebrow cocked again, he cast a disapproving look at me and swept his hand around the contrived temple. "Would the gods be pleased to know they are reduced to the level of entertainment?"

"I hope so." I kept my tone light. Considering the seriousness of his expression, I didn't want to accidentally insult him. "Otherwise, they'd have to be content with staying dead, right?"

His gaze swept over me and I shivered again as if the touch had been tangible, a brush of fingertips against my cheek.

"Well, I'll leave you to your worship. I mean, your wanderings." He gave me a conspirator's wink. "Unless..."

He hesitated, with a quiet clearing of throat as he tucked his notebook and pen into an inside pocket. "You wouldn't mind a companion? Sometimes one sees things differently when seeing through another's eyes. I would appreciate a new perspective."

I mulled it over, listening to the rain spattering the windows and distant voices echoing faintly from other rooms. Although I'd looked forward to a quiet afternoon, it might be nice to spend it with someone who seemed to share my interests. He certainly was attractive, and his pleasant voice intrigued me.

I realized I'd become used to living inside a shell. This man made me want to step outside for once.

"I'd like that." I smiled at his pleased expression. "I'm Sophie, by the way." I stuck out my hand in introduction.

Instead of shaking my hand, he bent his head over it and pressed polite lips to the backs of my fingers. The quaint gesture would have seemed strange and out of place had we been elsewhere. "I am Marek. Pleased to make your acquaintance."

Fingers tingling from the unexpected kiss, I fought the urge to curtsy. "Well, Marek. Lead me into the past."

His almost-smile sent a thrill down the back of my neck. "That's exactly the sort of thing I'd hoped you say. Shall we?"

He turned on his heel and swept out a hand with a

slight bow, indicating the archway to another exhibit. For the first time since I'd been coming to this museum, I wondered what I'd see on the other side, and was surprised to realize I wasn't afraid to find out.

We exited the temple exhibit through a side chamber, a brightly-lit, white-walled box of a room. An entire wall showcased a painting of a brilliantly colored and bejeweled goddess, golden *ankh* in hand.

"Oh, look." I hurried over to a set of suspended carved and painted slabs. In all its winged glory shone a portrait of Isis. "My lady."

Marek glanced at me in surprise. Approval added a light inflection to his voice. "A fan, are you?"

The goddess's painted eyes gazed passively from the splendid carvings of her many forms: the out-stretched wings, the horns and sun disk, the empty throne of Osiris. "Isis wasn't some god high above and far removed from the world and its ordinary mortals. The ancients worshiped her as a living queen. Who wouldn't be endeared to her?"

I glanced over my shoulder. Marek, arms crossed across his broad chest, watched me with wide eyes.

"Sorry," I said. "I didn't mean to sound like a zealot. I'm quite Catholic." I tugged my collar aside to reveal a

Crucifix. "She's a favorite of mine, that's all."

He pondered the pendant lying below the base of my throat for a few moments. "Don't apologize. Isis has been worshiped and adored by countless people throughout thousands of years. Many still believe she is the mother of us all…" His voice trailed off when he gazed up at her countenance. The harsh lines of his brow and mouth softened, a lightening of his weighty demeanor.

I recognized that look. My own faith gave me similar peace. "Are you one of them?"

After a thoughtful pause, he nodded. "Sometimes."

"What about right now?" I took advantage of the moment to admire once more the cut of his profile and the green of his eyes shining brightly under the fluorescent lights. I would have killed for a professor this striking in college. I might not have learned anything but, oh well, the sacrifices one made.

He turned solemn eyes toward me and caught me in his gaze. "Right now, I believe the Goddess walks among us. All we have to do is find her."

Marek's tone held such gravity I didn't dare make light of his response. The mood had grown considerably heavier, thick and congested with an undercurrent I didn't understand. I nodded in vague agreement and turned wordlessly to a different set of paintings.

As we explored the other exhibits, I decided that accompanying Marek was one of my more brilliant decisions. His knowledge of ancient Egypt seemed intimate, his pronunciations lending an exotic sound to the names of peoples and cities I'd only previously read.

He had to be a professor. Nobody went this far with a hobby.

We drifted from room to room, chatting and browsing. At times his hand politely guided me along, a soft pressure at the small of my back. Normally I didn't tolerate such closeness from a stranger but I had to admit: this guy was hot. Marek acted somber and academic and I figured him for a gentleman. An intelligent, alluring gentleman.

Of course, I kept my saucy thoughts to myself. It wouldn't do to let him know I was such a wild thing. *Slut* was usually not a good first impression.

Looks and brains aside, his sheer size made me feel protected. A man of his build, wearing that occasionally grim expression and steely gaze, should have made me wary, at the very least. If he intended harm I wouldn't stand a chance. I just didn't get that feeling.

Not that he couldn't put it out. I had distinct impressions of warning whenever we passed other people. Marek was a master of body language. His expression never changed, and his voice never rose from the quiet conversational tone he used when we were alone, but if someone approached, he stood in front of me in a subtle but unmistakable attitude of ownership.

It was strange, but not strange enough to alarm me. Surrounded by warrior priests and treasured queens, I imagined ourselves falling into similar patterns, assuming the roles of the relics around us. After so many years of coming here with my daydreams, I had finally met someone who fit right into them.

When we turned the last corner of the corridor and stepped through the doors of the mock Burial Chamber, I practically shivered with anticipation. My enthusiasm must have been apparent because he turned to me with an appraising glance.

"You are not put off by the notion of death," he said. The statement sounded like a curious question.

"Well," I said. "Death is a sucky thing for the most part, but I like mummies."

He glanced at my throat, perhaps looking for my Crucifix. "You are Christian. Surely you believe in eternal life."

"Sure I do. I just don't like to think about the dying you have to do first."

Marek nodded. "Not everyone is fortunate enough to die peacefully."

The walls were painted to recreate the interior of a New Kingdom tomb; figures and hieroglyphics danced across walls plastered and textured to resemble cut stone and false doors. Long glass cases, each holding mummified remains and descriptions of each step in the preservation process, stood along the perimeter of the room.

Other smaller cases and stands displayed funerary items, papyrus scrolls, and tools used by ancient embalmers. Somber lighting, provided by electric torches with flickering bulbs, created deep shadows while bright track lights shone down with distinct rays of light, an effect that was both ethereal and clinical.

"The Egyptians feared death but they celebrated it as well." Marek's voice took on the patient instructional tone I'd already come to recognize. "How else could one enter Paradise?"

Gesturing toward the center of the room, he urged me toward one of the smaller cases. "Life, Sophie, is an unending river. It continues after corporeal death and moves on into the afterlife. The Egyptians wove countless spells around their deceased to protect the soul on its journey through the underworld, which is dark and treacherous."

I contented myself to play the student's role. Marek's method of explaining history made it seem alive and real, as if he himself had stepped out of a painting to grant me a glimpse into the past.

"See?" He pointed into a glass case at his side. "There are spells to protect the soul, spells to guard the heart, and spells to pass through final judgment unscathed. Collectively, they are referred to as *Spells for Going Forth by Day.*"

Strolling over to where he stood, I peered into the glass case. He moved aside to make room and we stood side by side, examining the handwritten scrolls inside. Marek briefly brushed his hand against me, a gentle touch on my lower back that sent shivers in all directions. I smiled, enjoying the shivers as they faded into delightful tingles.

"The *Book of the Dead*," I said. "I like Chapter 125, myself. The whole Ten Commandments connection, you know?"

"You've read the *Book of the Dead*?" He sounded surprised. "It's not book club material."

"It's not like I memorized it. Names, names, names." I shrugged. "It's an ocean of names."

"You must realize how important names are, Sophie. Notice the cartouche? The drawing of a cartouche is the casting of a protective spell. Names have great power."

"Sure they do." I tapped a finger on the glass, pointing to a piece of carved red jasper, described beneath as a Blood of Isis amulet. "That's how Isis got her magic. She tricked Ra into telling her his name."

"Many cultures still believe surrendering the knowledge of their name would give someone power over them. Some assume false names to keep their inner secrets safe from those who intend harm."

I glanced at him. "Are you one of them?"

"No." He almost smiled. "Marek Thurzo is my right and true name." Marek paced along the edge of the room, pausing to peer into several of the longer glass boxes.

Marek gazed intently at each mummy as if urging some secret from their long-closed mouths. I wondered what he sought to learn from them.

"Without their name, they couldn't be judged or allowed to enter eternity. To erase a name..." The corners of his mouth tightened. Marek's tone became condensed and chilled. "To erase a name is to destroy a person's existence."

I didn't expect cute and fuzzy bunnies but this was depressing. I turned, eyebrows lifted in a politely quizzical expression.

"I know the ancients erased names from monuments," I said. "It implied what those people did should be disregarded and it removed them from public record. But you make it sound worse, Marek. You equate erasing a name with destroying a soul."

"Shouldn't I?" He paused in a shadow created by the beams of two ceiling lights. Darkness flowed down his body like a shroud. The shadows and the mummies and the whole tomb décor were actually starting to feel gloomy. "Forgetting the name of someone you've known—wouldn't it be like forgetting their existence? Who exists if they are not acknowledged?"

He rubbed his jaw in a pensive gesture. "If someone you loved forgot all about you, how would you feel?"

That did it. His melancholy finally penetrated my happy almost-on-a-date mood. I felt like I'd donned cement shoes and a fog-lined coat, and the dreariness made me droop. "I'd feel abandoned. Worthless."

Marek closed the distance between us with a few smooth strides and took up my hands. The melancholy drifted away as I warmed to the comfort in his nearness. "That's why the ancients took such pains to keep their names, even in death. So the gods wouldn't turn away in abandon."

I lifted my chin and my gaze. Marek contemplated my upturned face, permitting the intimate closeness. I felt the warmth of his body and breathed in his scent, a vague mix of sandalwood and leather, exotic and confident.

His throat, so smooth above his collar, rising like a column toward his jaw, practically beckoned for a touch of lips. If I just stood on my tiptoes, I could probably...

An alien idea intruded. Damn. I hated when intellectual thoughts interrupted the lewd ones. "Unless…"

My outburst startled him and his eyes widened. Shock loosened his grip on my fingers and I drew my hand back, pressing the base of my throat.

"Unless they wanted to be forgotten by the gods. Right?" I backed away, running my fingers along the top of one of the glass coffins. "They were just people, after all. And really, how much could human nature have changed over a couple thousand years? There had to be a few low-life jerks running around, don't you think?"

He cocked his head and followed me with his eyes. Light glinted off his green irises, a flash of emerald in the shadow.

Turning to the wall behind me, I flicked a finger at a painted scene of Judgment. Osiris presided, scales ready, punishment waiting. "Criminals hide behind aliases so the law doesn't catch up with them. I'm sure there was an Egyptian or two so vile they'd rather avoid eternity all together than risk getting eaten by that hippo-crocodile guy. Maybe they'd erase their own name. On purpose."

Marek remained silent, lips pressed tightly together. I still suspected he had serious academic tendencies so my tirade must have sounded ridiculous.

At least he didn't come right out and say so. When at last he spoke, his voice was mild. "It's a distinct possibility. I've never come across any accounting of the theory. Have you?"

"Nah." I shrugged. "Pseudo-educated guess."

To my relief, he smirked.

"Such wisdom. Incidentally, you should be wise, if you are aptly named."

"Huh? You mean, Miss Know-It-All?"

He exhaled through his nose with exaggerated patience. "Sophia. The Greek word for wisdom."

"Oh, right. No wonder I'm so smart." I fluttered my

eyelashes and dimpled. "How about you? Are you aptly named?"

"I sincerely hope not." His voice turned dark again and for a moment I felt that peculiar sense of danger around him, the threatening gloom. When his eyes found mine, however, it diminished and his expression seemed to lighten. "Perhaps not. Now I have your wisdom to guide me."

Funny. I heard what his mouth said but a voice echoed something different in my head.

I hope not, now I have finally found you.

Smiling, I slipped my arm around his, delighting in the firmness of his bicep. Sigh. Muscles. It didn't take much to thrill me. "Let's go, then. My wisdom tells me there's a gift shop downstairs. I'm in the mood for a souvenir."

"Yes, my Sophia." His laughter sounded warm and mellow and together we headed for the stairs, leaving the dead to their exhibitional afterlives.

When we reached the main staircases, I led him toward the commercial side of the museum, where a cafe and gift shop were located, and offered him a drink.

"What?" He seemed shocked and glanced around with concern. "Here?"

"Um, well, actually, over there," I said and pointed to the door of the cafe. I disapproved of museums that built their own mini-malls. It cheapened the whole learning experience by turning a history course into a side order at a malt shop.

He had the same opinion, if his reaction was any proof. Marek offered his arm, the gesture smoothly dispelling the awkwardness of his hesitation. Holding open the door, he ushered me inside and we chose a table by the windows.

I ordered coffee and a sandwich, although Marek only sipped at a cup of tea. Conversation flowed so effortlessly that anyone watching us would find little indication we'd been complete strangers only an hour or two before.

Eventually the darkening sky told me I had stayed much longer than I intended and I reluctantly brought our interlude to a close. When I stood to leave, he again offered his arm and escorted me to the main doors. Marek helped me into my raincoat, which by this time was dry despite having been sandwiched between other damp garments. A gentleman, through and through.

"Thanks for the tour, Marek," I said. "I'll see you again, sometime?"

"You can count on it, Sophie." His voice blended with the sound of the rain as he pushed open the door, turning into a melody that echoed in my mind long after I stepped out under the shelter of my umbrella and began the journey home alone.

For the first time in weeks, I fell asleep without agonizing over the letter I'd gotten from a dead man. Marek must be a hell of a guy if he could distract me from the one thing that haunted me most.

5

Early Monday morning, I swung my feet over the arm of Barbara's big red chair, cradling a huge wide-mouthed mug of hazelnut brew. I'd recently figured out how to use the milk steamer and a frothy layer of sugared foam floated like a cloud in my coffee.

Barbara's glasses did little to hide the crease between her lowered brows. The cap of a pen jutted from her mouth and she wagged it from side to side as she scowled at a much-abused stack of copy. She was on her second red pen of the morning.

I tried not to glance over even though I was dying to know who wrote the crap. It wouldn't have been professional of me. And hey, I was all about being professional.

"Were you sober, Sophie? He doesn't sound like your type."

"What—smooth, smart, and sexy isn't my type? Thanks a bunch."

"Physically, he sounds like a dream, okay? And you know..." She tugged her glasses down and rubbed the spot between her eyebrows, trying to dispel her aggravation. "I don't even care if you're embellishing. About time I got a vicarious jolly from you."

I stuck my tongue out at her. "I'm not embellishing. He really was all that. And a bag of chips. And a huge bowl of three-cheese-sour-cream dip on the side."

Sliding her glasses back up, she leaned over the copy again, crossing off an entire block of type. "He just sounds so dark. I guess it's true when they say opposites attract."

I'd told Barbara every detail about my afternoon with Marek. Recalling our conversation in the cafe, I decided *dark* was too mild a term. He was a tremendous pessimist, hinting at a tragic soul. His views, especially concerning himself, were intensely negative. It surprised me, considering he was the most handsome man I'd bumped into— literally––in years.

Usually I steer clear of nay-sayers and doom-criers but I was drawn to him. Had it all been an elaborate pick-up line? The overall impression I'd gotten from him was *I am damned, who will save me? Does it even matter anymore?* Truly told, there probably wasn't an easier way to rope in a sucker like me. Marek must have noticed the tattoo on my forehead that read *bleeding heart.*

Barbara's voice interrupted my reverie. "What did you say he did for a living? A professor or something?"

"Uh, no." I tapped my front teeth with a fingernail as I tried to remember. "He sort of explained but I didn't quite follow." Actually, I hadn't followed at all because I'd been incredibly distracted at the time. The conversation went something along the lines of:

"I am in business with my family. We control several local enterprises, as well as others in the country and abroad. Yadda yadda..." *Wow. Look at those eyes. I mean, did you ever see a shade of green like that? They practically glow.* "Yadda yadda... and unfortunately the role of ambassador usually falls to me. It is no terrible thing, as I am fortunately blessed with yadda yadda..." *Martha Stewart would kill to get her hands on paint that color, I bet. What would she call it? Spring? Emerald? And those lashes. Oof!* "...yadda yadda difficulties when dealing with the executive boards of other... interests... but such is the nature of politics."

So, no, I hadn't caught the whole thing. Hell if I told Barbara that part, though. I tried my best to look responsible in front of her and that bit would totally have blown my cover.

"And anyways, Mother," I said. "Aren't I old enough for a wild mysterious encounter with the occasional dark and alluring stranger? I could have asked him for his *curriculum vitae* but it would have seemed so—I don't know. Forced."

Barbara didn't answer. Shaking her head at the pages, she streaked an entire page with red from corner to corner and scrawled a brief note before dropping the pen with a sigh of disgust. She punched the button on the intercom, holding it down like a recently-squashed but resilient bug.

Her secretary answered immediately. "Yes, Ms. Evans?"

"Oh, God, Amanda." Barbara huffed out the last of her patience. "I can't take any more. Call Donna in here in fifteen minutes and tell her to bring her resume. I need to be reminded why I let her talk me into this."

"Yes, Ms. Evans." Amusement colored her voice, making it even harder for me to maintain an *I'm-not-be-ing-nosy* expression.

Barbara released the button. Her forehead creased, revealing her frustration. Rubbing her brow with the heel of her hand, she looked at me from behind her wrist. "Hope your day goes better than mine. Take my advice, kiddo. Be careful when offering to do someone a favor."

Laughing, I swung my legs down and slid out of the chair, hoisting my coffee cup. "I told Research I'd help fill in a feature on the latest tax debates. See you."

I walked out and shut the door behind me. I couldn't resist a furtive glance toward the far side of the office, where a white-faced and thin-lipped Donna flipped through her file cabinet. Apparently Amanda had relayed Barbara's message verbatim.

I chortled wickedly. *Can this day get any better?*

Blinking, I stepped out into the sun, wishing I'd remembered to grab my sunglasses before I'd left for work. The afternoon sun shone high overhead and the sidewalks were crowded. After a moment's hesitation near the main doors, I slipped into the stream of walkers, heading uptown.

Shouldering my bag, I set off at a comfortable pace. My apartment was about ten blocks away but it was too nice out for a bus.

It wasn't long until I arrived in my neighborhood in the east side of town, close to the harbor. My apartment had a clear view from the fire escape and in warm weather I kept a portable hammock outside for myself and my room-mate, Euphrates. We'd spent many evenings out there over the last few years, Euphrates licking my fingertips with his lazy tongue, rumbling contentedly as he dozed against my chest...

I did tell you he was a cat, didn't I? I usually called him Fraidy. Euphrates sounded more like an accusation.

He was a kitten when I found him, drenched and half-starved in the alley behind my building. Fraidy was my most favorite intervention. It wasn't long before he had taken complete run of the place. He's a cat and therefore genetic-ally predisposed to being the boss. Who was I to interfere with nature?

Now, if I could get him to help pay the rent, he'd be the perfect roommate. Oh well. Beggars can't be choosers.

The buzz of the can opener brought him thumping

into the kitchen, mid-whine, scolding me for taking so long to fill his dish. I spent a few moments stroking his back, enjoying his rough rumble of a purr, before heading into the living room.

I'd dropped the mail on the couch when I first came in. Picking up the stack, I flipped through the various bills and SASE responses before coming to the handwriting that made my heart thud. My fingers went numb and I lost hold of the letter. It slipped to the floor.

Patrick. The dead just wouldn't stay dead.

That night I dreamed.

I crawled through the living room window onto the fire escape. Instead of being surrounded by black-painted metal grates and the smells of springtime city air, everything was fog. Nothing above or below but a thick gray haze that could have held little or hidden much.

I longed for the safety of my living room. I backed up, intending to crawl back through the window but Marek stood behind me.

Don't go. Marek's green eyes were the only color in the sea of gray.

The fog's so thick, I said. *I can't see the rail.*

It's there.

I can't even see my feet.

Yet you stand on solid ground.

That supposed to be symbolic?

Your dream. Marek spread his hands and half-grinned. *You decide.*

My dream, eh? So maybe if I. . . I slid my hands boldly along his sides and pressed against him, braver for the fog and the safe confines of my fantasy.

Nice, he replied. *You feel good against me.* He stroked his hands up my arms, cupping my shoulders, brushing my hair away from my face and pushing it back. I felt the thrill of his fingers stroking my throat. *You surprise yourself.*

I do, actually. I wouldn't normally do this.

Embrace me?

I shook my head. *Stand in the fog.*

It's mysterious. He lifted me by the waist and spun, gently. Lost in the fog, I forgot up and down. I forgot the way back. Here with Marek, I forgot why the way back even mattered.

It's hiding something, I said. Turning in his arms, I peered at the solid gray everything. *I can sense there is something. . . big out there.*

So, see through it.

The fog is too thick.

You have to take a chance. He lowered his face next to mine, his chest against my back, arms crossed in front of me.

Wait. Holding rather tightly. Faint alarm bloomed. I'd hoped the dream would take a rather different direction. *And do what?*

Fall. Marek jumped off into the gray unknown, taking me with him.

My scream was a tight squeal that echoed long after the gray faded to black.

I woke, sitting up in bed, the scream still in my throat. Euphrates, straight-legged and yowling at the bottom of the bed, arched and hissed at the shadowed corner of the room by the window. My heart pounded, my brain replaying the dream.

I grappled with the bedside lamp, flooding the room with light. No one. Nothing. The cat's siren snapped off and he crouched, trembling. Nothing there.

Or was there? It felt like the dream lingered, gray wisps of memory hovering, watching, waiting for sleep to provide another opportunity to descend.

Feeling like any moment something would pop up

behind me, I shut off the light and dragged the cat to my chest like a teddy bear. Together we hid from the remainder of the night, deep under the covers, waiting for sunlight's rescue.

"That's why I love to do what I do," Marek said. "It's the chase, the hunt, the challenge. Every day is an opportunity to go out and prove myself again. There is no chance of becoming complacent. If I want to survive, I must keep going."

We sat at a fountain side table at one of the patio restaurants downtown one Wednesday afternoon, talking about our work. He'd shown up at *The Mag* earlier with an offer to take me to lunch. Even though we'd been seeing each other for about two weeks, he'd never come to my office before. I was pleasantly surprised by his unexpected arrival. The rest of the office got an eyeful as well.

Even Donna lost her composure, stumbling and unashamedly staring, slack-jawed, when she spied us outside my cube. I supposed it gave her another reason to hate me.

Thank God I'd worn what I did—a flirty skirt in fruit salad colors with a slim fit tangerine tee shirt. Since I was five-foot-seven and somewhat knobby, I didn't usually show off my legs. However, the shoes I chose—buckled round-toed pumps with a smart heel that reminded me of silver-screen starlets—stretched my legs and made them look like proper gams. I'd pinned my hair up in a bun with lots of loose strands, so artfully tousled it was impossible to tell if I spent seconds or hours doing it.

I was desperately glad he hadn't shown up the day before on "Roll Out Of Bed and Drag Yourself To Work In Any Old Thing" day. I'd actually worn flip-flops. They weren't even real shoes.

At lunch, birds took advantage of a free meal, hopping on the tiles beneath our table, while Marek described in detail what he did for a living. This time around I vowed to pay close attention.

I'd retained at least the basics from our chat in the museum café. Marek described his dual responsibilities as financial overlord and political mastermind (my slant, not his). His words sounded mild and polite but his aura—for lack of a more sensible word—had a taste of aggression I couldn't imagine being faked.

Just as I had that first day we'd spoken in the museum, I received more vague impressions of threat; it felt as if he stood, arms wide, to hold back a tide of danger behind him, protecting me from it even as I knew he could unleash it upon others. I shuddered to imagine what he might do in a stressful situation.

Still, he appeared respectable and polite, if not tremendously cheerful or overly appreciative of the other men sitting near our table.

Here in the sunshine, the mist from the fountain keeping it cool enough to keep my sweater on, he sat across from me in black Ralph Lauren pants and a dark green dress shirt, sleeves rolled to mid-forearm, unbuttoned at the throat. No tie, of course.

Marek didn't favor the metro style favored by most of the stock jockeys who devoured their thirty-minute lunches

and chatted urgently into cell phones around us. Yet, he
seemed more powerful than all of them put together, even as
he lounged in the wire-grid chair, legs crossed and relaxed.

I mulled over his words as I moved on to the other
half of my sandwich. He made his work sound stimulating
and exciting but it wasn't at all my style. "Not me. I like the
confinements of a nine to five. Well, okay, maybe not strictly
nine to five. *The Mag* is pretty lenient with my time card."

"Do you enjoy your work?"

"I like work, it likes me. I'm kind of destined for it. I
grew up with a little voice inside me—sort of like emotional
radar. Once it makes up its mind about something, it's
impossible to ignore."

"Destined. Hmm. Odd word." He pursed his lips in a
thoughtful frown. "You are fortunate to have a strong
internal guide."

"I'll say. My little voice is entirely responsible for
keeping me out of the kinds of trouble that makes you turn
to someone for advice in the first place."

He gazed at me with a hungry attention, making me
feel like I was the most fascinating person on the planet.
Nobody had ever been this curious about my life and times
the way he was. I didn't even think it was possible to be
interested in my line of work. It wasn't like I was an astro-
naut or an assassin. Marek made me feel worth knowing. It
was a nice change.

He shifted his feet and pushed back in his chair.
"Reckless people do not give stable counsel. I see why you
are suited to your occupation."

"It was a lucky break. I'm not aggressive enough to
prove myself every day. I like being needed in a certain place
at a certain time to do a certain thing."

The ice clinked in Marek's glass when he lifted it.
"You crave security."

I nodded. Boy, did he hit the nail on the head.

"Knowing I have a place to go lets me focus on putting everything I have into my performance. I don't have to worry about holding back part of myself as a reserve for my survival."

"What about your freelance work? That's not guaranteed."

My pulse quickened and fizzed like a shot of Mountain Dew. I was pleased he'd remember a tiny detail I'd only briefly mentioned. "No, but it's not my bread and butter, either. I write that stuff because my mind is always going. Typing it out kind of clears my head."

"You make it sound more like a hobby than a trained profession."

"I guess it is. I used to work in nursing but my last job was so stressful that to keep from worrying, I started talking to myself. I imagined dialogs, stories, discussions—anything at all, just to avoid thinking about work. Eventually I'd walked away from it all. Hardest thing I ever did."

I trailed off before my voice could betray the sadness I still felt. All the good I'd done, all the satisfaction I'd gotten from really helping people—I gave it all up because policies became increasingly focused on making money rather than practicing safely. I couldn't work for a company that made me feel I walked into a war zone every day.

Blinking, I glued a grin on my face, hoping he wouldn't call my bluff. "The freelance stuff makes money out of a bad habit I never dropped. I can't believe people pay for my ramblings but I'm glad they do, anyway."

"I wouldn't call them ramblings. Some of your articles are quite... insightful."

My phony grin drooped. "And you would know, how?"

"Internet."

I wanted to fling something at his nonchalant expression. *Mental note: Google yourself ASAP.* "And you're sure it's all me? I'm not the only Sophie Galen, you know."

"I read through some of your published work. Why are you upset? You're a writer. Isn't it the goal to be widely read?" As he suppressed a laugh, the edges of his eyes crinkled.

I didn't know if I should feel flattered or infuriated. Truthfully, he was right about wanting to be read, so I grudgingly restrained myself from lobbing something at him. Besides, the only thing within reach was my lunch and that was too good to waste.

"I don't know, Marek, I guess... I guess it seemed so personal to hear you talk about it. I mean, I do want to be read; it's my job. More readers equal more paychecks. But the freelance stuff tends to be kind of personal. Soul-borne. The people who read it don't know me so it's no big deal. But maybe if you read it, it is a big deal."

Marek gently held my gaze, his eyes full of warmth and acceptance. "Are you afraid of what I'll think? Is my opinion important? Do you fear I'll see more than you want to show?"

Bravely, I maintained eye contact. *Answer, letter D: All of the above.*

I wasn't ready to reveal so much so soon. Truthfully, I already was seriously *in like* with him. His company seemed to satisfy a need inside me I hadn't realized still existed. At first I had been drawn to him because he seemed so dark, so melancholy, another person to "save." It put me in complete control of the relationship.

I was surprised to discover the real chemistry between us, an attraction that seemed to be mutual. It changed things entirely.

I should have felt happy and confident spending time with someone who felt like all sorts of right to me. Instead, it terrified me. Wanting more from him made my soul feel exposed, wide open to the hurts I tried so long to avoid.

Being with him made me fear for my heart's safety.

I didn't know how to take chances like that anymore.

Swallowing hard and trying to look cavalier, I nodded. It was a big giant step to admit my vulnerability but I wouldn't cheapen whatever chance I had with him by lying.

Marek reached across the table toward me, pressing his hand to mine in a gesture that was both comforting and intimate. "Don't worry, Sophie. I'll never judge you by what you write. Words are just words. Right?"

Relieved, I nodded again, more enthusiastically.

He squeezed my hand before letting go. Standing up, he flicked his shoulders to smooth his shirt down into place.

"I've got to keep reading then." The smirk he wore was nothing short of playful. "There must be some really interesting stuff out there for you to look so worried."

"Marek," I whined. "I thought you understood."

"But I do." He chuckled deep in his throat. "I can't wait for you to reveal yourself to me, inch by maddening fraction of an inch. I want to know your entire splendor, your bared soul, your wellspring of inner self. I want it all and I want it now. If this helps me get it, then I'll do it."

"But they're only words—"

"Yes, but words tell stories. Even if the stories aren't true, they reveal much about the one who tells them. Perhaps your writing is not autobiographical, Sophie, but there surely is a bit of you in everything you write." Marek's eyes flashed, a green glint of amusement, a hint of tease that pierced his somber expression. "I seek the back story."

Defeated, I dropped my hands into my lap. "I can't change your mind?"

"I want all of you. This is another part to want."

"Can't I just distract you with more obvious parts?"

"You do more than distract." He regarded me with intensity. As his eyes swept over me, I felt a nearly-physical caress that made my pulse quicken again. "But my mind must be sated, as well."

Sated. The word invoked sudden images of strewn and tangled sheets, perspiration and exhausted satisfaction. Thank God he wasn't a mind reader.

I busied myself with gathering the remnants of our meal onto the plastic tray. "All right then. Satisfy whatever curiosity you have but, please, I'm not comfortable discussing those writings. I'm not ready to hear what you think of them."

"Agreed." He flashed a triumphant grin, completely ruining the usual severity of his expression. That quick smile, so rare for him, stole my breath away and left me feeling off balance.

As if I could ever prevent him from doing anything or from being smug about it.

Some things I just knew by instinct.

7

St. Joseph's Cathedral was an ancient stone and stained glass Catholic church standing smack-dab in the middle of downtown. The stout giant seemed to have been transplanted into a sleek, modern garden of steel and diesel fumes.

Ever since I was young, I believed the Church offered some sort of sanctuary; St. Joseph's completely re-affirmed those feelings. A broad public garden sprawled from front steps to sidewalk, while its walled-in cemetery gathered behind; the grounds helped to set it apart from the surrounding wilderness of office buildings and parking lots.

Once safely inside, I was submerged in tranquility, like a cool touch on an anxious brow. *Relax and find peace, no harm shall find you; no trouble shall reach you here.* Even the most obstinate soul could sense the asylum.

I passed the main entrance and rounded the corner, following the sidewalk to a flight of steps on the side of the building. These led down to a basement-level set of rooms that housed the Adoration Chapel, open from dawn to sunset. I often visited when I needed a little drive–thru sanctuary.

I'd spent a good part of the morning on the phone with Marek, who'd agonized over difficulty with clients or coworkers or somebody. Apparently his work involved a lot of ethics. Funny, since I thought his work was politically–inclined; politics and ethics usually avoided each other like plague.

To make matters worse, his dark mood spread an overtone of *damned if I do and damned if I don't* upon every word.

Since a degree in counseling wouldn't manifest itself and help me cure Marek's self-image problems, it couldn't hurt to ask the Big Guy for some guidance. Slipping inside, I dropped my bag on a chair and crossed the room to a kneeler.

The air was faintly perfumed with the spice of incense, a soothing fragrance that settled me into serenity. I blessed myself and knelt, reaching to light one of the votive candles. Peace nestled near the little flames warming blue glasses in front of a contented statue.

When the flames leapt and danced in place, I knew someone else had entered. Rising, I turned to see the priest holding out his hands and greeting me with a warm smile.

"Father Jared..." Peering up into his eyes, I noticed with a twinge of sadness the weariness in them, the little wrinkles beginning to bloom. I'd known him since high school but sometimes I forgot how many years had passed. To see time etched in an old friend's face is to acknowledge those years that slipped by, nearly uncounted.

Grasping my hands, he smiled wide enough to show his crooked bicuspid. That one tooth, only slightly misaligned, gave his smile a hint of adolescent innocence. "All these years and it still sounds strange to hear you call me that."

"Sorry, Jare. It's the collar."

"I know, I know." He tipped his head in rueful agreement. "But please, friends first, Sophie."

"Friends 'til infinity," I replied.

"So what's brought you here?" He settled into one of the folding chairs. "I thought you worked all day on Tuesdays."

"I quit early. I've been trying to help a new friend out. After a morning of that, I couldn't seem to get anything else done."

"Ah," he nodded. "A new friend. Do you go looking for these strays or do they just manage to keep finding you?"

"I don't know." I smiled wryly. "How was it with us?"

"Hmm." He leaned back, tapping his chin in a parody of deep thought. "I think you found me. You were suddenly there, shaking sense into me. My little savior."

"Some savior. Cigarette hanging out of my mouth, leather jacket and an Ozzy shirt..."

"And the boots! Remember the blue bandana you wore around your ankle? And don't even get me started on the hair. I mean, Holy Bon Jovi, Batman!"

"Knock it off." I chuckled, remembering the cruel big-haired late 80s and the things we wore for the music we loved. "So, yeah, another stray, I guess. But this one is different. He's so dark, Jare. It's like he stands at the edge of some great abyss and part of me is saying if I get too close, he might grab me and jump off."

I tried to make a joke of it but the ominous dreams I'd been having made it difficult. The comparison felt too close to the truth and my voice betrayed me. I rubbed my fingernail against my lower lip, trying to prevent anything else from emerging.

"I've told you before your soft heart could lead you to trouble one day. You have to walk away if he's dangerous."

I shook my head. "I mean, some of the things he's told

me, okay. He definitely isn't Playing-It-Safe Guy. I can... I can feel he's dangerous. But not to me."

"How do you know? You aren't psychic and you aren't a shrink. Worse yet, you trust people too easily."

I looked away, watching the candles flicker and sway. "You're right,. All I know is there's good in him and he needs me to help him find it."

He ran a hand over his short sandy curls. "Sophie, I've always admired your compassion. But you can't put yourself in harm's way. You can't save everyone. You have to understand that."

"I've never given up on anyone." I put my hand on his arm. "I didn't give up on you."

Jared seemed to consider that and something unspoken passed briefly between us before he leaned forward to kiss my forehead. "No, you didn't. If it wasn't for you, I probably never would have gotten my soul back."

Peering up into his eyes again, I thought I glimpsed the shaggy-headed seventeen-year-old boy I had once known, but it was only a trick of my memory. That boy had grown up a long time ago.

Jared's expression settled with resignation, the mature patience he'd developed after many years of tending his ever-straying sheep. "The look in your eyes says you're going to help him anyway, no matter the price. Okay. You need anything at all, call me. But at the first sign of bad, you turn around and you run. I can't always be there to fight the bad guys for you."

"And I can't afford to bail you out of jail anymore."

He scratched the back of his head and grinned. "I guess we outgrew the whole *Bonnie and Clyde* phase, didn't we?"

"Hey." I raised my hands. "I was only guilty by association and you know it."

He laughed. "You still are. Anyway. There's real danger

out there these days. If you get close to it, you turn and run. Promise?"

"Yes, Father." A visit with Jared was always a return to happiness. It was so easy to love him and, quite frankly, I liked being with a man who wasn't out for something more. No pressure, no need to impress. Plus, I figured I scored bonus points with God because my best friend was a priest.

I found my purse where I'd dropped it and hoisted it onto my shoulder. "I have to go, Jared. Thanks for being here for me."

"Sophie, be careful," he said. "I couldn't bear it if anything happened to you."

"But the Mass would be lovely, I'm sure." I smiled over my shoulder before I sprinted up the stairs and back out into the sun.

8

A few days later, I leaned back in my desk chair, reading over some text and thinking. Well, trying to think. A loud and obnoxious conversation took place on the other side of my partition. Normally the office noise doesn't distract me. When I'm working on my column I kind of zone into it, tuning everything else out. It's probably why I got too involved with the work.

I couldn't block this out, though. Donna's voice was a Zen killer for me.

"There is something so mysterious about him," Donna said. "I love the bad boy attitude. When I'm with him, all I can think about is sex and danger."

I gagged. I hurried to print my work so I could go hide in Barbara's office until lunch. Listening to Donna's sexcapades ranked dead last on my list of Things To Do Before I Die.

A rude beep from the printer told me I forgot to load paper and I reached desperately behind me for a new ream.

"Where did you meet him, Donna?" I couldn't match

the voice to a face. That might be for the best.

"At Folletti's," Donna said smugly. Small wonder. No place but the best for Donna. "He's upper management there. Usually, we just go upstairs to the club."

"Ooh, I heard of it. It's pretty exclusive."

"It is but this guy is on the inside. He's smooth, suave, and so seductive. When we're together we nearly incinerate. He told me I'm so hot, I smolder."

Ugh. Beyond gag and two seconds from throwing up into my mouth. He'd have to be dead if he thought Donna was hot, because she was one cold bitch. Printer refilled, I clicked OK and managed to keep from shaking the monitor to speed it up.

"His mouth... there are no words to describe what he does with it. It should be illegal. You know, he's got a friend who is just as tempting... you could double with me sometime."

I guessed the unintelligible squealing the other girl emitted represented agreement. Then again, I didn't speak Pig. The printer spit out the sheet and I grabbed it, scrambling out before I heard anything else about Donna's love life.

No wonder I preferred working from home.

My mood didn't improve despite the prospect of a quick date with Marek that afternoon.

"I don't get you," Marek said. We sat at a high table near the front window of Abbie's Ice Cream Emporium. I had an hour before *The Mag*'s monthly issue review meeting and Marek had met me on my break.

It would be a long meeting. It always was, hence the ice cream. Abbie's Chocolate Buzz contained enough caffeine and sugar to help me fake an alert and interested look. A single cup of coffee during the meeting would push me over the edge to the realm of "engaged."

I looked up from my bowl. "What, you never saw anyone eat potato chips with ice cream before? You deprived child."

"Not that. Sometime, you say the strangest things." He held his hands up to prevent me from arguing. "This is the twenty first century. Your ideals don't exist anymore."

"Mmm," I mused. "Maybe I have an old heart. It doesn't keep time with the world I live in anymore."

"Ah. You spend much time in your books. You like to be dramatic."

"No," I replied indignantly. How vaguely insulting. Picking out a wide chip, I scooped up a lump of chocolate. "People and things seem shallow when compared to a heart's true depths. Things like honor, courage, trust, promise —those things are merely words. Even faith is a watered-down echo of the original passion of the early religions. I mean, organized religion today is more business than anything."

I popped the chip into my mouth before it got soggy. Waving at the window, the busy street beyond, the city folk moving in an endless stream, I dismissed them all. "Complacency is king these days. Forgive me if my heart is stronger than that."

"Don't apologize. Few people find strength to keep living their individual lives when the world itself has become so automatic. You are an oddity, that's all."

I wasn't sure I liked the term *oddity* but I let it go. "Maybe. But it's who I am."

"I wonder." The words came out slowly, as if a new thought crept up on him and he attempted to sort it out. He leaned his chair back against the wall and regarded me shrewdly. "Are you other than what you would lead me to believe? Are you reincarnated? An old soul, perhaps?"

I graced him with a smirk that said *I think I'll call the nice men with the nets now.* "Why, yes. Yes, I am. I'm an age-old creature, a remnant of history, doomed to walk the earth, surrounded more and more by people who resemble me less and less."

"Now you make a joke."

"Well, what about you? You have a curious detachment from the world, considering how involved you are with your business and your finger on the pulse of political persuasion and what-not. What kind of modern man stalks around each day with your great big *this is a good day to die* attitude?"

"Well, now." He lowered his chin and toyed with his keys where they lay upon the table. Light from the overhead fluorescent bulbs sparked a green glint in his eye. "If I told you, you'd just think I was being as flippant as you are."

"No, really, Marek. You seem to court destruction. Do you have an old soul?"

He shook his head and pressed his lips into a humorless line. "I have no soul."

"Oh, you don't." I played along. "All right, a modern excuse then. Military, right? You know a lot about other cultures so maybe you served on foreign missions. Hit man?"

He shook his head so I pressed on. "Terrorist? Certainly not a martyr. I can't imagine you dying for anyone or anything. You'd be the one causing the dying."

"If you only knew." His tone warned I had wandered onto a conversational minefield: one wrong step and I'd be blown to bits. Back off. Back off now.

The impression was unmistakable. However, I heard the secret lurking behind the words. I had to pursue it. "Then tell me, Marek, and I would know."

His voice was hard, telling me I'd hit more than a conversational wall. "Don't try to solve a mystery that doesn't exist. I am what I am and there is no changing. Not myself, not my outcome, not my destiny. Telling you the truth wouldn't change anything."

I used my napkin and gave a baleful glance to the spreading chocolate puddle in the Styrofoam bowl. "Look, you know what I'm like. You wouldn't keep bringing up these heavy topics if there wasn't something you wanted from me. What is it, if not peace or relief from carrying a burden alone?"

"Can't it be I find you attractive and like to spend time looking at you?"

"It could be but it's not. Guys like that are less talk and more action. I think you want me to figure something out for you."

"You're wrong." Anger locked his jaw. Only his lips moved when he spoke and the words slid out on edge. "I am not one of your charity cases."

"Yeah, you are." A glance at my watch showed it was nearly time for my meeting. Standing up, I pulled money out of my wallet and dropped it on the table, knowing it would aggravate him. "When you're ready to admit it, give me a call."

9

I grumbled all the way back to the office and endured the staff meeting with a scowl plastered upon my face. How did I get involved with impossible men? Why did I bother? Who was I, Don frigging Quixote?

Marek had a darkness in him, some heavy weight that kept him from enjoying—I don't know—simple things. Like ice cream and chips. My sarcastic witty charm. Simply being alive. Didn't he get what I was about? He knew I was an advice guru. Why couldn't he tell me what troubled him so? Complete strangers did it all the time without a second thought. What kept him from opening up to me?

Didn't he trust me? It made me mad at him and mad at myself and mad at everyone who had the misfortune to glance my way.

I left work shortly after the meeting ended. I shudder to think how my letters would have sounded if I had column work to do. Might say I felt less than charitable.

I didn't know what I could do besides get a major grump on. So, grump firmly in place, I headed uptown to my sanctuary. Maybe Jared could tell me what to do with this roadblock, besides firebomb it and bribe a bum to pee on whatever smoldered.

Our friendship was a double-edged sword. I depended on him for objective honesty that always had my best interest at heart. Regular friends couldn't provide the extra assurance of God's Honest Truth, Guaranteed.

But sometimes when I was with Jared, I stared at the collar rather than looked at his eyes. Sure, he's my pastor. Sure, he's my best friend. Sure, I had enough emotional traumas without adding an audition for the *Thorn Birds* to my repertoire of Tremendously Stupid Mistakes.

But still, I trained my eyes on the collar, or his shoulder, or the tree behind him because sometimes, one look at his denim-blue eyes would cause my brain to stop registering *priest*. I'd see only the man, the grown-up version of the boy who, at seventeen, had convinced me we could have more fun together if we undressed.

And he'd been right. A lot.

I'm Catholic enough to know a special level of Hell was reserved for anyone who sundered a priest. But I was human enough to know how rare it was to connect to another soul, to transcend love. I knew how desperate a person could be to feel that love again.

Only human. Nice collar. Amen.

Jared was in the garden with one of the retired sisters who lived in the adjacent convent. The sisters were responsible for the churchyard's thriving year-long beauty. Jared usually ended up lugging the soil and the wheelbarrow and the big pots around, but he said he didn't mind.

A half-lifetime ago, however, if I had suggested he'd be planting flowers with a bunch of old nuns, he'd have responded with an expression of disbelief, an invitation to do something impossible to myself, and perhaps shown me the middle finger.

Jared waved as I passed through the gates and spoke a few words to the elderly sister before crossing the grass to meet me. He brushed at the soil clinging to his jeans before raking his hair back, oblivious to the smudge of dirt he left on his forehead.

"Father, mind the lawn," the nun called. "You'll crush the new grass."

Jared hot-footed it over to the path, resuming his rambling stride once he was on less sacred ground.

"How was work?" Jared caught up to me on the sidewalk and we strolled along one of the garden paths. The maple trees had finally uncurled their broad leaves and sunlight dropped through in spots that wavered with the light breeze.

"Eh. I go. I write. I drink coffee. Then I go home. For some reason, they pay me."

"The pay good?"

"I still have a place to live, at any rate. Hey." I nodded toward the sisters walking toward the Church doors. "Do nuns get paid a lot? Maybe they're hiring."

Jared pulled a nail clipper out of his pocket and began to clean his fingernails. I guess he took the cleanliness/Godliness thing seriously. "The sisters take a vow of poverty."

I wrinkled my nose. "That shouldn't be too much of a stretch."

"They give up their worldly possessions."

"All of them? Shoes too?" I craned my neck to see if Sister Mary Whatsherbutt wore strappy heels. Ugh. No.

Jared leaned closer and gave me a stern look. "They don't drink coffee. It's a sin."

"Ack! Forget it, I'm no saint. I'd rather be broke."

"You wouldn't be broke if you'd stayed in nursing."

"No," I admitted. "But I'd be miserable."

"I don't get it. You were born to do it—the way you care, the way you made a difference."

I scowled. This was a subject I'd deftly evaded. People didn't usually like bragging about their epic failures. "I cared too much."

"I don't follow."

I sighed, not really wanting to continue. "I had a great job, Jare. Every day I went to work and thought: this is the best day of my life."

"So what changed?"

"It was gradual. I mean, I didn't walk in one day and suddenly everything sucked. The changes were so subtle I never found that *aha, now I quit* moment. Stress built, you know, little things I could handle at first."

I pulled a lock of hair over my shoulder, twisting it and studying the split ends. "But it kept building. Management wanted profit. Increased quotas. Budget cuts. Scaled back support staff. Missed lunch breaks. That's when mistakes began to happen, mistakes I could objectively prove occurred due to the lack of help, and the supervisors just—blew it off."

"Everyone makes mistakes, Sophie."

"Not me, okay?" My heartbeat picked up, the re-membered stress manifesting. "I can't make mistakes, Jared, not any kind, not ever. But no one listened. I pleaded with the supervisors to give us what we needed but they turned a deaf ear. Someone higher up was twisting their arms even tighter. So screw the little people further down the food chain."

Jared reached out and squeezed my arm. "Sophie, slow down. You're getting..."

"Stressed out?" I dropped my hair and moved on to my cuticles. Anything to avoid eye contact. "I helped a lot of people, I made good relationships. I was part of the com-munity. I made a difference. I did."

I summoned a strained smile as I remembered old faces, old names, old times.

"But it was so hard," I whispered. "Whatever made me strong enough to deal with challenges at work, it had turned brittle. In Church I prayed for patience and tolerance and strength and peace. Well, at least until I had to start working Sundays."

He glanced away and drew a cross in the air with his fingers.

"I cracked, Jared," I said. "I failed. So I quit. It wasn't worth the pills or the sleepless nights I spent worrying about what I could have done wrong that day." I rubbed my eyes with the heels of my palms and pushed my hair back. "I quit. I left all the good behind because I couldn't handle the bad anymore."

"That was one job." he said. "Why not find a different one, someplace that didn't have the stress? Why not medical writing? You could still be using your knowledge and expertise somewhere."

"No. I can't."

"Because?"

"Because my career wasn't the only thing that ended. I had a relationship, too." Another reason to erase that entire section of my life. "Stan was a good guy. But the stress spilled over into my private life. I'd become my career. There was no nine-to-five then go home."

Jared whooshed out a breath and chuckled in sympathy. "I can understand that."

"Yeah, well, we worked together. When I started getting fed up with the job, he took it personally. He figured if I didn't want the job, I didn't want him, either." I tucked my hair behind my ears and watched ants on the sidewalk, waiting for the tears to sink back in. "It was a clean break. I don't regret it more than anything else."

"Are you still friends?"

"He's not who I knew five years ago. Neither am I. It's pointless to think about going back. It wasn't him—he gave a hundred percent. But he didn't need me. I never loved him the way I love when I'm needed. He merely wanted me. It wasn't enough. Maybe that's why I never settled with anyone else. Nobody ever needed me like…"

I trailed off, feeling like I'd painted myself into a corner. Last thing I needed right now is to lay a guilt trip on a priest.

"Like I needed you?" Jared supplied the words my cowardice couldn't.

"Yeah." I shrugged and tugged my sweater tightly around me, pulling at imaginary fuzz balls on my sleeve. Soon, I'd run out of things to fidget with. "I never found something like that again. You were kind of a benchmark."

I braved a glance in his direction. His gaze held the understanding a teacher gave a struggling kid. Patience, encouragement, acceptance.

I was grateful for his silence. This was a conversation I never intended to have with him, especially not on a day he wore a well-worn black Hanes pocket T-shirt instead of the safety net of the clergyman's collar. Our past was past. Our past had no place in the present. Our past was not something to discuss, especially not in a church garden. God forgive us.

"Maybe it's silly," I said. "I mean, we were seventeen. Trying to find our way on our own but still not ready to give up the security of somebody taking care of us, right? Teen angst, raging hormones, all that."

"Oh, I remember, all right. Lots of high-emotion circumstances at the time." The distant look in his eyes told me he remembered his own troubled past clearly.

"And this…" I gently traced the edge of a tattoo peering out from under the cuff of his shirt sleeve. He didn't have it when I'd first known him, although I'd watched him doodle it a half-million times. A stylized mathematical symbol, a combination of a loop and an arrow.

"Infinity." He lifted his sleeve to give me a better look. The bluish line had grown fuzzy the way most cheap tattoos did as they aged. "I got it the week I moved away. Math is supposed to be logical, right? I'd figure out how to get back to you and the infinity we tried to find. You know how far I got."

His eyes lost focus. "Time went by, though, and infinity came to mean other things. Like with my vocation, my studies at the seminary."

"You have to take math classes to be a priest?"

"No, silly. Theology classes. You know." He pointed a finger at the sky. "God? Infinity?"

"Oh, yeah," I grinned. "I heard of that somewhere."

"Right," he drawled. "Infinity. Nothing is permanent. We're a blink in a grander scheme. Our whole life is one tiny moment in infinity. Even if something is really bad, it's not forever."

"Even when it feels like forever?"

"Even then. We've nothing to fear, except maybe screwing up so badly we lose our chance to rejoin infinity. You'd have to be completely damnable. That's a hard thing to achieve."

"You didn't go to the same school I did," I said. "The nuns said we were hopeless."

"How can we be hopeless? We have souls, little slices of infinity inside us, and anyone with a soul couldn't be forgotten by God. He'd never leave behind a part of Himself." He made it sound comforting. So easy to forgive myself for the things I couldn't release. I wanted to believe him, to submerge myself in faith, to surrender.

Jared smiled, emphasizing what made him a charismatic pastor: gentleness and patience, wishing with his whole heart for me to believe. To just let go of my fear and believe.

I didn't feel quite that brave, but he encouraged me to think someday I might be. For now, I'd settle for a single peaceful moment in this lifetime of hectic coffee-fueled stress. Leaning back on my elbows, I turned back to the gardens, admiring the play of sunlight upon the leaves and grass, content to be momentarily content with life.

The temperate winds convinced me to skip the bus and walk home instead. My brain tried to sort out pressing questions along the way. What would it be like to abandon everything for my faith, like Jared had? Would I feel secure trusting God to take care of me?

My mom used to say that when things got to be too much to handle, we should "put it all in God's hands, and let Him take care of it." As a child I found it easy to have that kind of faith. After all, my parents took care of me and my brothers; it seemed natural to believe God was there too, taking care of the invisible things.

As I grew, the theory unraveled.

My twin brothers died when they were seven. My parents said *illness* but I don't remember anyone being sick. They didn't want to talk about it. I didn't, either, at first. By the time I was ready, the topic had long been forbidden.

I remember how quiet my dad became, how strong my mom tried to be. They were constantly preoccupied, too busy for the little things that made things normal. Smiles stretched thinner, faded faster. Meals became silent, functional tasks.

Everyday life lost sound, color, taste. I had to work harder at living, for me and for them. I couldn't bear to merely exist.

Outside my home, things were no more optimistic. Half my teen friends had lousy parents who left them to fend for themselves. I remember standing outside Jared's house, listening to his mother's aggravation spurt out the open windows as she berated him for yet another infraction, knowing I faced another long night of convincing him not to run.

So much uncertainty, so much pain, so little hope. Why didn't God take care of us?

And the one time I needed Him most, when I got the call at college, my Aunt Marie telling me I had to come home, my parents were in an accident—

my parents were dead

I'd blindly put everything into God's hands. He dropped it.

My world shattered. I watched it fall to pieces all around me, heard the discordant ping of sanity and hope as they blasted into oblivion. No words could describe my desolation. *Grief* wasn't strong enough. *Raw* wasn't strong enough. No word for that feeling when breath was pulled from me like a taffy string, making my lungs bunch up and stick shut. No word for that shallow breathing as I tried to learn to breathe again.

I put myself back together, but it was hard work, almost too hard for one small person like me. No word for that sense of being orphaned. *Orphaned* just wasn't strong enough.

So maybe I did believe in safety nets and security and avoiding risks. I had no choice. I couldn't blindly believe anymore. I needed proof and the only proof I found was what I could do. Feeling like this made me think I was an unfit Catholic. I did believe in God. I simply believed in myself more sometimes.

Is this what drove me? Is this why I had to be the one who made everything better for all those people? Is this why I had such a savior complex—because I didn't want people to realize He might not be there for them, either?

The sun set behind the artificial horizon of lofty

buildings and the tiny warmth it gave this time of year vanished. I pulled my sweater tighter and tried to ignore the chill as I hurried the last few blocks to my apartment.

I understood why a strong, capable man like Marek believed he wasn't good enough. As I fell asleep, a single thought of speculation curled itself into familiar patterns of self-doubt. No bedtime prayer could banish it and, as usual, peace eluded me.

Was I a saint for helping people the way I do?

Or a devil, for insisting God needed me to do it for Him?

10

"That you, Fraidy?"

I'd been in the bathroom when I heard an odd scratchy noise coming from the living room and went to investigate. The cat had a penchant for pushing over my paperwork, sliding over the neat stacks so he could sprawl across them. It was his way of insisting he was more important than my work. If I didn't stop him, he'd make a mess out of my articles.

I hurried out, hissing a *kissst* in warning but he wasn't anywhere near my desk. Nothing seemed out of place. Standing stock-still and straining my ears, I tried to identify the sound but it had ceased. The entire apartment had fallen dead silent.

Strange. Even with windows shut, it never sounded this quiet. Traffic and neighbors and house sounds constantly intruded. Now it seemed as if the apartment had been sealed off. The air had the texture of summer humidity without the heat or moisture. It caught in my throat, coated my mouth, curdled.

Something just wasn't right. I had the creepy feeling someone was watching me.

That Euphrates. He probably hid under the couch, pretending to be a jungle cat stalking his prey again. Like I couldn't squish him with one foot tied behind my back. Peering under the couch, however, I found only the usual collection of dust bunnies, ink pens, and kitty toys. I walked back toward the bedroom but the oppressiveness didn't dissipate.

Dumb cat. *Witness the mighty hunter,* I thought with a documentary-type voice, *bringing down his hapless victim and rubbing it to death.* I had a brief flash of an image of Marek and Euphrates stalking prey together. The absurdity of the thought made me laugh out loud.

My sudden laugh seemed to pop the bubble that had been squeezing down on me and I breathed deeply at the sudden release of tension. Everything sounded and felt normal again.

Euprates meowed, scowling at me from the hallway.

"S'matter, Fraidy Cat?" I squatted and held out my fingers to him but he flattened himself, ears back and whining. Poor thing acted spooked.

Maybe a storm was moving in. He hated storms and usually took his nervous tension out on the side of my couch. I walked over to where Euphrates hunched in a tight ball of anxiety and scooped him up.

Two tight taps sounded at the door. The cat twisted, a sudden fury of hiss and hind claw.

"Christ, Fraidy!" I wrestled with him for a second before dropping him, earning three deep scratches in my forearm.

The rap sounded again, an impatient demand. Euphrates crouched facing the door and issued a low constant caterwauling that sounded like a siren. The cat that usually ran from his own shadow wanted to fight. Puzzled by his odd behavior, I pushed him out of the way with my foot and went to the door.

"Who's there?" I bounced up on my toes to look through the peep hole.

"It's Marek." He stood like a shadow in the bright hallway and seemed to stare back at me through the peep-hole.

I whooshed out the breath I didn't realized I'd been holding. I didn't know who I'd expected but I was glad to see him. Surprised, yes, but still glad.

"Hang on." I flipped the myriad locks and swung open the door. I pushed my bangs back with my fingers, conscious about my appearance but powerless to do anything about it. "I really didn't expect you."

Euphrates stalked in front of me and pressed himself against my legs, rigid and hissing.

"Knock it off, Fraidy." I pushed him into the bedroom. Closing the door on the furious beast, I glanced at Marek, who seemed to reconsider his intention of visiting.

"Sorry about that." I flashed a sheepish grin. "I don't know what got into him. He's spooked."

I stepped aside to make way for Marek but he remained in the hall, staring at the adjacent bedroom door. It sounded as though there were a chipper-shredder on the other side.

"I promise he can't get out." I wiggled my fingers. "He has issues with the doorknob."

Marek showed no intention of moving either of his feet. Either he really didn't like cats or I had underestimated the force of Euphrates' wrath. I didn't want to give the neighbors a floor show tonight. "Marek, will you please come in, so I might close the door?"

Marek tipped his head in a genteel bow and strolled inside, paying no more attention to Euphrates the Destroyer. "I was not sure you would be home but, since I passed this way, I took a chance."

As I led him back to the living room, something in his voice caught my notice. I had the impression this wasn't simply a social call. I threw a questioning glance at him but he just shrugged. "Fortune favors the brave, right?"

"I wouldn't know," I said. "There isn't a brave bone in my body." Totally the truth. I'd suffered a total system failure as a young adult and rebooted in safe mode. Being with Marek was like taking every chance in the world at once. What was I doing, letting him in?

Remembering our last conversation and considering his gloomy tone, the tortured look in his eyes, I figured he was finally ready to pour his soul out to me. I pushed my own apprehensions aside and concentrated on doing my apparent duty.

I waved at the sofa in an invitation to sit. "Something to drink?"

"Maybe later." He toyed with the fringe on a small hole in the knee of his jeans. "Why don't you sit down?"

I must have appeared dismayed because he chuckled, an indulgent throaty sound. "You don't have to fuss over me. I only hoped for a chance to talk."

"Oh, all right." I sat down at my desk and swiveled the desk chair around to face him.

"The view..." He gestured toward the windows. "It's magnificent. I bet you could see all the way out to the harbor."

"Yeah, I guess. I considered moving a few times but I couldn't find anyplace else that compared. Besides, we're allowed on the fire escape here. Poor man's balcony."

He nodded, as if he understood how precious a commodity it was for a city dweller. "How are your neighbors?"

A perfectly-timed glass-trembling thump, followed by a heavily-accented debate, spared me the trouble of replying.

I shot him a baleful look and he glanced up at the ceiling, pretending to cringe in worry it might come down on our heads.

"They don't have any carpeting. Drives me batty," I said. "Actually, they're okay. The neighbors seem nice but pretty much they leave me alone, I leave them alone."

"That is a city attitude." He sniffed and shook his head. "The more people who are around, the less they have to do with each other. In a city this size, you can disappear. Crazy, isn't it? Someone can be lonely when they never have a chance to be alone."

Candles burned on the coffee table, the gold light captured in his green eyes. He regarded me with a piercing gaze, his eyes pale and bright. His intense scrutiny made me think he could see past my expression and delve deep into my secrets.

"That's what makes you so rare," he said. "The city is full of strangers who want to be left to their lives. Then there is you, actually giving a shit about them. Why?"

I blinked. Hard. "It's my job."

"No, it's not. Your job is to write, not to care. You can do one thing without doing the other. Why do you bother?"

"Why not?" I answered slowly. I hadn't expected such a confrontational question, but I didn't have anything to hide. "Aren't we all connected? Don't we depend upon each other to survive? Don't our relationships with other people define us?"

"No. Others come and go and eventually all you end up with is yourself."

"That's a pretty fatalistic view."

He set his jaw in a mulish line. "I'm a pretty fatalistic kind of guy."

"I don't believe that. I get the feeling you're looking for the same thing as everyone else."

Marek avoided my eyes and rested his elbows on his

thighs, hunching forward and studying the fringe on his jeans again. I tried very hard not to do the same thing but I'd never seen him in denim before. It distracted me. The fringe stood out like a spot of foam on a midnight sea.

His voice brought me back to the living room. "No, I don't think I am. Not at all."

"Sure you are," I pressed. "If you didn't want your family around you, would you mourn the ones you've lost? Would you spend so much time and effort helping the ones who remain? If you thought everyone's destiny was to end up alone, would you have bothered to come here?"

His voice slid into darker tones. "Are you implying you have something I need?"

I was slightly alarmed by the thread of threat that insinuated itself into the sentence, infusing it with the nameless danger I'd come to associate with him. I decided to ignore it and continue on as if we still discussed human dependency issues.

"Maybe. Perhaps I see things differently and you were ready for a new perspective." I deliberately repeated what he'd said the day we met.

"You sound like a psychiatrist." Lifting his head, he almost grinned. The hairs on the back of my neck relaxed. "Perhaps you have a point. I've been so busy trying to distance myself from my past I forget what it's like to actually connect with anyone. Sometimes I feel like a ghost, or worse."

"It's not too late, you know. You have so much to offer to the world."

He curled his lips but directed the sarcastic expression to his hands as he clasped them around his knee. "Do I?"

"Yes," I said. "You know, I enjoy spending time with you. You've traveled to places I've only dreamed of. You make me realize there's a whole world out there I never knew about. Your stories are fascinating, even if they tend to be a little..."

"Dark?"

"Yes, dark," I replied firmly. "It wouldn't hurt to let sunlight into your life, you know."

"Easy for you to say."

My God, was he a pessimist. Worse. He was the guy who criticized the pessimist for being too hopeful. "See? That's what I mean."

"Some things aren't meant for sunlight. The only place for them is in the shadows."

"You sound like you're so evil, so wretched."

Marek stretched and leaned on the back of the couch, spreading his arms to rest along the top cushions. Even sitting down, he gave a distinct impression of height and fierceness. "That's because I am."

"I don't believe it." Well, I mostly didn't. "You have depth and it speaks of a great soul. *Wretched* and *evil* are shallow characteristics for shallow people, meant for someone who doesn't put any effort into living. That's not you."

"Do you think I've exaggerated? Or lied?" The words could have been menacing but I detected only curiosity in the tilt of his head, his direct gaze.

"No... but somehow I think your dark perception of yourself colors everything you do and think. There is good in you. I can sense it."

Thoughts sprang unbidden to my mind, like flashes of revelation. Despite the dangerous layer he wore like a second skin, a true heart kept time in him.

Marek could be bad, terrifyingly bad, but it took effort. It had to be necessary. When it was, he was a lion. Walking, hunting, the embodiment of watchful death. When there was peace, he was simply a good man. Balanced.

My inner voice was at it again. The epiphany rein-forced my gut instincts, my first impressions.

Marek looked up at me for a long searching moment, treating me to another glimpse of the candlelight dancing in his eyes. His mouth moved silently as if he struggled to choose his words.

He swallowed whatever unspoken thought he'd contemplated. Standing, he cleared his throat. "I think I'm ready for something to drink."

"Oh, jeez. Sure." I sprang up apologetically and sprinted toward the kitchen but he intercepted me, grasping my arm when I passed.

"No, don't go through any trouble. Would you—want to go out for something? There is a café at the top of the bank building on Tenth. It's a splendid night. Definitely not one to be wasted indoors."

His enticing offer was punctuated by an obscene screech from my still-imprisoned cat, which had grown quiet while we talked. Euphrates had found his second wind.

Marek still gripped my arm and I grew warm under his touch. I grew squirmy, too, because, despite the pleasure of his touch, my arm still throbbed from Euphrates's parting gift.

When I winced, Marek looked down. Concern bunched his brows when he saw the rents.

"What happened?" Gingerly he turned over my arm to examine the deep scratches. Blood had welled up along them like strings of scarlet beads. I had forgotten about the scratches in the surprise of seeing Marek but his unintentional contact woke up the wounded nerves.

"Fraidy did it when you knocked. Scared the hell out of him, I guess."

He clucked his tongue. Pulling out a handkerchief, he unfurled it with a flick of his fingers and dabbed off the wounds. Before I could stop him, he pressed a soft kiss to my arm. "To make it all better."

My face grew warm and I made a joke to cover my discomfort. "Thanks, Nurse Marek."

My skin tingled and a rosy glow settled over the scratches, chasing away the sharp pain. Reluctantly he released me, perhaps as unwilling as I was to end an accidental moment. I swooped to grab my shoulder bag and keys and followed him to the door.

"Oh, wait," I said. "I forgot to let Fraidy out."

"I'll just, ah, wait down the hall, then," Marek said. Couldn't say I blamed him.

Stepping back into the apartment, I closed the door behind me before opening the one to the bedroom. Instead of a frontal assault, I encountered only stillness. Euphrates looked up at me mournfully so I scooped him up and snuggled him. "Cheer up, Fraidy. I'll be back soon."

As I turned the key in the door, I heard a sad wail from the other side. Funny, through the thick wood it almost like Euphrates cried *don't go...*

11

I had never before been to the Skytop Café.

Okay, to be perfectly honest, I never even knew it existed. The street level of the National Bank building was unremarkable. I walked down Tenth Street at least once a week, never giving the skyscraper more than a passing glance. It was an ordinary mass of concrete, glass, and steel.

However, a pleasant express lift to the top proved otherwise. The top floor opened onto a spacious patio, lined in neon lights and chrome trim that flashed in stark relief against the blackness of the night sky beyond. Metal tracks embedded in the floor hinted that the majority of the restaurant could be closed off against poor weather.

Tonight, everything was exposed to the crisp night air.

Passing the DJ booth and crossing the open floor, Marek lifted a finger and indicated a table at the far edge, away from the crowded bar. Only a sleek rail separated us from the empty arms of the night. As I slid onto my seat, I peeked over and down the side of the building. The streets seemed so far below us...

...ah, a little too far. I pulled back from the edge and realized Marek had sat down next to me, rather than across the table.

"Takes your breath away, doesn't it?" He leaned against me, his voice finding my eager ear, his breath stirring against my cheek. A wave of chills sweep over me. I could smell him, his skin, his hair. I would've agreed with him but I had momentarily forgotten how to speak.

I gazed back over the city again, concentrating on the heights rather than the unyielding depths. A light breeze played with my hair as it carried faint sounds of city life from below, mixing it with the sounds of the people behind us. Marek slipped his arm around the back of my chair, surrounding me as he leaned closer.

I couldn't remember the last time I'd been this close to someone and actually felt comfortable. It felt more like exquisite clothing—secure, natural, and pleasant. I couldn't recall being this content with anyone before and the simplicity of it amazed me.

"It could be like this all the time." His whisper broke through the layers of my trance. He stroked his fingers up my arms, bringing them to rest on my shoulders, playing his thumbs along the back of my neck, under my hair. Shivering, I turned my head, my temple brushing against the line of his jaw as I searched for his eyes.

His pupils were large and bottomless, irises reduced to thin rings. They resembled twin pools of night, wearing bright green halos. His eyes glowed, the irises shining like neon.

Averting my gaze, I leaned away from him. I squeezed shut my eyes and shook my head. What did I see? There was no candle here, no light to reflect itself. Why did his eyes look so strange?

He drew back and gently rapped the table with his fingers. "I will order our drinks."

Marek pushed away from the table in a decisive move-ment and headed to the bar, offering the perfect distraction. Damn, but I liked watching him walk. He moved with masculine grace, his strides strong.

He paid the bartender and returned, flashing a grin when he noticed me watching. I wasn't the only one; almost every female in the place had him on her radar—faces uplifted, heads turning to follow him. He paid them no notice. His eyes never left mine and the closer he got, the more I could *feel* his eyes upon me. They were their usual green once more.

Marek's scrutiny made me feel self-conscious, as if I were being watched by many. I busied myself by looking at the drink menu, the view, my hands—anything but him. Acting casual took so much effort.

I smiled, accepting the glass he offered and set it down on the cardboard coaster, grateful for something to do with my hands. Any other time, we would have chatted, laughed, bickered even. Why now did every movement, every gesture mean so much more?

The speakers burst with sound as the DJ began his set. The music wasn't loud enough to drown out conversation but it provided sufficient excuse to not have to talk. I enjoyed this rare kind of peace. Sometimes a mood was so right I didn't need to pad it with words.

Apparently, Marek didn't seem to share my content-ment. From time to time, he appeared ready to blurt out something, before resetting his jaw in a resolute line. Some-thing heavy weighed on his mind and I could almost feel his tension.

One thing, though—whenever he looked at me, his eyes held me. His gaze made me feel as if part of me already belonged to him. And I liked it. I liked it a lot.

I should have kicked myself. I should have left right then and there, making an excuse to use the bathroom but sneaking out altogether. I should have stood up and said, *Thanks for the drinks and the lovely physical caress of your eyes. See you around.*

But I didn't.

Maybe I suspected he'd figure out my plan and slip into the elevator beside me. Maybe he'd just follow me home. *Maybe* didn't matter anymore. I sat at the table, knowing I should leave. Things had gotten too intense. Instead of obeying my inner voice, I pushed those thoughts clean aside.

How long had it been since I'd spent time with anybody? My heart was lonely, my body practically needed dusting off, and I'd already imagined a whole lot of fun stuff with Marek. Maybe my heart and my mind didn't connect on the whole Marek subject but I had to face it—my mind tended to play it safe.

Marek and "playing it safe" were mutually exclusive concepts.

I couldn't lose anything when I didn't have anything. For years I contented myself to live sparsely, material and immaterial things alike. The mere threat of loss—any kind of loss—paralyzed me.

Sitting here with him made me realize what I'd been living without.

I wanted Marek in my life. I wanted to know his touch, to be anchored once more in the present instead of blown around by the past. I wanted the thrill and the stability and the pain of hanging up the phone. I wanted to have someone worth losing.

I'd lived alone and untouched since calling it quits with Stan. He was only an interruption in the drought left in Jared's wake. The solitude should have made me immune. I had no one but my cat and my priest and the occasional pity date with Barbara and her husband.

And yet. Patrick. Guilt. Pain. Memories haunting and

hurting and hollowing me. I still wasn't safe. Giving up everything didn't protect me. I starved myself of closeness and companionship and the pain still found me.

Enough of the martyrdom. If I was destined to bleed anyway, I might as well do it with someone who could peel off a Band-Aid.

Reaching for my glass with one hand, I lifted my chin and met his gaze. I stretched out my other hand to him and he grasped it, pulling it to his mouth. Leaning to kiss it, Marek gazed back up at me from under his black lashes.

A flash of triumph surged into his eyes.

I trembled but blocked out the warning sounds in the back of my skull, turning instead to listen to the din of the night. Its empty arms still waited and I faced it with a mixture of anticipation and dread.

"I want to show you something." Marek squeezed my hand and stood, pulling me up.

Behind him people drifted in twos and threes to the space in front of the DJ's set-up. Please, anything but dancing. To my immense relief he lead me in the other direction. Tucking my hand into the bend of his arm, he guided me away from the crowd, toward to the far end of the patio.

Leaning close, he spoke. "We can get up to the roof from here. It's spectacular."

People glanced our way as we passed them, the women openly admiring him. One by one they lost interest and went back to their smoky conversations and trendy drinks. Beyond the open booth where the DJ checked his equipment, I could see Marek's destination.

A white steel door, painted with big red letters.

EMERGENCY EXIT ONLY. ALARM WILL SOUND.

"Um, are you sure about this?" I dragged my feet. I

didn't want to cause a scene. Alarms tended to cause scenes.

He never faltered or even acknowledged I did. "Don't worry. I go up there often."

Before I could pull him back, he pushed open the door. No alarm, except the pounding of my heart. We slipped through and I glanced behind us as the door closed quietly.

Our footsteps made dull thuds on the steel staircase, the sound swallowed by the concrete walls. Relieved by the lack of trouble at the door, my trepidation gave way to anticipation. This type of miscreant behavior was so unlike me. Recklessness sped my pulse and I let him lead me up the stairs.

The steps ended at another massive door and Marek leaned into it with his shoulder, forcing it open. Fresh air rushed in like cold water. We emerged from the stairwell and stepped out into pure night.

"Amazing," I whispered.

The city lay too far below us to intrude. We had risen high above sight and sound. The wind sang a gentle melody as it ran laughingly across the top of the building. Nothing stood between us and the night sky that hung around us like a tapestry. The stars—could I touch one if I reached out? And how did the blackness of the velvet sky get deeper with every moment? Was I the only one who knew what the night looked like?

I wanted to preserve this moment, bottle it up, store it for the times I grew weary of ordinary sunlight. I threw back my head and slowly spun, delirious and delighted. I laughed into the wind. It rushed around and through me, refreshing me with its clean sharpness. Throwing open my arms, I embraced the night as it had beckoned me to do from the first moment I came here with Marek.

Night returned the embrace. I found myself in Marek's arms.

"Got you," he whispered.

My laughter was the sound of release from unknown bonds as he lifted me. My arms slipped over his shoulders and he held me up into the night.

For a perfect moment, we'd become a monument to joy.

12

As Marek set me back onto my feet, I slid down along his body. His sly smile told me there had been nothing accidental about it and I blushed to think how many parts of mine had become briefly acquainted with parts of his.

His arm forming a protective mantle around my shoulders, we circled the large cooling units that created the landscape of the roof and wandered toward the edge overlooking the same part of the city we'd seen earlier from the patio. We were only about twenty or thirty feet higher but everything seemed so much farther down. Maybe the lack of a guard rail created this illusion.

Releasing me, Marek strolled to the edge and sat down, swinging his feet over. Raking his hair back, he grinned at me and beckoned me to join him. He lounged on the edge of the skyscraper as if he sat on someone's front porch.

Not me. I really didn't like heights. Call it self-preservation.

"And you come up here a lot—why?" I stalled,

although I knew I couldn't risk looking like a sissy. The threat of humiliation lent me false courage and, although I crawled on my hands and knees to get there, I eventually scooted my way over to sit beside him.

Once I was firmly anchored, it didn't seem so bad. As long as I didn't lean over and look down, that is.

"The view doesn't impress?"

"Oh, it impresses, all right." I kept my eyes trained on him rather than the big empty space right in front of me or, worse yet, our table far below. "But what in the world possessed you to come up here? Do you make a habit out of trying alarmed doors?"

Marek reclined slightly, leaning back on his arms. We sat close enough so our sides touched. "My business has offices in this building. I explore every building we use, top to bottom. The tops are generally more enjoyable to visit."

I nodded and surveyed the cityscape. Lights dotted the sides of buildings and traffic lit thin streams of red and white glow as it flowed through the canyons of downtown labyrinth.

His chest made a spot of warmth into which I nestled my shoulder, a sharp contrast with the cool nip of the night air. Time slipped by us momentarily, offering sanctuary, a place where we could enjoy a single, peaceful moment. No pressure, no demands.

Perched up at the top of the National Bank building, one of the tallest in the city, I had a fleeting feeling of how it must have felt for an old king to look out over his great kingdom and find everything to be well.

Contented, I tipped my head and rested against Marek's shoulder. My anxiety from being close to more than six hundred feet worth of free fall had dwindled away to a vague tremor. He turned his head slightly, his gentle expression mirroring my own. Closing my eyes, I wished I could keep a piece of this feeling with me forever.

"You can..." Marek whispered into my hair.

My eyes snapped open as the daydream disintegrated. I stiffened as if I had a clothes hanger in my shirt. "What did you say?"

Marek remained still, his expression indecipherable. "You can keep a piece of this forever."

"I don't think I said anything." Puzzled, I tried to think back. "What was in that drink, anyway?"

I could see it on the table, where my jacket draped over an empty chair. Did we sit long enough to drink anything before coming up here? My confusion turned into frustration. I must be tipsy. But I hadn't drunk anything.

"No, you didn't say it," he admitted after a few moments. "But I can hear the words of your heart as plainly as if you'd spoken them. I hear the wishes you offer to the stars while you sit here, dreaming with me."

"I don't understand, Marek." I struggled to find words and I struggled against the placid mood I drifted in. "Why do I feel like this?"

He shifted so he could look straight into my eyes. We were still so close and it was hard not to be aware of my attraction to him—his broad shoulders, his high cheekbones and slender nose, his alluring mouth. My pulse raced, my mouth ran dry, and a hundred other clichés manifested themselves, right down to the clenching deep inside that betrayed my deepest feelings.

He leaned close, temptingly close, and I could almost taste his breath. His soft voice wrapped around me, drawing me closer still. "Do you long for me, Sophie?"

I closed my eyes and drew a wavering breath. My loins all but screamed out affirmations but this was about more than screaming loins. Every nerve in my body buzzed as if I'd been plugged into an electrical outlet. My arm shivered with cold now that we no longer touched.

I remembered how my insides tightened in pleasure

when he had his arms around me, even for that single innocent moment. I contemplated the grim line of his mouth
and knew, more than anything, I wanted to see him smile. I
thought about how much better my life was with Marek in
it. About how much Marek was in my life.

"Marek..." I could barely whisper past the knot in my
throat. Tears blurred my eyes and I found myself in the grips
of a powerful emotion, one so much bigger than I, so much
more than I could possibly hold.

Who was this man, to unlock such things within me?

I did long for him. I wanted to say *yes* but was afraid
to. Something wasn't right. The menace that swirled around
him, the threat that radiated from him, even if it never once
seemed like I myself was in danger... I'd be foolish to ignore
my instinct.

His rugged hand reached up to cradle my face.
Closing my eyes, I laid my hand over his, pressing into his
warm touch. A tear broke loose and slid down, becoming a
streak of quicksilver as it cooled in the night air.

"Sophie, I must tell you something." His eyes
appeared full of urgency. "I would give you so much. I
would reveal your heart's desires and grant them all to you. I
would keep you from pain and disappointment all the days
of your life." Leaning close, he brushed his lips against my
cheek, resting them next to my ear. "Would it be worth any
price to have that?"

His voice, melodic and mesmerizing, ran like cool
water through me, soaking down into thirsty places. It was a
mixture of sound and texture that I felt as well as heard,
wrapping like crushed velvet to clothe me and drawing me
to him, into him.

Lost in the sensations of being so close, so desired, I
pieced together my dreamy thoughts. What price would I
pay to be with him? To be coupled with a man who defined
the ideal essence of a man, a perfect balance of conflicting

qualities: strength and gentleness, danger and security, mystery and honesty?

Yet I was not all of one accord. My mind struggled against the bliss the rest of my senses floated along in. What price had I paid to be with others, only to receive faulty goods, no guarantees, bad investments? I'd paid terrible prices in the past, and some days the debts still haunted me.

Looking up at Marek, I fought to free myself of the spell my hungry heart had cast and tried to determine his true intentions. I looked past the strong jaw and soft green eyes, the black hair hanging like a veil over his shoulder, blown back from his brow by the winds sweeping around us. I looked into those eyes, the supposed mirrors of the soul, pushing my way in to peer into the depths of the man who had so captivated me.

Perhaps misinterpreting my intensity as eagerness, Marek smiled to encourage me. I ignored my inner voice no longer and saw everything.

A predator coiled like a sleeping beast inside, stirred by my nearness and the scent of my skin. His danger was real, his stories all true. His ever-present threat wafted like wisps of smoke from a banked and resting fire, subtle but sure. A small glimpse of teeth, like tips of icebergs.

My instinct rang with a clarity I'd never before experienced, and the world spun a quarter turn around me. I gasped and grabbed Marek's arm to steady myself, keep from pitching forward and falling. These secrets were never meant to be revealed.

Not until this moment, when something about his intentions changed. The veil lifted and the truth exposed, the realization of it all settled upon me like cold spring mist.

Marek had been hunting me.

Full of conflict, I searched his face for something that would make sense of my thoughts. I wanted him to deny it, to once more wear the puzzled expression he wore whenever I uttered aloud these strange feelings, these emotional vibrations I detected when we were together.

I begged silently to be wrong about what I felt. Marek only nodded, almost imperceptibly, his eyes firmly trained on my own.

Oh, my God. He'd been hunting me.
So why did I long for him still?

I might have offered him my soul and undying devotion had there not sounded a crash of metal on metal as the roof door clanked open.

We froze.

He gripped my shoulder in a warning to be silent. The large cooling unit blocked our view. If we couldn't see the door, then there was a good chance we hadn't been spotted yet, either.

Harsh male voices came in pulses as we crept back from the edge of the roof and crouched against the cold metal box. Marek moved like liquid.

Craning his neck while trying to remain undiscovered, he stretched to see who had opened the door. Apparently, his view was not obstructed. His eyes widened and he swore a quiet but deadly curse.

My heart knocked, punctuating my breath. I sure as hell didn't want to get arrested. That would be bad. Oh, shit. I knew we shouldn't have come up here.

Marek slid over me, covering me, hiding me between his massive frame and the cooling unit. Dipping his head, he barely whispered. "Don't even breathe."

Cops? I mouthed up at him.

He shook his head once. *Worse,* he mouthed back.

Air solidified and jammed my throat. Worse? What could possibly be worse?

I could discern two voices now. One sounded deep, hard. Rage rolled the words around, making them impossible to understand. The second voice pleaded, explaining something while the first interrupted with angry barks of accusation.

Marek pressed up against me, watching over my head through a gap in the machinery. I was trapped between steel and steel.

Suddenly, the argument escalated. A protest, cut off in mid-scream. Wet choking.

Silence.

Marek froze as if he'd turned to stone. A sharp tang flitted by, a weird smell I couldn't identify. He inhaled sharply, one last time, before he ceased breathing.

Alarmed, I twisted beneath him and stood on my tiptoes to look.

Two men stood chest to chest, one nearly eclipsing the other. His broad back made him appear as wide as he was tall. The other's knees were bent at right angles, jutting out to the sides like a broken puppet. Broad Back held him by his shoulders, pulling him down to his face as if he spoke into his ear.

After a moment, Broad Back shoved him away. He sagged like an empty coat to the ground, legs folding beneath him like stiff wool.

His shirt was saturated with blood. It spread down his chest like a second garment, oozing like syrup, slow-moving and sluggish. My eyes zeroed in. Slashed throat.

He hit the ground with a thud, head lolling, limbs bent underneath him. Open eyes stared unfocused at a sky he no longer saw.

Broad Back hunched over him, swiveling at the waist to scan about. When he faced the cooling unit that sheltered us, I saw him.

Not him. It.

Its face barely looked human. Bone and skin rose in ridges that formed pits around its eyes. Eyes glowed as if lit from within, cold silver light. The gaping twisted maw, full of impossible teeth, gleamed crimson.

That thing had torn open the throat of the fallen man. With its teeth.

My mind refused to cooperate and my heart twisted into an unending contraction. It fisted, cramped, crushed. I fought to breathe. I forgot how to think.

"We have no choice." Marek shook off his catatonia and backed away, hands firm upon my shoulders as he pulled me back. As he moved, he kept the metal box between us and the creature on the other side.

I noticed how close to the edge we stood. I realized what he planned. As if there were possibly room inside me for it, new horror surged, reanimating my heart with a jolt. I shook my head desperately and dug my fingers into his arms, back-pedaling. No, no, no—

He bent close, mouth on my ear. "Deep breath."

Wrapping his arms around me like a straitjacket, he jumped off the roof backwards, pulling me with him.

I couldn't scream. Descending at nine-point-eight meters per second squared ripped every coherent thought from my mind and the air from my lungs. Time slowed in that peculiar way that meant events were unfolding too fast. I slipped from Marek's grasp and watched as he pushed away from me, falling faster below.

The tables on the patio rushed up. The air sliced my eyes.

I squeezed them shut. No time to pray.

I crashed into Marek with a shattered force. He caught me like a parcel, clutching me in his arms as he stood upon our table. A moment of stunned silence passed as everyone in the bar turned and stared with open mouths and wide eyes. In the silent vacuum of shock, a glass rolled off the table and smashed.

The crowd erupted.

People pointed and shouted as their disbelief faded. I locked my arms around Marek's neck, fearful and speechless. He calmly stepped off the table like a groom crossing the threshold and set me down.

He bolted, pulling me off my feet and dragging me behind like a balloon.

We ran past the bar, past the exclaiming patrons, past the DJ who, wedged safely between his headphones, hadn't noticed our crash landing. We ran to the elevator but the cars were floors away. We ran down the stairs. At the sixtieth floor we exited the stairwell and caught the express elevator that waited, doors open and expectant.

No talk. Just panting. The elevator car might run out of air before I got my breath back.

In less than a moment we landed. Marek threw me a look to get ready and seized my hand once more and we stormed through the lobby, out the doors and down the street.

My adrenaline lasted four blocks before failing. My lungs demanded air. My legs screamed. I ran out of fuel, staggering to a stop. My hands on knees, head hanging. Air. Need air.

Raising my head, I saw we were close to Saint Joseph's. Instinct nudged me. Sanctuary.

Marek scanned behind us, around us, searching the shadows for things I couldn't see. I tugged at his arm, pointing to the cathedral. He turned in the direction of my gesturing and nodded, pulling me across the street toward the church.

The trees lining the sidewalk cast deep shadows from the glare of overhead street lamps. He guided me down the darkened steps to the basement chapel entrance. Using his body as a shield, he pressed me into the recess of the doorway.

Marek's voice was hard, allowing no argument. "Go in. You'll be safe."

"What was... that thing?" My breath and voice, ragged gasps around the *ba-ba-ba-ba-ba* of my heartbeat. "That man. The blood—"

"Sophie, listen to me. Go in. Stay until morning. Don't let anything in." He glanced over his shoulder again and pushed me against the door.

"You." The air burned my throat. "Come with me. Don't leave me alone here."

Marek backed up a step, lifting his head and snarling with impatience. "I said, go in, unless you want to die, too."

"We can keep running. My place. We'll be safe, we can call someone..."

"No!" he roared. He turned into me with such force that he shoved me against the door, trapping me once more beneath his hard body. His chest heaved and his words came out rushed, stuck together, sounding like a continuous growl. "I resisted before. I resisted so many times. You're not safe now."

"Keep me safe!"

"I cannot." His voice dropped, sounding both reasonable and ominous. "I am the danger now."

Marek lowered his chin, looking up through his lashes at me. His eyes glowed bright green. Pools of night, wearing bright green halos. He smiled a predator's smile, deep with teeth.

I jerked back, hitting the door jamb with my shoulder. Sparks of pain. Nowhere to go.

He swept his brilliant eyes over my face to my bare throat. He shook his head as if to clear it and rubbed his hand over his mouth but never lifted his eyes. "Go. In. Now."

I should have done it but I froze. That creature. Marek was just like him.

"Yes." His clenched teeth turned the word into a hiss.

Marek dug his fingers into the flesh of his cheek and gripped his jaw. "I cannot resist much longer. Please!"

Releasing his mouth, he ran his hand down the side of my face, to my neck. His jaw was tight with bunched muscle, the exertion pulling his mouth into an exaggerated frown. "I don't want to mourn for you, too."

Pinning me against the chapel door, he pressed his forehead to my temple, bending my head to my shoulder. His voice little more than an anguished groan. "Oh, gods, please."

"No! Marek! This isn't you!" I was wedged into the corner of the doorway. I squirmed to evade him and only wedged myself tighter. Desperately, I snaked my hands up between us, trying to push him away but he grabbed my wrists and pulled my arms straight, pressing my hands back against the door. I cried out as my arm bent at a sharp angle across the frame.

Marek's mouth hovered over the pulse on my neck, breath blasting across my skin. A drop splashed onto my shoulder; sweat or tears, no way to tell. He inhaled deeply, groaning and pressing tighter against me. His heart was pounding, his every muscle taut.

"Why? Why would you hurt me?" My sobs melted together, shaking my shoulders. Marek would hurt me. The shock of it spent my last reserves of strength. I had nothing left with which to fight, not after that torturous flight. My legs tingled and buckled. My face slipped against his silky black mane.

"It's me," I whimpered. "Your Sophia."

With an anguished cry he sprang back, horror in his fiery green eyes, his face twisted in revulsion. He streaked up the steps and his voice was a scream. "Get inside!"

Sense returned with a blinding crash. The lock clicked behind me and the door slid open. I fell inside, threw myself against the door, fumbled with the deadbolt, slammed it into place.

The room was all inky blackness lit by spots of trembling votive candle flame. I knew the room as well as I did my own apartment. Staggering on jelly legs and succumbing to a cold shock that steadily rose like flood waters, I felt my way toward the altar.

With fumbling hands, I grabbed the monstrance and clutched it to my chest while feeling for the door to the storage room. Once inside, I curled into a ball as far from the door as I could get. I eventually fell into an exhausted near-sleep on the floor.

My last thoughts were a single prayer, repeated over and over.

Dear God, whatever they are, please protect me.

I awoke the next morning to Jared's hand on my shoulder.

Disoriented, I struggled, striking out before I realized it was him. At the sight of his worried eyes, I broke down. Kneeling on the floor, Jared stroked my hair, whispered comforting nonsense, and asked nothing.

Thank God. There was absolutely nothing I could have told him.

Jared left only long enough to say Mass. I was still in the corner when he returned; I'd retreated deep within myself and hadn't noticed the passage of time. He didn't ask what had happened. He knew me well enough to know I'd talk when I was ready.

He chatted about unimportant things as he drove me home, flipping through the radio stations and trying to rouse me. I couldn't meet his eyes and stared out the window instead.

Jared fished my keys out of my purse when I made no move to do so. Inside the apartment, he whistled as he made a pot of tea and made friendly noises at Euphrates, who interrogated him loudly. I sank onto the couch and drew my knees up, tucking my feet into the cushion.

Jared set the tea pot onto the coffee table. "Sugar?"

I shrugged.

He disappeared into the kitchen, returning with the sugar bowl and a mug. Tugging once on his pant legs, he sat beside me. "What happened last night?"

My jaw trembled. I wanted to tell him but where did I start? I chewed my lip and stared at my knees.

"Did someone hurt you?" Anger and worry added an edge to his tone.

I looked steadily into his eyes and shook my head, a tiny negation.

"I can't help you if you don't talk to me."

"You can't help me."

"Bullshit, Soph!"

I flinched, ducking my head and hiding behind my arms. The sudden noise itself was enough to startle me. Adding to the surprise was the fact I hadn't heard him say that word since high school.

Perhaps noting my new distress, he softened his tone and reached out to stroke my arm. "This is me you're talking to, remember? I know that look on your face. Are you forgetting we lived through stuff like this before?"

I was pretty sure we never encountered a man-eating monster before. Stuff like that, you tend to remember. Lifting my chin, I peered at him over my arm. "It's different this time."

"So different that you just shut down on me? What happened?" He worked his hand up to my shoulder, kneading my neck with his thumb. The touch was so warm, so real, it helped pull me out of my racing thoughts, the constant replay. "Who hurt you?"

The darkness in his voice sent a coldness through me

despite his warm touch. The last time I heard him use that tone, someone ended up in the ICU and he ended up in jail. His eyes were large and dark, the blue irises swallowed by his pupils.

"No one." My voice wavered. Even I wouldn't believe me. "I swear, no one hurt me. I got scared, is all. The city is full of scary things, remember."

"Not hurt?" he echoed. His shoulders relaxed. "You ran like I told you?"

"Oh, I ran, alright."

His shoulders dropped as he released a big breath and he rubbed the tops of his legs before resting his hands in his lap, palms up. "Will you call me when you're ready to talk?"

"Yeah." I let my gaze drift away. "I will."

Seeing as I was pretty much as good as I'd get, he left.

I sipped the tea. I sat on the couch. I watched the sun grow and bloom and fade into twilight. I measured shadows as they lengthened on the floor. I dreaded the approaching night.

I got up only to pee and to check and recheck the locks on the door and windows. My brain had flat-lined; wiped clean as if the world didn't exist anymore. Euphrates enjoyed my lassitude and sprawled on the couch next to me, digging his feet into my legs when he stretched. The jabs of his claws came as a shock; I was surprised to feel anything at all.

I lapsed into another staring spell as I sat on the toilet sometime around seven. A thump startled me; Euphrates barreled down the hall and charged into my room. The racket reminded me to stand up before I had permanent ring around the rear end.

Leaning over the sink, I washed my hands and rubbed my face with my wet fingers, breathing in the lemon verbena scent the soap had left behind. I needed to wake up,

snap out of this stupor, decide what to do. Figure out what I
had seen.

Where did I start? The only person I could ask was
part of the problem.

I decided to call Jared. When in doubt or moral peril,
call a priest, right? Maybe he'd heard something in confession that would help this make sense. I tried to remember if
he'd ever mentioned monsters.

I guessed it was true that citrus was an invigorating
scent. Having made that one small decision, I felt renewed. I
needed to take action, to regain control. Staring at my
reflection in the mirror, I realized my loss of self-control
frightened me as much as anything I'd witnessed the night
before.

I'd become enthralled with Marek, stepping out of my
self-protective bubble and allowing him to get to me. I'd
known it wasn't safe.

I pinched my cheeks, mottling them with blotchy
spots of pink. My face seemed ghastly pale beneath my
brown hair and dark swipes under my eyes gave me a not-
so-chic heroin chic appearance. My reflection looked only a
few degrees warmer than dead.

What had I been thinking? Didn't he feel dangerous,
right from the beginning? I knew the risks I faced in a relationship. In the rush and thrill, I probably just imagined the
monster stuff.

Who was I kidding? Being pulled off the roof—I
didn't imagine that. I didn't imagine waking up in the
church, either. The tea pot still sat on the coffee table, proof
enough Jared had been here: I'd never have gotten the dusty
thing off the top of the cabinet on my own.

I couldn't wrap my brain around all of it. Bad enough
I might have fallen in love with someone. Turned out he
might be some kind of monster. I gave myself one last grim
look, hitched up my mental pants, and went to find the

phone.

"Fraidy, come eat something," I called over my shoulder toward the bedroom as I headed to the kitchen. Of course I didn't watch where I walked. There shouldn't have been anything to walk into. Or anyone, for that matter.

Such as Marek, who stood in my living room, arms folded, waiting.

14

"Marek!" I stumbled backwards a few steps, almost losing my balance. "How did you get in? The door's locked."

I was sure. I'd checked and rechecked about a hundred times since Jared left. Windows. Did he come up the fire escape? No, no, no. I had checked and rechecked. Everything was locked. Yet here he stood in my apartment. Did it matter? He got in. Everything was locked and he still got in.

"Sophie." He used the same non-threatening tone Jared had and raised his hands in front of him. "I just want to talk."

"Uh-uh." My pulse hammered. He took a careful step toward me and I backed away. "Stay back, Marek. Don't come any closer."

He froze statue-still. "Sophie, I'm telling the truth. I only want to talk."

"Fine. Stay there. Talk. Then get out."

I didn't know what to do. My idea of keeping safe from strangers involved locking the door. Unfortunately, my survival plan didn't include a contingency for when the stranger showed up inside. No plan B. Damn it!

With a careful step, I slid closer to the kitchen doorway. Behind me, on the counter next to the microwave was a butcher's block. Plan B. Would a kitchen knife stop a monster?

Marek tapped a temple with the heel of one hand, closing his eyes. "Sophie... no. Come in here. Sit. It's only me."

"You and your teeth."

"I swear I will keep my teeth to myself. You are in no danger."

"And if I don't believe you?" The tiny voice didn't sound like me. Timid. Trapped.

"Please..."

One gentle word, so vulnerable. Before me stood a pillar of strength, a mountain of a man, a beast. And he begged. His mournful plea went right through me, straight to the part inside that couldn't deny him.

My resolve weakened. I closed my eyes in defeat and hung my head. I allowed him to draw me back into the living room, but made a wide berth around him to get to my desk chair.

Just like old times. Except now, instead of too far apart, we were too close.

Marek nodded, accepting my avoidance. He inhaled deeply through his nose, mouth reduced to a grim line. "You're afraid of me."

I snorted. "Brilliant deduction, Sherlock. You almost ate me."

His eyes widened. "How could you be flippant about this?"

"You mean now? When there's some sort of monster sitting across the room from me?" I pointed at him but my hand trembled.

Something like pain clouded his expression. "I told

you, you are in no danger from me."

"And I asked you, why should I believe you?"

"I... I've given you no reason to trust me. I only ask you do."

"What can you possibly say that would explain everything? Look at my arm." I pulled up my sleeve and thrust my fist out, revealing my forearm. Where there should have been deep scratches, there was nothing. The skin was smooth, unmarred but for spider-thin streaks of pale scars. Normal people didn't give magical boo-boo kisses.

"That guy on the roof. The fall off the roof that should have killed us. The teeth a-and the way you... you..." My voice failed as I remembered. I didn't want to remember. It would be real if I could remember. "What could you possibly say?"

He hunched his shoulders, staring down at his hands for a long while. When he finally spoke, his voice was quiet and solemn and final.

When he spoke, I heard some invisible door inside my head slam shut, separating me from whatever had been my life.

Without looking up, Marek uttered one word.

Vampire.

15

"No." I shook my head and looked away. "No."

But I knew he wasn't lying. Knew he couldn't lie, not about something this terrible. Deep inside, my gut knew he spoke the truth.

"Will you listen, Sophie?"

His need shone plainly in his proud, pleading eyes, so much emotion in those few words. This was what he'd been trying to tell me: all those half-spoken things, the times he'd begin to speak but pull away at the last moment, the truths he held back in effort to invoke protection.

He couldn't keep them from me any longer.

I turned back to face him, meeting his gaze. I heard the need in his voice and saw the need in his eyes. Resolutely, I sighed. Of course I'd listen. This was my place in life, wasn't it? People needed me and I'd sit and listen and make everything all better.

Encouraged by my reaction, he began to unravel his secrets.

I hoped I'd still be breathing when he finished.

༄ၹ ၹ༄

The creature on the roof had been a vampire with a solid reputation as assassin.

"I knew him by sight," Marek said. "He works for one of the territorial masters of the East Coast. That was the closest I've ever been to him."

"I can't believe what I'm hearing. Vampires?"

"Yeah. Sorry."

"Sorry?" Somehow, in this context, it came off a little contrived: *sorry I said vampires are real, and one almost got us, and I am one, too.* Sorry didn't really cut it.

"We keep our personal affairs separate from those of humanity. Usually humans only come in contact with us when we prey and even then, they aren't aware of too much for long."

"Marek!"

"I'm sorry," he repeated. "Look. I need you to hear me out in entirety. Once I start, I must tell you everything. If I didn't need you so badly, I'd never have put you through all of this."

I scrubbed at my brows with the heels of both palms, figuring it would be a long night, and shuffled into the kitchen. I tugged the coffee pot from its perch on the hot plate but reconsidered. Coffee wouldn't do, not tonight.

Instead, I pulled a wine bottle out of the fridge and took two glasses from the cupboard. As I passed the butcher's block, I lifted one of the blades. I could hide it up my sleeve and if he...

"Sophie, you don't need that. Just come back out."

Sighing, I slid it back and trudged back in with the wine.

He talked and I listened and I drank. Two glasses was usually enough for me to pass out laughing but tonight the wine didn't work. His words were too sobering. Marek wasn't human.

"My species," he said, "are precursor to vampire, which is the final stage of our evolution. Not many of us survive long enough to Fall. Once evolved, the vampire is immortal because the transmutation has spiritual as well as physical ramifications. The soul is eliminated."

Without a soul, there was no afterlife. No soul meant no reason for a conscience. A vampire existed on hunger and instinct and the fulfillment of desires. No ethics. No rules. Very, very, very bad.

"But," Marek stressed. "Full vampire is rare. The oldest and strongest vampires struggle for the rank and privilege of Master. They gather soldiers and slaves, layering themselves with insulation against those who would knock them from their seats of power and destroy them."

"What about you?" For an hour or so since he materialized behind me, I'd sat and listened, trying to pretend this was another of his lectures. Right now, I wanted more practical information—where did Marek fit in?

It was a very personal question. Only the day before he'd been the object of my intense desire. I wanted to know what Marek was because I wanted to know what I would have given myself to. I wanted to know what it was I might have become.

He smiled with familiar self-loathing. "I'm demi-vamp, Sophie. I am truly alive. I am not vampire, although I have the ability to evolve." He cleared his throat, his restless hands tapping the couch cushion beside his legs. "Demivampire is a species, just like human or feline or Were."

"Were?" I squeaked. "Like werewolf?"

"A species." He ignored my exclamation. "You cannot be bitten and become vampire."

His gaze held me tightly and I couldn't look away. Brightness seeped into his eyes, the same glow I'd noticed the last time he'd sat on my couch, the glow I'd assumed was candlelight reflection. No candles burned now. The light came from within.

"Humans who have been preyed upon cannot turn into vampire after being drained of blood. They just become corpses." Marek shrugged and his eyes dimmed back to their normal green. "It is important you know. I'm sorry it's unpleasant."

I scowled and stared into my wineglass so I didn't have to look at him. *Unpleasant* didn't seem to even touch it.

So. His big news was finally out. Marek was demivampire. Could have been worse. I tipped back an unladylike mouthful and reached once more for the bottle. At least he hadn't told me he was married.

16

The night slipped away, stealing my energy. Between the lack of sleep and the multiple adrenaline surges, I drooped. Still, as much as I wanted to crawl into bed and hide, I didn't want him to leave.

For some reason, my alarm had faded and curiosity peeked out its timid head. I wanted to know more. I ducked back into the living room through the fire escape window. I'd needed a breather and the breeze did wonders for my spirit.

"So... you DV..." I couldn't use the word *vampire;* saying DV made it possible to have this conversation. "You're like humans with extra teeth?"

"No. We are similar to human as far as our bodies are designed. Head on top, legs on the bottom, all the usual parts in between." He paused to taste the wine that sat on the coffee table, the condensation dripping down the sides of the glass as his fingertips disturbed the surface. "Legends say we're descended from the son of Horus but, scientifically, the demivampire have more earthly origins. We simply have evolved faster than you."

"Evolved as in lost your vestigial tail faster?"

"Evolved as in developed heightened abilities. Greater speed and greater reflexes. Sensitive hearing. Night vision sharp enough to rival day sight. Enhanced sense of smell."

"They sound like animal characteristics."

"I prefer to think of them as shared traits." He arched a neat brow and favored me with the stern glance that had originally convinced me he was a professor. "We also possess talents that, to you, might appear to be supernatural."

"You aren't about to tell me that you're double-jointed or rub your belly and pat your head at the same time, are you?" I mean, it was hard enough figuring out how a man worked, especially a man like Marek who was all still-waters-running-deep. Now I probably had a bunch of super-human problems to deal with. Fantastic.

He frowned as he concentrated. "Our gifts can be described as mind-to-environment. I can manipulate the physical. You've seen me do it but you didn't realize. I also have compulsion abilities that are common to all DV, since they are basic survival traits. I cannot move your will but I can move your body. If I want you to do something, I can make you do it."

He cocked his eyebrows with a deep slant as his usual commanding arrogance surfaced.

"And to think, all along I figured you just had tremendous leadership skills."

"I do, but that's not the point. If I compelled you, you'd know you did something against your will. You'd try to fight it and fail. I can cloud your thinking so you wouldn't be aware of the manipulation. I can also distract you with pleasure so you would enjoy doing what I wanted."

Pleasure. Normally the word caused all sorts of naughty ideas to surface but tonight a second, unspoken word echoed in its wake: pain. "You know," I said. "People would probably do what you wanted because of the fear you'd, oh, I don't know, tear their limbs off or something. Why use the compulsion stuff?"

"Because DV are hunters. Humans are the preferred prey. We must consume living blood to survive." So matter-of-fact. "Compulsion aids us in obtaining and placating our prey. If we terrified people when we fed, we'd be hunted down and destroyed."

Marek stretched against the back of the couch and cracked his knuckles. The humanity of the gesture reassured me. It also skeeved the daylights out of me. I couldn't stand that sound. If he cracked his neck, I'd throw something.

As I considered the aerodynamics of the phone book on my desk, something occurred to me. "How many times have you done it to me?"

"I cannot control what is my nature. But I swear—I've never used my mind to force you to do anything you did not want to do."

"What about jumping off a roof?"

"That was physical force, not compulsion. I admit... I have placated you but only to reduce your anxiety. You drink too much coffee. Little stresses toss you right off the edge."

"Hey. I don't bust your chops about being inhuman. Leave my coffee alone."

"At any rate, I never caused you to feel anything you weren't going to feel on your own."

"Like desire?" Too late. My mouth was leaking words.

The side of his mouth tugged up in an insolent grin. "You desire me?"

My face aflame, I tucked my chin to my chest and hid behind my loose hair, smoothing my eyebrows with a finger. Walked right into that one.

"You're not psychic, are you?" I wasn't confident enough to let him into every corner of my mind. Bad

enough he performed a background check on me; I didn't
need him taking an inventory of my brain.

Marek shrugged. "DV can pick up the scent of sudden
emotional thought. Little things like surprise, sympathy, or
fear cause physical changes that are simple to detect."

He ran his finger around the rim of his glass, creating a
hollow hum of sound. "Mind-to-mind powers emerge as
one gets close to the brink of evolution. When the line
between life and death becomes blurred, so do the bound-
aries between individual minds. The Fallen can not only
read minds but can also manipulate thoughts and desires. A
vampire could make you strangle your own child and you'd
believe it had been your idea in the first place."

If he wanted to terrify me, he'd succeeded. I needed
another break. I trudged into the kitchen for a new bottle of
wine. Marek's glass was still more than half-full; he seemed
to be merely wetting his lips.

Aw, crap. Should I have made him a Bloody Mary
instead? I glanced up at a plaque that hung on the wall, the
shape of a teapot bearing the letters "WWMD?" They stood
for "What Would Martha Do?" I wondered if she ever
hinted at etiquette for entertaining DV in one of her
magazines.

Shit. With her supernatural skills, I'd bet Martha was
more than familiar with DV etiquette. It would explain why
she could do anything and make a fortune doing it. I'd
watched her make meatballs once. It was uncanny.

My thoughts returned to Marek. I tried not to think
of him feeding. I'd already spent a fair amount of time
imagining what it would be like to kiss him but now it
would be hard to imagine kissing without also imagining
bloody teeth. Just—yuck.

Bottle in hand, I returned to my seat and he
continued. "Think of the food chain. Humans raise domesticated food sources. Since humans do not breed as quickly

as, say, cattle, we have to be more discreet. Instead of preying on a human to its death, we more or less graze."

I didn't like the comparison he made between me and a cow but I let it go. It wasn't a battle I needed to wage tonight.

"Just as many humans squander the Earth's resources for power and greed, many demivamps consume and destroy life out of lust for power and advancement. Some kill their prey intentionally in order to force their own evolution."

His voice dropped into a more reverent tone. "When a human dies, his soul leaves the body and begins its journey to the afterlife. But, death is more than a simple ending or beginning. When the life-force leaves a human body, energy is released. This energy triggers a biochemical process in a demivamp. Like an enzyme, it catalyzes a chain of reactions that speeds evolution."

Marek watched me with his startling bright eyes. "The more traumatic the death, the greater the energy of the catalyst. A death powerful enough would affect not only the killing vamp but also anyone close by."

Kicking off my shoes, I tucked my feet up underneath me and followed the thought to its most obvious conclusion. "So... last night on the roof. You were affected by that man's death."

"Yes." Marek's voice was soft and thick. "The scent of blood had a strong effect but the death was overwhelming. The church was the only safe place for you."

"You were going to prey on me, weren't you?" I spoke with a calmness I did not feel.

He looked away, as if shamed. Silently, he summoned his courage and met my eyes again. I could have drowned in the regret that pooled in his eyes. It must have taken several lifetimes of pain to accumulate that amount of remorse. His sorrow was palpable and dripped down my soul.

"That man's death..." Something flashed across his face,

as if he indulged a terrible craving. The brief rapture passed, replaced by his grimace, his self-hate. "It weakened me, indeed. I already desire you, in so many ways, and the call of your blood held so much promise. I am sorry, Sophie."

Out toward the harbor, the sky slowly took on a gentle hint of light, softening the edge of crisp, sharp night. In all the years I've lived here, I'd never been awake to see the sun rise. It seemed so metaphorical I could've cried.

I thought I had myself pretty well figured out, confident I knew exactly what my big picture looked like. Tonight, all the pieces that made up my life had been tossed up into the air and I found myself trying to sort them out like a jigsaw puzzle. Some fell easily back into place but others wouldn't fit unless I altered the edges of the pieces around it.

I did the best I could for now. Too many pieces missing. Even so, I realized my big picture had been drastically altered.

"You are a strong woman, Sophie. Your depth of character anchors you. You strive to put the world right. A lesser woman would have given in to hysterics."

"To be perfectly honest, there were lots of hysterics." Wrinkling my nose, I waved my hand dismissively as I spun the chair to face him again. "But that's not important. I want to ask about something you said. You 'resisted before.' When exactly do you mean by 'before?'"

What I wanted to know fell more along the lines of whether or not I was ever more than a Happy Meal. I wasn't sure how to ask without offending; I wasn't sure if I could handle anything other than the answer I wanted.

"That is a personal story, rather than an anthropological one." Standing, unfolding his great height, he shrugged his shirt down into place. "Dawn approaches. I need my natural ability to return home unseen."

I remembered how he'd simply appeared in my parlor. "How will you get home?"

"Same way I came." He dropped a wink before striding toward the door. I trailed along behind, half-expecting him to turn into a bat and flutter off like a drunken bird.

He didn't. He opened the door and walked out into the hallway. Signs of life from first-shift workers drifted down the hall: showers and kitchen noises, coffee smells, something spicy and totally un-breakfast like wafting over from the vegan next door.

"There is more to my story but it must wait for another night. Do not draw hasty conclusions while I'm away."

Following behind, I stopped at the doorway and leaned against the frame, arms wrapped around myself, trying unsuccessfully to dispel a stubborn chill. "Marek?"

He turned, his hair sliding over his shoulder, a stark contrast of darkness against light skin. "Yes?"

"Knock first when you come back."

Marek laughed his stormy laugh, smooth and deep, the one that made waves crash inside me. He leaned to kiss me goodbye, but I hurriedly backed away out of reach. Checking himself, he merely nodded and retreated down the hallway. "Good night, Sophie."

I watched until he rounded the corner and disappeared, listening for his tread on the stairs but hearing nothing. He was gone. For a moment I lingered, half-wishing he'd reappear, half-dreading some other monster might.

I turned the deadbolt and hooked the chain, despite knowing it couldn't keep them out. Habit, I guess. Pressing my back against the door, I slid slowly to the floor, a crumpled arrangement of arm and leg and disquiet. I was alone, plunged into a foreign, deadly world and it was all right outside my door.

How long did I have until it came knocking?

I woke up with a headache and a sick sense of dread that knotted my stomach and killed my appetite. Kind of like college finals all over again, except there was no kegger to look forward to at the end of the week. Thank goodness for that because, right now, the last thing I wanted to think about was anybody drinking anything.

I spent the next day in tremulous anticipation, preparing my arguments, getting ready to expose the hoax. By the time Marek knocked, I was wary, I was skeptical, and I was armed to the teeth with logic. I never stood a chance.

Euphrates, in the middle of his meal, suddenly bolted for the window and disappeared down the fire escape with a clatter. A split second later, a rap sounded at the door.

I tiptoed toward the door, deftly avoiding the squeaky floorboard near my bedroom. My heart pounding, I peered through the viewer to see Marek, a looming shadow in the brightly-lit hallway.

"Good evening, Sophie," he murmured. "May I come in?"

"Marek." I sounded reasonable, considering. "I don't know how to ask this politely, so I'll just flat out ask. Are you crazy?"

"Maybe I am. Does it matter?" The view distorted his image but I thought he appeared amused. He crossed his arms and leaned against the opposite wall.

"I'm not sure." It came out as a thin whisper.

"Then let me remove your doubt." Like a striking snake, Marek rushed the door, his palm raised to slap the peephole.

Panicking, I backed away from the door, afraid he would knock it down on top of me. Anticipating the impact, I scrabbled backwards up the hallway.

I crashed into the wall of his steely flesh and frantically spun to face him. A scream began as I recoiled. His hands slid around my arms, catching me and preventing me from crumbling. He held me up so I could see his face, his expression one of patient determination, willing me to believe. My scream never emerged. Only the sinking feeling it was all real.

As the adrenaline drained, I realized my feet and legs still worked and I pulled out of his gentle grasp. Reluctantly, he released me, with his usual expression of grimness.

He kept his word, knocking politely each evening thereafter. When I invited him in, he gave me a wry glance that acknowledged the pleasantries as farce. I needed him to pretend to be something he wasn't and he patiently obliged. Marek spent the hours until dawn describing his version of the world. Everything had been right there in front of me, yet completely hidden from view.

With each revelation, each story, each tiny detail, I realized the danger I'd suspected was worse than I ever could have imagined. Why did I think I would be safe with him? Safe from him? What made me think for one single moment I was exempt from the harm he and his kind pushed in front of themselves like a wicked sandstorm?

Why did some animal trainers think it was okay to live with tigers as if they were friends or children? Trust? Stupidity? Hope? A belief that affection given would unfailingly be returned? I wasn't sure but even Siegfried and Roy found out the hard way that sometimes animals acted like animals. It was their nature.

Whatever made a trainer feel immune from the worst an animal had to offer, it must have been the same thing encouraging me to welcome Marek into my home night after night.

I became a student of a brand new history. After an uneasy sleep in the morning, I'd sit at my computer, working like a woman possessed, emailing my text to Barbara. Sometimes I'd sit and stare at nothing, reliving his words, applying his principles to the specifics of the world I knew and absorbing the implications. All that time, I wondered why I wasn't horrified.

I knew he wasn't a nut job, or his stories the fabrications of a demented imagination. He'd proven it.

So I listened night after night; I accepted that his stories were true, all true. I also accepted, without putting it into precise words, that the aura of danger that covered him like an oily cloud was also real. That second night, I had hidden behind a door, boldly daring him to prove himself. The door may as well have been a sheet of paper snowflakes.

The exhausted sleep that claimed me when he departed in the morning offered no real rest. My dreams were full of him and his lessons.

Over and over I relived the moment when he appeared behind me in the hall. Over and over he caught me and pulled me up against his chest. Sometimes his mouth would find mine and my body would betray me and I'd lose myself in his kiss. Sometimes his lips parted to reveal sharp teeth. Sometimes his mouth pressed itself into its familiar grim line, his eyes filled to overflowing with hope-lessness and severity.

Before I'd wake, sweating and gasping, he'd speak one sentence. *Did you really think a door could stop me?*

And he'd smile.

18

One night, Marek arrived as he'd done every night for about a week. He knocked, I hollered "come in," and he manifested out of sight in the hallway. It saved me the trouble of getting up to answer the door. As long as I didn't have to watch the hocus pocus, I could deal.

Instead of assuming his usual spot on my couch, he disappeared into my room.

I was baffled. So was Euphrates, who thumped down the hallway and stalked into the parlor with his tail straight up like a chipmunk. He looked so affronted at having been disturbed that I laughed. Euphrates had gradually allowed Marek to enter the apartment, but his tolerance did not extend to hospitality. He stayed in my bedroom, well away from Marek.

The cat slunk his way around the perimeter of the room. I bent down and reached under the desk, trying to coax him out of the corner, when a polite cough made me jump, straight up and into the bottom of the desk.

Rubbing my head and wincing, I noticed Marek in

the doorway. Euphrates took off like a rocket and seemed to evaporate in a cloud of dust bunnies. *Meep meep!*

"You okay?" Marek asked.

"Yeah. Uh..." I gestured vaguely with my free hand. "What are you doing with my laundry?"

"It's not laundry yet. These are from your closet." Holding up his hands, he displayed two outfits. "Pick one and put it on."

"Bossy much?" I noticed he wore a sharp suit of exquisite charcoal. I didn't need to look in a mirror to know I looked like the second week of summer camp. A week of staying up until dawn, sleeping like crap, and still trying to work the day shift left me no more ambitious than t-shirt and sweats.

"I'm not bossy. I'm just telling you to do something." He didn't flinch when the pillow I launched thumped into his chest. "Or I can do it for you. Either way is fine with me."

Twenty minutes later I was dressed (on my own, thank you) and reasonably groomed. Marek made coffee while I showered and emerged from my waking coma. He'd even toasted a bagel for me. I had no idea he was so domesticated.

He stood in the hall outside the bathroom as I finished getting ready, hands in his pockets, leaning in his deceptively lazy manner. I twisted my hair up experimentally and reached for a clip. "So, you gonna clue me in?"

"Not like that." Marek craned his neck and stared intently at my hair. "No need to put that pretty neck out there for all to see."

My eyes grew as wide as saucers and I hastily shook my hair down again.

He nodded in approval as I settled my hair down around my shoulders. "I know the last week has been difficult. But you seem to have been cooped up here. Have you even left your apartment?"

I tried to remember. Come to think of it, no. I hadn't really left. All the work I accomplished, I emailed to the office. Barbara suggested I work from home when I called her Monday about my raging stomach virus, a true case of two-bucket disease that was probably virulently contagious. She didn't even want details, which was a pity because I had a great cache of them; as an ex-nurse, I have a fertile imagination.

I hadn't been to *The Mag* all week. Apart from running to the corner deli, I'd pretty much become a hermit. Of course, the main reason was the awful schedule I kept. Now I realized something else. I'd been afraid to leave.

Feeling guilty, I shrugged and toyed with my bangs.

He sighed, a deep regretful sound. "It's my own fault. I went about all this all wrong. You withdrew from the world, not embraced it as I had hoped."

I shot him a look. "Embrace it? Is that what you wanted? Because, I gotta be honest—I don't go around embracing things that want to kill me."

He pinched his lips together. "That's what I mean. Yes, okay. Much of what I told you is... savage... compared to what you expect from the ones who surround you. But, tell me, are meals the defining characteristic of your society? Is there more to you, Sophie, than what you consume to stay alive?"

I dug through my make-up bag in search of eyeliner. I've been trying to keep an open mind but it disturbed me to hear him say things like *meals* and *consume*, knowing he meant *people*.

Uncapping an eye pencil, I considered his point and reluctantly conceded. "What about the savagery?" I countered. "How can I go outside, not knowing if the taxi driver or the stranger asking directions really means to take my life?"

"Sophie, this is the city. Those threats existed long

before you learned of the DV."

I said nothing. He was right.

Staring down at my trembling hand, I figured it'd probably be best to go with no make-up at all, rather than doodle shaky lines over my face like some epileptic crack whore. My brown eyes, dark with anxiety, ringed with lack of sleep, looked big enough. Make-up would only make it worse.

Pushing away from the wall, Marek slid in behind me and met my gaze in the mirror. He gently brushed my shoulders with his hands, stroking them slowly down my arms.

The comforting motion soothed my nervous trembling. I felt my tension slip away as if he'd pushed off an itchy cloak. Calm and coolness smoothed over my jangling nerves and his expression confirmed the comfort wasn't imagined. He intentionally used compulsion, enforcing that whatever he might be, he wasn't completely scary.

"You're tired, and the coffee really got you buzzing," he whispered. "Relax so you don't stab yourself with that pencil."

I leaned back, allowing his hands to hold me against him. Exhaling, I smiled. He couldn't be evil and feel like sanctuary at the same time. There had to be rules about that.

A moment passed in contented silence. He squeezed me gently before letting go. "Finish up. I made reservations."

As he backed up to leave the bathroom, I stopped him, sliding my fingers around his biceps. His eyes, expectant and surprised, brightened momentarily, a pulse of light.

"Marek, tell me... promise me... I'll be safe with you?" Everything I've worried about since meeting him was embedded in that question.

He returned my intensity with an intensity of his own. Swallowing hard, he spoke with a rough voice. "As safe as any woman is with a man who wants her."

His mouth was a seductive line that invited closer inspection, but I felt a mental push as he compelled me to turn back to the mirror. "Finish painting your eyes," he insisted playfully. "Tonight, I'll introduce you to my world."

19

The valet opened my door, outstretched hand sheathed in a spotless white glove.

I ignored it and got out on my own. I didn't like the thought of a stranger touching me. I tried not to look suspiciously at him and summoned a phony smile, grateful when Marek appeared at my side.

I'd never been inside Folletti's although I'd read plenty about the restaurant. Whenever *The Mag* published a list of hot spots in town, it always mentioned Folletti's as one of the top attractions. It had been the subject of an in-depth write-up more than once. Despite its popularity, I'd never had enough interest to venture inside.

The outside had the appearance of its original business; it had been a shirt factory until the late seventies. A massive four-story building of faded red brick, it took up a full third of a city block. Now remodeled into a multi-level entertainment complex, it boasted a classy restaurant, a more casual pizza parlor, a game room, two nightclubs, and a penthouse bar.

Folletti's was a popular spot for the underage crowd, who were granted admittance to the first two floors. Security guards conspicuously patrolled and kept trouble to a minimum. In fact, I'd never heard of a single incident ever happening at Folletti's.

Access upstairs was limited to the over-twenty-one crowd and management had a reputation for enforcing age restrictions. As a result, Folletti's was big with parents, too. They'd drop off their kids at the pizza joint and drive around to the restaurant side.

It was family-friendly yet trendy enough to keep the singles crowd more than satisfied. Their managers had to be MENSA for sheer marketing genius.

As I preceded Marek into the foyer of the restaurant, I saw why I'd never been invited here before. Folletti's was out of my league. I'd suspected the place would be high-end but until this moment I didn't realize just how nose-bleedingly high. The inside had been decorated in tasteful gold and crystal. Not overdone, just elegant. The staff sported tuxedos, the waitresses wore little black dresses *sans* aprons.

A glance into the dining room revealed it was definitely a couples' place. Table for two by candlelight seemed to be the prevailing theme. Good thing I hadn't argued Marek's choice of apparel; even better I'd improvised with a string of pearls. Marek had seemed pleased and smiled at me in a way that seemed both indulgent and confident.

He checked our jackets and was immediately recognized by the *maitre d'*, who dipped his head in courtesy and dispatched a passing waiter. Marek stood with hands clasped behind his back and wore a look of patient expectation.

I touched my necklace with tentative fingers, hoping my lipstick was even and my slip wasn't showing. The specials board appeared to be hand painted in oils on scented wood. The places where I normally dined taped a photocopy in their window or used a marker board.

I swallowed against the dryness of my mouth. Chilean sea bass? Wasn't that on the endangered species list? And what exactly was *guanciale*? I couldn't even pronounce it. I meant to ask Marek but a ruddy-complexioned man in a tux approached, catching my attention immediately.

I usually had a knack for sizing people up. I put on my politest smile but within moments I had to struggle to keep it in place.

First impressions tend to be the strongest, and his was one of sheer force. He pushed his aggression in front of him like a snowplow. Striding purposefully, he didn't greet Marek —he confronted him.

"Marek." The man's black eyebrows, like smears of greasepaint, drew severe lines over glittering black eyes. The insincerity in his voice was not quite concealed. "To what do we owe this great pleasure?"

"Do I need a reason to drop by?" Marek replied without looking down at the shorter man's face. He seemed more interested in watching the dining room than speaking with him.

"I assume you're not here to dally with your playthings." He shot an appraising glance at me, his eyes flicking up and down, taking all of my appearance in at once. "Although, I saw several of your brood upstairs..."

"My manners are atrocious." Marek cut him off, but not before I'd gotten a clear idea of exactly what the guy meant. "May I present Ms. Sophie Galen. Sophie, this is Andre Caen, the evening manager."

He pronounced the name *Khan*, as in *Genghis*. Suited the jerk, anyway.

Caen bristled at the manner by which he'd been introduced. Apparently, he thought of himself as being much more important. Marek didn't seem the least bit upset by Caen's attempt to intimidate him so if he could blow him off, then by golly, so would I. Try, I mean.

"Pleased to meet you," I said. I smiled as vacantly as I could, watching a smug look settle upon Caen's face. Marek dismissed him, turning toward the *maitre d'* who had hesitantly drawn near, waiting to take us to our table. Breathing out a sigh of relief, I didn't dawdle as he led us into the dining room.

Our table nestled in a quiet niche behind a fountain. Water flowed down over tiny silver bells, chiming a soothing melody. Marek had just drawn out my chair for me when a younger man called his name. I'd hoped this guy wouldn't be as annoying as the last.

However, Marek's eyes were warm when he turned to greet him and I relaxed. "Rodrian," he said. "This is Sophie. Sophie, meet my brother."

He wasn't as tall or as broad as Marek, but still nicely built. His dark brown hair had been styled sleekly but might have been chin-length and wavy if left loose. Hazel eyes glowed briefly at the sound of my name and amber sparks smoldered as he turned to me.

I held out my hand to shake but instead he turned my hand, kissing it. Looking up at me, he winked. "I've heard much about you, Sophie."

I liked him immediately. "All good, I hope?"

"My brother is not the least poetic but what he's told me sounded like pure verse. Still, he didn't do you justice." Marek cleared his throat and Rodrian released my hand with a grin. He tucked a smart little bow. "Welcome to Folletti's. It will be my sincere pleasure to serve you."

"You're a waiter?"

"No, the owner."

Figured. Bossy Marek would, of course, have a bossy brother. I sat down and smoothed my skirt as Rodrian stepped closer to Marek.

Glancing over his shoulder, Rodrian waited for a woman to walk past, nodding and smiling like the perfect host. When he turned back, the playful mood disappeared and he became all business. He spoke quietly but made no effort to conceal his words from me.

"Brother, I must speak with you soon. His men were here earlier. They insist we reconsider our position on the new legislation. I know what you said," he whispered hurriedly, as Marek made an exasperated noise. "I sent them away. They knew I stalled. I don't know how much longer I can keep it up."

Marek looked undaunted. "Just ignore them. They'll stop coming when they realize we won't be coerced. The Master's gaze will soon be drawn from us."

"But the tributes? They won't leave us alone forever, not when we can be made to pay to keep peace. They'll be back. They always come back."

"Rodrian, trust me. Everything will work out the way we planned. Worse comes to worst, you sell the place and we begin anew elsewhere."

Rodrian's expression fell. He didn't seem to like the idea but made quiet noises of acquiescence; it seemed more habit than actual assent. Summoning a smile for me, Rodrian switched gears and once more played host.

"I hope you enjoy your evening, Sophie. I look forward to seeing you again. Marek." Rodrian nodded to his brother and left.

Marek took his seat as the wine stewards appeared. They served us from separate bottles, although the hue of the libation appeared similar. Marek watched me carefully to see if I'd react, but I didn't. I didn't want to contemplate the contents of his glass too much.

"Well." Marek set down his glass and leaned toward me. The gesture lowered his head and he gazed at me from under his pitch-black lashes. "Are you enjoying yourself, yet?"

A glance at the people surrounding us did little to

relieve my apprehension. Everyone but me seemed elegant and relaxed. I sat on eggshells, worrying that I'd spill my glass or use the wrong fork.

Then I realized: so what if I did? Unless I set the place on fire or threw holy water on someone, Marek wouldn't care. His brother was the owner and Marek personified force. Even Caen's demonstration couldn't challenge my conception of who truly mattered here.

Since no one else here oozed strength the way Marek did, I decided I didn't care about anyone else's opinion. I only needed to concentrate on Marek. With that pleasant task in mind, I smiled back at him, sincerely and full of anticipation.

"Good," he chuckled. "For a moment I worried Caen had upset you."

"I know men like Caen," I said. "Little boys make lots of noise. He didn't impress me."

He reached for his glass. "Think no more of him. He's hardly representative of what I want you to experience tonight. He is not an ideal DV."

"Is Rodrian?"

"Not as much as I." His tone sounded sullen.

I laughed, goofy smile spreading. "Are you jealous?"

"Not jealous," he said firmly. I didn't believe him. "Rodrian is a ladies' man to be sure, but he knows better than to draw your attention."

I smirked at him and picked up the menu.

"Not jealous," he insisted.

What a liar.

20

"Marek." A well-dressed man called out he passed near our table, his voice a pleasant tenor that matched his build. "How are you, friend?"

Marek raised his head at the sound of the voice and smiled. He used his napkin hastily before dropping it next to his plate as he stood, reaching to take the man's outstretched hand. Their handshake seemed familiar and warm and Marek leaned to clap him on the shoulder.

"Frank, it has been far too long." He indicated me with a sweep of his hand. "Let me introduce you to Sophie Galen. Sophie, this is Frank Levene and his wife Annette."

A pretty blonde emerged from her husband's side and we exchanged hellos. Annette had an admirable grip for a woman—confident, direct. Not wilting or flimsy. She didn't make it a contest, either. Her husband shook as well, matching his pressure to mine.

"Senator Levene," I said, and received a smile for recognizing him. "It's an honor."

"Please, call me Frank. 'Senator' is a working name and my wife doesn't allow work during dinner."

Frank Levene was an influential Senator who'd held his seat for several terms. He had a knack for humanizing political issues so common people could understand the consequences. Constituents admired him, lawmakers respected him, and anyone on the other side of his campaigns faced a rough battle.

Right now, he was the center of media attention regarding the tax hikes. His opposition to the issue was well-known and he had tremendous support behind him. I'd only read his name about eight million times in the last month at work.

Marek knew him personally. Why wasn't I surprised?

Marek and Frank talked briefly, inquiries about family and vague references to business. After promising to speak again soon, the Levenes continued on their ways and Marek returned to his seat. Obviously he hadn't been kidding when he'd told me he was involved in politics.

"He seems really nice," I said.

Marek reached for his wineglass. "He's a good boy."

"Boy?" I laughed. "He's fifty, at least. Someone that dignified-looking kind of surpasses *good boy*, don't you think?"

"You're right. I've known him for so long I sometimes forget."

"You two go back far?"

"Mmm hmm," he assented while he drank. "I met him when he was in elementary school. He was nine, I think. Scrawny, never seeming to fit into his clothes. Quiet, unassertive, used to being told to behave. His potential, though... that I could see plainly. He had an inner spirit. You could say I mentored him."

Marek mentored him? But how could that be? The Senator had to be a good ten or fifteen years older than...

"Keep an open mind, Sophie." His voice was quiet. "I'm older than I look"

"Oh," I said lamely. "How much older?"

"Much older."

I hugged my ribs and glanced around at the other patrons. Everyone seemed so normal, so human. How much of this was illusion? What was reality? "Is the Senator DV?"

"No, human. Why?"

I shrugged and lifted my fork. "Just wondering."

"Would you think less of him if he were demivampire?" It sounded innocent, but I had a clear impression of the depth of his question.

I answered truthfully. "No, not less. Just different."

"Different, how?"

"Well, I always thought politicians were blood-suckers. I guess it gives new meaning."

"Oh, that was lovely. Now answer seriously."

I really didn't want to. This was my first night out after a really tough week. I wanted to relax and have a good time. However, his insistent gaze didn't let me off the hook. I sighed and surrendered.

"DV are different. I had people pretty much figured out despite having this sign on my forehead that reads *sucker*. Now I find out there are new rules for some people. New danger. New potential. Like you."

"Am I different than everyone you've met before?"

"Oh, yes. Without a doubt." I met his gaze, needing him to understand. "When we're together, I—I feel you. I suppose I've always had an instinct for people's emotions but this is so strong. I only ever felt like this once before but he was human. I used to think love made me so aware of him. Now I wonder—was it love or magic?"

"You're sure he was human?" Marek bristled and looked like he wanted to spring to his feet and flip the table. Well, hell. If we were going to talk life stories, Mr. Jealousy needed to accept the fact I didn't exactly hatch out of an egg the day before we met.

Ignoring the jealous vibe I answered his question honestly. "Yes, I'm sure. First, I've bled in front of him and he never acted like Fraidy on catnip. You, my dear, could probably find a paper cut on me with your eyes closed."

"True. I could. Second?"

"Second." I let the word drag reluctantly, unsure of how it would go over. "You know him. You know he's human."

"I? I know him?" A change came over his expression like a cloud passing in front of the sun. "The priest."

"Yeah."

He said nothing, staring at me with stony eyes.

I squirmed under the hard look. "We knew each other when we were teens. He was my first serious boyfriend. When he moved away we lost track of each other. A few years ago he transferred to my parish and we renewed our friendship."

"You love this man as well?" His voice was neutral but his power churned with unease.

"Not the same way. Even if he weren't a priest now, he's different. I'm different. We've grown up. Away. Apart. Our friendship and history remain. But the history's just history."

Marek glanced around, seeming to settle. "I knew I didn't like him for a reason."

"He's a priest, you caveman. Get over it."

"I am not a caveman," he protested. "I didn't even see the Renaissance."

"Oh, there's a relief. So I only have to deal with male chauvinistic patterns developed over the last few centuries, is that it?"

"Men will always guard their women from other men. Women should be appreciative."

"Well, I'll be sure to let you know if that ever happens." I raised my glass in a mock toast.

Marek must have taken my gesture as a sign of his victory. His eyes twinkling and bright once more, he reached across the table to take my hand. Pulling it to his lips for a lingering touch of lips and breath, he whispered. "So, you feel me, do you?"

"Yes." I shivered, goose bumps chasing each other up my arm.

"Even when I don't touch you?"

"Especially then, because I'm not distracted by your physical touch. Sometimes it's like I'm wearing you somehow."

He nodded. "It is my power. It seeks you out, knowing you are mine."

"I am, am I?" I laughed. "You sound awful sure."

"Would you have such attentions of mine were it not true?"

"Well, I am pretty charming. Guys treat me like this all the time."

His eyes narrowed.

"Not since we started dating, though," I hastily added.

He waved his hand dismissively. "Does not matter. You are mine. There will be no others."

"What? Are you taking me off the market?" I pouted. As if I'd ever been a hot commodity.

"Unless you'd be more satisfied with someone else." I grew butterflies at the look of heat he poured toward me. "Can someone else make you feel... like this?"

It was like a slow fog that crept in late at night. The sensation was thick and soft and incredibly hot. Not temperature hot—more like the kind of hot that melts away protest and inhibition and leaves a woman ready to do anything her lover asks.

I gasped for breath, surrounded by his desire, pinned down by the light in his eyes. "Oh," I whispered. "I like that."

He smiled and tilted his head, pulling back the fuzzy mental sex blanket. "Mine."

"Maybe we'll argue about that later." I shivered in the afterglow of the intimate contact. A waiter appeared to clear our dishes and I used the moment to get back into sorts.

Marek waited for the man to leave before speaking again. "Is it ever uncomfortable? Sensing me?"

"Only when you're unhappy," I admitted. It was easier to discuss my strange sensing now he'd confirmed them, validating my suspicions. "Sometimes I get caught up."

"Well, then. Your primary goal should be to please me. It would benefit us both."

I laughed at his heart-of-the-matter style of logic. Kind of like going for a walk with a big German Shepherd who spotted a rabbit and chased it down. "Thanks for keeping it simple, sweetie."

Dessert was served, warm apples, crunchy crumbs and gooey caramel. The splendid down-home stuff eclipsed the pretentiousness of the dinner itself. I believed in good simple things. This was the basic goodness of which all other goodness was made.

When I finished making an unashamed glutton of myself and contemplated the last sips of my coffee, Marek drew my attention back to the previous discussion. His eyes grew serious as the waiter finished clearing the table. "How long have you been sensitive to my presence?"

"From the beginning, I think. I didn't realize it was you, though, until the other night."

He tilted his head and waited for me to continue.

"I felt you in the museum. I thought it was my imagination—I was in a pensive mood that day so I figured it was a combination of that and your larger-than-life-ness. Your formidability. Your mysteriousness." I paused, remembering, feeling my gut-sense click into focused agreement. "I felt you every time since. Sometimes, even when you weren't around. I figured it was infatuation. That maybe I'd been thinking about you way too hard."

"You think so?"

"Yeah, I mean, that night. Before you knocked on the door, before I had any idea you'd show up. I felt it then, too."

I described the oppressive sensation of being watched —the muffled sound, the paranoid cat, and my assuming it had been caused by the weather.

"Ah," he said. "That explains your remark about a storm frightening your cat."

"Right. I didn't really think too much more it since the feeling disappeared. When you knocked, the cat flipped out and ripped me up, which was a bit distracting. And of course, the night ended in a mind-consuming way." I shuddered. The image of blood and teeth only flashed through my memory but it was a staggering flash. "I didn't think about it, period, until now."

"So when I arrived, it seemed as if my presence got there before me?"

Didn't he know? I mean, his power was a part of him, not like wisps of cologne that floated unknowingly around. Wasn't it? "No," I said. "It went on for about five minutes or so, long enough to get Fraidy worked up. Then it just, *poof!* went away and everything returned to normal. And then you knocked."

I sat back and waited for him to say, *Oh, right. That was me.*

He didn't. He leaned forward and squinted. "It lasted for several minutes, then dissipated suddenly, just before I knocked."

"Yes. Why?"

"Nothing," he said. He sat back, face carefully neutral. "I'm simply curious."

"Bullshit," I answered sweetly.

Marek glanced around with alarm. I was loud but, anyways. Simply curious, my ass. I didn't believe him because his words didn't match his feel. For the first time in my life I had an advantage over a man. I could pick up his emotions. I knew he had lied.

Marek's "feel" was usually dark without being sinister. It was protective without hiding the danger he held at bay, like a thick glass wall. But suddenly, his back-off feeling and his watch-out feeling and his oh-the-sexy-things-I'd-like-to-do-to-you feeling took on a new sheen—a naked feeling of being threatened.

This couldn't be good.

"Marek," I said firmly. "I'm old enough to prefer knowing the truth over being protected from it. This week I've learned many truths—about DV, about vampire, and about you. You may as well tell me why you're threatened because I can feel it."

I crossed my arms stubbornly. He stared in complete astonishment and temporarily forgot to close his mouth.

"You'll catch flies," I said.

Marek shut his mouth with a snap and exhaled through his nose. "Sophie, did it feel like me?"

I considered it. "No. Not really. I mean, I did think it was just the weather. Or the cat watching me. It didn't feel like a someone."

"Well, it was someone. But it wasn't the cat. It wasn't me, either."

A tiny thrill of carbonation fizzed through my chest, the buzz of anxiety. "You think it was... that vampire?"

"No, no," he said. "I'd have known if any vampire were near. Of course, there would have been your corpse as evidence." His mouth made a grim line. "No, you weren't being hunted, but you were being watched by someone who was chased off by my arrival. I intend to find out whom that someone is."

21

After dinner we went upstairs to Dark Gardens, the nightclub that sprawled over most of the fourth floor. As we rode the elevator, he told me where we were headed. I balked, lingering in the car when the doors slid open.

I don't dance. Really.

Marek laughed and draped his arm around me, steering me along the hall toward the club entrance. "We're going to watch, that's all. I don't expect you to be able to move in those heels."

He nodded to the men who checked ID at the entrance and pushed open the door. Music poured out in a wave of solid sound.

If I'd felt conspicuous walking into Folletti's, I might as well have been naked with my hair on fire now. I hated when people watched me. I was self-conscious by nature but the moment I walked inside I became downright paranoid. Memories of Marek's DV lessons reminded me I was a human in a DV world and I worried someone would stop by for a bite.

I stepped closer to Marek and pressed my hand to his ribs, too apprehensive to move further into the club. He waved to someone behind the bar while casually reaching his hand under my hair to stroke the back of my neck. The comforting gesture eased my apprehension and a glance up at his face encouraged me to relax.

Dark Gardens boasted a sunken dance floor. Three wide levels, dotted with tables and booths, ringed the circular dance area, creating a bowl. True to his word, he steered us to a table on the upper levels. We could see the entire floor and most of the seating. The music beat insistently but not loud enough to drown out conversation.

Marek pointed out DV and human in the rolling crowd below. Black lights mixed in with the gelled ones and the room flashed with bright color. Occasionally I caught the glow of bright eyes glinting among the neon sparks.

When I commented on it, he only shrugged. "The black lights are camouflage. We can bring the light to our eyes by will, the same way you'd wink at someone. Blood also calls the light. Dark Gardens is a feeding ground, a safe place for DV to satisfy their need. The brightening cannot always be controlled, not here among such temptation."

Nodding to a group nearby, he leaned closer. "Watch."

Three college-aged girls scooted into a nearby booth, looking sophisticated, trendy, and sharp. A man soon approached the table, appearing to recognize them, and slid in next to them. The girl closest to him laughed, covering her mouth. With a smile she reached up and stroked the back of his neck, playing with his hair.

"Did you see that?" Marek said.

It looked like flirting to me. I shrugged.

"She claimed him," he said.

"For what?"

"For feeding. The humans who are drawn here are susceptible to compulsion. If they weren't, they'd just feel a general not-my-kind-of-place vibe and lose interest in the club. Up here, the DV come to feed. Only suitable donors would linger."

He slid his gaze toward the booth. The couple snuggled as the other girls in the booth ignored them. Instead, they waved to other patrons and laughed with each other.

"By claiming him," Marek said. "She's announced to other DV only she will feed on him. It prevents fights and keeps the human from being over-preyed. Even if she had no intention to drink from him, no other DV would dare approach him."

"I didn't see you make any gesture on me."

"That's because no one here would cross me."

"Because of your power?"

"No," he said. "Because I'm the biggest guy in the room." He casually stretched, showing off the muscle beneath his fine shirt. I had to agree with his logic. Power or no power, Marek didn't look like someone to kick sand on.

He rose from his seat, captured my hand, and drew me along with him. I realized he was leading me down to the dance floor.

The look simmering in his eyes made me forget how much I loathed dancing. That look held me, his hands held me, his arms held me. We didn't dance. It had become much more intimate. He pulled me up against him and we swayed to a rhythm he picked, slower than the one that played. People bounced and twisted around us but we were alone, separate.

Marek stretched out his power. He sent a stream of pleasure through me, tickling my insides and brushing against soft secret places. It started a slow fire within, one I wanted him to quench only after the fire had burned everything else away.

I surrendered to my senses, opening myself up to the

touch of his power. I took a deep breath and closed my eyes. I submerged myself in what he felt, now so much more than mere impression. Pleasure mingled with other emotions. Possession. Desire. Need.

Not just the need to have me, the need to have his urges met by mine. A desperate need cried out from deep within his soul. He needed me to help him find salvation.

It called to something inside me. It made me reach out to him instinctively, to stretch out my awareness like fingers caressing his depths. I drew his needs to me, filtered them through my own essence, and returned them to him, satisfied.

My eyes closed, my mind inundated by swimming emotion, I whispered. "I promise."

I opened my eyes to find him staring down at me, eyes bright like sunlight on grass. His lips parted rapturously and he ran his tongue back and forth between his sharpened canines.

"Would you call my desire, here, Sophie?" His voice was husky, as if words were difficult to form. "Gods, you can feel me, my power. You know what I am. Do you mean to tease me?"

I stretched up against him, lacing my fingers behind his neck and drawing him down to my face. My skin tingled from the memory of the strange feelings I'd just experienced. "I know what you are, Marek, and it doesn't matter. Who you are, whatever world you come from, it doesn't matter. I want you."

He seemed stunned, even as he wrapped his arms tighter around me. "You don't know what you're saying."

"Maybe but I do know what I'm feeling. Let me be your sunlight. I'll show you what love and hope truly mean. You'll never be lost in the dark again."

His power quickened, thinning out into a triumphant ribbon that surged up into his eyes. They burned with a violent emerald fire and I laughed with delight.

Marek shuddered and pulled me tighter.

"Mine," he growled. "You will be mine."

"Mmm," I said, and slipped my arms up around his neck. "Just shut up and dance."

PART II

22

We sat in Rodrian's office, high up in the National Bank building on Tenth Street.

I should have been concerned, considering we were halfway up to the same roof Marek had once pulled me from. However, it was daytime, the sun shone like a golden promise, and since neither Marek nor his brother masked their power around me anymore, I sat amidst their supernatural arsenal and felt quite safe.

Marek sat in a dated leather armchair, newspaper spread imperiously in front of him as he made disapproving faces at everything he read. I curled up on the couch, my bare feet tucked under me as I browsed a book on ancient Egyptian spirituality. I hoped to better understand some of what Marek told me during his DV lessons.

Extra-credit Sophie, that's me.

One of the chapters listed a genealogy of Osiris. Marek had said his race descended from Horus; this text stated Bastet, the cat-headed goddess, had been the half-sister of Horus. I read a passage aloud and turned to Marek.

"So is this why Euphrates hates you? Sibling rivalry?"

"*Hate* is such a strong word."

"Who is Euphrates?" asked Rodrian.

"My cat."

"Oh." Rodrian's lip curled in faint disgust.

"All cats are part of Bastet," said Marek. "Her spirit lives in each of them. That's partly why they're singularly disagreeable animals."

"Because they think they're gods?"

"No," Rodrian interjected. "Because they think they're women."

I made a face and a sarcastic sound at him. What a brat.

Rodrian had spread his accounting books across the desk, scribbling notes and punching at a calculator. I once asked why he didn't use Quicken or some other computer program; he'd replied he liked the feel of pen and paper and preferred to use his brain.

It drove me crazy. He apparently preferred fountain pens with loud scratchy nibs, too. The noise couldn't have been more annoying had he used a quill on sandpaper and an abacus.

"You need a life, Rode," I said at last. "Computers are faster."

"And you carry a notebook, why?"

I looked down at my spiral-bound journal, which lay on the couch next to me. "It's portable."

"So are laptops."

"You're such a pain."

"Because I make sense." He cracked his knuckles. "Why argue against hand writing when you do it your-self?"

"In my case, it's different."

"No, it's not."

"Please," interrupted Marek. "You sound like hens

pecking at each other. My ears grow weary."

Rodrian smirked at me once before going back to his work. He sent a tiny pulse, a touch of mocking, as close to a poke and *I got you last* as any dignified DV would let himself get.

"Yeah, well, Marek just called you a chicken. So there," I hissed back.

"You know..." Marek dropped his paper and gave us each a reprimanding look. "When I said I wished for you to consider Sophie your family, I didn't mean school-aged siblings."

"Oh?" Rodrian grinned, inappropriate hope in his tone. "What did you mean, then?"

Marek sighed and retreated behind the financial section.

The door banged open and a giggling mass of girl whirled in, a blur of long blonde hair and Express jeans and expensive handbag.

"And how is the most important, most incredible, most generous man in my life today?" She sang the words as she hopped onto the desk, scattering Rodrian's papers beneath her perch.

He tilted his head up at her. "I'm fine, though suspicious."

"Suspicious? Why?"

"It sounds like you want something. Again."

"Can't a girl just be appreciative of someone and heap lavish praise on him?"

"I'm not a king, Shiloh."

"That's right," called Marek. "I'm king."

"Yes, you are." She laughed over her shoulder toward him, and as she turned, she noticed me. "Oh. You have company. Sorry, I didn't see you there. Am I interrupting something?" She eyed Rodrian, pursing her lips and lowering her chin like an expectant school teacher.

"Just my work, dear. Is there something you want besides an opportunity to adore me?"

"Now that you mention it, I could use a little cashola."

"Shoes again?" He sighed and reached for his wallet.

"You mean you don't like my shoes?" She pouted and held up one foot for inspection. The sunlight sparked off her gold Baby Phat sandals. I stifled a sound of admiration: I'd seen them in last week's Cosmo and had been talking myself down ever since.

"I like your shoes just fine. It's your closet space and its nearing extinction that I dread."

"Typical man. When will you learn a woman's closet has magical properties that accommodate many, many shoes?"

"Maybe when you're a woman, you can teach me."

"Beast."

"I love you."

"You better." Shiloh plucked away the money Rodrian held out and slid off the desk. "Who'd love you back, if not me?"

"Oh, I could think of a few people."

"You'd better not." Her voice held a playful but warning tone and I caught the doubtful glance she gave me. "I don't share."

"Get." He straightened out his ledgers. "I have work to do."

"Love you, bye." She pulled the door shut with a bang.

"Wow, Rode. Isn't she, ah, too young for you?" Once the sound of her footsteps had faded, I couldn't resist asking.

Rodrian looked up from his spreadsheets, confused. "What do you mean?"

"What do I mean?" I echoed with a weak laugh. "Shiloh—she's, what, nineteen? Twenty?"

"No. She's fifteen."

My jaw dropped. "You're kidding. That's sick."

"What's sick? Marek, what is this woman talking about?"

Marek dropped the pages low enough to peer over the top. "Apparently Sophie thinks Shiloh is your lady friend."

"Oh." Rodrian sat back in his seat and didn't say another word. Picking up his pen, he resumed scratching numbers.

I pulled a paperclip off my notebook and threw it at him. Better that, than the whole book. "Isn't she?"

"Sophie." Rodrian plucked the paperclip from his shirt and set it on his desk. He had such a superior air about him I almost threw another. "Shiloh is my daughter."

Speechless, I shot an accusing look over my shoulder at Marek. Cripes, you'd think he'd clue me in before I made an ass out of myself. Marek remained silent, although the newspaper bounced. He was laughing behind that damned paper.

"Your... daughter?" Open mouth, insert foot. "Oh. Right, then."

"My youngest daughter." He emphasized his words with a wicked smile, twisting the knife of embarrassment just a teensy bit more.

My mouth opened and closed a few times but no words came out. My foot must have been in the way.

"Is it so hard to believe, Sophie?"

"Rode, you're, like, college boy pin-up of the century."

"Ah, Soph?" Marek's inquisitive voice held a bit of warning not to drool all over myself.

"No, Marek, really. He's too scrumptious to be someone's old man."

Inquisitive became anguished. "Soph, please."

Rodrian slouched back in his chair and smirked. His brother's girlfriend waxed poetic over him and he absolutely loved it.

Marek, on the other hand, hated it. Knowing he was jealous made me love him even more. Wasn't it twisted? It was like saying *I love you because I know I can hurt you.*

"My brother is quite the family man." Marek's tone was stiff. "If not for him our family line might have died out by now. Brother, remind me—am I a great uncle, yet?"

"Great uncle? Holy crap, Rode. A grandfather?" I dropped my head back on the couch and groaned. "You? I gotta say, it's easier to believe you drink blood. Hell, it's easier to believe you have three nipples or something."

"Jeez, Marek." Rodrian looked distressed. "Did you have to tell her about that, too?"

"Ew!" I shrieked and leapt to my feet, scrambling to the door with my fingers in my ears. "Not listening! La-la-la-la-la!"

Rodrian chased me down before I could open it, laughing like a kid who'd dangled a spider in front of a little girl's face.

"C'mon, Soph. I was just kidding." Pulling my arm, he spun me to face him. "I only have two nipples."

He stepped toward me, stalking like a panther. I backed up, wary of the sudden change in Rodrian's power, and thumped against the door.

I slowed my breath, hoping to slam the brakes on my thudding heart, trying to not react. It wasn't easy. Rodrian's sexuality demanded a lot of attention. His voice sank deeper, rougher, and his eyes filled with amber heat.

"Want me to prove it?" He hooked a finger around his tie and tugged it loose, unbuttoning the top button of his shirt with a hot grin. "You can look. I don't mind."

A growl from the other side of the room threw a figurative bucket of cold water on Rodrian and he backed off, playful once more. "Do I feel like a grandfather to you?"

Fluffing my hair to hide my relief, I flopped back onto the couch. "Hell no, you don't."

I laughed and fanned myself, stealing a glance at Marek, whose paper lay in a heap on his lap. I blew him a kiss. "Relax, sweetie, or your face will stay that way."

He glared back at us, jaw clenched hard enough to break teeth, before ducking back behind his paper.

Rodrian took his seat, pulling off his tie and dropping it on the desk. "Shiloh is my youngest. She lives with her sister."

"So, you have kids, huh?" This time I kept the utter disbelief out of my voice.

"Mmm," he assented. "Sophie... let me tell you about my children."

Something in his voice brought down Marek's paper. The playfulness had well and truly disappeared. Rodrian's tone sounded serious. Reflective.

Sad.

"When Boxer was born," he began, "I thought I'd explode with joy. My firstborn, a son. The moment I saw him, held him for the first time, kissed his copper lashes, touched his fingers, admired his lips, curled like tiny rose petals... It took my breath. Love crushed me. Everything I had lived through had led to him, to that moment where finally, my life lay bundled in my arms."

He looked down at upturned hands, as if gazing once more upon his newborn son. Rodrian's eyes glowed with warmth, hazel irises throwing off glints of amber and forest, the light emphasized by his warm smile.

"But our family wasn't destined for a peaceful existence. Father had been a clan guardian and we were all targets, all the time. I couldn't abide the idea of losing Boxer and I put all my energy into keeping him safe. That was my mistake. I became too protective, too smothering. I didn't let him grow into his power."

Marek shook his head, regret showing plainly in his

eyes. "Boxer was talented. He came into his cusp early. His gifts had great potential, such tremendous strength behind them."

"They did," Rodrian agreed. "But instead of encouraging him I held him back. I sheltered him, repressed him, and kept him out of danger instead of preparing him to face the world. And so, he rebelled. Typical teenager."

Rodrian paused, chewing on a knuckle and staring at nothing. His voice dropped and the mood of his power sank with it.

"Marek was in Asia. I couldn't bring myself to call him, to admit I needed help raising my own child. Boxer fell in with a bad crowd and started experimenting with blood rush. His strength convinced him he was strong enough to take anything. I constantly pulled him out of trouble, using anger to hide my fear. He lashed out, fighting me, seeking thrill after killing thrill. The rush twisted him and he became a 'lution junkie. By the time Marek returned, it was too late. Boxer Fell. He had to be exterminated."

I gasped, tears rising. Sympathy chilled me as if the AC had kicked on full blast, and I rubbed fruitlessly at the goose bumps on my arms. "Oh, Rodrian, I'm sorry..."

He raised his hand. "He evolved, Sophie. By the time he'd been tracked down in Germany and put to the sword, he was vampire. There was none of my son left in him. My only pain comes from not having been a better father. His end is my fault."

"You are an admirable father." Marek interjected firmly, raising from his seat and standing in front of Rodrian's desk. "You have strength and talent and depth of heart I can never hope to possess."

"Right," Rodrian responded. "This is why my son is dead."

I could hear self-loathing in his voice, similar to what I'd often heard in Marek's. How could these amazing men have such pointed feelings for themselves?

His guilt and sorrow was so thick it made me dizzy. I couldn't imagine what it did to him if I only got the run-off. How could he store all this inside and remain so mischievous on the outside? How could someone with so much light in his eyes have such darkness surrounding his heart?

"You don't make life when you create a baby," I said. "You're blessed with a gift. When that life ends, it goes back to the big miracle it came from. You can't blame yourself when life is lost, Rode. You can only appreciate it while you have it and remember it when it's gone."

Rodrian swung his chair around to face the windows. "What if you chased it away?"

"You didn't chase it away. You were being a parent. You didn't hurt him, Rode—circumstances did. Don't blame yourself."

"You make it sound easy."

"It's not," I said. "You figure it out only after you've hurt enough to last a couple lifetimes. I know."

"You've hurt like this? You've buried your own child?" He spat the words like poison.

"No," I answered quietly. "My family. My brothers. My parents. It doesn't hurt any less, not when they were all you had."

Marek sat down beside me, concern in his deep green eyes. I could feel him surround me with a soothing touch of power but I reassured him with a pat on his leg. "It's okay, love. Rode needs the comfort, now."

With a curt nod, Marek addressed him. "It was all so long ago, brother. You must get past it. Death is a part of life. No sense mourning what you cannot control. It makes you weak."

"No, Marek," I corrected him. "Pain has its own rules. It's a mountain, a big one that gets in the way of living. You can't just go around it. You have to find the tunnel and go through it. It's dark and scary but if you try to avoid it, you're just walking uphill the rest of your life."

Rodrian still had his back turned to me. "I can help you, Rode. You don't have to go through it alone."

He stood and stared out the window for a brief moment, tugging his sleeves down into place. Turning to me, he gave me a doubtful look. "How?"

"Well, for starters, tell me about your daughters. Shiloh and her sister."

"What can I say? I'm not even raising Shiloh. Brianda is. Brianda—now, there's a girl." His mood lightened and her name seemed to invoke a sudden glint in his eyes. "She's like their mother. Strong, clever..."

"Vicious," added Marek.

"Yeah," answered Rodrian with a dreamy smile. "My sweet girl."

Marek rolled his eyes and turned to explain. "Brianda never showed an interest in taking a mate, at least not in a traditional sense. She may not be thinking of children of her own but she enjoys mothering Shiloh."

"Don't you worry about them living alone in the city?" I remembered the arguments my parents had made when I moved in with a couple girls during college. They flipped, to be precise. The battles ceased when I offered to move into a house full of boys. Lesser of two evils.

"Not as much as I worry I'll screw them up like I did Boxer."

"Besides," added Marek, "Brianda is skilled enough to keep them both safe, as well as their neighbors. I've considered taking on Brianda as part of my guard. Beautiful and deadly. Just like her dear old uncle."

I groaned. These guys were true proponents of healthy egos.

"At any rate," Marek continued, "there's absolutely no

need to worry about Shiloh while Brianda takes care of her."

"See?" I said. "If there's one thing I almost learned, it's when Marek says don't worry, you don't have to worry much. Turn your attention to enjoying your daughters. Shiloh seems so bouncy, so fun, so full of life."

"You haven't the faintest idea." Rodrian chuckled in spite of himself.

"Then celebrate her. Use the joy to guide you through the pain. See how life goes on, all the more precious now because you know it's fragile and temporary."

Marek reached up, smoothing my hair back from my face, over my shoulder. His touch seemed tentative, as if I, too, were fragile and temporary.

For a long moment, no one spoke. Rodrian stared back out the windows, down at the teeming streets below us, the harbor further off. With a sigh, he pushed in his chair and approached me, crouching pensively. Gently grasping my hand, Rodrian placed a gallant, almost sacred, kiss on my skin.

I reached out to him with my compassion, wishing to comfort him.

Resting his cheek against my hand, he shuddered. His sadness and pain spilled into me, as if desperate for release. How many mornings did he wake in a cloud of regret? How many evenings did he sit alone, finding new depths to his despair? His eyes betrayed his anguish and I sent my heart out to him, praying for the pain to back off long enough for him to regroup and face it standing.

I rested my head against his and closed my eyes.

I could feel something else behind his grief, something bright and warming, something he'd forgotten. By releasing some of his hurtful guilt he uncovered it the way you'd find a favorite sweater when unpacking a bunch of heavy old blankets you'd put away for the season. It was bright and beautiful and buoyant.

Hope.

An encouraging sign. "I'll help, Rodrian. I promise."

A strong arm slipped around my waist and Marek leaned closer to me, adding his confident reliable power to Rodrian's healing haze. "We'll help, brother."

Rodrian looked up at him, surprised. His wide eyes revealed the child within, the younger brother who depended so much upon the older. "You, Marek? You will?"

Marek let out a big breath, pushed his hair back from his forehead, and waved a dismissive hand. "Fine. You got me. She'll help. I'll just keep telling you what to do and expecting you to do it. What else is family for?"

When we left Rodrian's office, Marek suggested a walk instead of heading straight home. We paused at the Overlook, a stone-walled ledge built along the outer wall of an old retired cemetery near the river's edge. The view showed the river below, the brightly lit bridge far beyond. Sunlight glinted off water and windshields as both streamed by in the distance.

Marek leaned on his elbows, hands clasped. He'd loosened his hair and it tumbled over one shoulder, catching the slight breeze. "You are, in so many ways, truly an image of Isis."

"I'm no goddess. If anything, I'm as far from one as I can get."

"Ah, but the goddess is in you. *Isis knows the orphan, knows the widow. Isis seeks shelter for the weak, justice for the poor.* You do that. All those people to whom you've been kind, for absolutely no reason. All those people for whom you've shown compassion, who give you nothing in return."

"All those people were weak or poor. What do they have to give in return?" I countered.

"Yet, you champion them." He laughed, the sound harsh and full of disbelief.

I shrugged. "Someone needs to."

He shook his head and pulled his hair back over his shoulder. "Everyone has a choice. The test comes with accepting the consequences."

"Fine, then." Crossing my arms, I leaned back against the wall. "When I became an advice columnist, I took an oath to save and protect."

"Strange choice of words. Why *save*?"

As spontaneous as the word had been, it was accurate. "I made a mistake a long time ago. A big one. Not a day goes by when I don't think about it and want to kick myself in the head."

"The past is past."

"Well, maybe yours is. Mine seems to be right behind me every step I take."

"So. You made a mistake. What happened?"

I chewed my lip and toyed with my rings. Funny how the breeze seemed to die down. Suddenly, the cemetery behind me ceased being a piece of scenery. The crumbling stone monuments seemed oppressively close, as if waiting for me to speak. "We don't need to talk about it, Marek. I'm past the point where therapy will exorcise my demon."

"We do need to talk about it because it is your demon. I promise I won't try to fix you. Just tell me what drives you."

"Fine. You want to know, fine." I balled my hands, steeling myself for the story. "When I was in junior high, a boy in my class hanged himself in his closet. His little sister found him."

Marek dipped his head. "Suicide. That's harsh. How old was he? Fourteen?"

"Fifteen."

His expression clouded. "Shiloh's age."

"Right. And I was the last person he spoke with before he did it. He was nice enough to thank me in his suicide note."

"Oh, gods." He reached up and rubbed his face.

"Damn straight—one God isn't enough to swear by. He wrote, 'Tell Sophie she's right. Life is hopeless.' My demon is the spirit of a fifteen-year-old boy who committed suicide because of me."

"Not necessarily. What did you talk about?"

"Everything. I had no idea he'd do it, you know. He didn't sound depressed. Kris called me after supper and said he was grounded again. Got caught stealing cigarettes from the deli near his house. The owner made a big deal, called the cops and everything. Cop read him the riot act and told him it was a black mark that would stay on his permanent record. Kris was afraid he wouldn't get into college because of it. The cop later said he was just trying to scare him straight."

"What did you say? Can you remember?"

"I can't forget. Every word is seared into my brain. I was feeling pretty low when he called. My parents were together but dad worked all the time. Mom belonged to all sorts of groups. They weren't home a lot. After my brothers died, I felt abandoned.

"I became a one-man salvation army. I rallied my friends when they were down. The class clown. Miss Sunshine. Kris called me, hoping I'd cheer him up. But I didn't. I was too busy pitying myself."

I stooped and gathered a small handful of rocks, throwing the biggest one out at the river. There was no splash. "I was in a pissy mood. I yelled at him for being stupid. We all smoked behind our parents' backs. If he got caught, we'd all get caught. 'Sorry,' he said. 'It was just a prank.' I said I hoped they at least let him keep the smokes because he'd pay for them for the rest of his life."

Marek turned to face me, still leaning against the wall, resting on his elbow. "You didn't know you were his last hope. You wouldn't have said it, had you known."

I let the rest of the stones slip through my fingers, listening to the spatter when they hit the water below, and rubbed my empty hands. "I damned him, Marek. I told him God wouldn't forgive him. No redemption with the cops who said he'd never get into college, no redemption with his parents who grounded him for the rest of his life. No redemption with God, because Sophie says the Almighty Merciful One doesn't care about a petty thief. My fault."

"You didn't damn him."

"Then why does he keep coming back? Why am I still haunted, if I'm not being punished? Kris keeps coming back. He's reincarnated over and over and over. The last time, he was Patrick."

Marek's subtle shake of chin and shoulders revealed incomprehension. I thought everybody knew about Patrick.

"He used to write to the column every week. Depressed guy, personal problems. We corresponded. It was evident he needed therapy, a counselor, something more than a bleeding heart pen-pal. I encouraged. I cajoled. I mailed him lists of groups and clinics. In the end, what did I get?" I tightened my hands into impotent fists. "Another suicide note. Another note and a reminder of my failure with Kris. It never stops. I try, and I fight, and I keep losing."

"I see why you feel the way you do. Your strong words found an easy target on a wounded soul."

"If I knew he'd—if I knew—"

His voice held more warmth and understanding than I'd ever received from anyone before, the simple sound of his love. "You wouldn't have said it. I know. The unseen future has a way of making us hate ourselves for an innocent past.

It was an unfortunate thing. But it drives you to be better."

I nodded, lifting one shoulder in half-hearted agreement.

"It drives you to save and redeem others."

"I don't deserve—"

"It is noble." His firm voice was malleable with acceptance. "It's a quality of Isis. You prove my point for me."

"Isis wouldn't convince someone they're past hope."

"Isis was human. She wasn't perfect. She injured Horus when she meant to assist him in battle. Did she do so intentionally?"

"What mother would intentionally hurt her child?"

"Exactly. An error of judgment, a miscalculation of future movement. She did not aim for Horus but she struck him all the same. Sometimes terrible things happen. We accept our punishment and continue forward."

"So, basically, a kid commits suicide and tells the world it's because of me, and your response is 'deal with it'?"

"Sophie, it was tragic. It changed your life. It restructured your soul. Because of that, many people benefited. How many people gained confidence because of something you've said or done? Think of the greater good."

"Someday. Maybe. Today, Kris is still just a demon."

"Don't say demon. Angel is more appropriate."

"Angel or demon, they're both dead. A nice word doesn't change it."

"You're right. But remember, you have to live with yourself. If pretending lets you find a semblance of peace, then you must pretend."

"What are you pretending?"

"Hmm?" He made a harsh sound and shook his head to clear his thoughts. His power turbined tighter around him.

"I know you're haunted, too, Marek. What demon drives you?"

"I'm not sure you'd understand."

"Try me."

"Then I'm not sure you'll forgive me."

"Well. Now you have to tell me or I'll always think the worst."

Marek let out a long, slow breath, like a patient preparing for the pain of resetting a broken bone. "I've been around a long time. Long before Wall Street or Washington, DC. I was originally schooled in the art of war. I trained with militants of other cultures. I fought. I protected. I destroyed. And war, Sophie, is a messy thing. Blood doesn't wash from one's hands."

I knew Marek had a violent past. I knew his conscience was a burden he continued to carry. I knew I had to be supportive now, because this weight made up much of the mass of his spirit. "Who did you fight?"

"Vampire."

"Oh." The muscles in my shoulders twitched. I didn't realize they'd tensed until my purse slid down my arm, and I hitched it back up. "Well, that's okay. It's not killing if they're dead already."

"True. But their daylight agents are not."

"Oh."

"War makes decisions for us, Sophie. Missions dictate our actions. A soldier has a light conscience as long as he keeps things in perspective."

"But that's not what tortures you, is it?" I slid my hand along his forearm to the crook of his elbow, into the warmth between his arm and side. "There's something deeper."

He placed his hand over mine, curling his fingers around mine and drawing me closer. "Yes. I coordinated slayer patrols. Our strength and training is still no match against vampire, so we hunted the newly Fallen. Their power is weak, when the young are overwhelmed by sensory over-load. We seize the opportunity to destroy them while they're vulnerable."

"Vampire is vampire, Marek. Why is that bad?"

He released my hand and turned back toward the river, avoiding my eyes. "Because I was on patrol when we learned Boxer had Fallen."

Boxer. Rodrian's son. My chest stiffened, mid-breath, mid-beat, mid-thought.

"I exterminated him." Marek's voice shuffled like leaden shoes, the sound of his soul dragged helplessly behind. "Boxer died on my sword."

"But... he was already dead."

"We knew our target was on the brink of evolution. We knew he belonged to a local family. That's all. The tips led us to Germany. He was holed up with a group in Mannheim, a Were stronghold. Traitors, the lot. When he evolved, we pounced. I didn't know it was Boxer until I faced him at sunfall."

Marek bowed his head, bending to rest it on his hands like a sinner in the back row at church, far away from the glory of the altar, unsure if he was worthy to even raise his eyes. "He died with the sun. When he re-opened his eyes, he was vampire. I staked him to the floor. But he recognized me. His last word was my name."

I reached out with my compassion as I'd done for Rodrian, encountering his stubborn barrier. I nudged at him, asking him to open up to me. "Does Rode know?"

"No."

I inched closer so that I could lean into him. Feeling him against me, warm and solid and sure, gave me back some of the confidence I'd lost talking about my past. "Could Boxer have been saved?"

"No. At sunfall, the DV dies. No resurrection."

I tried not to dwell on the hopelessness of such an ending. "You did what you could."

"I tell myself that. I pretend Boxer died at sunfall. I

killed a vampire. Boxer's soul is somewhere safe. But every vampire I killed since wore his face and spoke my name. He is the demon who chases me."

"I don't suppose the term *greater good* is consolation?"

His power softened somewhat under my persistence, losing a layer of despair. "You give me consolation. Your scent and your smile are enough."

"I have more to offer than that. Don't sell me short because I smell good." I smiled my come-on-you-know-I'm-cute smile. It worked a peculiar magic on him, as if big and tough and hard could be undone by a tiny flash of something sweet.

"I still don't get it," he said. "My world is so different. It's about gain, power, survival. Yours isn't. And yet..." He stood and threw out his arms toward the magnificent view. "We share the same world. How?"

"Opposite ends of the food chain, I guess. You take, I give. Same could be said for our species in general."

In a swift movement he pulled me against his chest and engulfed me in his embrace. The heat of his bright eyes, the touch of so much of his body against mine, the suddenness of it all stole my breath.

For all his intensity, his voice was as playful as it was deep. The bass notes rumbled in his chest, making my skin vibrate. "That's right," he growled. "I feel you haven't given me nearly enough of what I want. And I..." He leaned down to press his lips against my throat, inhaling deeply. "I want so much."

I caressed the sides of his face, feeling the roughness of his sideburns contrast sharply with his perfectly clean shave. I coaxed him away from my vulnerable throat and brought his face even with mine. "Who am I, Marek, to fool with nature? It's my place to give, so take a little of me, now."

"Just a little?"

I couldn't respond. Not because I surrendered to his kiss but because I hadn't figured out exactly how much I was willing to give.

I'd just have to trust he didn't take more than I could handle.

24

"Turn off your computer and lie with me." Marek lay on the couch, one arm tucked behind his head as he watched TV. He'd been flipping between CNN and The History Channel. "You need a break."

"I wish I could." I rested my weary head in my cupped hand and rolled the mouse in aimless circles. Even though it was after eight o'clock, I sat at my computer, wearing no more than a camisole and sleep-shorts. Since meeting Marek I'd fallen behind on the extras I usually contributed at work. It was odd. Until I met him I never had anything to do except write.

Usually it made me smile. There was so much more to life now that someone special shared it with me. However the closer deadlines got, the less I smiled and the more I worried.

I had it easy at work and I knew it. I didn't want to jeopardize it by slacking off. Donna's comments had been a lot more pointed than usual and I didn't want the sentiments to spread. I might have the world with Marek but loving him didn't pay the rent.

"I promised to get some research done for an article on the new tax legislation. Vote goes to the House this July and *The Mag* wants to spotlight each side of the issue. I'm organizing material on Senator Levene since he's been a major force behind one of the State Reps."

"How is it going?"

"Too many unanswered questions," I admitted. "The 'pro' side is carpet-bombing with all sorts of happy horseshit about how many benefits the taxes will bring. But it's the Senator's voice we need—he just doesn't give in to Q and A too often." I stood up and stretched, then walked over to the couch.

Marek reached up and tugged me down onto him. As I wiggled into a comfortable position, he stroked my hair and rumbled contentedly. "Better," he whispered.

"One good interview with Levene would have the state running behind him like rats behind the piper. Instead, I'm trying to piece together quotes from a bunch of different sources. It's making me nuts. I wish I could get into his head."

"Good idea," said Marek. "Do that."

I lifted my head and shot him a look that said *oh, yeah, right.* "Good idea, maybe, but an impossible one."

He nudged me, urging me to get up. I did so very reluctantly; Marek made a comfortable cushion. As I trudged back to the computer, he sat up and dug his hand into his front pocket.

"Not impossible." He pulled his cell phone free. "Get dressed."

"Why?"

"We'll get your answers. Then, your work will be done and you can go back to lavishing your attention on me."

"I don't understand."

"I'm calling Frank. We'll stop by for a drink and you'll

ask him what you want to know."

"What? No. I can't do it." I sprang from the chair to grab his hand, which already had his cell phone flipped open. "I don't interview. Let me call Tammy. She can do it justice, not me."

"No. Not Tammy. You. Frank will do this for me as a favor." He closed his phone and gave me a serious look. "But, I want you to handle it carefully. *The Mag* can't discover you or I have such connections to Frank. Our public relationship has been meticulously developed. Can you publish this information without revealing our involvement?"

"Sure," I said. "We'll use a pseudonym. *The Mag* does it all the time."

"You can arrange this?"

I shrugged. "My editor can."

He nodded with satisfaction. "You're okay doing this?"

His insistence puzzled me. "Why wouldn't I be? I get paid either way. I write a lot of extras at work but the only thing I put my name on is my column. It's part of the reason they love me. I help them look good."

"So modest," he said with a laugh.

"So true," I agreed. "And so sad. I bet I'd get paid a lot more if I were an attention-grabber. But then they'd expect more and I'd have to work more. So I cut my losses and remain satisfied being broke but happy."

"As long as you have plenty of time to spend doting on me, I, too, am satisfied. Now, get dressed. I'd like to get this done quickly."

"Why?"

His smirk was full of smoldering promise. "All the sooner to get you undressed again."

We were on our way to Frank's within the half-hour. When Marek wanted something done, it got done straight away. He'd called Frank and said he'd like to drop in, if it was convenient. Of course it was okay. Flipping his phone shut he gave me one of those *what else did you expect?* kind of looks.

"So Frank is involved in your political business?"

"Yes. I'm a lobbyist of sorts, the same as any other in Washington. My issues simply tend to go beyond gun control and earmarking funds."

I nodded and drummed my fingers on the armrest of the passenger side door. "It makes perfect sense."

"It does?" He sounded guarded, as if he were afraid their relationship might be more apparent than he thought.

"Sure. I just didn't think of it until now. Senator Levene sounds like you. He speaks as if he grew up listening to you preach."

"I guess he did, in a way. I never had any children of my own. It would have been unfair to sire a son when I constantly put myself in harm's way."

"Rodrian has a family."

"Rodrian was content to put down roots, to find a mate and sire children. We were the only sons. While I pursued and protected, Rodrian took care of our family and our interests. He did well, after all. It would have been good fortune if his sons had lived to sire sons of their own, but there's still hope. There's Shiloh and, should the hells decide to freeze over, Brianda. Our line will continue. Somehow."

He drove a while, lost in thought. I patted his thigh, a comforting connection, and watched the raindrops zigzag along my window, battered by the wind.

Marek stretched his arm across the top of my seat. "I never sired children but I've encountered many special people. Over the years I've taken some of them in. I've arranged for better homes, for education and employment, for protection for them and their families. Not all of them knew my true nature but some did. Some knew the truths of the DV. Frank is one."

His voice held affection and I felt a sense of pride and joy emanating from him. It was the feeling I got from Rodrian when he talked about his daughters.

"Frank is a rare man. You say he sounds like he grew up listening to me 'preach.'" Marek cast a sidelong glance at me as if not quite appreciating the phrase. "He's a foster-child, raised by a DV pair who had no children of their own. They allowed themselves to age as humans would for the sake of illusion. I was the uncle who spoiled his nephew and encouraged him to go to law school. As Frank grew, I faded into the background, re-emerging as his colleague and acquaintance. I sat at his wedding feast, witnessed the religious dedications of his children. He knows the DV."

He drummed his fingers against my headrest and sighed. "I never had a son of my own. If ever I did, he would be Frank."

"I'd always wondered how someone involved in politics could manage to maintain the attitude of a knight. The whole good versus evil thing. There's no dirt on him, anywhere. Not even a single muddy statement. People say he's an angel of God."

He didn't exactly snort but it sounded close. "Frank is no angel. He's as devilishly mischievous as any boy. I mean, was. He's matured somewhat but you still wouldn't want to go fishing with him. It's his excuse to get the badness out."

"Fishing?" I choked. "You?"

"Why not?" His voice rose indignantly.

I laughed and waved my hand, trying to imagine a Mr. Marek Outdoors Guy. Nah.

Eventually, we pulled up the driveway of an elegant colonial in an upscale suburb. My pulse hummed with anticipation. Reaching down, I pretended to adjust a pant cuff and rubbed my palms on my leg.

I reorganized my articles and notes and pulled down

the vanity mirror to re-check my teeth. As I dug out my lip gloss, Marek shifted the car into park, switched off the ignition and turned to face me.

"There is another reason why I'd like you to pass on taking credit for this interview. A much more important reason." His eyes, shadowed and dark, matched his voice.

"Oh?" I was always wary when he used that particular tone. It usually meant he would say something I'd rather not hear.

"Frank's opposition—the legislators pushing to get the legislation passed—are also lobby-funded. The most influential of these groups uses vamp money. The territory Master is footing the bill."

"The Master?"

"Master vampire. The tax increase will fund his tribute. It's a bribe. Give the Master his money and he keeps his vamps underground, away from humans. The taxes will hit the hardest-pressed people. This legislation is as much a DV-vampire battle as it is one of politics or economics. Associating with Frank can put you in danger. Mortal danger."

Suddenly, I wasn't worried so much about bungling the interview.

Despite the late hour, Frank's wife cordially showed us into his study. She was dressed in a robe and slippers as if ready to retire. Staying long enough to remind her husband to remember to come to bed sometime before dawn, Annette gave Marek a knowing look. He had the decency to look chastised before kissing her on the cheek.

"Frank," Marek said. "You remember my Sophie."

"Of course." Frank reached out to grasp my hands. "It's not often someone shares Marek's table. He keeps a 'Fortress of Solitude' ward around it." He dropped a knowing wink at me.

"Of course I don't," disagreed Marek amiably.

It was easy to relax amidst their comfortable manners. Here in the privacy of his home, Frank left off the Important Politician Attitude and became simply Frank, the man who'd been raised by Marek and his family. He poured drinks from a cabinet bar on the side of the room and gestured to make ourselves at home.

"You must be made of sunshine, Sophie." Frank settled himself into a high-backed upholstered chair. "I rarely see Marek without his customary black cloud."

"You mean he usually feels grumpier than he does right now?" I wanted to know how another human perceived the power Marek and other DV emitted.

His smile was blank, as if he didn't understand my question. "Probably. At least his eyebrows aren't touching tonight. He usually looks much more forbidding."

I smiled back but glanced at Marek, who returned my questioning look with an indecipherable one of his own.

"Frank, you know I wouldn't call you away from your wife's bed if it wasn't important," Marek said. "Sophie works for *The Mag* and she's researching the tax debate. She had some questions."

"Of course. I'm a politician. I appreciate any chance to talk about what's important to me. It's a familial trait." He nodded toward Marek, who cleared his throat in reply.

I'd never seen anyone joke around with Marek before. Rodrian teased, but Frank played with him. Marek actually seemed to enjoy it. I could get used to this.

Marek lifted his eyebrow, using his stern expression and a slow shake of his head to try to dissuade me. He'd picked up my mischievous vibe at once.

"Another tax increase, right? What else is new? But what will we gain from it? Not new roads. Not better schools. And not safety, not by any means." He made a fist and tapped his hand with it. "We shouldn't have to pay for the right to stay alive."

Marek tapped his finger against his mouth and nodded.

Frank's eyes lost their youthful glint. "The reason for the increase isn't public knowledge, not even among my colleagues. I don't even think the Senate committee knows who is behind the legislation. I just happen to have an inside lead."

"Marek," I said.

Frank nodded. He leaned forward slightly, extending an entreating hand. "Big business won't pay, even though they will benefit from the protection. The common man will—they are the ones most likely to be lured into the shadows. It's a godless game and most don't even know they are playing because they are completely unaware of the Underground."

At the sound of the word *Underground*, Marek released a jarring spike of threat, making me sit forward in alarm. It must have been unintentional because he followed it with a tiny wave of apology.

Frank didn't seem to notice. He sat back and reached for his glass. "All this is off the record, of course. You understand it's not prudent to make such arguments in public. It's no easy thing, living in two worlds at once, being unable to publicly acknowledge things that are so much a part of your life."

Even though we'd been sitting in his study for a fraction of an hour, I found I had developed a sense of kinship with Frank. I supposed the streams of pride and familiarity I caught issuing from Marek might have enforced it.

Someone else knew about the clandestine race of DV. Frank was someone else who had to keep it all to himself, without any of his own kind to share it.

"Would you ever want to talk sometime?" I asked shyly. "There's so much I want to know—about the DV, about Marek—"

"Haven't I been forthcoming enough?" Marek interjected.

"Yeah, but..." I shrugged. "Frank's on the home team. It'd be nice to have a human perspective."

Frank smiled. "You don't need to explain, Sophie. I know what you mean. When Marek took me in, I felt like an outsider, too. It gets easier. You can't remain a stranger to him for long."

Marek passed a simmering stare at me and my pulse quickened. He thought about knowing me in a Biblical sense and I wasn't talking Sunday School. His power insinuated itself around me like silken sheets and it chased a blush upwards through me, warming as it went.

You will be mine, his power whispered.

It wasn't fair Marek used his DV body talk with me, forcing me to fight to keep a neutral face. Then again, Marek would never have covered me in sexy if Frank could detect it. He wouldn't do something so exhibitionistic. It confirmed what I'd already suspected. Frank couldn't sense Marek's power.

But I could. Why? What's wrong with me?

Thankfully, Frank didn't seem to notice the heat in my cheeks or my quick streak of self-doubt. At least I wouldn't have to cover it up. Never thought I'd say it but talking with regular people was so much easier.

Frank sighed, oblivious to my internal dialogue. "Price we pay. Some secrets, some truths, can never be made public. A balance must be maintained, one that goes beyond what's right for any one or any group. The balance must be maintained for everyone's sake."

"Balance is essential," Marek said. "It is worth the sacrifice."

Frank's eyes wrinkled when he smiled. "Besides, Marek wouldn't let me tell you everything, anyway. He's much too fond of his stern reputation. If word ever got out he lets his guard down..."

"Frank, Sophie likes my tough guy image. Why so intent on shattering it?"

"Because, sometimes, you're much more human than you'd like to admit."

Marek scowled, as if firmly disagreeing but not willing to engage in the debate.

"I look forward to getting to know you, Sophie," Frank said "You must be someone special. He's always kept himself too isolated. Looking at you makes me think there's hope for the old boy."

"*Old boy,* Frank?" Marek sounded wounded.

"You're right. Don't stand us both before a mirror. I hardly recognize myself anymore. Who's the guy with the wrinkles, the grey hair, the dignified public smile? I've grown from a gawky kid to this... well, this old guy sitting here with you," he said with a laugh. "The world we worked so hard to build has gotten in the way."

"The world we have successfully built," Marek said. "You mustn't look at it so negatively. This is destiny."

"Destiny or not, sometimes I wish I was seventeen again and it was summer forever and we could fly off to some new country or unexplored mountainside or European city like we did when you wanted to disappear."

Frank's voice grew rough and unsure around the edges, his laugh-lines glistening. I found it difficult to sense human emotions, compared with DV, but Frank's longing for the past was so intense I knew without a doubt what he wished. He wanted to go back to a simpler time.

I reached out with a soothing mental touch because I knew all too well what those wishes felt like. Sometimes it is hard to accept that we can't go back..

He smiled, looking over at Marek with appreciation, perhaps assuming it was compulsion that comforted him. Frank didn't realize the comfort was mine. Marek gazed back at him with affectionate benevolence but sent me a small pulse of gratitude.

"I envy you, Sophie," Frank sighed. "Enjoy every moment you have with Marek, even the dark ones. You'll miss them should they end. And be sure to live. Live, so he lives. He's too stubborn to do it alone. Marek is content to merely exist."

"Untrue," Marek protested. "I live plenty."

"If you need me, Marek will call. You understand the need for secrecy, of course, but I'll consider you family, Sophie, because Marek considers you family."

"Thanks, Frank. I'm grateful knowing I'm not the only human living in DV Land anymore. Sometimes I feel like a kept woman."

"You are," Marek said. "I keep you. You are mine." He let his eyes take up their glow, an emerald flash that punctuated the surge in his power that wrapped me in his embrace. For a moment, we were entwined together, even though the room separated us. We were simply together.

"Good luck with Lord Marek," Frank said. "His relationship skills are primitive and his chauvinism is legendary."

Marek dampened the glow and arched an eyebrow at Frank. "And his memory is perfect to the point of being photographic."

"And his point is taken," Frank said with a laugh. "Now, I guess we better get serious and give Sophie the information she wants for her magazine article before my wife storms in and drags me off to bed by my ear. I'm too old to burn the midnight oil, despite my upbringing."

An hour later, I had notes out the wazoo. Frank was generous, well-spoken, and answered every question. He'd even looked over what I'd written earlier and made some helpful suggestions. By morning I'd be looking at a powerful piece of public persuasion. This could be the article to put the final nails in the pro-tax coffin.

Eh, maybe a bad choice of words.

As we made our way to the door, Frank hugged each of us warmly, and asked after a few people he knew. As they chatted, I noticed a framed photograph on the bookshelf near the door.

A younger Frank bedecked in thick sideburns and a heavy mustache perched in a wooden rowboat, green summer and lemon sun on the distant shoreline. His mouth was open in a whoop of delight as someone else appeared to have difficulty reeling in a fish. That someone had his back to the camera but I recognized the long black ponytail.

Marek cleared his throat behind me. I grinned impishly. "You?"

"I told you I fished."

I peered at the picture, noticing the muscles bunched under the tee shirt, the veins bulging in his forearms. "How big was that thing? It must have been a monster."

"Oh, it was a monster all right." His voice was a sullen growl.

Frank laughed like a teenager. "Rodrian hooked Marek's line to an old tree on the bottom. We almost capsized with the effort Marek put into raising it. That tree wouldn't come up so he was determined to take us down to it."

"Can't just fish like a normal boy, can you? Every-thing is a joke."

"I have to make up for you, don't I?" He laughed when Marek's expression sank into more sullen lines.

"I hope you do the same, Sophie." Frank waited on the porch as Marek opened the car door for me. "Don't be afraid to shine on him. He keeps to the dark places too much. I don't think he'll ever tan but he won't burn either. Don't be afraid to shine."

Although the next morning loomed wet and dreary and I'd only grabbed a few short hours of sleep, I beamed, full of sunny smiles, while I knocked on Barbara's office door. Swinging the door open at her unintelligible reply, I sauntered in.

"Here you go, Barb." I held out a file folder.

"What's that, hon?"

"A present."

I handed her the folder and she slipped her glasses down from their perch on top of her head. She scanned the page, her eyes getting wider with each line. She re-read the first lines in complete astonishment before looking up.

"Sophie, this is an interview with Senator Levene."

"Crap. I gave you the wrong one. I meant to give you a review of the new strip joint uptown. Give it here." I reached to take it back.

She pressed the folder up to her chest and stepped out of reach. "Oh, no, you don't. How on Earth did you get this?"

"Oh, you know..." I waved my fingers in a vague

gesture. "I've got connections."

"Since when? Or should I say, 'since who?'"

"Never could keep a secret from you, Barbara." I turned to pour a cup of coffee as she poured over the text. Curling up in the big red chair, I sipped at my cup of sanity and let her read in peace.

"It's all here. I didn't know you could give such good interview. I must have overlooked one of your gifts. And this..." She waved the pages briefly. "I heard it was next to impossible to get an interview with him. That alone will get you noticed. I'll send it right over to Tammy. You'll earn a nice byline with this."

"Actually..." I interrupted her as she reached for the phone, remembering Marek's warnings. "I'd rather make it anonymous. Can we give it to Jonathan Albert?"

"Are you crazy? It's a huge feather for your cap."

"I know. I'd just hate unwanted attention."

"You can't be ashamed of this. Senator Levene's rep is spotless. It's no bad thing to be associated with him."

"Of course I'm not ashamed. He's a good..." I almost finished it with *boy* but caught myself. "Person. I'm grateful to have the chance to speak with him. But some people might mistake a chance interview for something more and try to get something from me I can't provide."

Barbara gave me a long, measuring look. "I'm not sure I understand. But if that's what you want... just seems a waste of a fabulous credit."

"I know. But I promised to protect my, um, connection, so I have to insist."

"Okay." She punched the intercom and called Amanda in. "I'll keep your secret, and tell Tammy to credit the house ghost for what's probably the interview of the year."

"Lucky ghost," I said.

I'd get to keep my neck. Luckier me.

లల ౨ా

Later in the week, I received a letter. It was addressed to the column, but inside was a handwritten note.

Dear Sophie,

While visiting Budapest as a young man, I came across a small church before the start of services. Wishing to experience every last drop of that amazing culture, I found a seat inside. Thankfully, my tour guide spoke the native language and translated much of the sermon. The words I heard that day have been with me since. I don't know if it was prayer or advice but, at any rate, it was truth:

"The difference between mystery and darkness, challenge and despair, doubt and defeat is love. Unconditional love surrounds us, strengthens us, and saves us from ourselves. Love offers itself to us like a gift even when we feel most unworthy. This love we may gather unto ourselves and this love we return even as we share it. Love is the line that draws the shape of God."

I hope you find as much meaning in these words as I have. May the truth light the way for you, and ultimately bring you peace.

Warmest regards, Frank

I slipped the note back into its envelope and tucked it into my purse. Something told me his "tour guide" was a mutual acquaintance. I recognized the truth in those words and smiled, grateful for the note and the reassurance I was no longer alone.

26

City dwellers know that running a few simple errands is never a simple thing.

Take this particular afternoon, for instance. I had to go to the bank because if I didn't make my deposit my car insurance payment would bounce. I needed to pick up some dry-cleaning before the place decided to eBay my stuff. I wanted to pick up pizza for dinner and get back to Marek's townhouse in time to eat, fool around, get dressed, and go out.

Always sounded simple but never actually was.

The dry cleaning pick-up would have been a breeze had they actually known where my garments were. They were like the Keystone Kops in there. I used the delay to phone in my take-out order and twenty agonizing minutes later I was on my way to Folletti's. I usually loved the sound of Cantonese arguments they sounded like opera. Just not today.

Karma threw me a juicy bone by opening a parking spot right around the corner from the entrance to Slices, the pizza joint at Folletti's. As I dropped coins into the meter, I heard a familiar voice call my name.

Shiloh ambled along with a few of her friends. Once she realized I wasn't out for her dad, she more or less adopted me. Marek adored her in his hug-me-and-get-it-over-with way, fending off her affections with gentle gruffness. Shiloh's spiritedness was therapeutic for Marek.

"Hey, Shy." I answered with a wave.

"Are you here to see Uncle Marek? Because I don't think he's here. She's in love with my uncle," she said to her friends. As the girls dissolved into ripples of laughter, Shiloh tugged me aside. "Are you staying long, Sophie?"

"No, I'm only picking up dinner. I'm supposed to meet Marek at his place."

"Great. You can give me a ride home." She spoke with the confidence of a child who knew she'd be cared for by a trusted adult, without question. "Please?"

I liked Shiloh a lot. She was the only DV I knew who didn't go all power-feely on me. She seemed like any other teenager I've ever known. Marek had explained that DV adolescents didn't adopt their power until they reach their cusp, usually somewhere in their teens.

I could only imagine what someone like Shiloh would feel like: a bucket of confetti in a tornado, maybe, with Justin Timberlake blasting in the background as it cut a mean swath through the middle of my psyche. The thought of picking up a teenage DV vibe was a terrifying concept, especially from a bouncy ball of life like Shiloh.

I'd gotten used to her hanging around her father's office at Folletti's, where Marek spent a lot of time when we were together. When Rodrian and Marek had business to attend and I had work in the morning, I usually ended up driving her home. She lived with Brianda near Marek's townhouse in Chaucer's Square so it wasn't out of my way. Sometimes a meeting would pop up or Marek would take an out-of-towner and Shiloh and I'd go someplace to eat.

Come to think of it, wherever Shiloh was, so was food. That girl must have hollow legs.

Anyways, Shiloh was a fun, sweet kid who treated me like an aunt. Aunt Sophie, that's me. Too bad it made me sound like an old spinster.

"Of course, you can come with," I answered.

"Great!" She issued a squeal of delight. "Let's go get your food and I'll tell Dad I'm going with you."

Waving goodbye to her friends, she linked arms with me and skipped along, telling me about this boy and that teacher and every dramatic thing that happened since I last saw her. She had enough to dish on throughout my stop into Slices and the ride up to Rodrian's office, finishing in more subdued tones as we walked down the hallway to his door.

Without a knock, Shiloh flung open the door. "Dad, Sophie's here. She said she'd drop me off at home. That okay?"

The door banged open against the door-stop with a thud. I could see Rodrian behind his desk, looking taken aback. His eyes found me and my pizza boxes and I shrugged an apology.

I could also see the two men sitting in front of Rodrian's desk. Nice suits, I noticed. One turned toward the sound of her commotion, his expression neutral. Lawyer, I figured. Who else managed a dead face like that? Or new Botox. That too.

"That's fine." Rodrian lay down a pen he'd been holding and clasped his hands on the desktop. His curt nod dismissed me completely. "Thank you, Miss."

"Love you, bye." Shiloh laughed and yanked the door closed. "Let's go before he changes his mind."

"Why'd he call me 'Miss?'" I wrinkled my nose. He'd called me lots of things, some of which made Marek angry enough to almost knock him on his ass, but never *Miss*.

"You've never seen Dad in action." Shiloh blew her bangs out of her eyes. "He could be such a bossy jerk. He called you 'Miss' so those two stiffs would think you're part of his workforce. I'm never going to work in business or in politics. I'd suck at pretending to be some powerful hot-shot."

"Me, too." I balanced the boxes with one hand and summoned the elevator. Those lawyers probably thought I was a pizza delivery girl. How terrifically glamorous.

Shiloh turned mock serious eyes on the cardboard take-out trays. "So, uh, are you going to eat all that yourself?"

I rolled my eyes. Hollow legs, I swear.

Once outside, she took the trays from me so I could rummage through my purse for my car keys. Traffic had gotten heavier and an endless stream of cars slid past, their drivers looking for a spot to park.

"Excuse me," called a strong pleasant voice. A long black luxury sedan, glided to a halt near us and a tinted window slid down. It drew my attention and I looked up. "Are you leaving?"

"Yeah." My spot had been a tight squeeze to begin with and I drove a compact but it didn't mean I couldn't be polite. I pointed toward my car. "Red Cavalier, three from the corner."

"My thanks, Miss." The window slid back up and the car pulled away, disappearing around the corner.

"You're way too nice," Shiloh said. "I'd have let him drive around all night. There's perfectly good valet around the back. Get a move on or I'm going eat this here on the street. It's bad enough I have to smell it all the way home."

I didn't know what she was worried about. She ate two slices before we even got to the parkway. She knew I wouldn't let her starve.

27

The waiter cleared away the last of the plates and set a cup of coffee in front of me with a wink. I didn't need to order out loud anymore. I smiled back with appreciation and reached for the sugar bowl.

I'd only met Marek about a couple of weeks earlier but it seemed as if I've known him much longer. The comfortable way we joked about things, as we had earlier about me actually cooking something or him actually eating it... it was like we'd known each other forever.

Now a sugar bowl sat on Marek's table. That little porcelain dish, with its cheerful blue flowers and delicate handles, got just as many smiles as I did when we dined together. Little DV pulses of warm approval often accompanied the smiles.

The DV thought I was good for him. Ironic, because I thought it was definitely the other way around.

"I have something for you," Marek said. The barest hint of a smile tugged the sides of his mouth.

"Really? What's the occasion?"

"Not that I need one, but... one month ago today we had our first date here."

"Marek!" I laughed. "I had no idea you were so sentimental."

"Good to know I can still surprise you after all this time." He pushed a small jeweler's box toward me.

I lifted the lid and made a tiny gasp. "Oh," I breathed. "It's beautiful."

I tugged out the tiny pin securing the trinket in place and removed the necklace from its cushion. A dark red pendant dangled from an intricately-wrought gold chain. The pendant seemed to be stone rather than jewel, and more careful inspection showed it was decorated with tiny Egyptian symbols. "Marek, this looks like the one at the Science Institute."

He nodded. "You remember."

"Sure I do. It's a Blood of Isis amulet."

"That's right. If you were able to read the hieroglyphs, you'd see they are words from the Book of the Dead. You need a magnifying glass to see them but I assure you it is accurately crafted."

"Would you read it to me?"

Marek took the pendant from my outstretched hand and peered at it a moment before glancing at me from under his lashes. "Do you read hieroglyphs?"

"No," I said.

"Neither do I." He smirked and handed the pendant back.

I fastened it around my neck and, lifting my hair up, I showed him how pretty my neck looked. Marek swept his eyes over me and I felt the weight of his glance as if he'd touched me with his fingers instead. He rumbled seductively, the purr of a lion, and my pulse quickened.

"I wish you could. I'd love to know the words," I said.

"Well, I can tell you how the spell is worded. *Blood of*

Isis, words of power of Isis, glory of Isis. It is a protection for this great one, a protection against wickedness. I pray this amulet will protect you just as I swear I will protect you."

I gazed down at the pendant, feeling its smooth weight in my hand. Turning it over, I noticed another design. I tilted my hand to catch the light and saw a tiny cartouche. "Is this my name?"

"No," he said quietly. "It is mine. Remember it always and keep me alive in your heart. The Egyptians believed speaking the name of dead would bring them back to life. It's how I feel, in a way, since I met you..."

He gazed longingly at the pendant lying against my skin. "I entrust my soul to you, Sophie. Will you keep it for me?"

"You mean you admit you still have one?" I smiled in response. "Not so long ago you came to me, convinced you were damned."

"Being with you has changed my idea about many things, some of which are quite apparent." He ran his finger over the lid of the sugar bowl. "But many private things, many hidden things, have been rearranged within me as well."

His voice grew softer, more intense, and his eyes brightened with jade highlights. "No one has ever touched me the way you do. I don't understand it, but you get inside me somehow. You make me better. Never in my long life has anyone touched me like this."

I loved him even more for having said those words. My heart swelled with fulfillment and I swallowed against an emotional lump in my throat. Marek was the love for whom I'd searched, the one who satisfied my need to be needed. "Well," I said, my voice swollen, "I won't take your soul. It's not yours to give away. I'll help you enjoy it, though. Somehow."

Marek reached across the table, taking my hand and

drawing it toward him. He seemed on the verge of speaking again when Rodrian strode over.

28

"Hello, Rodrian." Marek greeted him, without taking his eyes from mine. His power felt tight and urgent and I had the sinking feeling the night would shortly be heading downhill.

"Marek, Sophie." Rodrian gave me a smile but it disappeared quickly. He leaned toward his brother and spoke in low, urgent tones. "His men are here, Marek."

Marek lowered his eyes and pressed his lips together. His sullen expression matched his deep exhale as he released my hand and sat back in his chair. "Most inconvenient, brother."

"I did not invite them."

Waving a hand, Marek pushed his chair back and faced him. "I didn't mean to imply you did. So. They are here. Why?"

"They wish to speak with you."

"I figured as much." Marek rubbed his brow and frowned apologetically. "They won't take no for an answer, I suppose?"

Rodrian swiped his hair back and shifted his weight.

"Short of staking them, I don't know how else to persuade them to leave."

"Well, then, I suppose we talk." Marek stood and tugged his cuffs down. "I'm sorry, Sophie. It won't take long. Why don't you wait upstairs in the club?"

The second we walked into Dark Gardens, that invisible spotlight blared down on me again. All of a sudden I felt exposed, as if everyone was watching me, waiting for me to be left unguarded.

Marek deposited me in a booth, an unhappy look on his face. "On second thought, I don't like leaving you alone here."

I didn't like it either. I felt like an item on the menu. However, I didn't want to look like a puny human in front of Rodrian and the Beefcake Brute Squad.

"It's okay, Marek," I lied. "I'm a big girl. I survived this long without you, haven't I?"

His scowl indicated he emphatically disagreed.

Rodrian cleared his throat, urging him along. "Mark her, Marek, and come on."

I didn't like the sound of that. "What do you mean, 'mark me'? You're not going to, ew! Like, pee on me, or something?"

The scowl became disgust. "Certainly not. We are not dogs. That type of behavior is for animals."

"Now you did it," said Rodrian. "If we weren't in such a hurry, this could've gotten interesting. I love it when Marek goes anti-Were."

"You have to explain that, too, Marek. But not right now." I added the last part in a hurry, catching the impatient glance Rodrian passed at me. "Mark me or whatever, as long as it doesn't hurt, and go."

Marek regarded me pensively and rubbed his jaw. I watched his hand, imagining the mist of stubble against my own skin. He stretched down, caressing my neck and shoulders, stroking my hair aside to reveal the bare skin.

The touch sent shivers cascading downward like a shower of sparks and I almost forgot we were surrounded by so many people. The sense of being watched diminished. The room and crowd fell away, leaving us alone in the sensation. I wondered what passed through his mind, knowing my own thoughts would be plain upon my face.

I gazed up at him expectantly, waiting for him to mark me, completely trusting him not to hurt me. When Rodrian spoke, I jumped.

"About time." Rodrian sounded impatient.

"It's not a thing to be rushed," Marek protested, his grin a hungry innocence.

"Wait," I said. "You mean, that's it?"

Rodrian's voice took on a more teasing tone and he leaned closer, flirty-close. "What did you expect, paint?"

"Well... something."

"Do you feel everyone's eyes upon you?"

"No." Come to think of it, the oppression had disappeared.

"Do you feel like you're in danger?"

"No."

Marek shrugged. "Then it worked. Let's go."

"Enjoy the club," added Rodrian. "Feel free to explore; no place is off limits to you, and no one will prey on you."

"Because of that gesture." I couldn't keep the skepticism out of my voice.

"Yes, precisely so."

"But if I leave the room, won't I be around other DV who didn't see him make with the Harry Potter?"

"Trust me." Rodrian smiled, mischief lighting his eyes, and his men exchanged amused glances. "We're clever enough to accommodate for not being around when something happens."

"Sounds mysterious, and not the least bit reliable." I

frowned up at them. "How about a wristband? Or a shirt with big block letters reading *I'm with Marek*? Or..."

Cutting me off with a swift kiss that made me forget where I was, let alone why I babbled, Marek shushed me.

"Now, that's a marking anyone would understand," I said when he let me come up for air.

Marek treated me to another of his rare grins but, as he stood to leave, it melted from his face. Standing next to Rodrian and his men, he'd become dangerous again. The men flanked him as if he were a weapon.

"Soon, Sophie." Marek winked at me before they strode away.

I watched them until they disappeared from view, then turned to watch the crowd instead. They looked normal. As normal as expected, anyways, I amended. I spotted one guy dancing like he had Jell-O in his shirt and wanted to shake it down and out through the bottom of his pants.

Apparently, it was a cool dance, because admiring girls surrounded him.

Somehow, I refrained from banging my head on the table for feeling so old and out of it. Thankfully, I'd worn a corset under my sheer blouse. It gave me a false sense of security, as did my backless heels.

Especially the heels. God bless Steve Madden for his age-negating miracles.

It seemed like a nice enough crowd. I'd been in clubs before. My college friends talked me into going and for lack of anything better to do, I'd go. Two things always convinced me to swear it off again.

Number one, I couldn't dance. The biggest lie ever told was that to dance, all you did was "just go out there and have fun." Forcing a rhythm-and-tone-deaf body to move in a way that looked natural was not *fun*. I looked ridiculous when I danced and I was stupid enough to forget this important fact from time to time. It was a wretched cycle.

Number two, girls were vicious cats. They traveled in packs and picked fights everywhere they went. Most tried to conceal the ugly side of their natures but eventually the level of competition and jealousy overwhelmed the entire purpose of "going out and having fun." Even when I minded my own business, my big mouth got me into trouble.

Glancing around the room, I added a third reason: my being an old broad. Thirty-four was old compared to a crowd like this. I felt like a classroom mother on chaperone duty. Number three was enough of an argument to talk me out of doing just about anything.

It was different at Dark Gardens. I could make eye contact with other girls despite catching approving looks from the hot-looking men with them. Apparently, Dark Gardens was the exception to the usual nightclub rules.

I recognized the next song as a favorite of mine; a metal song had been mixed with an infectious *thump-thump-thump* that made it impossible for me to sit in the booth. I got up to explore the place just for an excuse to move. If I didn't move, I was going to sing and then all bets would be off.

Circling wide around the seating level, I surveyed the scene. The ring of booths and tables sat four wide steps higher than the round dance floor. Smart, I thought, since part of going dancing was sitting and watching, scoping out likely prey.

Eh, wrong choice of words. I swallowed against a dry spot in my throat.

A group of young women got up from a nearby booth and started down the steps. Flashes of colors glinted in more than one set of eyes as they glanced around. Spotting me, they waved at me to join them.

I didn't really want to, but as far as I understood Marek's intentions, I had to mingle with the DV. One of these girls might be his niece or cousin. I couldn't risk insulting anyone by being standoffish. If my lack of grace embarrassed them, so be it.

Turned out, it wasn't so bad. The sociable girls didn't act like silly kids, which in turn didn't make me feel like nursing home fodder. I discovered I could actually move despite the fantastic shoes I wore, and, even more surprisingly, I enjoyed myself.

Our little group expanded a little at a time and new people mingled through. As the songs changed, so did the crowd. By the third song, I realized one of the newcomers seemed intent on dancing with me. Alone.

He was roughly my height and had short dark blond hair ruffled up in tousled waves and soft spikes. A mischievous grin was framed by a devilish goatee, and he danced like a show-off. I brushed him off with a small shake of my head. I didn't want a partner.

Instead of moving on, he changed tactics to keep my attention. He'd dance mockingly behind someone else's back, smoothly switching moves if they'd turn around and spot him. The other girls caught on, giggling and pointing out suggestions for his next target. He'd stop just as they turned around to see the commotion behind them.

Eventually, his luck ran out and, needless to say, the victim wasn't as amused as we were. Grabbing the imp by his collar and his belt, the offended man hoisted him easily over his head and threatened to toss him up over the booths. The girls rushed to the rogue's aid, pleading for his release even as he laughed and dangled upside down over us.

"For a price," he said. "Since you deprive me of sport."

"Name it," I said boldly.

"You'll dance with me." He stared right into my eyes.

His own eyes remained dark. Since they didn't flash or glow, I agreed. I was "marked" and he kept his fangs hidden. What's the harm? "I'll dance. Just—set him down already.

He's looking down my friend's shirt."

"Damn!" The troublemaker's voice was drowned out by the girl's indignant shriek as she tried to jump up and club him. He didn't look like he suffered too much, considering the jumping animated her cleavage.

"On second thought, maybe he's safer up there..." I grinned up at him as he tried to fend off several well-aimed swats.

"Think so?" Mr. Muscles set the kid down as if he were a marshmallow. Still gripping him by the collar, he growled into the younger man's face, "Perhaps you'll find a worse fate in her hands, terrifying little thing she is."

"Thanks a bunch, Tanner!" The little demon yelped as he took off, Chesty Girl in hot pursuit. Her friends rolled their eyes as if they'd seen it all before.

I tried not to stare slack-jawed at Tanner. I couldn't get over these muscles. Marek hadn't lied when he said the DV had accelerated strength. It was obscene.

"Now we dance." He drew me away from the rest of the girls. The beat picked up with the next song and, lights flashing above and below, the crowd bounced along.

Tanner must have been born to dance. He glided and rolled with a fluidity I'd never seen. At one point I tried to imagine Marek dancing but laughed and gave up.

Marek could move, but not as serpentine-like as this guy. Tanner was a preternatural John Travolta *a la* Saturday Night Fever, right down to the dark wavy locks and hairy chest peeking out of his open collar.

Gradually, the beat relented, winding its way down into a slow song. Not wanting to close-dance, I smiled a thanks-and-so-long smile. Tanner blinked lazily and grabbed my hand, tugging me off the floor.

"Let's go shoot some pool." His white teeth, straight and non-pointy, glinted strangely under the black lights. Climbing the steps out of the bowl, he tugged me toward the hall that led to other parts of the club.

I didn't want to, but I was here to mingle at Marek's command. Reluctantly, I nodded my head and tried to look like I thought it was a great idea.

The hallway leading to the pool room was crowded with canoodling couples and laughing girls. Tanner draped his arm around my shoulders and squeezed us through. His hands were getting too nosy and I had to keep moving them out of forbidden territories. I hated grabby guys and he was definitely one of them. Wishing I had my cell phone, I began planning a polite escape.

Halfway through the hall Tanner drifted toward a corner. When he nuzzled my neck I put both hands on his chest and pushed him away. "Thanks, but I'm not interested."

"Yes, you are. I can smell it." He grabbed my arm and pushed me back against the wall, pressing against me and shoving his face close to mine. "You aren't going anywhere without me. What I want can happen right here."

Apparently, I thought with disgust. I could feel his eager parts springing up against my hip. I shoved him with effort. "Get off me, creep, or I'll scream."

Rubbing his obscene interest against my hip, he laughed. "Go ahead."

I screamed. B-movie perfect every time.

Every girl around me screamed back, playful, mocking, echoing it and canceling it out. No one moved to stop him. My mouth hung open in dismay as I wildly scanned the disinterested crowd. No one looked. No one cared.

"I love vamp security." Tanner growled, showing teeth. He darted his head down for a kiss, hard and rude.

Twisting my head away I slapped him, the snap of the impact hurting my hand.

"Do it again, bitch." He slitted his eyes. "I'll bite you so hard you'll wish you woke up dead."

"As if. You can't turn me vamp. I'm not stupid." I pushed my way past, but he stood his ground, forcing me to slide against him.

He caught me around my waist and wrenched me back, thumping me into the wall. "Neither am I."

He grabbed my jaw and twisted my head up, forcing me to look at his face. His eyes were wolfy, the color of burned oranges and Autumn rust.

Eyes wide, I fought in earnest. Instinctively my knee slammed into his crotch. It barely fazed him.

He grabbed my wrists and yanked me up to his face. He had more teeth than any person had the right to have. "That's it, bitch. Consider yourself bitten."

"Not if I bite you first!" Using his momentum, I jumped up at him. I found his ear with my mouth and clamped down with everything I had. Flesh crunched and ripped between my teeth as I toreaway.

He dropped me and grabbed at his ear, screaming in pain. This time, no one screamed back, because Tanner howled like a wounded dog.

I spit out a mouthful of blood. Salt and uncooked meat and wet dog, possibly the worst combination I ever tasted. All I wanted was a glass of something so I could gargle. I spit and wiped my tongue off until it was bumpy and dry, all the while mentally screaming, *so much for universal precautions, moron!*

Unseen hands drew me gently away from Tanner, who warily watched the circle of men closing in on him. I stared at him with a bland catatonia, craning my neck when a couple of bouncers hustled him backwards through a service door. A woman spoke next to my ear. "Let's find your booth."

The soft voice behind me sounded a lot nicer than Tanner so I didn't argue. Her hands on my shoulders, she guided me through the thickening crowd, nosy humans trying to peer past the thick wall of Rodrian's men.

The music, the light, the dancing continued without a skip. No one paid any attention to me; everyone seemed determined to act like nothing had happened. I knew they knew. The anxiety was tangible.

She guided me to my booth. As I slid in, I saw my rescuer. The pretty Latina, dressed head to toe in a leather suit that didn't hide any of her roller-coaster curves, glanced over the top of the booth before sitting next to me. Intense concern crowded her delicate features.

"Need a drink?" At my wordless nod, she motioned over my head. "Are you bitten?"

"No. I don't think so. He just... well, humped me a little."

"Are you sure?" She peered worriedly at me. "Let me see."

"I'm fine," I insisted, as she turned my head this way and that. I impatiently endured her examination, rapping my hands against the table, trying to drain off the high tide of tension.

"I saw blood on you. I have to make sure." She wiped at my shoulder, the napkin coming away with a bloody smear. Accusation lit her eyes, a flash of deep violet.

"Not mine. I bit him. Oh, shit." Something awful occurred to me. "Will I catch wolf?"

Finishing her inspection, she released my chin. "No. Lycanthropy is transmitted by saliva. The beast has to be in animal form, at least in part."

I remembered his pumpkin-colored eyes and shuddered. When the shudders didn't cease, I hugged myself and rocked. Cold. I remembered this kind of cold. It was panic. Shock would follow. I whimpered and tried to breathe over my lobbing heartbeat.

She wrapped her arm around me in a comforting gesture. "You did a smart thing. I never would've thought of it."

"I was scared silly. I still am. Marek..."

"Has been called," she interrupted. "Already on his way."

The sound of his name summoned him out of thin air. He gathered me against him and rocked me, cradling my head to his chest. I held onto him and listened to his heartbeat, feeling my tremors slowly settle. Relief pushed away the horror of what happened.

Rodrian was furious. My hearing muffled by Marek's embrace, I could faintly hear his voice as he interrogated someone.

"Not here." I heard Marek's voice through his chest, hollow and distant. "In the office."

He released me, and I sought the girl who'd rescued me. She was talking with some of the girls who'd originally danced with me. I caught her eye. "Thanks for helping me."

She beamed back in reply, shrugging as if it were nothing extraordinary.

Rodrian's eyes flicked over her. "Yes, Dahlia. Our thanks."

Dahlia blushed a deep rose and lowered her eyes, seeming both embarrassed by the praise and flattered by the notice.

"Okay, everyone. Let's just have a good time tonight. Right?" Rodrian dispersed the small crowd. On cue, they turned and drifted away.

As they scattered, I caught a glimpse of the rogue who started it all. His hands were shoved into the front pockets of his jeans, his shoulders hunched. He looked at me with troubled eyes, worry drawing creases in his brow.

Our eyes connected. *You and me both, kid.*

He melted into the crowd as Marek steered me away. I suppose I just added Number Four to the list of why I hated clubs. Frigging werewolves.

29

The calm evaporated once the door clicked shut. Everyone clamored to be heard.

Teeth firmly set into my lower lip, I huddled in the corner of the big leather couch. It wasn't as comfortable as the one in his office at Tenth Street. This one was old, the leather hard and unyielding, slippery and crunchy at the same time. And it was cold. It felt like sitting on a frozen cow.

Marek stood in front of me like a monolith, almost daring anyone to come closer. Rodrian paced behind his desk, speaking on his cell phone, while the guards argued amongst themselves. Caen sat next to the desk, his eyes making a circuit around the room, watching everyone. His gaze slid over me as if I wasn't even here. What a charmer.

Eventually, Rodrian lowered his phone and raised a hand. Everyone grew quiet, voices ceasing mid-sentence. The silence was brittle.

"The bottom line is: he shouldn't have been admitted. The 'No Were' policy is well known and should have been enforced. I want to know where he got in and why it never reached my attention. Greco, take two men and question every door guard. Report back to Caen."

The men left without a word as Rodrian addressed those who remained. "Where is he?"

A voice spoke from the back of the room. "Wine vault, sir."

"Good." A smile, hollow and mean, ghosted across Rodrian's visage and a pulse of vengeance colored his power. Younger brother but not lesser. "I want answers. Keep a dozen on him at all times. Use whatever means necessary to keep him alive."

"What will happen to him?" Startled heads swiveled in my direction. They'd apparently forgotten I'd been involved.

"Does it matter?" Marek didn't turn around. His anger had settled around him as if he wore a thundercloud. "He assaulted you. He earned his death."

"You can't kill a guy because he tried to..." Only two words would have fit the end of that sentence and I didn't want to say either one.

Rodrian strode over and knelt next to the couch, reaching over the arm to touch my shoulder. "He wanted to rape you, Sophie. No, look at me. He also said he'd bite you. That would have been so much worse."

He glanced up at Marek who, at this point, could have thrown off lightning. "What do you know about the Were?"

When I shook my head, Rodrian spat an impatient curse. Marek whirled around. "There is still much for her to learn, brother, and I haven't taken the time to teach her about dogs and their filthy tricks. Certainly I did not think a lesson in Were was prerequisite for a visit here."

"This is our world, Marek," Rodrian countered. "The Were are as much a part of it as we are, as are vampire or human. We are all part of the Balance. You may not like them, Marek, but you can't live in a world separate from them."

Marek didn't like being lectured and his power grew bruised and swollen with anger. Rodrian was on his feet, squaring off to face him. He was just as angry about what happened and his anger sought a target. Between them I caught a glimpse of Caen.

He smiled and laced his fingers over his stomach.

It really pissed me off to see Caen enjoying the brothers facing off, so I decided to put an end to his fun. Spoil-Sport Sophie, that's me.

I stood and wedged myself between them. Facing Rodrian, I reached backwards to find one of Marek's hands, entwining our fingers. His other arm draped across my collarbone as he relaxed behind me. I shifted my concentration to his brother.

"Rode, it's okay. Marek's right. There hasn't been time to tell me everything." I kept my voice gentle, trying to talk him down. "Tell me why biting me would be worse."

"Because, Sophie." Rodrian glanced from me to Marek and back again. "When you're bitten, you become immediate possession of the Den. You go to a safe house until the next full moon. If you turn, you become part of their Den. If you don't, you get an amnesia treatment and you go home. They claim that at the safe house, you're surrounded by people who can prepare you for what would happen if you'd been infected."

"You keep saying 'if.' There's a chance even if he bit me I might not have turned, right?"

"In theory," Marek said. "In reality, safe houses are anything but. You would be kept captive and repeatedly bitten to ensure your turning." His voice dropped and he spoke through gritted teeth. "You'd be brutalized and treated like an animal so you would be Pack-broken by the time the moon grew."

His hand squeezed mine tightly. "They are animals. They behave like animals."

Fear turned my knees to water and I wobbled. Rodrian blanketed my free hand in his. I felt the last of his tension drain away; mine, however, was an altogether different story.

"But you're safe, Sophie. Whoever this guy is, he won't get another chance to hurt anyone." He raised my hand to his mouth, his kiss a tender oath.

"Tanner," I mumbled. "His name is Tanner."

"He told you his name?" Caen rose and stepped closer, a different kind of interest filling his face. Caen's dark eyes and penetrating stare made me uneasy. I didn't like being under his scrutiny. He made me feel as if he could take something away from me if he stared hard enough.

"No." I avoided eye contact. "Someone else called him Tanner. Some kid who danced funny." I couldn't think straight. Too much bad stuff all at once. Again.

"We must find him." Caen motioned with his fingers to draw two more men forward out of the group. "Describe him. *Funny* isn't helpful enough." He pushed his power at me, demanding I relinquish the information. I shrank, leaning into Marek's embrace.

Marek released me and drew me behind him. He batted away Caen's intrusion with a push of his own, causing Caen to reel.

Undisguised hatred flared in the smaller man's eyes. "Don't push me, Thurzo."

"So you do remember my name." Marek stared him down until Caen backed away. He stood near the rest of Rodrian's force, who watched with neutral expressions.

Regular people didn't do things like this. Regular people didn't fit themselves into places on a food chain. I knew nothing of this world. I was helpless.

"Talk to me, Sophie, and tell me what you know. Every detail." Rodrian stroked my cheek and gazed into my eyes. His patience and desire to help me felt like a liquid warmth behind my eyes, soothing and relaxing.

Without hesitation, I poured out everything: the descriptions of the girls, the kid who angered Tanner, the chesty chick who went after him when he took off. I told him details I didn't realize I remembered until they spilled out. I remembered details I didn't realize I had blocked, including the way everyone screamed back, ignoring my cry for help.

"He said he loved vamp security." Still not understanding the remark, I glanced from Rodrian to Marek and back again.

Both men appeared unconcerned and Marek only offered the briefest of explanations. "It is camouflage. Sometimes a feeder loses their nerve. Sometimes a guest sees something that shouldn't be seen. If someone screams, humans become alarmed. If a group of girls scream together playfully, it diffuses the fear, the danger."

Rodrian shrugged in agreement, as if saying *it is our way.*

"Yeah, well." I couldn't hide the pinch in my voice. "I almost became someone's lunch."

"And that's the problem we need to investigate." Rodrian left me to Marek, and faced the group again. "Go, you all have work to do. Caen..."

His mild tone halted the man at the door. "Please remain. We need to speak."

Rodrian smiled, a gesture for my benefit alone. He wore his mature businessman facade but darkness slid beneath the smile. Things would turn ugly when the door closed between us.

"G'night, Rode." I tugged Marek toward the door. "Thanks for the swell evening." I gave him a wry smile to let him know I was okay, that his phony smile had worked; I would survive this, too. Marek hugged my shoulders to lead me out.

I hoped the room was soundproof.

We didn't talk much in his car. I slumped in the Lincoln's heated seat, leaning my forehead against the window, watching the cars and people and buildings streak by in a blur of light and color.

Marek didn't waste time comforting me with words; he knew I'd be okay, eventually. I needed time to sulk. He draped his arm across the back of the seat and from time to time he'd touch my hair. His power, protective and subdued, hovered around me. It was all I needed, so much more than empty words.

Eventually, I had to say something. "Tonight pretty much sucked."

"Yeah. But it will be worse for someone else." Marek's tone was dark, even for him.

Marek tapped the horn at a taxi that had cut in front of us. Just once, I'd like to see him act a little human. I'd have thrown a flock of finger birds at the driver and yelled out the window. Marek's reserved composure made me feel like I had zero self-control by comparison.

"Why is there a nowhere rule? At Folletti's, I mean." Now was as good a time as any to learn about yet another species.

Marek cleared his throat. "No-Were," he emphasized. "Certain places are off limits to other species. Folletti's is a restaurant for humans and feeding ground for DV. The No-Were policy maintains the Werekind cannot show up unannounced. They have to be checked in and approved before they are admitted, and even then only under certain conditions."

"Are you at war or something?" I thought of the movies I'd seen, since I didn't have a tremendous experience pool when it came to werewolves. The analogy might have merit, since people of the same species went to war, often over trivial differences.

"Nothing so dramatic, no, but we generally don't mingle. For one thing, Weres are only slightly better than curs. They act like animals. They're content to waste their gifts and run about on all fours whenever the moon swells. It's pathetic."

"Is this what Rode meant when he said *anti-Were*?"

"Point taken." His voice lost the contemptuous tone as he continued. "There is a more practical reason why the Were are unwelcome in DV feeding grounds. Granted, it's a reason based on legend rather than fact but no one is willing to test the theory."

"Which is?"

"I'm getting to it." He took a deep breath, a sure sign of a long and detailed lecture. "I've told you a great deal of our Genesis lies in Egyptian mythology. We are descendants of Horus."

"Yes."

"Legends say Horus had several children. Burial practices describe the 'Four Sons of Horus' as gods who protected canopic jars. Not all of Horus' children were benevolent, however.

"Our legends focus on the eldest two, born as twins yet as different as night and day. One son was vampire. The other, you can now guess, was Were. Horus' line combined the humanity he obtained from his mother, Isis, with the supernatural gifts of being god-begotten and magically conceived from the dead."

Marek's voice took on the cadence of chanted prayer. "Horus, our falcon-headed forefather, is a pillar of strength, a storm of revenge. His eyes are the sun and the moon, and his eyes follow his children everywhere.

"Horus bequest great gifts to his children but never intended for them to become stronger than he. The sun controls the vampire, driving him into unconsciousness, destroying him should he grow defiant and challenge its power. The moon controls the Were, giving him power only at her command and whim. The gods may be forgotten in these times but Horus lives on. His eyes are watching and controlling his children's children. Although legend may have spawned it, for us it is no myth."

"So. The Werekind are your cousins?"

Marek's upper lip curled, as if he was repulsed by the suggestion. "Maybe centuries ago, when our lines were young. Certainly not now."

I leaned over and poked him. "You can't pick your family."

"No, but I can pick my next meal." His threat was disarmed as the corners of his mouth tugged upward in a grin. I laughed and looked out the window.

See how much my world had changed? Crap like that wasn't usually funny.

A sharp ring cut short our respite. Pulling his arm away, he flipped open his cell phone.

"Yeah. News?" He listened, then lowered the phone momentarily, as if he'd throw it. A long pause as he listened and his face grew dead calm once more. "Yeah. Fine. We'll talk then."

He flipped shut the phone with an angry snap and dropped it onto the seat. Gripping the wheel, his hands tense, his knuckles white. The air grew heavy with tension. I held my breath.

A long moment passed. Eventually, he stretched his fingers, consciously relaxing them. With one hand, he touched his hair, raking it back from his temples. "The mutt is dead. We got nothing."

"Dead? What happened?"

"He pulled a suicide. Apparently he smuggled a silver bullet."

I had to be missing something. "Don't you need a gun

in order to use a bullet?"

Marek slowed with traffic as we approached a red light. "It's not a real bullet. A silver bullet is a glass capsule filled with silver nitrate. If a Were eats one, it's fatal. They chew the glass and swallow it. The shards cut their mouth and throat, which allows the silver to come into direct contact with their bloodstream. The anaphylaxis is nearly instantaneous."

"What kind of animal eats glass?" This was the guy who'd rubbed up against me? God, I couldn't imagine it.

"Now you see one of my many points." The light turned green and he hit the gas. I sank back into the leather seat as we shot forward.

Wanting to change the subject, I remembered what we'd been talking about when the phone rang. "So, apart from all that, why are there No-Were rules?"

"Ah. I never finished. See, because of our origins, it is forbidden our bloods should be combined. If one fed upon the other, legend says it would manifest a phenomenon known as Horus United—both of his bloods co-mingled in a single vessel. The person would shape-shift, irreversibly but not into wolf. There's only one animal that person could become. Falcon."

"Like Horus."

Marek nodded, keeping his eyes on the road. "No one wants to volunteer for testing. Can you blame them? Who'd want to live as a bird? Tiny brain, weak, helpless..."

"Able to fly, living simply as nature intended, free from humanity and the pettiness and the ugliness."

He shrugged. "Still. No volunteers. Accidental transformation has never been formally documented. The rules are as old as tradition, and tradition is as old as our existence. Weres and DV do not share blood. Period."

"So that's it?"

"Pretty much. We cooperate but, for all intents and

purposes, our societies don't mix. No-Were zones aren't hallowed grounds so Weres may enter, but they are searched and monitored and expected to be on good behavior. They have enough good people that we can't ban them." He added the last part grudgingly.

Too bad. Folletti's did a hell of a job making sure Tanner behaved himself. "I think it's weird the DV haven't pursued it. You guys are the smartest of the smart, aren't you? No one's ever looked into it? No research?"

"On the contrary. We have people doing *in vitro* research, but it's not showing any conclusive results. Millions are spent each year in joint ventures. Were relations are getting strained because of it but that's another story. Still, fact remains. When the bloods are combined, nothing happens. Something is missing."

Grateful for something else to think about, something clinical and impersonal and easier to deal with, I turned back to the window. As light streamed past, it colored my memories from my countless hours in the museums. I pondered the first time I met Marek, wondering if he had given me any clues that day about these truths of his.

He'd gazed at Isis' image with such tenderness. It really was love, I supposed now, if she was, after all, his mythological grandmother. Isis, with her wings, her disk and horns, her empty throne. Isis, with the *ankh* in her hands. The *ankh*...

"Life." I spoke out loud as my gut-instinct tugged at me to follow the thought.

"What was that?" He, too, had been deep in thought.

"Life." I repeated. "Life is missing. That's the difference between *in vitro* and *in vivo*, isn't it?" Scooting to a more comfortable position, I rested my head against the seat. "Horus is a God of the living, not of the dead. Horus's existence reaffirms life beyond the point of hope. Osiris was already dead when Horus was conceived."

The thought fed itself and gut-sense nudged it along. Maybe I'd hate myself in the morning for ruining perfectly good mythology but tonight I needed to sort this puzzle out, to be distracted by something that wasn't an immediate and personal threat.

"Instead of studying blood samples combined after they are taken from people, why not study blood samples of falcons? You might come across one of your, I don't know, hybrids. You can work backwards from what you find."

I glanced down at the pendant I wore. Marek had given it to me only hours before, and yet it seemed so long ago. Time flies when you're having "fun." I separated a lock of hair and twisted it around my fingers. "The merging must happen in a living vessel. Horus's miracle can't be worked in a test tube."

Marek pulled the car over to the curb and shifted it into park, and we rocked to a stop. He stared at me with a penetrating glint in his eyes. "How do you do that?"

Startled, I ceased playing with my hair and dropped my hands. "Do what?"

"That thing you do. You take a foreign idea and open it up. Unfold it. Clarify it, as if you'd been thinking about it all your life."

"Oh. I thought you were going to say something about tying knots in my hair."

Leaning over, he wrapped a hand around the back of my head, pulling me onto his mouth with a kiss that made me see stars. I obliged by kissing back. It was either that or suffocate.

Releasing me the smallest bit so he could speak, he whispered in a husky voice. "I am going to find out who you are, Sophia Galen. I swear to it." He inhaled my breath from my lips, and it seemed he drew me in, ever so slightly. Marek redefined the word *intimate*.

Marek tasted my lips, teasing me into kissing back.

Eventually we were interrupted by a group of laughing kids who tapped on the window as they passed, braying with laughter and cat-calls. Marek pulled from me with a tiny smirk and swung the car back onto the road.

Out of the corner of my eye, I watched him adjust himself covertly. I pretended not to notice but, pleased with my own ability to tease, I chuckled all the way home.

30

As I'd suspected, sleep didn't want to be in the same room as me.

Marek wanted to spend the night, insisting I shouldn't be alone. I had to practically shove him out the door with two hands and a cattle prod. He made no effort to conceal his disapproval. On and off until dawn I caught touches of his power, as if he lurked close by, keeping a watchful "eye" on me through the night.

I'd jumped in the shower as soon as he left, desperate to wash away the oily stain that still seemed to cling to me. I knew it was all in my head. It was the memory of the Were's hands on me and not real dirt. Nonetheless, I applied the bath poof with such force my skin tingled.

I didn't fall asleep as much as eventually lost consciousness. Even unconsciousness didn't linger once the sun came up, despite the exhausting emotional ride I'd been on. Euphrates, who curled up along the other pillow, woke when I finally gave up pretending to sleep. He leveled a disgusted glare at me as I rolled out of bed.

Stroking away the disapproval in his yellow eyes, I scratched behind his ears. "Relax, Fraidy," I told him. "I ruined your sleep for one morning. I think someone ruined my sleep for a good while to come."

He seemed to accept that I'd be sufficiently punished and graced me with his presence while I went out to the kitchen to get coffee started. What a sport.

After the first cup had time to sink in, giving me that false yet lovely sense of being awake, I lamented over the terrible waste of a Saturday morning for sleeping late. Accepting the cruel fact my Saturday would be several hours longer than usual, I wondered what to do with the extra time.

Picking a yoga outfit to match my blue trainers, I went for a walk to clear my head. My feet picked out their own path, my brain still preoccupied with the events from the night before.

That little bit of restless almost-sleep had mercifully put some distance between my interlude with Tanner. At least I could evaluate the existence of shape-shifters without only reliving the part when one almost chewed on me.

I stopped at a donut shop for a bagel and a brew, chewing automatically as I walked. Too many brain cells were consumed with churning thoughts.

Why was it when something bad happened, I later found out about a whole new species pretending to be people? What was next? If I tripped on this sidewalk and fell flat on my face into the bushes, would I discover a race of tiny beings, ready with ropes, *a la Gulliver's Travels*?

More disconcertingly, why was I taking all this in stride? I must be some kind of freak if I could walk around town at an ungodly hour sorting out what I learned the night before when I had been accosted by a werewolf.

As I tossed the empty bagel wrapper into a trash bin, I realized I hadn't tasted a single bite. Thinking too much again. Brushing my hands together, I saw St. Joseph's down the block. I guessed when I put my feet on auto-pilot, they picked the destination that would bring me the most peace. Huh. Good to know my subconscious mind looked out for my best interests.

Rounding the corner and crossing the street, I peered through the fence to see my madrigal hard at work once more in the church gardens. As I steered myself up the main walk, he spotted me. "Hope you brought your work gloves today."

I glanced behind me at no one before giving him a *who, me?* kind of look.

Brushing his hands together, he laughed and shook his head. "Come on and sit a while with me, Sophie. Sister Johanna is working me to an early grave with these seed-lings. You must be exhausted yourself, keeping your eyes open at this hour on a Saturday."

I smirked. "Isn't sarcasm a sin, Father?"

"Not if it's not sarcasm."

The sun was already warm, though it was well before ten in the morning, and the weather promised another bright June day. He indicated a shady spot, away from the sister who planted petunias around a statue of St. Joseph and the Infant.

St. Joseph, foster father of the child Jesus, held the boy carefully, protectively, yet each face wore a serene expression that implied the child somehow took care of the parent. The statue represented an invitation to have faith, to believe we are cared for in a way our modern mentality found difficult to accept. After all, wasn't that what faith was about?

"Oh..." I reached down to brush my fingers against a shrub gracing the corner of the path. "A bleeding heart . Think Mother Nature Superior over there will yell if I pick some?"

"No," Jared said. "I'm sure she won't." He reached

down and carefully snapped off a strand of flowers for me.

We sat down on a wide stone bench under one of the red maple trees, and I pulled off one of the blossoms. "I haven't seen these in years," I said. "Let's see if I still remember how to do this."

I peeled the delicate pink petals apart and began to separate the pieces of the flower. I'd learned the game as a child and had taught it to Jared the summer I'd met him. If disassembled carefully, the flower could be reduced to a bunch of parts that resembled miniature toys. Jared watched with a bemused expression.

Rabbits, slippers, baseball bat... drat. What's that last pair called?

I grinned as I lined up the pieces on my pant leg. These tiny visits to more innocent times delighted me. "Remember when we used to do this? There was a bush in the old cemetery we hung out in. We'd set up little bunny armies on the blanket..."

Whoops. Probably not the best memory to relive now that half the memory was a priest. My face burned, probably as pink as the blossoms in my lap. "Sorry."

"Sophie, it's okay." He glanced over his shoulder at the nun who was hopefully out of earshot. "Memories aren't sins."

"Even if what you're remembering was a sin?"

"Sophie, we were just teens. What we shared were important moments, because they made me who I am today. It couldn't have been evil."

I fidgeted with the tiny baseball bat and clucked my tongue as I swung it. "Even the home base part?"

"The whole game," he said firmly. His eyes crinkled with a suppressed grin. "Don't worry. When I do my youth ministries, I only preach against about a third of what we did together that summer."

I applied myself vigorously to the rest of the blossoms.

"Only a third, huh? So odds are my bleeding hearts and I won't go to Hell?"

He laughed, eyes twinkling. Sister looked up from her flowerbed with a shrewd expression. She'd soil herself if she knew her pastor was discussing his past sex life with an ex-girlfriend.

"I should hardly think so. I mean, that's what confession is for, right?" He picked up the filament whose name I'd forgotten. "Ice skates," he said. "I can never get these things out without ripping them. They're too delicate."

Jared turned it over in his palm to admire its slender curve. "You know, I never cease to be amazed by this little blossom. Such a tiny heart, yet when you open it and examine its contents, you finally see how much that heart can hold. Never underestimate the depths of a heart, Sophie. It's a miracle in and of itself."

"That's eloquent."

"It was part of my first sermon when I was ordained," he added shyly.

"Oh. I wish I'd been there."

"I'm rather glad you weren't," he admitted. "Seeing you would have been too much a test of my faith."

"Why? Would you have changed your mind?"

"I didn't join the Church because you or someone else wasn't there. I was meant for this. Father Mac let me help with his Youth Group back home and I felt like I'd found my place. He directed me, gave me focus, a goal. One person, if he's very special, has the power to reshape the person you become. One relationship can affect how you approach every relationship thereafter. I wish you could have met him."

I remembered him at age seventeen. I remembered how lost he'd been, like a dry leaf in an autumn wind. The kid had been shipped back and forth between his parents and each time it ended up worse than the last. He liked cutting school and ditching the cops and I'd caught him with dope more than once.

Anyone Jared admired deserved my respect, because I knew the list of people who could claim that honor was short.

"So, no," he said. "I don't think I would have ripped off my vestments and raced out the back door with you. I accomplished something on my own, you know? If you'd have walked in, I might've turned to you for help the way I always did, instead of standing on the Altar and letting people look to me for help instead."

My affection for him was a warm glow, a swell of nameless emotion, a pulse of soft comfort that came from being with someone who meant the world to me. Once, there'd been no barriers between us; we needed few words.

Now, I wasn't sure if we had the same connection. My relationship with Marek seemed so much more intimate, so effortless. The contrast made me feel as if I'd suddenly become a stranger to my best friend. "I'm proud of you."

"Well..." He stood, reminding me he'd grown up after all. "That was long ago. That kid is just a memory. Who we are now and what we've become is what's important today."

My smile wavered. It wasn't that I didn't agree with him but... I wasn't sure what I'd become since I'd met Marek. I'd discovered things about myself I never knew were there or at least significant enough to notice. The previous night just made it even more obvious.

"What's wrong?" Jared used his pastor's voice, the one that coaxed out the most resistant of confidences. I'd always caved when he invoked the voice of God's mediator.

"Eh," I said. "Nothing that wouldn't sound like a confession. God knows you hear enough of those."

"Yeah, but if you ever want to talk about something..."

I chewed my lip. This was my chance to be honest. Once upon a time I told Jared everything. I wasn't sure I ought to be sharing those secrets, even with someone who could never and would never tell. Even with someone who knew me better than anybody. I had to keep the demivamps a secret.

Giving him a false smile to encourage the belief I had nothing to share, I blew off my chance to confide in him. "I know. Thanks. And anyways, Sister Johanna looks like she's getting a hernia. You better help her with that wheelbarrow."

I scooped up the flower petals and stood, tossing them into the bushes. With a small wave good-bye, I started down the path. "See you later, Farmer Jared."

"Don't be so hard on yourself." Jared called after me. "You're only human."

"Yeah," I scoffed. "At least I have that much going for me."

At least until the next bad guy came along and tried to bite me, anyways.

The sun fell, the moon rose, and when the night unfolded, it found us in the lower levels of Folletti's. To be exact, we were in one of the basement storage rooms, standing between long rows of wooden shelves bearing industrial-size cans of tomato paste and stacks of pressed table linens. The far wall was lined with a series of metal doors; the heavy latches and lit control panels next to each one implied they were freezer units.

We were centered around one freezer in particular. Although the door remained shut the entire time, I knew what they had on ice in there. Or, more specifically, who.

Gross. I mean, I ate at this joint. How sanitary was it to have a dead werewolf hanging up next to the steaks and the chops? I considered asking Marek if they kept a special meat locker just for bodies, but I didn't. I was reluctant to find out how often they had dead assassins in storage.

It was chilly down there, so I lingered at the back of

the assembly, closer to the doorway leading back upstairs. Even though I wore Marek's jacket, I longed for the heat of the main floors. Plus, I didn't need a front row seat to tonight's show.

Caen was going to punish one of his guys for the Were's suicide.

This little soiree was a DV-style apology for my nearly getting raped-Wered-killed-whatever the night before. Rodrian didn't want me to lose faith in him or his security. Tonight they'd excise the weak link and he wanted me to witness it.

It all sounded ominous. It felt even worse when I'd skimmed Rodrian's power and realized how deep and dangerous he anticipated things would go. I tried to beg out of it but Marek insisted. This was an apology that the DV needed to provide.

I did the only thing I could. I wore Marek's jacket, wrapped myself in his scent, and all but hid behind him.

Caen's inner beast, usually kept in check around his employer, had been unleashed. He wasn't over-acting for my benefit. He'd been given free rein tonight, and Caen never missed an opportunity to display his power. He furiously paced a tight circle around another DV in front of the freezer door.

Chal stood his ground, looking worried but not scared. Maybe Caen was a better boss to Chal than underling to anyone else. Could be. I didn't care. I didn't like Chal from the start. If he ended up in the meat locker next to Tanner, I wouldn't send flowers.

First off, he mistakenly thought he was hot shit. I'd become accustomed to seeing plenty of wolf whistle-worthy male specimens since becoming a charter member of DV Land. But Chal didn't fit the bill. I guessed he was the token loser.

He stood maybe an inch taller than me and was out of

shape. I mean, total beer gut, flat butt, and man-boobs. Short brown hair in a fifteen dollar buzz-cut. Muddy brown eyes and a near-sighted ass-kissing lapdog look.

And the name. *Chal.* Like he thought he was champagne when he was barely Mad Dog minus the paper bag.

When Caen wasn't around to keep him in line, he acted like everyone else's boss. He'd swagger around Folletti's with his arms folded, bullshitting with guests and watching everyone else when he should have been working the door.

I'd first met him on my way up to Rode's office one afternoon, outside the private elevator. "You can't use that one, sweetheart," he called out. "Try the common lift in the lobby."

"Oh, hi," I said in my nice-little-Sophie voice. "Actually, Rodrian is expecting me in his office. You could call upstairs if you need to clear it."

He sauntered over, arms crossed and chin up so he could look down at me. No easy feat, since I wore my tallest pair of *Sex and the City* heels, which put me two inches taller. He accomplished it by not making eye contact. I had to put my hand over the opening of my blouse so he couldn't look into it.

"You are...?" My patience thinned. He repulsed me, both visually and, as he edged into my personal space, aromatically. Was it Miller Time already?

"Chal. Unlike you, I belong here." He tossed an authoritative compulsion at me.

I ignored the flimsy mental push and laughed in his face.

"Chal? Is that short for something?" I added an insult by pointedly looking him up and down and emphasizing the word *short*.

"No," he sneered. "It's just Chal."

"Oh. Well, then, just Chal, if you have a problem with me, take it up with Rodrian. Better yet, go right over his head to Marek. He's expecting me, too."

The door dinged open and I stepped in, paying him no further notice. The little coward made no move to stop me, but stood with arms crossed, staring me down. Turning to push the button, I noticed he was staring at my ass. At least I hadn't given him the finger until the doors closed between us.

So, yeah. I'd say Chal had made quite an impression.

It was sort of nice watching him get dressed down now. Sorry, but even a Pollyanna like me felt petty and vindictive once in a while.

Chal had been in charge of the Were's custody. As Caen's toady, he commanded the dozen who took Tanner to the wine cellar. Just one job to do—and he'd botched it.

Now Caen's rep was on the line and he didn't like being made to look bad. Chal would suffer for Caen's injured pride as well as his mistake. Everyone here knew it, and from the scant tastes I took of the guards' power, they anticipated what would come next.

However, Chal didn't look scared. Truthfully, I'd have been petrified. No one could ever accuse Chal of being too smart.

"A silver bullet," Caen said. "What was your first clue this wolf wasn't here to dance?"

"He concealed it," Chal insisted. "The door crew said they searched him. They never found it. Neither did we when we brought him down He was stripped, searched, and scanned."

"Then where was it? In his ass? Because, if necessary, you'll start looking there, too."

"No." Chal wrinkled his nose as if repulsed by the idea. Personally, I was surprised he'd take offense to the suggestion, ass-kisser that he was. "It was under a bandage."

Caen ceased pacing and cocked his head as if he hadn't heard him clearly. "A bandage? Is that what you said?"

"Yeah, boss. A Band-Aid or something."

"A Band-Aid. Hmm." Caen seemed to think that over. "Of course, you wouldn't look under a Band-Aid."

"No, of course not. I mean, who would, right?" Chal gave a shaky laugh.

"No," said Caen. "You wouldn't. Because why would a shapeshifter be wearing a fucking Band-Aid in the first place!" Caen roared and splintered the air with a ferocious crack of angry power. He went from *Zero* to *You're Dead!* in three seconds flat. "You never detain a Were for questioning without stripping it down completely. Completely!"

Caen lunged, stopping nose to nose with Chal, who appeared to have forgotten how to breathe. The sudden movement, too quick for a human, disoriented me and I sidled up to Marek, craving the security of his touch. Not human, I reminded myself. Caen's not human.

"You told me you could handle this, Chal." Caen's lips were thinned and stretched back, baring his teeth and slicing his words. "You are the most incompetent DV I have ever met."

Chal's jaw dropped. "Wait a minute, Caen, you—"

His voice was cut off by a sharp gasp. Chal doubled over, holding his stomach and keening. The air thickened with tension, crackled with apprehension.

Caen's right hand was fisted at his side and he wore a smile. A happy, contented smile. One that spoke volumes about his character, how deep and ragged his bloodlust ran. "I what?"

Chal sucked in a breath and raised his face, straightening a bit. "You said—"

Caen twisted his wrist as if he wrung out a dishrag.

Chal's distress pressed down on me and I buried my face in Marek's arm, silently begging escape. Marek's power washed over me as he tried to shield me from the rush of painful emotion.

The power made Chal recede but it couldn't block his voice. Protests bled into wails that raised the hairs on my neck. I heard a thud and knew he was on the floor. I didn't watch.

Those few short moments stretched to impossible lengths. Eventually the pain-filled sounds reduced themselves to ragged breaths and I dared to look. Chal was once again on his feet, his posture now far from cocky. Shoulders drooped with submission, he pressed both hands to his belly.

"Get out." Caen's voice rolled out in a growl. "Get out, before I paint the walls with you."

Sweat soaked dark spots on Chal's shirt and his breath was choppy. "But you said. . ."

"I said, now." Caen's rage was unmistakable, his eyes gleaming sallow gold. His power felt more beast than man and I cringed. His eyes reminded me I was still just food. I didn't want to be here any longer.

Apparently neither did Chal, who decided to leave while he could still walk. Without a glance at anyone else, he ducked his head and slunk to the door.

Upon seeing me, though, he regained a healthy portion of his chump's constitution and wrinkled his nose like he smelled something rotten.

"Geez, who let the human in here?" His voice was a mumble but he made sure I'd heard. "Aren't you supposed to be on a leash?"

If he could forget he'd been writhing on the floor in agony only a moment ago, so could I. I stepped away from Marek and squared off to face the pig. Caen blamed him for the Were attack. I should, too.

"Hey, Chal," I used my Shirley Temple voice and fluttered my lashes. "Was Tanner wearing a Snoopy Band-Aid?"

He narrowed his eyes, as if he could possibly even consider retaliating with Marek right behind me. "Drop dead, bitch."

"Go to hell, Count Chuckula."

"Sophie, darling?" Marek sounded somewhat amused as he interrupted our pleasantries and I couldn't resist a smirk. Chal shot me one last deadly look before hurrying upstairs and I wiggled my fingers goodbye. "Do you have to do that?"

"Do what?" I turned to him, hoping my face was resplendent with wide-eyed innocence.

"Bait him."

"Eh, he's a dope. Is he fired?"

"Worse," said Caen, his voice portentous. He stomped out of the room.

We waited on the side until everyone else filed out before heading upstairs to the staff elevator. The ride up to Rodrian's office was a silent one. Rodrian's power felt hesitant and unsure and I knew whatever weighed on his mind, it wouldn't make Marek happy.

31

"No."

Marek's voice held no room for argument. It was the sound of a massive unmovable weight slamming into place. Absolute and final.

Rodrian apparently heard otherwise. "You are being unreasonable, brother. It's completely legitimate and absolutely guaranteed."

Marek turned and stared at him in disbelief. "Why not lay out the welcome mat for more problems? We've enough trouble dealing with the Underground the way it is. Do we need to ease the way for more vampire? More Masters? Another territorial battle?"

"We've kept vamps under control since the Civil War, Marek. Hells, even the seventies couldn't give them the advantage they needed to overrun us. They can't do it now."

"No, Rodrian."

Rodrian didn't seem to hear him. "Worries about a Master conflict are baseless. I don't like him any more than you but don't you say 'keep your enemies closer?' Better to keep a familiar Master in control than a new undiscovered danger."

"I do not even want to know what you're hinting at."

"It's obvious, Marek. We help to keep the Master in place. We hammer out an agreement. We lend to his security for the ultimate augmentation of our own."

"Are you blind?" Marek whirled on him in sudden fury, eyes blazing and teeth bared. "Are you stupid? Or have you absolutely no regard for what I've done, or what we have gone through, to keep the vampire as far as possible from our families? What have we lost to them, Rodrian? Whom have we lost to them?"

Marek's ferocity lashed out like a hurricane as he paced around the office. He'd never attack Rodrian but he made no effort to conceal his anger. "You don't see any of this, do you? You can't see past the business, the cash, the power. It makes you an aggressive businessman but it keeps you from seeing the spider web of effects your actions will have. The ramifications will spread out in every direction and I will have to rectify each and every one."

Rodrian boldly met him eye for eye. At length, his defiance deflated. Shaking his head, he sank down into the couch, elbows on his knees and head in his hands. Seeing this, Marek assumed a much less aggressive stance near the windows, his power drifting back down to its usual feel. I knew better than to think he would be any less immovable.

"You are right, Marek." Rodrian pushed his bangs back from his forehead but they only stayed a moment before slipping back down. With his hair loose, he appeared younger, less arrogant. "I don't see the things of which you constantly warn. I see profit. I see the increase in blood traffic from human business. Gods, the blood alone. Humans out to drink and seek pleasure—ideal prey..."

I suspected he hadn't fed yet, wanting to remain lean and hungry and dangerous for Chal's chastising. Now the thoughts of preying distracted him. He drew his brows as if trying to concentrate on his argument. "A casino would solve all of our problems. If it attracts undesirable behavior, those who seek such activity are prey as well. We augment the local police with our own forces, we give the Master a tribute to keep himself busy, and we all benefit."

"See past it," Marek said. "This is our city. Our home. Think about the residents and the effects casino trade will have on them. Look at what happened in New Jersey. Who lives there anymore?"

Actually, I knew plenty of people living in New Jersey but I had a feeling they weren't talking about average Joe Human. I crossed out a line I'd written and started over, keeping silent and busy.

Marek crouched before Rodrian, putting one hand to his brother's shoulder and urging him to meet his eyes. "I do hear what you say in terms of the Master and a possible guarantee against a play for power. If he were human, I might consider it. If he were DV, it would be a sound plan because he'd hold up his end of the bargain with honor.

"But he's not, Rodrian. He's vampire." Marek gritted his teeth and he emphasized each word with a slight shake of his hand. "I spent your entire lifetime fighting to keep you and our family and our race and our humans and our world safe from him and his kind."

"So, what do we do, Marek? Just watch while dirty politics wreck our home? Humans will leave Balaton. The city isn't big enough to support a new tribute. We'd lose control of the financial sector."

"No, we won't," said Marek, as he pushed back to his feet. "We'll fight. We will use our power to divert the legislation and redirect it toward another of our goals."

Rodrian leaned forward as if to protest but Marek didn't give him the chance to get a word in. Crossing his arms, Marek stood once more at the window. "Concentrate on your businesses. Don't get involved with Underground politics. That's my problem."

"I wish you'd keep an open mind about this, brother." Rodrian's voice was plaintive, the child trying to wear down the parent's resolve. "An opportunity like this is unprecedented. We can't afford to be obstinate."

Marek pressed his lips together, making an exasperated sound, his frustration leaking through his control. "Rodrian, can't you see? I cannot afford not to be obstinate. It is the reason we have survived."

"You have old-fashioned ideals. We have to keep current if we want to survive. You can't fight all the time, Marek. Sometimes you've got to bend. We don't rule the world; humanity does. If they want change, they'll get it."

"You are right, Rodrian, we do not rule the world. Gods willing, we never will. But as long as I have my ideals, no matter how 'old-fashioned,' I will use them and live by them, so I can continue protecting us and improving what I am."

"I do not possess your strength, Marek."

"You don't need to. Go. See to your hunger."

Rodrian stayed only a moment longer before getting up and walking out.

As the door closed behind him, I cleared my throat. "Do you... ah... need to go with him?"

Marek shook his head. "No. I took care of things earlier."

I swallowed and didn't push it. Don't ask questions you don't want answered, right? Trouble was, sometimes I wanted to know who spent those intimate moments with him. I knew I'd be jealous. I knew I'd probably get pissy. But the whole blood thing—as much as I feared pain I wanted to know just a tiny bit more about who gave him what he needed. I stole a glance at him, wondering if now would be a good time to finally put those questions to rest.

Maybe... not.

Marek abandoned his authoritative stance and flopped into the desk chair, leaning back and staring at the ceiling. He didn't so much resemble a breathing stone of power now as he did my mom after she'd gotten the twins off to bed when they were toddlers.

"You'd think he'd get the general idea by now." He sounded a trifle irritated. "He's what, one ten? One twenty?"

"One twenty what?"

Marek waved a hand. "Years old."

I gulped, at a complete loss for a reply. Here all I was worried about was a probably heated discussion about his blood dates. But no.

I had never directly asked Marek his age, let alone his brother's. He'd made enough leading comments to convince me he was older than anyone had a right to be and I religiously avoided the topic.

Rodrian was a hundred years old? And still looked that tight? Oh, good Lord. What can a man learn in that time?

Marek swung the chair back and forth, rocking. "I know he is the younger. I know my duty is to provide for him. I raised him when our father. . . died." He clasped his hands over his forehead, clearly vexed. "You'd think he'd be ready to assume more responsibility by now."

"Well, you said you raised him, that all his life you've fought to protect him. Was the fighting obvious? I mean, did you let him tag along to your bloody conflicts?"

Marek stopped rocking. "Of course not. I wanted him to grow up in a better world. I wanted to keep the ugliness away. Banish it if I could."

"Then see, you've done your job too well. Your family prospered in a garden of tranquility, one you fought to give them. You're the stone wall surrounding that garden. They never see what the wall keeps out, or how battered the outside of the wall is, or how thick and strong it is. How can Rode be ready to fight something he doesn't know exists?"

He sat up, crossing his arms and staring at the door, contemplative.

I pushed myself out of the shallow dent I'd formed on the hard cushion, and leaned forward on the edge of the couch. Reaching behind me, I collected my notebook and pens and stowed them in my tote bag. "I guess it's like the way my dad lectured me when I was in high school. He didn't want me to find things out the hard way. If I'd been smarter, I'd have listened to him."

I got off the couch and perched on the desk near him. "Don't be mad at him, Marek. You gave him a better world than you yourself knew. Rode sees nothing but possibility and security. He's brilliant and enthusiastic. He's more than ready to go out and seize every opportunity he can find because he's confident. Those are blessings, love, and you made them possible. Isn't that what you wanted?"

He slid his chair toward me and with one arm tugged me off the desk and onto his lap. I settled against him as he accommodated my body. Burying his face in my hair, he lipped my neck, making me shiver with pleasant goose bumps.

"Of course it is," he said. "You are right. What would I do without you, Sophie? You keep me sane." He exhaled deeply, and his breath stirred the tiny hairs on the back of my neck, tickling. "And how did you ever get to be so wise?"

Pulling back to look at me, Marek seemed to expect a response.

I shrugged and took the facetious way out. "It's a God-given talent. How else do you think I got my name?"

His expression changed, as if he remembered something that should have been apparent all along. "Sophia," he whispered. "That's right. Greek for *wisdom*." He made an appraising sound deep in his throat. "Funny, too. Humor, beauty, compassion, wisdom... I guess opposites attract, don't they?"

"I wouldn't say complete opposites. You're pretty, too."

"Like I said, funny." He leaned his head back over the top of the chair. "You should spend time lecturing my brother. He would benefit from your wisdom as well. Although..." His voice held warning. "Do not sit on his lap to do it. You are already far too fond of him."

"Relax." I laughed at his flash of jealousy. "I've told you before, I think of him as a brother. A one-hundred-and-twenty year old brother."

Okay, that didn't even sound convincing. Brothers didn't take your breath away when they smiled. Rodrian was harmlessly flirtatious and I knew he'd never make a move on me, but he was beautiful and we all knew it. Especially him.

Marek growled, oblivious to my internal dialog. "That better be all. If he ever meant to take you from me..."

"Relax," I repeated. "No one will ever take what I don't want to give, not ever again. And speaking of giving..."

I ran my hands across his chest once, enjoying the feel of muscle and bone beneath his shirt, before pushing myself off his lap. I stood before him and innocently wiggled my dress down into place.

His eyes ran down me hungrily, and light glinted off his sharper teeth as his mouth opened slightly. God help me, I loved baiting this predator. What kind of person had I become?

I silenced the thought and walked to the door. "I have something to give you."

"Do you, now." He stood and leveled a heated glance at me. "What is it?"

"I can't tell you. I can only show you."

"Show me, then."

"I can't."

"Why not?"

"I don't have it here."

He looked puzzled, as if he had misinterpreted me after all. "Where is it?"

I smiled and opened the door, leaning against the jamb a moment before turning to saunter out. Over my shoulder, I flashed a wicked smile at him. "At home. On the couch."

Out in the hall, I heard him trip over the chair in his rush to follow me and I hid a grin.

The next day I hummed my way through a longer-than-usual workday. Earlier in the morning I'd gotten a call from Marek, saying he'd meet me at *The Mag* at four. It was easier to enjoy work knowing something nice waited for me afterward.

He asked how my day went as I smoothed the seat belt and suggested dinner at some quiet corner of a bistro. Before I had a chance to respond he casually dropped a large leather-bound book onto my lap.

"What's this?" I joked. "My homework?"

"No," he answered. "Your destiny."

I rolled my eyes even as I tugged on the bookmark. I turned to a page he had marked with a thin velvet ribbon and pulled the book open to reveal ancient-looking text and woodcut prints. The word leapt from the page, drawing my gaze.

Sophia.

"Sophia," he said. "The one hope any DV has for salvation."

I searched his face, hoping for an explanation or at least a punch line. He gazed back at me so serenely I could have wept.

"I spent my life looking for this salvation, Sophie. I think it's you."

I looked down at the page without comprehension

and felt a wave of dizziness.

The Sophia Oracle. Me?

"I don't understand, Marek." My voice trembled. "What is this? This book has to be about a billion years old."

"Sophie, where did we meet? In a museum. I told you it was personal research. This is the research. The origin of the DV. Who I am. And now, I realize who you are, too."

"You're wrong," I said. "This is bizarre. I'm not special."

"It's you." He touched my arm, and the sense of his power became clearer with the physical contact. He believed what he said. Every ounce of his power pulsed with insistence. "The Sophia's qualities are your qualities. Don't you recognize a part of yourself in those words?"

I scanned the text, feeling carsick despite the fact we were still parked. Compassion, wisdom, emotional vessel, blah blah blah. "Okay," I said. "Some of it. But this says the Sophia has bright blue eyes. Mine are dark brown."

"Please," Marek said. "Please, keep an open mind. I spent a good part of my life researching this Oracle, looking for her. I need to know. Be patient? For me?"

His plea tugged at my heartstrings, making me answer with complete sincerity. "Marek, don't you see?" I reached for his hand. "Everything I do is for you."

"I love you," he whispered.

He'd never said those words before. I mentally framed the moment. Blinking back sweet tears, I gave him a reassuring squeeze. "I know."

"You do?"

"Sure. Wisdom here, hello."

Marek seemed relieved. "You'll go along with me on this?"

"Sure, if it doesn't hurt."

"I'd never hurt you."

"Okay, then." I looked down at the book again,

thinking it might not be so bad, especially if I got a Sophia outfit. I liked the Grecian robes. And the shoes were so cute.

We didn't say more about it as we drove to the restaurant. I'd be anything he wanted me to be because he was everything I'd ever needed. It only seemed fair.

32

"I don't know if I can do this." I bit my lip. Maybe one more deep breath would help.

Marek chortled, a deep muted sound. "Yes, you can."

We stood in front of the main doors of the Federal Archives building downtown. Its outside was sheeted in bluish mirrored glass that reflected back traffic and building and sky. Inside was a courtroom full of DV councilors who waited to evaluate me and my Sophia-ness. Streams of busy people flowed past, paying no mind to the two of us standing in the middle of the sidewalk and talking to each other's reflections in the glass.

Earlier Marek had announced that he'd met with members of the DV council. They were enthusiastic and wanted to meet me immediately. It didn't leave me much time to prepare.

Prepare for what, anyway? It wasn't like I could've bought a Sophia SAT prep book and crammed. I had no idea what they expected from me.

On the car ride over, Marek had shared information. For once. "We haven't had a Sophia here in over three centuries. There are rumors of one in Eastern Asia somewhere, and at least two in Europe. DV tend to guard them jealously."

He glanced over at me, a grin almost tugging the corners of his mouth. Marek tended to guard me jealously so at least he acknowledged the coincidence.

"The trouble is that Sophias manifest where they are most needed. They can travel but they seem reluctant to do so."

I could relate. I've lived in maybe three zip-codes my whole life. "So the only way the DV here in the States can get a Sophia is if they find a homegrown one?"

"Yes."

"So, today's pretty important?"

"Pretty much," he admitted.

Gah. More pressure please, I wasn't quite totally shattered by my nerves yet.

Now we stood in front of the blue-mirrored building and I wished I could just stay out here on the sidewalk with my reflection. We were happy out here. "Okay, then." I straightened my shoulders and tried to look confident. "We have to do this right now before I lose my nerve."

"You have nothing to worry about. They're just people. Why are you nervous?"

Truth? I didn't want to let him down. Something had come over him since he got this big Sophia thing idea in his head. His power had changed in the slightest of ways. It had lost some of its desperation, its doomed oppressiveness.

In short, Marek had lightened up, just a bit. I loved him either way but, I have to admit, this way was easier. I didn't want to burst his happy bubble.

"What if they're scary? What if they call me a fake and flatten me with mean blasts of *you suck*? I'm not sure I can do this."

He reached for my hand and squeezed, sending a

sweet throb of encouragement. I loved the way he reached into my brain and tapped the endorphins. "We are going to talk. That's all. They'll see what makes you special. Just be yourself. Act naturally."

"No way. If I'm going to do this, I need to act like a Sophia."

"You already do." He gave my hand another squeeze before letting go to open the door.

I wished the walls were mirrored so I could appraise my appearance one last time on the way down the hall. I rubbed a finger across my front teeth and Marek laughed. "Relax. You look fine."

"I need to look wise." We took a rear staircase up a floor to a mezzanine where he card-swiped the lock. The door opened into a short hallway that led to a large set of double doors. "So, how long has it been since the last American Sophia?"

"Seventeenth century. New England." He hesitated. "She was a midwife from Massachusetts."

Maybe he was nervous, too. "Babies are nice. And she was technically a medical professional. So, this Sophia was loved and respected and, after living happily ever after, she passed on without a successor and you've all been alone ever since?"

Marek squirmed. Okay, he flicked his eyes away. For him, that was squirming. "We can talk about this later."

"No, we can talk about it now," I said almost sweetly. My Sophia-senses, or whatever he'd call them, were tingling. "You're hiding something, I can feel it. Spill."

"Fine. Her abilities made some humans suspicious, even though she was an exemplary citizen who was greatly loved and respected by all who knew her. Humans don't remember such things when hysteria strikes. She was persecuted during the Salem witch trials and executed in 1692. Oh, look, we're here."

At the word *executed*, my legs locked and I froze. He dragged me the last few steps to the massive doors and pushed me through the same way I often shoved my cat into the bedroom.

A moment later I forgot all about it because when the door closed behind us, I experienced what it must have been like for an early Christian to find herself in a Roman coliseum. The doors *boomed* shut with a sound not unlike the crack of doom.

If this was a courtroom, then I'm friggin' Judge Judy.

This was an amphitheater.

When we entered the room everyone inside dropped their conversations and turned to face us, breaking off from their little groups and standing separately like statues. One man, an older gentleman with short hair the color of sunset on silver, greeted Marek, his voice carrying across the room. I guessed this was Epidauros, after all.

A second later his power reached me. I gulped. Not acoustics, then. Acoustics didn't make every hair on your body stand up. Marek's power usually felt like threat and danger and impending storm; this man was different. Powerful, yes. But this was authority, not force.

One touch convinced me that whatever he said, I'd trust it, I'd believe it, and I'd do it. Not because he compelled me but because he felt like one hundred percent boss of everything and it would never occur to me to do anything else. He didn't inspire fear—just obedience.

The feeling subsided when he saw me, as if he remembered his manners and pulled himself back. Maybe he pitied the human trying to hide behind Marek's arm. He smiled at me, benevolence warming his eyes, and strode to meet us in the orchestra of the room.

When he drew closer Marek greeted him. "Dunkan, it's good to see you again."

"And you, Marek."

"Your brother, is he well?"

"Pontian is as well as he ever is. Then again, healers don't have excuses to be anything but. Well." Dunkan glanced at me but did not address me directly. "This is hopeful news you've brought me."

His smile seemed genuine and his power felt honest so I relaxed a notch. Marek and Dunkan exchanged a few more personal words before Dunkan stepped back, adopting formal manners and resuming his authoritarian stance.

Several others filed closer to extend greetings. The rest of the assembly drifted up the aisles to sit in the semi-circles of benches rising up and around the room. No one else's power announced itself to me and it started to feel more like a job interview.

Okay. This isn't so bad. Smile and wave, girl. Pretend you're in charge.

As I shook the last proffered hand and returned the last polite hello, I turned back to Marek to show him my can-do smile. However, Marek was no longer at my side.

No one was. I stood alone on the tiled circle. The room fell silent and it all happened so quickly I didn't even have time to react. By the time my brain told my adrenal glands to sound the Oh Shit! Alarm, Dunkan commenced the proceedings. Faces fell to impassiveness. Even Marek wore his neutral game face.

Dunkan stood at the center of the half-circle, his back to me as he addressed the council. "By the gods, our witnesses: we, the One Hundred and Fifty-First Conclave, do convene on this date for the purpose of hearing the petition of one citizen, by right and true Name of Marek Thurzo. Rise, Citizen Thurzo. Do you wish to address the Conclave?"

Marek stood, hands folded in front like a pall bearer, and answered in baritone. "I do."

I succeeded in wrestling my eyebrows down to their usual place on my forehead. Citizen Thurzo would get an earful from me later when I petitioned his ass six ways to next Sunday. *We're going to talk is all...* yeah, right.

"Members of Conclave, my thanks for your time and attention." Several heads tipped in his direction. I did my best to keep from frowning at him. "The American demivampire have been without the guidance of the Sophia Oracle for several hundred years. Few possess substantial information regarding the nature of this elusive muse. Several Conclave members may remember my role in previous examinations of Sophia candidates, none of whom have been deemed true Oracles."

He paused, making eye contact with one or two people. "For the first time I bring forth a candidate of my own. To the Conclave I present Ms. Sophia Galen, her right and true Name."

Every pair of eyes found me, some flashing a brief light, others scrutinizing me intently. Dunkan gestured, indicating I should step forward, and addressed me. "Ms. Sophia Galen..."

"Sophie." I interrupted without thinking. "Just Sophie."

"Ms. Galen." The amendment was accompanied by an expression that implied he'd prefer not to be interrupted again. "What do you know of the Sophia Oracle?"

"Only what Marek has told me," I admitted. "The DV are subject to the process of evolution, which marks both physical and spiritual changes. I have to say, I still don't understand it well but the gist of it seems pretty simple."

I took a deep breath and held my composure. Public speaking sucks at best, but this was infinitely worse. This crowd might eat me if they didn't like what I said.

"Evolution is like every little sin brings you one step closer to being damned. Thing is, even if you're sorry, you can never be forgiven. No absolution. No starting over. No second chances. God must have realized how terrible a fate it was, so He created the Sophia to compensate. You might not get a second chance but, with a Sophia's help, you might not ever need one."

I clasped my hands and rocked back on my heels, more confident now. My gut told me I was spot on and, when I peeked at Marek, he didn't have his head buried in his hands. Good sign, right there.

Dunkan, however, didn't hand me a gold star. "A passable, if rudimentary, definition. Your choice of words likens it to a children's story rather than the sacred ideology of our people. However, you speak honestly and with sensitivity and we detect no malice in your intent."

I didn't think he wanted a response, which was good because I wasn't sure I had a polite one. Silence seemed the prudent way to go at the moment.

"Based, therefore, on your interpretation of the Sophia, tell us why you have come forth as a candidate."

Technically, I didn't come forth—Marek dragged me in here—but I had a funny feeling it was probably an unacceptable response. "Marek thought some my qualities are Sophia-like in nature. He trusts the combined experience and knowledge of the Conclave will be able to make a determination."

A woman spoke from her seat in the rings of benches. "What do you seek to gain?"

"Me? I don't seek to gain anything."

"Ms. Galen, everybody wants something. Are we to believe you are simply being generous in seeking the title of Sophia?"

I surveyed the strange faces, at a complete loss for a response. Something in Marek's eyes encouraged me to continue. He purposefully refrained from reaching out to me with his power so it wouldn't look like he was coercing me.

I knew holding back was a strain on him. I wore his essence the way I wore his jacket. His presence was always there, keeping us in constant contact, reassuring and comforting. His willingness to endure this separation was a big indication of how important this was.

"I understand your reservations. Marek said it's been lifetimes since the last Sophia. I understand why it's important, even if I don't yet understand the details. I don't seek a title, or honor, or..." I faltered, unsure of the right words. "Please. I'm just Sophie. I care for people. I try to better this world the only way I know how: one person at a time. Marek knows this and believes this is what the Sophia must be. I want him to know for sure, to follow this to the end, so he doesn't spend the rest of his life wondering."

Marek watched me, unmoving, eyes gleaming. No one had ever held me in their gaze with such love, such acceptance. My heart swelled, almost too big for me to stand without running to him.

"I'm not here for me. I'm here for him. If I am what he thinks, fine. I'll do whatever it is I'm meant to do. If I'm not..." I shrugged. "Who cares? I'll still do what I've always done. I can't change. If I can help, all you need to do is ask. It's what everyone else does."

Their eyes weighed me, silent and cold, and I lost some of my resolve. Rather than look at the emotionless statues, I studied my feet, waiting.

Look at me.

Someone's power called to me. It wasn't Marek. Someone in the Conclave.

My head snapped up and I scanned row after row of blank faces. No one spoke or moved or gave any indication they knew someone had used their power to touch me.

Look at me, girl. Seek me out.

I took a step, then two, closer to the rows of benches.

The words carried on a ribbon-thin hum of power, one I could track back to its source. I paced along the edge of the orchestra as I played a game of hot and cold.

When I followed the touch up one of the aisles, halfway up it snapped off. I bit my lip, stretching my awareness out, reaching around for it like I searched for something in a darkened room. When I detected it again, I seized it, tracing it to an iron-haired woman. She didn't acknowledge me but I knew the power was hers. Everyone in the room sat motionless, staring at the circle as if I remained below.

Placing my hand on her shoulder, I whispered. "You?"

She turned her lined face to me, the creases between her pale blue eyes deepening. For a moment I doubted myself. I hastily looked toward Marek, who hid his mouth behind his hand.

When she spoke, her voice shocked me and I almost left the ground. "She has the gift of empathy, as proven by this trial."

What? A frigging test? Son of a... Wait. I passed. Woo-hoo me!

Dunkan stood. "Ms. Galen, please resume your place."

"What happens now?" I could have skipped down the steps.

"Why, my dear." The older woman smiled thinly. "It's the inquisition."

The next half-hour passed in a blur. It was like SINCERELY SOPHIE: LIVE! except I'd have included a house band and some great audience giveaways. I supposed this was the talking Marek had said we'd do.

Dunkan briefly spoke about the traditional role of Sophia as oracle, and the next thing I knew they subjected me to the most grueling session of Q and A as ever I had the misfortune to endure. Person after person asked question after question on every conceivable (and more than one inconceivable) topic.

It was worse than work, Donna included. At work, I had the luxury of time, consideration, and coffee. Here, the questions flew, *bam-bam-bam*, one after another. As soon as one person would sit, another would stand up and throw a complete spin on the previous topic.

All in all, I held up my end, even under the circumstances. I gave awesome advice, and in fact more than one time I hoped a stenographer took notes because I was on fire. Even when they pummeled me with the more bizarre DV questions, I found something to which I could relate, something I could be helpful about.

When at last they finished grilling me, I wanted to sag with relief.

I hoped there would be some sort of adjournment because now would be a good time for a potty break and a cup of coffee. I was tired of talking, tired of standing, tired of looking at the impassive faces. Still, I was proud of myself, which gave me the buoyancy I needed to maintain my composure.

"Ms. Galen." Dunkan called out my name, startling me. "You have demonstrated a strong gift of empathy. You have satisfactorily endured the inquisition. Citizen Thurzo, we have given your petition full and measured consideration."

"So," I said. "Was Marek right? Am I what he thinks I am?"

"My dear..." The old woman stood and folded her hands gracefully before her. "You are wise, you are practical, and you desire to help those in need. However admirable these qualities may be, they are not enough to make a Sophia. I am sorry."

The verdict came as a shock. It took a few heartbeats for it to sink in. Halfway through this I had started to believe that Marek was right. Something cold and hard hit the floor of my stomach. I think it was my pride.

The faces lost some of their impassivity. Pulses of regret and disappointment seeped down toward me. Pity crept toward me and I did my best to push back that ugliest of emotions before it made me break down in front of everyone.

Disdain glowered, pointing out the irritation of a man near the top of the benches. *This?* I felt his power clearly. *This is the best humanity has to offer?* Angry tears stung my eyes and I stubbornly held them back. Lifting my chin, I boldly met his glare. He didn't even blink. Maybe he was a million years old and could knot the hairs on my arms from where he sat but I wouldn't let him cow me down, not after all this.

I am still me. I am still Sophie. I didn't do any of this for you. I did it for him.

Before I could look at Marek and see the awful disappointment I knew he must have felt, I thanked the Conclave with terse words, spun on my heel, and walked out.

33

"What was I thinking when I let you talk me into this?" I kicked the door when it didn't open fast enough. Embarrassment burned my face, stung my eyes, tightened my jaw like a cramp.

The looks they'd given me—the pity, the contempt. What had made me agree to this? It had been like taking an oral exam I never studied for. How was I supposed to prove to them I could do whatever it was Marek was convinced I could?

I was an advice columnist. So what. That made me a Messiah? The embodiment of wisdom? What kind of idiot was I? If I was so goddamned wise, why didn't I foresee the disasters life dropped on me at fairly regular intervals? Why didn't I know what a dope I'd look like before Marek's great big important council? Why couldn't I figure out how to deal with that bitch at work?

"Sophie, relax. Relax!" Marek had caught up to me on the stairwell, and I tried my best to outrun him. He grabbed my arm and interrupted me in mid-mental-rant. "You're overreacting. It didn't go the way I thought it would. That's okay. It doesn't change what you are."

"Great, that's great. Because I am nothing but a total asshole to have thought for one second I was your Sophia." I wrenched my arm free and glared up at him. "I give good advice because it's my job, not because some god made me special."

"You have that job because of the gift you already had," he countered firmly. "Wasn't your previous practice was successful because of your advice? What about your thing with the priest?"

Something about the way he said *thing with the priest* set my teeth on edge again. I doubled back on him, catching him off guard. He pulled up to avoid steam-rolling me.

"Don't even." I pointed a finger and poked it into his chest. "You don't know anything about it. Don't cut it down. Don't bring it up at all."

"I'm not cutting it down, I am just reminding you. Your heart changed the boy's life, as it has changed many others." He turned away but not before I saw his dour expression. "I cannot stop being unhappy knowing about your past together. I believe you and he will not carry on the way you once did but I will not pretend to like knowing you're still close. It's not right."

"Marek. He. Is. A. Priest." I bit off each word and spit it out. "And he is my best friend. And, he is a priest!" Several heads turned in our direction. "Men don't come any safer."

"My brother is your friend. I trust him above any other man alive. He well knows what would belie him should he ever overstep his bounds. Still, I would not like you to be alone with him, either."

"Way to show how much you trust me. Some Sophia I must be. I'm the one you say will guide your race but you can't trust me alone with any one of them. Is that it?"

"It's not you I do not trust. It's them."

"Same thing."

"No, it's not." He raked his hair in frustration. "Look. You have a special quality, Sophie. It drew me to you. It made me follow you until I could devise a way to meet you. One hint of your scent and I could think of nothing else. I didn't know I'd be the one consumed, Sophie. You conquered me. You do that to everyone who gets close to you. My kind would love a chance to taste you. It makes me insane on countless levels of countless issues."

I was dumbfounded. "What are you saying? I'm—I'm vamp bait, is that it? That DV will sniff me out and chase me down? That's horrifying."

"No, that's not it." Marek broke off with an aggravated noise. "I'm not saying it right. It's not a pheromone; it's a quality. It shines through your actions. Your words. Your determination to set everything right. I saw it one day, before we officially met. You gave money to a man on the street for food. I told you it was futile but you refused to see anything but possibility. You couldn't change a damned thing for him but you were still determined to try."

"Wait, wait." I glared up at him. "You told me so?"

My mind raced back to before I met him, trying to remember. Trouble was I gave money to a lot of people on the street. But when did someone ever say something?

Then it hit me. The pizza shop. The guy on the corner. I'd ranted to Barbara about it. She'd told me to blow it off and I did. Did try, I mean.

"That... was you?" I knew I hadn't looked too hard at the guy. I had been too flustered to see, too embarrassed to look him in the eyes. That's why we met?

He nodded, following my thoughts in his uncanny way.

Uncanny, shit. He's demivampire. It wasn't uncanny, it was predatory. He'd stalked me. I frowned in accusation.

"No!" Anguish flooded his face. "Never prey, I swear. If

it were that, I would have compelled you to forget anything and everything about me. Prey would have been blood and nothing more. It was never like that."

He shoved his hands in his pockets and hung his head. "I saw what you did. I saw an eminence in you as I have seen in no other before. You try to save the world in your own way. I thought maybe you would save me."

When he at last turned so slowly to face me, he reluctantly met my eyes. "I should have been damned long ago. My soul hangs by a thread. I have done so much to hate myself and I don't want to end up like the Fallen. Your spark convinced me you'd fight a ferocious battle to save someone, even if it was a losing one. What am I, if not that?"

Marek spread his arms. "Sophie, I'm not wrong about you. I've lived in isolation—desolation—for so long. You changed me. You brought me back from a terrible edge."

He reached for my hand with both of his, pressing it first to his mouth then to his chest. I could feel his heart beat under my fingertips, a steady, patient rhythm. "I know who you are, Sophie. Believe me, even if you won't believe in yourself."

"Believe in myself?" I whispered. Blinking hard to quell the tears, I shook my head. "I let myself down more than anyone else does."

Protest crowded his face, furrowing his brow and pursing his lips. In a swift movement he sprang to his feet again, attempting to pull me toward him but I backed away.

"And now, back there, I just let you down, too. My God, I love you so much, Marek, and I want so badly to be what you want me to be. But I'm not. I'm just plain old Sophie, and I am so sorry I disappointed you."

The last words were strangled by a sob that refused to remain inside any longer and I succumbed to tears. Turning away before he could see me break, I blindly twisted away from him and stumbled into the stream of people.

Even while I tried to lose myself in the crowd, he sent out his power to me—a touch of sympathy and love, a silent request to return. Truthfully, part of me wanted to. Part of me wanted to run and cling to him and let him wrap himself around me and hide me until I felt better.

But I didn't. I wasn't strong enough to do the right thing. The rest of me needed time alone to hate myself for a while. I kept walking.

Funny. It'd been so long since I'd given myself a good self-berating. I hadn't done this since... well, since I met Marek. Ever notice how we had to relearn good habits but the bad ones always came right back to us? Shaking my head, I pushed aside the touch of his unseen gesture and tried to put the city between us.

Rounding a corner, I cut through a narrow service street I knew would lead to one of the bus routes. Apparently, the city had been busy redecorating, though, because one of the buildings that had bordered the street was gone, replaced by a courtyard park.

Paved paths streamed from several directions to meet at a circular court, a tiny haven of benches and dwarf trees. I headed through, too blinded by my thoughts to appreciate the new scenery. These little corners of my city never failed to surprise me. Every now and then I turned a corner and bumped into something new and unexpected. A new skyscraper, a new parking lot, a new something that hadn't been there when I walked by six months earlier.

The city never ceased changing. A living thing, it grew and died and constantly redefined itself. It was a phoenix that rose from its own ashes. It was a girl who couldn't decide what to wear. It was fickle.

My mood soured. People were fickle, too. You woke up thinking you had something figured out and *wham!* Your life wasn't anything like you'd thought. All the tiny unnoticeable changes you'd gone through have somehow added up and the person in the mirror didn't even remotely resemble the person you saw in there the last time you'd looked.

The world kept changing, too. Not too long ago I'd looked out my window and thought, yep, that's my city, this is my life, here it all is, just like always. Then a guy walked into my life and turned everything on its ear. "Hi there," he said. "Did you know? Vampires and Werewolves are real, my family and I drink blood and have magical powers, and if that's not enough to make your eyes pop, I'm in love with you. Oh, and by the by, you're a god-gifted oracle destined to save my entire race from eternal damnation."

People weren't meant to constantly redefine themselves. They found something that fit and they stuck with it. I haven't changed in fifteen frigging years. Why did I have to do it now? I wasn't that fickle. I wasn't that resilient. I wasn't that strong.

You are, came the whisper of Marek's power, dimmer for the distance between us.

"No, I'm not," I said out loud.

I could live a fairy tale life with Marek because I loved him, every grimly beautiful and deadly and perfect inch of him. I could deal with the whole DV thing, no sweat. Any culture outside of middle-class Irish-American was pretty much foreign to me, so DV was just another ethnic group. My talent for giving good advice was a simple combination of common sense and imagination but if he wanted to call me a goddess when we were alone together, fine with me. I loved pillow talk. I did, however, have a huge problem with having to prove something like that to a bunch of strangers.

"You shouldn't have to prove anything to him. Not if he loved you."

A nearby voice startled me so much I jumped. I'd been emoting so intently I forgot I was still out in public. I detected a DV vibe at once and glanced around to see who'd picked up my bad mood.

A group of teen-aged girls was hovering near a bench up the path from me. No one seemed to be looking in my direction, so I guessed they weren't actually speaking to me.

What a relief. I'd always been a mental screamer, although lately I'd learned to tone it down, what with DV power and the ability to scent out what I felt. Marek had once said my empathic nature went both ways when I thought hard enough.

As I approached the girls, I recognized several of the faces as Shiloh's friends, and, of course, wherever her friends were, so was she. She looked up and waved when she saw me, breaking away from the little group to bounce over.

"You okay?" She peered into my face, and I hastily smoothed the telltale crease from between my eyebrows.

"Yeah, Shy, I'm fine," I lied, then nodded to one of the girls who huddled on the bench, crying. "What's up? She okay?"

Shiloh shrugged. "Boy problems. Problem number one being the boy."

"Shiloh..." A tear-soaked whine issued from the miserable girl on the bench.

"Please." Shiloh rolled her eyes and held up her palm. "Don't even. I told you, Tess, he's a bum. I don't know why you don't listen to me. You know I'm right."

I forgot all about my pissy mood and almost laughed. She sounded like she'd been taking classes at Marek's School for Bossy Maniacs.

"You don't understand," said Tess. "You can't help who you fall in love with."

Her voice sounded mournful and her faint power swirled with confusion and sorrow. Her pain radiated so distinctly it brought back memories of my own misery fests when I'd been her age. It was all too easy to sympathize with her.

"In love with a bum, huh," I said. "Sucks, don't it?"

Sighing, I sank down onto the bench across the path from the small crowd. Eh, I had nothing else to do, really. Maybe if I talked with Shiloh's bunch I'd forget some of my own angst. Nothing like someone else's problems to help me ignore my own.

Tess right away put on her smug teenager face. "Hardly."

When she met my eyes, though, she broke down and smiled weakly. "Okay, bummy, but not a total bum. He's a nice guy. He's just got... problems."

"Ha! What an understatement." The brunette standing closest to her barked a short laugh. Swinging her head in my direction, she put her hands on her hips. "He's a junkie."

"Ugh," I said. "A junkie?"

"He's not a junkie." The tone of Jess's voice told me she was accustomed to arguing this point. "He just uses with his friends. He never does blood rush when I'm around."

"Ahh." I nodded my head like an old wise woman. Well, I was twice their age. "Classic case of bad influence."

She shrugged admission. "When he's with me, he's so good. My parents adore him."

"Your parents don't know about him." The interjection sounded from somewhere in the mass of girls.

"My parents see his goodness. It's not fake," Tess shot back. "He's cute. He's smart. He's so sweet. You should read his emails. He texts me poetry during class. He even has my picture on his Facebook page and says he's 'in a relationship.'"

"But?" I prompted.

"But... he's hooked. I know it." Her voice fell quiet and fat tears slid down her cheeks. "I know he won't stop, even though he says he loves me. I come second."

How sad was that? Tess was just a kid but she knew how the world worked. When I had been growing up, sure, kids had problems, and there had been lots of "bad" guys around. But today the problems were so much bigger, so much deadlier. Kids had to grow up too fast. My problems hadn't been as bad by half but I also didn't see the world so clearly when I was her age.

If I had, would I have given up on people? If I didn't have my rose-colored glasses, my naïveté, would I have admitted defeat and given up, walked away from battles I couldn't win? Looking at the girls, thinking about why I sat here listening to their problems, I knew the answer. I wouldn't have given up. It was the way I'd been wired.

"So, what will you do now?" I leaned forward and rested my elbows on my knees. The sun had fallen behind one of the buildings, tilting shadows across the small park. I had a sudden yearning for Marek's jacket and rubbed my arms.

"How do I know? I love him and I know all he'll ever do is hurt me."

"Yeah," said the brunette. "Like when he evolves. He'll hurt all of us, then."

Tess hung her head, covered her face in her hands, and wept her broken heart out. Bad enough to betray your own heart, but when you betrayed your best friends along with it...

"You have to let him go," I said. "If your heart and your head are telling you two different things, you'll never have peace. I understand you don't always get to choose the person you fall in love with. But trust me on this one. Your heart isn't a good judge of character. It's too full of wishes and good intentions and second chances."

Rising from my seat on the bench, I crossed to her side of the path and squatted next to her. I peered up into her face as she knuckled her eyes. A sudden rush of dizziness hit me and I had to reach out a hand to steady myself. The girl felt so confused and upset she unintentionally leaked compulsion. Teens weren't as fine-tuned in their control as fully-cusped adults.

Considering I'd been too nervous to eat all day, I wasn't ready to handle the mental touch. Her angst made my blood run cold. Or was it the lateness of the afternoon? I felt crowded. I've picked up emotions from Marek and Rodrian before but hers had a feeling of density, as if she pushed her power into me somehow.

Tess gave me an odd look. I guessed if some nosy broad started giving me a lesson about life and love in the middle of a park, I'd look at her strangely, too. Especially if she knelt by me and wobbled like a drunk.

A touch on my shoulder made me look up to see Shiloh.

"Sophie, are you..." Her voice trailed off, eyes wide.

"I'm okay, Shy. I just need to sit. I've been through the wringer today." The girl sitting next to Tess scooted over, making room for me, and I smiled appreciatively.

"So..." Tess took a hitching breath as I unlocked my knees, stretching a moment before sitting. "Am I stupid for wasting love on someone like him?"

"It's not stupid. Love is never wasted."

"But... what if I don't find someone else? What if no one else ever likes me? What if I don't find someone who will love me without hurting me?"

"Tess..." I laughed gently. "There are plenty of soul-mates in the sea. There will be another. And if he doesn't work out, there will be yet another. You've a lifetime to find them all."

I looked around for Shiloh but she wasn't in sight. No doubt she went off in search of a food truck. The other girls had fallen quiet, listening, and Tess seemed to have calmed down, even though she had yet to rein in her accidental compulsion. I still felt crowded and cold.

Crap. Growing up was so hard. Bad enough to be

caught between youth and maturity. When your heart got tangled up in the conflict, the bad just got worse.

"Your mind, the voice of reason, is the counter-balance. When you find a good match, both your heart and mind will approve, because you'll have found the one who fits both. Don't despair. Love is confusing but it will make sense once you find the mate to your body and soul. Your heart and mind will be in accord. That's why true love gives you such a sense of wholeness, of being complete. It's because you can honestly say, with every ounce of your being, *yes*."

"Wow." One of the girls whispered as she peered into my eyes. "That's amazing."

"Thank you, Sophie." Tess squeezed my hand. "I know you're right. I know what I have to do. It's just... so hard."

"I know," I replied. "It's love that makes it so hard. If it wasn't love, it wouldn't hurt when you got it wrong. Then again, it wouldn't feel so good when you get it right."

She smiled, and when I looked in her eyes, I saw a shimmer of light within the DV glow. It was hope.

Something across the park caught her attention and I turned to look. Shiloh had returned with Marek and Rodrian and some of the people from the courtroom. They seemed to be marching over in a hurry.

"Her eyes. They're blue." I heard the murmur from one of the Conclave members. Did they see the hope reflected in Tess's eyes? Could they see it the way I did, feel it on the flow of her undeveloped power like I could? Did they recognize it for what it is?

But... they didn't look at Tess. One of the ladies covered her mouth and pointed. At me.

Desperately, I sought out a familiar face. Shiloh appeared frightened as she tugged on Rodrian's arm. Rodrian's mouth worked like a fish for a moment or two, before breaking out into his boyish bigger-than-face grin.

And when I looked at Marek...

Well, Marek absolutely shone. His power felt like the sun breaking over the edge of a storm front. I'd never seen him this way.

He crossed the grass and approached our bench as the others fanned out behind him. Shiloh's friends flanked me like a crowd of ladies-in-waiting, facing the adults. Only a single moment of silence passed before the line of council men broke and the old woman from the Conclave pushed through.

"Ah," she said. "There you are, Sophia."

"I told you." I tightened my lips to keep from frowning and dug deep for a patient tone. "It's just Sophie."

"Oh no, it's not." Her voice wavered. A brightness bloomed in her eyes too, the kind that had been in Tess's. "It's definitely Sophia. And we..."

She covered her heart with a weathered hand and dipped her head in reverence. "We are truly honored by your presence."

On some unseen cue, they all bowed.

All except for Marek, who gazed at me with unsurpassed love and utter faith. Marek gazed at me and smiled.

34

They paraded me back to the courtroom but this time things went much differently. I wasn't surrounded by cold impassive strangers. The high and mighty Conclave had been replaced with people who seemed genuinely awed.

Even the meanie from the back who'd sent such ugly vibes at me had changed his tune. His power felt humbled. Contrite. Usually, I'd be all for giving him a stiff dose of cold shoulder, considering the crap he'd been thinking earlier. Yet, I couldn't even muster a sarcastic smirk at him. Not a single ounce of spite. I felt like they were... mine. I didn't want to get back at them for their earlier humiliation. I wanted to help them.

It wasn't only the Conclave in the rounds of benches, either. Shiloh and her friends had insisted on coming along upstairs, proclaiming they "had" me first. As Marek escorted me on his arm like a bridegroom, Shiloh marched right behind us every step of the way and jostled her father out of the way for a better seat in the courtroom.

The room was noisy, the excitement palpable, their

expressions bright and eager. I didn't need to be empathic to feel any of it.

This time, they let me have a chair. Tess filched coffee from an office down the hall. Talk about showing the love.

A kinder, gentler sort of inquisition followed, honest concerns from real people seeking guidance. When I felt the genuine hope from each one, whatever made me the Sophia sprung forth, reaching out to them, so jubilant to finally be where it belonged. I never felt so good.

My gut instinct, my inner voice—I'd lived with it my entire life. I never suspected it would amount to anything more than a helpful hunch, a compassionate personality.

This Sophia thing, it leapt with joy to be needed. It surged up and out of me in a rush of windy eagerness. Something that had been content before to merely trickle forth now flooded me with purpose. It made me laugh with wild joy. This was where I was meant to be. Something inside me clicked into place, all the right doors were finally unlocked, and I became whole. For the first time in my life, I felt complete.

I forget half of what I said. There was only this feeling that at last... at last they found me. I found me.

And I remember Marek. My grim, dark love felt so different. Over and over I replayed in my mind the sight of his smile, that true smile that made him momentarily unrecognizable. His power hummed louder than anyone else's, holding my attention no matter who spoke, and washing over me with his proud love. I caught the appreciation the Conclave felt for him, their gratitude, their confidence in him answered by this blessing.

I knew I'd never again be the person I had been. Before, I'd been a shell. Now I was filled with something I can't believe I never noticed before. They didn't put something into me or teach me how to do something new. All those DV, all their need, called forth my true self.

Eventually, though, I drooped with weariness. The earlier nerves, the coffee on an empty stomach, and my newly-freed Sophia all took their physical tolls. That strange fullness receded, pulling itself back into the depths of my mind. However, the barricade containing it had forever vanished.

Marek remained by my side, his arm around my shoulders, and nodded at Dunkan, who called the Conclave to a close. We gradually succeeded in tearing ourselves away from the gathering of DV, who were reluctant to end the evening.

His stream of affection took on a different flavor as we drove home. Though he said very little, his power teased me all the way back to his townhouse and his glances gently twisted my insides, small tugs of intent. He felt so peaceful, so content, so satisfied. And so... hungry.

I'd never been in a more accommodating mood.

We parked in the spot that was always open and waiting for him. He held the front door open for me, leaning against it as I walked inside. His eyes followed me and I could feel their nearly-physical touch. Anticipation. He'd bided his time, accepting my past hesitations with agonizing patience.

As I passed through the doorway, I brushed against him, trailing my fingers across his chest. Once inside, I dropped my purse, missing the chair and not caring. I turned into him, matching his kiss and his embrace with an eager-ness that bordered on ferocity. He laughed into my open-mouthed smile, delighted and possessive.

"Stay with me." He whispered onto my mouth and glazed me with the sheen of his longings.

Something melted inside me and I grasped his shirt collar with both hands, tugging him closer. "How long?"

"Tonight. Forever. You don't need to be alone, not ever again." He held my face in his hands, stroking my cheek, smoothing back my hair. His eyes sparkled, and I smiled at his smile. He knew how to smile. I knew it.

"Hell, I took care of everyone else's needs today. It'd be selfish not to pay a little attention to you, now."

"Sophie..." As he murmured my name, he bent and brushed his lips against my ear. "Tonight isn't about need. This is pure desire."

Marek spent the next several hours showing me exactly what he'd meant.

Not a bad way to end the strangest day of my life.

The night was glorious. I'd never felt so loved or so cherished or so desired in all my life. I'd never fallen asleep so exhausted or so satisfied, either. His attentions and, em, talents made it completely possible to forget that an actual world existed outside his bedroom door. At first, I'd been a trifle concerned with the physical mechanics of loving a man so much taller than myself but, in the end, it turned out Marek was a perfect fit, no dirty puns intended.

Okay, maybe just one dirty pun, but one that was deliciously deserved.

The days and the nights that followed were just as glorious. With much reluctance, Marek allowed me out of his bed early Monday morning so I could go to work and earn my living. Conveniently, he'd managed to let himself into my apartment as I slept, retrieving work clothes and other necessities as well as feeding Euphrates (although I'm sure he spent more time perusing my underwear drawer than making nice with the cat.)

He looked so despondent when I got out of his car. As much as he would have liked to keep me all for himself, he knew there was another reason I had to work, one that had nothing to do with paying my rent.

Barbara noticed a change right away. After making almost all the right assumptions, as well as a couple lewd comments about my having needed some action, she began scrutinizing my work with new interest.

"Sophie, tell me." She set a folder onto her desk and leaned back in her chair. "How could a little nookie make you even better at what you already did well? If anything, I'd expect you to slack off like certain others."

She jerked her head once toward Donna's lair, where the Stapler Nazi slumped at her desk. Lately she'd been looking pale and tired and spent most of her day drinking those organic-looking energy drinks. I guessed her lurid night-life had finally caught up to her. She looked like death reheated in the microwave.

Not me. I felt incredible. No matter how much sleep I missed, thanks to Marek's healthy appetite and nearly-insatiable curiosity, I felt energized. Coffee had nothing on this Sophia thing.

Thank goodness, too. The DV decided they were my new best friends, keeping me busy with phone calls and luncheons and chance meetings galore. I never would have been able to keep up with it if not for the Sophia lending me strength.

As I went back to my cube, I saw Donna. She looked like she had a migraine—eyes closed, fingers to her temples, deep creases bracketing her thin-lipped mouth. I actually pitied her. Must have been the Sophia.

She cracked her eyes as I approached. "Yes?" Her tone implied seeing me were the last thing she wanted.

"You okay, Donna?" I stretched out my empathic awareness and tried to sense her. She was human—physically, at least—so it was difficult. Humans didn't emote as clearly as the DV.

"I'm fine." She bit off each word, their bitter taste pinching her mouth.

"You look... worn out. Can I help?"

"Yes. Leave. Your need to make everyone love you is

making my headache worse."

I stared back, open-mouthed, dismayed by her rude-
ness.

"Now would be nice," she snapped.

I rolled my eyes and walked away. Sophia or no, it was
more fun hating her. Some people weren't worth the price
of redemption.

35

"Damn shame, innit." Mrs. Park clucked her tongue in disapproval as she put my take-out tray into a plastic bag. I set my purse on the deli counter, digging out change to pay for my lunch order. I could've used a change purse rather than chasing quarters around through the mess on the bottom but that would've been too easy. "World's heading straight to hell."

"What's that?" I had no idea what she was talking about, although I always got a kick when the tiny Asian lady used foul language. So demure, so delicate, yet endowed with the vocabulary of a Brooklyn longshoreman. I tried my best to encourage her.

Mrs. Park made a jutting motion with her chin toward the newspaper rack behind me. "That Levene. All over the news today. How did you miss it?"

I know how I missed it, I thought with a smile. I'd been catching up on the sleep I'd been sacrificing. It was the first night I'd stayed at my place in over a week and I bagged work to sleep in. My paycheck could wait until Monday.

Right now I was looking forward to a three-day-weekend full of...

Then it clicked. Her words registered and I raised my head, quarter forgotten. Levene? I turned toward the rack.

My mouth went cotton dry as I took in the front page. Frank's picture. Big black letters shouted the headline: BRUTAL SLAYING SHOCKS HARRISBURG

"Oh no," I whispered.

"In the Senate building, too," she continued. "So much for security. What kind of monster would do such a thing?"

Ripping the paper from the rack, I scanned the story. There had to be a mistake. There must be an explanation. This couldn't be true. Frank couldn't be dead. He couldn't be.

I paid for the paper and my lunch, took the change with trembling fingers, and sprinted upstairs. My stomach twisted into a painful knot that rode high between my ribs, making it difficult to breathe.

I called Marek.

He answered on the first ring. "You're home? I'll be there in fifteen minutes. Dress for the bike." *Click.*

I didn't get a single word in.

As I dragged the bottom of my closet, I tried unsuccessfully to swallow down the butterflies making my stomach tumble. I knew he had a motorcycle. I just hoped I'd never have to meet it, much less ride it. I didn't like motorcycles.

Twelve minutes later I waited on the stoop, fussing with Euphrates. Sweet kitty knew I was upset and tried his best to distract me by climbing up my pant leg, leaving a score of itchy puncture wounds from his hind claws. Kitty love usually equaled tough love.

I had dutifully dressed in what I hoped would be considered "for the bike." Finally, a legitimate reason to wear my heavy black leather engineer boots. I didn't own many outfits that called for them, although they looked fabulous with jeans.

I bent to admire them, rubbing at a scuff on the left toe. Well, okay, they weren't exactly engineer boots. They came from Victoria's Secret, actually. Got them on sale nearly eight years ago. But they looked like engineer boots. That counted for something.

The black leather jacket I'd bought last summer totally rocked. Tapered waist and zippered sleeves implied hotness beneath. With my hair loose and sunglasses on, I looked like a total hard-ass. Did it even make sense? I owned clothes that reflected absolutely nothing about me. I supposed I always had a thing for costumes. This was another one. Today I had to pretend to be someone who rode motorcycles.

I heard his approach from the middle of the next block, long before I saw him. Marek swooped up to the curb straddling a jet black bike, presumably the Night Train he'd warned me about. His hair fell straight back, windblown and loose. No helmet. What possessed me to think he wore one? He didn't even use a seatbelt. Or the rear view mirror, for that matter.

Euphrates, startled by the loud rumble, discontinued his assault on my jeans as the thundering bike drew near. Upon seeing Marek, he beat it around the corner and thumped up the fire escape.

Marek leaned on one leg as he swung off the bike. His black denim jeans were faded slightly, like perfect highlights. And black boots, just like mine. Well, maybe not just like mine. I tried not to grin, thinking how unlikely it was we shopped the same catalogs.

"You look good." His voice sounded husky as if he'd been yelling.

I flipped my hair over my shoulder in a move I'd practiced in the hallway mirror, trying to look tough and sexy and wondering if it worked. "Thanks. You, um, got a helmet for me?"

"A helmet?" he repeated. "I wasn't sure you'd wear one. It's clipped on the side." He eyed my fidgeting fingers with suspicion. "You okay, Sophie?"

"Yeah, of course."

"You're nervous."

"A little," I said softly.

Marek closed the distance between us and reached for me, running his leathered palms down my arms to rest on my hips. Tugging me close, he murmured into my hair.

"Don't be. I've got you." I slipped my hands around his waist and rested against him as he encircled me with steely arms, all the harder for the stiff shell of his jacket. He sounded as if he spoke through clenched teeth. "Nothing bad will happen to you. I won't let it."

I was taken aback by his intensity. As he held me tightly against him, I had a sinking feeling the headlines were true. Frank was dead. I felt like I lost a dear friend.

I couldn't even begin to understand what Marek was enduring. He'd considered Frank his son. I stretched out a mental touch but only encountered a tightly coiled swirl of anguish. Marek was locked down. All I had to go on were his words and his voice and they didn't leave room for hope of a happy ending.

What kind of monster would do something like this? Mrs. Park had said.

Oh, shit. Monster.

"Marek?" Worry made my voice thin.

"Shh." He released me and walked around the bike, bending to unlatch the helmet. Tossing it to me, he pulled his hair back. "We have to go. Can you get on?"

He swung himself onto the motorcycle again. If I had a choice before, it had evaporated. I realized the implications of Frank's murder. No way would I be standing alone on this sidewalk when Marek and the only safety left in the world pulled away.

I managed to get on without making a complete ass of myself, fighting a wave of nausea as the engine burst into its throaty rumble. It wasn't simple nerves; I had a premonition things would be dire. Disastrously dire. Hurtling through the streets on a naked piece of steel didn't seem so awful by comparison.

My only comfort remained in clinging to the piece of steel who sat in front of me and drove the bike. I held on, eyes squeezed shut behind my sunglasses, and prayed he hadn't been lying when he said he wouldn't let anything bad happen to me.

I prayed if he was lying, let it be over quickly.

"It wasn't Were," Greco said as we walked into Rodrian's Tenth Street office.

He passed a glance at us as we entered and tipped his head with respect at Marek. As I trailed in attached to Marek's hand, I gave him a faint smile. His eyes widened before he tipped his head at me as well. "Tony was the first one in. If there had been any recent Were activity on the grounds, he'd have known. Paschel got onto CSI. She couldn't feel a thing."

"Feel?" I asked.

Rodrian turned to explain. The bruises below his eyes made him look weary and beaten. "Paschel's gift is psychic through touch. She reads life through her hands. If she didn't feel anything. . ."

"Then no living thing did this," finished Marek, voice strained with grief and quiet rage.

"Yeah, that's what she reported. And—she found this."

Marek raised his gaze to Rodrian's face, waiting.

Rodrian stepped over to his desk and took something out of the top drawer. He dropped it on the desk, where it wobbled a moment before lying flat and still. The coin landed face up, revealing the insignia of a heart pierced with two swords.

Marek stared at the piece. Something in his steely gaze told me he recognized it. Sorrow turned to slate and he spoke without looking up. "How was he executed?"

"Paschel said..." Unshed tears crowded Rodrian's voice. "It was bad. Only his face was unscathed."

I stretched out my awareness and my heart wailed at the feel of their power signatures. They both tried to be strong and objective even as sorrow shredded them.

Frank Levene, executed. He wasn't just a friend who'd been slain. He'd been so much more. Frank had been a symbol of hope.

He'd been an investment in the future Marek wanted to shape. Under the guidance and support of the DV, Frank had become powerful and influential, translating Marek's hopes into laws and reforms that protected, provided, and prospered. More than a trusted colleague, Marek loved him like a son and brother and friend. He'd been family.

Now family and investment and hope had been murdered. It was political defeat and personal loss taken to the highest degree.

We mourned silently together, a funeral party in a secured office high above a city that bred nightmare and agony below. We mourned a man who died because someone wanted to send Marek a loud message: *Play the game our way or you will lose.*

"What's our move?" Rodrian sank onto the couch, hands clasped between his knees, face upturned to his brother. Waiting for direction.

Marek rubbed a hand over his mouth, a grim thin line. "Nothing."

"What? You're joking." Caen shoved himself to his feet, staring at Marek as if he were insane. His voice could have cut through steel. Each word had a sharp edge that pushed its way into my attention, and there was little chance of ignoring him. I cringed, waiting for Marek's inevitable explosion.

It never came. Marek's voice was expressionless. "Nothing will change, with the obvious exception of security increases for our other interests. We will not be intimidated."

"That's it?" Caen argued in disbelief. "We must organize a retaliatory strike."

"Impossible," countered Rodrian. "We'd never win. There's no way to wage war without it spilling out into the open. No matter what we did, we'd lose. We have to compromise."

"Compromise with demons? Are we cowards or fools?" Caen's eyes swept the room for support. Greco turned his back to him, crossing his arms and looking straight ahead at Rodrian. Caen would find no alliance in him.

A few of the others shifted uncomfortably. I could feel the conflict trickling through their power—their loyalty to the Thurzo family struggling against their instinct to avenge.

Caen's power bore a point, a sharp focus of ambition. He saw opportunity. I hated Caen for seeing opportunity where the rest of us saw only loss.

"No. No war. No compromise. I'll go." Marek's voice was leaden, heavy and final.

"Go? You'll go where?" My turn for an outburst. Now, of all times, I didn't want him to go anywhere. Not when we were finally so happy. Not when I was suddenly so scared.

Marek turned to me, apology gleaming in his eyes and betraying his regret. His voice held its usual tone of absolute certainty of what needed to be done and how he had to do it. There was no room for argument. There never was, with Marek. "I will meet him. We will end this."

"You're only giving him what he wants—the opportunity to bring about your Fall," Rodrian said.

I held my tongue, afraid the next sound that emerged from my mouth would be a scream. Everything was spiraling out of control. I squeezed Marek's hand, desperate for anchor.

Marek shook his head. "No. I resisted this long. It will not happen now."

"There has to be another way," insisted Rodrian. "Send someone else."

"Send Caen," I blurted.

Caen blanched before issuing a warning growl and a spike of threat.

I huffed out an exaggerated sigh. "Tuck it away, Caen," I shot back. "I'm not in the mood for a demonstration of how big your manhood is."

The assault wavered a teeny moment before he receded; Caen was shocked I would say such a thing, much less stand up to him. I stepped forward to address Greco and the others. "Caen is the most powerful, behind Marek and Rode, even if he does lack finesse. As Rode's right hand, he knows everything he needs to negotiate a... cease fire, or whatever."

"This is true." Greco nodded slightly. Several others wore agreeable expressions.

Caen gave me a penetrating stare, trying to figure out where I was leading. Truthfully, though, as much as I'd argued for his competence, I just wanted him gone. Better him than my man. If I could have pulled off a Sophia trick to help convince them, I would have.

"It has to be me." Marek sounded weary. "He will be satisfied with no one else."

"Marek..." Rodrian raised his hands, palms bared, supplicating.

"No. Can't you see? This is what he wants. If I don't

go, he'll take someone else. He doesn't make mistakes, brother. Frank wasn't a mistake. Father wasn't a mistake. He'll hit us again and again until I have nothing left. I will not stand here and watch you Fall, one by one."

He turned slowly, looking into the eyes of the men who surrounded him—even Caen, who sullenly acknowledged his intent and lowered his eyes. Marek stood half a pace in front of me, sheltering me, excluding me from the threat.

Instead, he wrapped me in a gentle pulse of comfort. Even tinged by the turmoil raging through him, it helped. I squeezed his hand. He squeezed back.

Marek walked to the door and opened it, ending the meeting. "Arrangements must be made. We'll meet tomorrow after sunfall. Tonight, I will not be disturbed."

Rodrian's gaze flickered to me again, so briefly I'd have missed it had I not been watching him. Tapping his fingers on the desk top, he nodded. "Okay. Tomorrow, at Folletti's."

"Sir?" Greco ran a hand over the top of his shaved head and waited while the rest of the crew filed out. "Is there family who needs arrangements?"

"Not flowers," said Marek, before Rodrian could answer. "The only thing they need right now is protection."

We left shortly afterwards and waited at the elevator, silent and solemn. When the doors closed, he punched the button and found my hand again. I pressed against his side, needing the contact but not wanting to intrude. His eyes found me in the mirrored doors and he smiled faintly, a slight turn of the mouth that never reached his haunted eyes.

We hit the street at the start of rush hour traffic. Seeing the bike again gave me a more welcome type of stress. At the curb he pulled me to him and pushed my hair back from my shoulders, trailing his fingers down my throat.

"Stay with me tonight," he asked. "I have a cottage in the country. It's quiet. Secure." He leaned over me and his hair fell like a veil, cutting off the sight of everything but his face. "I need to gather myself. If you were alone in your apartment I would only worry."

Standing up straight again, he glanced at the passersby. "I don't mean to scare you. I just don't want to take any chances."

I leaned to take the helmet from its clip. "Do we have time to swing by my place first?"

"Of course." He mounted the bike but before I could get on he put his hand on my arm. "Sophie, I'm sorry. I never meant to put you in danger. I never wanted any of this for you."

I reached up and stroked the side of his cheek, giving him my best Buck Up! smile. "It's all right. I'm sure I'll think of something brilliant."

He pulled me closer and drew me down to his face, letting his eyes simmer with a gentle hint of light. His mouth hovered over my skin, breathing me in.

"I have no doubt you will, my little Sophia." His voice sounded husky again, but now with promise, rather than pain. Releasing me, he urged me onto the bike and soon we slipped seamlessly into the traffic.

We headed north. By the time we hit the parkway I was accustomed to the ride. The open road held fewer stationary targets so I wasn't nearly as afraid of colliding with things. Eventually, it became white noise and I relaxed enough to loosen my death grip around Marek's waist.

Marek's compulsion had a lot to do with the tension fading. I sure wasn't responsible for the positive attitude adjustment. One thing about the Wonderful World of DV I appreciated was the calming influence Marek exuded whenever I had more than I could handle.

Marek left the parkway and headed west. He took the curve of the off-ramp at a tilt that reminded me I wasn't brave or placated enough to let go. I flung my arms back around him, feeling him laugh.

The sky was turning toward the beginnings of sunset —what Marek had meant by "sunfall." The sun had dropped to that particular position that made it impossible to drive, its light creating a sheet of luminescence upon the highway that slid into your eyes and made you squint despite visor or sunglasses.

Sunfall was the time of the day when the sun makes the subtle change from a king of the sky to dying star of the horizon. Marek once told me all the names the DV have for different phases of sun and moon, spinning a tale of earth lore and vampire superstition unlike any I'd heard before. It was entertaining and engaging and altogether frightening.

Sunfall marked the beginning of the end for a fully-evolved DV, his body making the final physical changes that rendered him vampire. At sunset the sun died, the DV died, and the vampire rose. For the DV at the brink of evolution, sunfall was a time for pain and fear and damnation. For those who survived, it was a moment of prayer and reflection.

Despite sunfall's spiritual gloom, the sunlight was incomparably beautiful—passing from white invisible light to warm color, rendering shadows that enhanced the beauty of the remaining light. The irony was harsh; how could something so beautiful be so terrible?

I contemplated this as Marek left the main road. We passed through a set of tall gates and rode up a long sloped driveway, our destination hidden from view by trees and garden, full of life and dancing in the colors of a dying sun.

"So this is your 'cottage in the country'?" I doubted we had come to the right place.

We'd pulled up in front of a huge house about twenty minutes outside the city limits. It wasn't so much suburbia as a community of estates. Gates hid the driveway from the main road and the long driveway put a considerable distance between the house and outside traffic.

The sunlight washed the front of the house with its palette of heated watercolors, staining the edifice in corals and marigolds, the heat of a neatly-banked fire.

Testing my legs, I turned to survey the grounds. The driveway circled a small garden with a central fountain. Maidens of carved white stone held swords in various positions around the center piece—a dance of death parading around a gentler dance of water. The water leaped upwards and outwards, catching the sunlight and igniting with a molten glow.

No cottage I'd ever seen had a fountain like this in front of it. A vinyl goldfish pond bought at the local home do-it-yourself store, at best. Cottage, my Aunt Fannie. Try *mansion.*

Marek leaned against the now quiet bike, allowing me time to look around. Crossing his arms, he nodded. "Yeah," he said. "Quaint, huh?"

"Quaint?" I leaned back and squinted, trying to see the upper stories of the house and failing. The porch had columns, for crying out loud. "I guess. Maybe, though, 'palatial' might be a better word."

He laughed and pulled my tote from the saddlebag. "Well, technically, it started out as a cottage. I've had it renovated a few times since I acquired it."

I walked back a few paces, taking in the rows of elegant windows. "Renovated, right."

"Actually, the original structure still exists. It's the guest suite now."

"Right." I followed him up the steps. We passed through the massive double doors into a brightly lit foyer. Cream walls stretched toward high ceilings that scattered my voice in echoes. "Sounds fancy. I never slept in a bedroom as big as a whole cottage before."

"You won't tonight, either. My private quarters are much more suitable."

"What..." I chuckled. "Isn't *quaint* romantic enough for you?"

He dropped his keys on a high-legged antique table along the side wall. "*Quaint* isn't secure enough."

The teasing mood I'd been trying to maintain disappeared.

"I'm sorry," he said. "I shouldn't have said that. We're safe here, I swear." He sighed heavily and reached for me, rubbing my arms and softening the edge of my alarm. "We came here to relax and enjoy ourselves. And we will do exactly that."

He released me and unzipped his jacket, shrugging it

off and tossing it onto a chair near the table. I was lost—lost in the situation, lost in the aftermath of the killing, lost in the luxury of the quaint little mansion looming around me like an expensive crypt.

Marek unzipped my coat, pushing it down over my shoulders and slipping it from my arms before tossing it onto his own.

"The house is secure. I have both an electronic system and a mobile security force. There's no place you should be afraid to explore here, guest suite included. But I have wards upstairs, old ones that have never failed. We can relax up there. I'd like us to have time to ourselves, time not spent worrying for your safety."

"Marek, how bad will things get?"

"I don't know." For once, he sounded as if he didn't know the answer and not that he didn't know how to tell me.

"We'll be okay, right?"

His mouth softened somewhat, not quite a smile. The warmth in his eyes made the lie almost believable. "Yeah," he said. "We will."

A short while later I was neck-deep in hot water. For once, it was the pleasant kind that had a sunken tub to hold it. Sometimes good things came in deep, green marble packages.

Lounging in water so hot it stifled my breath, I was determined to endure the tub as long as it took for the tension in my neck and shoulders and mind to melt away. Marek assured me he'd pull me out before I cooked. I wanted to stay in as long past *al dente* as I could tolerate.

Much of the basement level was devoted to Marek's personal work-out space. I'd been in gyms before, having embarked on many a New Year's resolution down at the local spa. I'd also seen photos of home gyms, the kinds regular people set up in basements or spare bedrooms. This room was unlike either.

The hot tub was the most comfortable-looking thing in the room and even this thing breathed menacing steam. The rest of the gym was filled with what I imagined were torture devices for sick people who obviously liked to abuse themselves. I wasn't anti-exercise but these machines were intimidating.

I'd long suspected Marek's muscles weren't of the CGI-variety but for the first time I watched what he did to grow them. Right now he hung from a horizontal rack doing upside-down push-ups. Pull-ups. Well, whatever. They looked strenuous.

His workout kept him from chatting but I didn't mind; I was content watching him. No words existed for how nice he looked, right down to the bulge of vein in his forearms and the sheen of perspiration glazing his skin.

As a writer, I should have been at the top of my game when it came to descriptive phrases. Moments like this made me glad I didn't keep a journal. Right now I had trouble getting past words like *luscious* and *hunk* and a couple others that were equally embarrassing.

But oh, so appropriate, I thought with a salacious grin. God help me but I'd even shamelessly entertained a few clichés.

A contented noise escaped me as I sank further down into the big vat of Sophie soup. I hadn't anticipated when he'd said "pack for the cottage" he'd meant "prepare to stay at a spa resort." A bathing suit wasn't the first thing I tossed into my overnight bag.

I wore a tee shirt he'd cleverly sliced up in the back and tied more snugly behind me. At least it wasn't billowing out around me like a big wet parachute. Thank goodness I'd worn bikini panties. I thought the ensemble looked cute. He thought so too, if the frequency with which he looked me over was any indication.

With sounds of exertion he finished his set, dangling from the rack a few moments to stretch before dropping to the ground. He grabbed a towel and dried his face and neck, then stretched again.

Although he'd said we came here to relax, he now seemed to be pushing himself through exercises with a determination bordering on ferocity. I mean, Toto, I don't think we're at *Curves* anymore!

Did he always try to kill himself like this? Was he trying to distract himself from the horrors of the day? Was he preparing for something that lay ahead? Either way, he wasn't relaxing, even by his standards. I sighed and dragged my limp self out of the tub. Truthfully, I wasn't relaxing, either.

"We can hit the pool, if you like." Marek nodded at a frosted glass door at the far end of the gym. "I'll just shower off first."

The air seemed cool now in comparison to the hot water. A regular pool sounded more shocking than refreshing. "I'm kind of water-logged."

"I noticed." A pleasant leer curled his mouth and he lifted his towel toward me. "I like the wet shirt look. You have pretty goose bumps."

I made a face and grabbed his towel, holding it in front of me with belated modesty. "You go in. I'll sit on the side."

"Fair enough." He ducked into a side room and I soon heard the sounds of more water.

I toweled off while he finished and soon followed him through the glass door to the swimming pool. I could count the number of times I'd used an indoor pool on one hand. Okay, on one finger. How many people had a pool in their house? I didn't mean a big yucky rectangle like down at the YMCA, spackled on the bottom with lumps sharp enough to shred toes.

Oh, no. This was a sleek resort pool, kidney-shaped curves full of water the color of the ocean in the Bahamas— bluish-green and perfectly clear. The marble tiles had been seamlessly jointed together; it appeared the pool was carved out of a single piece of stone and polished to a smoothness of a soap bar.

Track lights in the water and around the edge of the deck area cast gentle light on stone and water. Elegant lounge chairs and full-size palm trees ringed the room. All it needed was a hammock and a waiter wearing Bermuda shorts and I'd swear I'd walked into Club Med.

I selected a spot at the edge while Marek walked over to a wall box in the corner. Flipping it open, he hit a couple switches. "What time do you want?"

That made no sense, so I responded with eloquence. "Huh?"

"What time of day do you want in here? I can adjust the lighting. You could pick the time of year, too, if you wanted but I generally let the control run on real time."

"No time like the present, right?" I joked. "Or is it too late?"

"Never too late," he replied. "How's this?"

A loud click sounded, followed by an electrical hum that faded as light panels in the walls and ceiling warmed up. The room glowed with the pinks, oranges and violets of sunset. Even the shadows slanted realistically as light shimmered through the trees to float across the surface of the water.

The light, where it reached me through the shadow of the leaves, cast a gentle glow upon my skin. "Wow," I said, my voice breathy. "I can feel it."

"That's because it's UV. You could tan in here if you wanted."

Marek turned a dial and the sounds of twilight rose

around us. Evening birds and crickets called from the trees. Delighted by this enchantment, I kicked playfully in the water and watched the sunset dance across its surface. "That's what makes it feel real?"

"Part of it. I keep the light company in business with the amount of electricity I pull when I turn on the lights." Marek stepped to the edge and dropped like a blade into the water, sending up a fizz of tiny bubbles before resurfacing. "What can I say? I like my illusions complete."

"Really? I figured you were spoiled for luxury."

"That too," he agreed.

"This place is amazing." I leaned back on my arms, admiring the scenery. "I mean, I like the townhouse in Chaucer's Square but it doesn't compare to this. Why not live here full time?"

He treaded the water so smoothly his head didn't bob. "It's more convenient to live in the city. Closer to work, closer to other things."

"Humanity?"

He agreed with a short nod. "All this is nice, but I don't need it all the time. I've spent most of my life living on much less. In Europe, I lived primitively, compared to this."

"Honey, I live primitively compared to this."

"True. Your bathroom is too small to call a closet. It's shameful." He slid sideways in the water to avoid the splash I aimed at him. "I don't need this every day. I keep staff here year round so I can come and go as I want."

He ducked under, swimming like a dart to the far edge of the pool. Kicking off at the edge, he returned with swift economical strokes that barely broke the water.

Marek drifted back and wrapped his hands around my calves. His sudden touch goose-bumped me again. "As nice as it is, it's not a place to be alone. It looks like a resort, and who goes on vacation alone?"

"Hmm. Good question. I can't even think of the last

time I went on vacation. Spring break in college, maybe?" I winced. "Pathetic, isn't it?"

He tilted his head. "What does that make me? I haven't been on holiday since the forties."

The thought made me dizzy and I lowered my gaze. "Don't say such things. There are some truths I can't handle."

"Sophie, I don't get it. You don't cringe when someone mentions blood thirst..."

"It's a simple fact of life. Blood is food." I interrupted with my now-familiar litany.

"...but the mention of my age disturbs you?"

"I like older men," I replied. "But you're practically a mummy. I don't want to be reminded you are really, really, really old."

"Do I need to convince you?"

I wrinkled my nose. "That you're a mummy? Yuck. No thanks."

"No, girl. That I am anything but." His hands tightened and he yanked me into the water. I yelped in surprise, sputtering protests and streaming water from my hair. He pulled me around him and I obligingly entwined my arms and legs around him.

The air was faintly perfumed with the scents of flowers and chlorine, a true oasis. I closed my eyes and hummed my delight, feeling secure in his embrace. Being in the water made it feel as if he caressed me everywhere at once.

"Now what do you think?" His voice rumbled through his chest into mine.

"Mmm," I said lazily. "That you don't feel a day over a hundred and twenty?"

I got a nose full when he tossed me up and under. I was so surprised I forgot to swim. Good thing he rescued me before I sank. I spit a mouthful of pool water at his smirk.

"You okay?" His apologetic expression was completely phony, and I saw the laughter lurking beneath the surface. How mature of him to suppress his insincerity.

"I'm fine. But you're lucky, mister. If I drowned, your whole race would be screwed."

"Mmm," he agreed, and pulled me back around him. "Can't let that happen, can we?" He swam toward the center of the pool, holding me while keeping us both afloat. I listened to the sound of water lapping the sides of the pool, admired the beads of moisture clinging to his skin, and played with his silky hair floating in the water behind him.

"You know," he said absently. "My brother is about a hundred and twenty."

"I know." He couldn't see my dimpled grin so I loaded extra sweetness into my voice.

He pulled back to see my face and his eyes searched mine, trying to decipher my response. "You know?"

"Yes."

"Oh. Okay."

Splash.

By the time I broke the surface, he'd gotten out of the pool. Between coughs, I called to him, trying not to laugh. "Cmon, don't be a baby. You know you feel way older than he does."

His response was to hit the power switch, returning the lights to dim pool glow. The birds and crickets vanished and the only sound left was the door banging shut behind him.

Sheesh. Men. And their egos. Looked like I'd be spending a lot of time making it up to him tonight.

The thought made me smile wickedly. I scrambled onto the deck and, grabbing a towel from the rack by the door, I hurried after him, eager to begin my apology.

37

I couldn't imagine a more shameful waste of a beautiful Saturday evening than having to work at The Annual Balaton Business Expo. It wasn't that I had better things to do; with Marek out of town on his awful business, I had nothing else I wanted to do, anyway.

Technically, I was supposed to remain at Wayne Manor or whatever Marek called the place. He'd forbidden me to leave the grounds until he came back from his negotiations with the territorial Master's representatives. He said that I shouldn't worry about him, that everything would go exactly as he planned; I should enjoy the facilities and think about how I would welcome him home. He encouraged me to think creatively before kissing me like a savage. Very inspirational, indeed.

He'd given me plenty of fond memories to peruse in his absence, despite my piteous farewell; I knew he had to go but I couldn't bear the thought of being left alone in the big house. Besides, as much as I would have liked to force myself to lounge at his pool, I'd catch hell if I didn't show up for work.

Work I wasn't paid to do. No words could describe my loathing for this damnable Expo.

I knew there'd be no point in arguing with him so I waited until he left, scrawled a brief note, and left it on a countertop in his suite before I sneaked out. I'd be back in less than four hours, no sweat. I took a cab to my place to change and get my car, planning on driving back when I finished at the Expo. That way I'd only have to sell one of my kidneys to pay for cab fare. Sure, he'd notice the Cavalier upon his return and give me a thorough yelling but this was definitely the occasion to say *sorry* rather than *please*.

At home, I had trouble finding a respectable business suit to wear. Working at *The Mag* meant a casual wardrobe for me, falling somewhere between Sunday morning church and Monday Night Football. I found a dark blue suit at the back of my closet, one I'd bought several years ago. Finding it still fit, I dug out navy pumps to match. Spaghetti-strap camisole, knee-length skirt, matching blazer. I looked nice but who was I trying to impress? Donna?

Ugh. This was all her fault.

I had to pay special event rates to park in the garage of the hotel where the Expo had been booked. I'd hoped for discount parking for vendors but no, of course not. My validation ticket promised I'd be charged in twenty minute increments. Gritting my teeth, I calculated I'd have to sell plasma for a year and a half to pay for it.

Great. Blood and a kidney. Non-reimbursable business expenses. Gotta love them.

I found our table and checked the assignment sheet as Donna and a person from Marketing spoke with another vendor. The poor man tried to focus on what Marketing Guy said but Donna kept butting in with her annoying attitude of *know-it-all*. Eventually, the two men exchanged business cards and promises to talk at a more convenient time, all the time shooting daggered looks at Donna. She was utterly oblivious.

Instead, she turned back to the table, wearing a satisfied expression as if she'd single handedly altered the course of publishing for years to come. Triumphant jubilation practically split her face in two when she saw me frowning at the clipboard. "Well. You're actually on time. I figured you'd skip out."

At this point, I couldn't even pretend to want to be here. "What does this mean? *Swag bags, entrance five?*"

"You take this box." She produced a carton from under the table and shoved it at me. I wasn't prepared for the weight and nearly collapsed into the backdrop of *The Mag's* banner. "You give out one bag to everyone who comes in."

As I looked down at the box, I noticed a huge smear of dirt on the front of my white camisole. I opened my mouth to protest as she pointedly scrutinized the damage.

An apology forthcoming? Could it be? Nah.

"Where's your name tag?" Her eyes were slitted. "Everyone else wore theirs."

"Name tag?" I echoed.

"I handed them out Friday at work. Oh." She sneered at me with flair. "That's right. You took the day off. I bet it's still lying on your desk."

Rummaging under the table again, she took out a sheet of labels and uncapped a Sharpie.

"This will have to do." She scrawled on the sheet, peeled a label, and slapped it onto my lapel. Crooked. I sighed. Her outburst generated a lot of unwanted attention from people in the aisle, and I wanted to evaporate.

"Entrance five is that way." Donna pointed toward the far end of the conference room. Turning away, she ignored me completely. I'd been dismissed.

Heels weren't meant to be worn while carrying thirty-five pound boxes, especially if walking on carpet. I got several odd looks from other vendors as I passed them, but salvaged the remnants of my dignity and suppressed my temper. By the time I reached the door I had a semblance of control.

And a dirty blouse that would have to go to the cleaners. And a name tag reading "HELLO MY NAME IS SOPHY" in big block letters. Not even the name of my company, let alone my feature. Hell, not even my name.

I thought about Donna's name tag and the gold lettering spelling out EXECUTIVE RESOURCE MANAGEMENT. I supposed *Stapler Nazi* wasn't classy enough for the occasion.

Smile, I scolded myself. *Hostile* was a bad first impression. Bad for business.

I opened the box and dug out a handful of plastic bags decorated with *The Mag's* logo and loaded with fliers and, oh look, a copy of the summer bonus issue. Far away from the hubbub of The Expo, I stood like a leper at the least populated entrance. Pretty much the only people using it were hotel staff and people looking for the bathroom or a quiet place to use their cell phone.

Determinedly, I stood my ground, handing out my vehicle trash bags to anyone with an empty hand. It might be a lousy job but I wouldn't give anyone named Donna the satisfaction of seeing me aggravated. One hour and twenty minutes until I could leave. Plenty of time to inspect my manicure, recall a particularly enjoyable moment or two from the night before, and plot my dastardly revenge.

She had an upcoming vacation. I'd acquisition everything in that damn supply closet of hers. I'd fill the cushion of her desk chair with petroleum jelly. I'd write her number on the wall of the men's bathroom in the fast food joint downstairs, as if half the city didn't already know it.

She'd pay, I promised myself, feeling much better. At least being the Sophia didn't mean abandoning my refined sense of spite.

Halfway through my shift, a gentleman in a nondes-cript suit approached me. Nice name badge, though, I noticed sullenly. Mr. Carey of Guest Relations had a nice name badge. Mine was still crooked and had started to curl at one corner. When he cleared his throat like a stutter, I surmised he was a tad uncomfortable. "Miss? From the magazine?"

I nodded as if I had an important reason to be standing near the least traveled door at the entire conference.

"There's a slight problem with your order for the presentation. I need someone to sign for the projector request."

I hadn't the foggiest idea what he talked about. "Our table is at C21. Ask for the office manager. She's probably the one who ordered it."

He rubbed his hands together and nodded. "Ah, she is the one I needed, actually. Donna Slate? I've checked the table. She is, ah, indisposed at the moment."

Leaning close, he whispered. "The bathroom."

As if anyone would overhear him in our little corner of Pluto. "Good luck with that. Once she goes in, it's anybody's guess when she'll come out. Enjoy the wait."

"That's the problem. I've been waiting for her. The deliveryman is getting angry. He said we put him off his route. If someone doesn't come down right now, he's leaving."

Hoo boy. If the guy left, I'd catch hell for not getting whatever Donna ordered.

"Fine," I said. "But you better vouch for me that I wasn't slacking off. This is a very important job I'm doing." He didn't deserve my sarcasm but mine wouldn't be the first war to incur a civilian casualty.

Relief flooded the poor guy's face. "Thanks so much, Miss..." He trailed off. Still being nice about my first-class name tag.

"Galen," I supplied. "Sophie Galen, at your service."

He smiled. "Well, follow me, Sophie Galen. The man who wants you is right downstairs."

I slid the row of bags off my finger and dumped them back into the box, not concerned that some of them spilled their contents. We took a service elevator to the first level of the garage, where a van marked East Coast Media Services waited at the loading dock.

An impatient man in gray coveralls waited at the back of the open vehicle, hollering into a walkie-talkie and preparing to stow some machine and its cabinet in the bay. When he spotted us, he shook his fist. "You really know how to keep a guy waiting."

He didn't sound like he was joking. Too bad.

I smiled a bright and annoying smile. "Fashionably late as usual. Where do I sign?"

"Nowhere." Mr. Carey stepped behind me and grabbed my arms, his grasp icy and solid.

"Hey!" I braced my feet and tried to twist loose but he lifted me off the ground. "Let me go!"

"Zip-tie her legs," Mr. Carey said. "Someone might detect a compulsion." The driver didn't waste a second. He threaded the plastic and yanked it tight enough to dig into my flesh.

"Help me!" I screamed.

A hand, then tape went over my mouth. They pushed me into the van and I landed on the floor with a thud, pushing the filthy carpet up in a bunch beneath my face. Something hard dug into my shoulder and the impact brought sharp instant pain. I screamed against the tape.

Hotel Guy held me down with one knee in the middle of my back, tying my wrists behind me while Coveralls slammed the vehicle into drive, throwing us back. I looked up as high as my position would allow me and I saw the glint of bright eyes spark briefly in the rear-view mirror.

The van sped out of the garage and raced through the streets. We squealed around a corner before panic set in. I'd been stolen, vanished without a trace.

PART III

38

I gave up trying to walk and submitted to being dragged between them. They seemed intent on it anyway, the jerks. Their grips were cold and unbreakable and they had little regard for what the dragging did to my legs.

Alternatively, I cursed myself for getting nicked by these two, for going downstairs with Hotel Guy—hell, for going to the Expo in the first place.

And for wearing a skirt with heels. I'd always known pride goes before a fall but apparently vanity goes before a tremendous dragging.

All but a small part of my brain was ransacked with terror. The little piece of my personality that survived my abduction chattered away like an ass. For instance, I thought: look what these assholes are doing to my shoes. I can't walk home with a broken heel.

Real helpful. You'd think logic and cunning would be hard at work, trying to devise a way out. Wasn't I the Sophia? The Embodiment of Wisdom? But no, only my sarcasm had survived.

Shortly I found out it wasn't a good thing, either. When I thought *these assholes*, Hotel Guy shot out a slap, smacking the impudence out of me. Rotten bastards could read minds, too.

Down, down, down we went. Stone steps, dank walls, musty dead smells—the whole *decor* screamed *lair*. I gave up on rallying my brain and let it sink back into terrified mush. The small perky part quietly continued to think hopeful thoughts. I might figure out a way to escape from two vampires. Marek might find me. Hopefully there'd be an elevator.

Gut instinct and Sophia alike kept quiet and tried not to attract attention. The less competent I looked, the better my chances to fool them.

For the duration of our descent, my companions remained ominously silent, their holds on my arms unrelenting. The only indication they acknowledged me came in the form of a mean squeeze or two when I inadvertently thought of something particularly uncomplimentary.

The steps ended long after I lost count and the bottom of the stairwell ended bluntly with a tremendous stone wall. That was all. Just dirty, dank wall. Coveralls raised his free hand and tapped it once before pushing it out of the way, swinging it open to reveal what I presumed would be the actual lair.

And not just any old lair. My eyes widened. This was no hole in the ground. This was opulence to extreme.

We stood in the rectangular foyer of a manor that rivaled the palaces of Old Europe, a vault of marble and silk and gold. Two staircases swept up and out to the sides, and the second level formed a balcony, lined with closed doors. The lower level, completely tiled in rose marble, seeped outward to touch the three walls, each bearing a massive door.

A tremendous chandelier was suspended over the

center of the room, a glittering mass of crystal and candle-light that cast a deceivingly warm glow onto the surfaces beneath. The light echoed in dozens of sconces circling the room on each floor, and although we were countless stories underground, it was as bright as July sunshine.

Simple combustion couldn't create this light; it was power. Someone's power.

I felt that someone as my captors resumed hauling me toward the center door, dragging me through the light pooling on the cold marble floor. I felt that someone the way one felt a lover at night, even if they didn't talk or touch. It was the way I had come to feel Marek, as if my body acknowledged him in a way separate from my conscious mind.

An even colder dread began to mist over me, soaking me to the core. This someone wouldn't be a lover, not like any I'd ever wanted. Like a rabbit in a snare, I instinctively struggled against my captors. Struggling pulled the snare tighter around my throat.

One of the bullies barked out a short command. When the door drifted open, the presence I'd felt in the foyer grew. Dread seeped like fog through my body, winding into every corner.

"You will kneel in the presence of the Master." Hotel Guy had long abandoned his phony polite voice. He'd also abandoned his phony polite human face. The bones had shifted, eye brows and cheekbones and chin becoming sharper, more pronounced. The skin looked thinner, stretched tightly over the protruding ridges. More primitive. More dead.

I had a memory flash of the rooftop vampire who started my entire journey to this terrifying end and jerked my eyes away. Hotel Guy shook me, interpreting my fear as refusal. "If you have difficulty, I will assist you."

He didn't mean *I will ease you to your sore, battered*

knees. He meant *I'll break your legs.*

I hung my head in unequivocal submission.

Marek had told me about Masters and the battles they waged in their lust for power, the tales sounding tall and mythic. I expected to find the Master seated upon a throne in a massive audience chamber, some haggard battle-scarred monster, like a Dark Ages king.

When the lights rose around us in response to some unspoken command, what I saw was nothing like what I expected. In fact, it was all the more terrifying in its normalcy.

No throne room littered with empty corpses, no dungeon or dais surrounded by old bones. We stood in an office. It made the threat more relatable, more immediate. Absolutely real.

My escorts dumped me in a boneless pile in the center of the room, ripping my blazer off. The sudden bareness increased my sense of vulnerability. The dark carpet was deep and plush, its luxuriousness making every scratch and scrape on my bare legs scream. The room smelled like dry soil and stale breath, despite the new appearance of the carpet.

Although we were too far below the ground for any actual windows, long velvety draperies hung upon the walls like window dressings. Rows of books with leather and gilded covers stacked from floor to ceiling. The entire room boasted of money and comfort and luxury, all of which would have appealed to my truest hedonist self had I not been brought here to die.

I took a deep breath, swallowed the greasy metallic taste coating the inside of my mouth, and pushed myself to my protesting feet, using the pain to focus.

The vamps growled with displeasure and I expected to be knocked down once more. Instead of hitting me, they backed off into the shadows behind me, necks painfully bent, chins to chests.

Not good. Something scarier than those two was in here with us. Straightening slowly, I turned back toward the desk to see a brilliant figure.

He stepped out of the shadows and the light clung to him, slender and pale like a streak of frozen lightning. His clothing seemed spun of actual silver, an odd mix of robe and trouser. Blond hair, braided, beaded and nearly translucent, flowed down his shoulders like a veil. Bright lavender eyes alighted with mild amusement as he appraised me. They would have been beautiful eyes had they not been rimmed with red. He looked like a Nordic god with a hangover.

Again a hand shot out, this time so forcibly my head rocked back with the blow. Dazed, I wiped at my nose. My fingers came away sticky with blood. My brain buzzed: *pain fear hate*

"Stop." The white man's voice was mild, a quiet sound that carried on a wave of power. "You're wasting it."

I realized he referred to me and the seriousness of my situation, the hopelessness and the inevitable pain.

Genially he smiled, knowing what I knew and pronouncing my plight insignificant. His eyes glittered, neon bouncing off ice, heating with a silver-white glow.

"I am known as the Still-Heart." His voice was liquid rabbit fur rubbing the insides of my head, muffling the sounds of my thoughts. All I heard was his voice. All that mattered was his voice. I stared, enraptured, swayed by his compulsion and infatuated with his deadly temptation. "Welcome to your death, sweet one."

My mind chased after his beautiful voice and I smiled.

The two vamps dipped curt nods and hauled me out. I clawed my mental way out the compulsion that had cocooned itself around my will. I didn't resist their rough handling, too preoccupied with clearing my head. They hustled me backwards out of the room and dragged me through a new set of doors.

The new scenery was even more unlikely than the office. As I finally dispelled the fog of Still-Heart's voice, I saw we stood in a massive stone-walled cathedral.

A church? A vampire had a church in his evil lair?

As my eyes adjusted to the torch light, I realized it was merely a caricature of a church. No saints, no crosses, no redemption—only arches and high ceilings and an inauspicious-looking altar. The shadowed walls bore Egyptian symbols, and the painted pictures triggered a recollection of one of Marek's vampire lessons.

Ancient Egyptians had been buried with their coffins in one room and a chapel in another, which provided a dwelling place for the soulless body. The survivors would bring offerings of food and drink to the chapel so the deceased could be sustained in death.

Sustained. Oh shit, I'm the offering.

Still-Heart mounted the maroon steps at the front of the obscene chapel and draped himself over a high-backed chair. At least he had the decency to fulfill one of my stereotypical expectations. Torches in sconces and rows of candles caused chaotic shadows to twist upon the walls, hinting at deeper shadows in the alcoves perforating the perimeter.

Some alcoves showed the bright white eyes of silent figures hiding, watching, waiting. Some contained things that scratched at the walls or rattled heavy-sounding chains. One dark space issued the low rumble of a large animal that sounded as if it had grown rather intolerant of its surroundings and wanted to be unleashed. All bad sounds.

The stone floor bore an uneven wash of reds and browns as if painted by a careless artist. Steel loops were embedded in the floor. I refused to speculate what purpose they served. Jared's church didn't have steel floor loops.

At the foot of the steps, the vamps tossed me onto the

floor. I landed on my side, my leg bent beneath. My elbow took the brunt of the blow and a current of electric pain shot down though my fingers. My position forced me to look up at the unmoving figure, subservient to him.

"What do you want with me?" Screaming against tape had roughened my voice, and even quiet speaking hurt. "I've done nothing to you. I can't do anything for you..."

Still-Heart lifted his eyes as if exasperated. It would have been a human gesture if he wasn't a corpse. "This isn't about you. You're almost as worthless as you claim to be."

"Hey, that's not what I meant!"

He waved a slender hand at me, white leather glove fitting like second skin. "Be silent."

The invisible fingers of a compulsion closed around my throat like a fist, crushing my voice. I glared at him. If looks could kill, he'd be even more dead.

"I'm not concerned with you. Only him." He smirked and gestured eloquently toward the nearest alcove. As Still-Heart's words bled into echoes and faded away, a pale light grew in one of the alcoves, illuminating the object within. I saw what had made the terrible beast-like sound, the animal at the end of its patience.

Marek.

Bound and chained, hair in matted snarls around his face, clothes bloodied and torn, Marek looked as if he'd been dragged through the woods and buried alive. I couldn't fathom the damage they'd done to him if he'd become this tattered in such a short amount of time. We'd been together less than twelve hours ago.

As the light grew around him, Marek opened his eyes, slowly rousing.

A wave of power flooded the room with a resounding crash. I tasted utter annihilation riding upon it and knew it was his. The force blasted like the heat wave of an explosion, solid and destructive, pressing me down. My head scraped against the floor.

Marek's assault cut off abruptly and I lifted my head. Still-Heart stood with one arm outstretched toward Marek, hand clenched in a fist, face twisted with the effort to quell Marek's outburst. Marek locked eyes with him, promising death and rage with his glare.

Marek flagged in his restraints, his head hanging slightly. It was the most defeat would ever dare countenance itself upon him. His eyes never left the vampire. They seeped a gleam of sickly green from behind thick locks of hair.

Seeing Marek in such a state almost unhinged me, but instinct kept me focused. I concentrated on the pain in my legs, the chill of the floor, the surrounding threat.

Still-Heart turned, a sinister smile playing upon his bloodless lips.

"Almost. He's almost mine. Did you feel his power, human?" Stepping down from the dais, he spared me a glance. "Of course you did. Crushed beneath it like an insect."

Before, his voice had been mesmerizing, beckoning me to follow and drawing me deeper into my head. At first, I'd chased it, a child after a butterfly. All I'd felt was the touch of his voice, running over my thoughts like fingers. The sound and the feel of his voice, all the things it promised. It was all I wanted, all I noticed.

As I struggled to focus, the Sophia crept forth and reclaimed my attention. It remained unaffected by the sweet lies Still-Heart poured into me, oil and honey, fur and pleasure. The Sophia could not be fooled by vampire illusions and it grabbed me, shaking me and freeing me from the compulsion before it took hold again. It delivered a resounding mental *slap*, the kind one gave a hysterical person.

I'd been set back to rights, my mind cleared. Scared but cleared. Focused.

I couldn't bear to look away from Marek. He was oblivious to anyone but the Master. I had to do something, to snap him out of his trance, to give him a mental slap, too.

The vampire whirled on me. "And what would you do, human? Fight me? My legions? Tear the shackles from the walls and save your beloved?"

Still-Heart sauntered down the steps and crouched before me, pulling my chin toward him, tearing my eyes from his prisoner. He stroked my face with his elegant fingers and the sensation of a fire's comforting glow oozed in slow trails down my skin.

"You are too puny, too weak, too stupid to realize..." He smiled as he scoffed at me, his mouth twisted in a teasing smirk. "He'll kill you when he gets the chance. He's mine."

His hatred leaked through the disguise of his smile, turning the warm lazy touches into pricks of pain. Wide-eyed, I shook my head. Never. Marek would die first.

"He certainly will." He gleaned my thoughts as effortlessly as spoken conversation. "And then at last, Marek, the warrior, will be mine. Mine to control. Mine to command. Mine to wield. As vampire, he will be second to no one, save myself."

Stalking toward Marek, he spread his arms wide as if proudly showing off a prized possession. "I've hunted him for ages. The bounty that had been placed upon him was too tempting to pass up. Now, I realize he'd make a more splendid prize."

Still-Heart tapped a lone finger to the side of his mouth. "He'll be nearly invincible. All I need to do is help him to cast off his soul. He's been rather stubborn about keeping it."

He remembered me, turning to look down his slender nose as I huddled on my knees, scraping at the invisible fingers still clutching my throat. "You won't want to miss this, darling."

With a flick of his hand, the constriction on my throat eased, his compulsion lifted. I rubbed the spots where bruises would likely bloom. "Of course," he said. "I wouldn't want to miss out on your screams. I've heard they are quite lovely."

Closing the distance between us in a matter of moments, Still-Heart drew me to my feet with the invisible fingers of his will and lifted me from the ground, my back arched and bent like a string puppet.

He insinuated himself along my twisted body, mimicking a dancer's pose. Pressing his body against mine, he slid an arm around my waist and pushed my shoulder back. Without his power seducing my brain with imagined sensation, the embrace felt like I'd become bound by living stone, his body bearing the coldness of a chilly waterbed. For a moment, I wondered what it might feel like had I still been under the power of his mind-spell.

Should I let his compulsion soften the dead reality? If I opened myself up a tiny bit, could I get through this? Would I be damned?

Still-Heart caressed the skin of my throat, my bared shoulders, the lacy top of my camisole. The amulet Marek had given me lay in the well of my throat. Still-Heart smirked and hooked a finger under the fine chain.

With a hiss, he ripped it off and flung it aside. Satisfied, he raked a wicked scratch across the top of my breast, smiling like a raptor at the hot streak of blood. The wound was the thinnest of scratches but it burned like acid.

Gasping with the flash of agony, I crumpled. Marek reacted at once, leaping forward but caught by the chains binding him. With a roar, he threw another wall of power at us.

Still-Heart shifted his own power, allowing Marek's attack to flow over us impotently. Bending his head, he lapped the blood away, his tongue searing my flesh closed as it drew its wet line across my skin. The pain tore a jagged scream from my throat, and Marek's roars added to the cacophony.

"Oh..." Still-Heart looked up from my breast to search my face. Desire burned in his eyes, a need to be sated. "Magnificent. Who are you, human, to taste so... complete?"

Licking his lips, he released me and drew away as if the touch of my skin scalded him. I fell back into the hard grasp of one of his flunkies.

"What a waste it will be to throw you to him," he said. His expression was a mix of wonder, of lust, of anticipation. "Oh, I could do so many things... perhaps I'll keep you. For myself."

An indistinguishable vampire secured me against the wall directly across from Still-Heart's dais. I twisted my face away, trying to avoid the scent of its skin, so much like old damp book.

Ugly creatures, those vampires. Their bony faces gave skeletal gauntness to their appearances, reminding me they were corpses. Almost mummy-like in appearance, the ridges of their pronounced brows emphasized their white gleaming eyes.

Their eyes disturbed me the most. Silver glow, devoid of color or warmth. Devoid of personality. I'd become fond of the bright eyes of the DV and delighted in the subtle shades that reflected their emotions. Vampires were different. Eyes were the windows of the soul, and the white gleam shouted the truth: vampires possessed no souls.

Their eyes held empty, white light. Cold. Clinical. Dead.

Still-Heart loomed like a monument before his altar. He didn't touch my mind, thankfully; perhaps I was too far beneath his notice for the moment. That could be good and bad; good for not drawing his attention, bad for negotiating my survival.

To my left was the alcove where Marek was bound. He hung in his restraints, deadly still, deadly quiet. His power felt like a disease.

Still-Heart's head snapped up as if he'd heard something. Rage seeped into his face and without a word he turned and swept out of the room through a large doorway to the right of the altar. The vamps streamed out in his wake, leaving behind only silence.

The light faded when the Master left the room, as if he'd stolen it all away. In his absence the darkness spread. A few eerie glows remained, enough to discern doorways and recesses.

An eternity seemed to pass, and my eyes grew accustomed to the darkness. Thin lines of illumination traced Marek's form. I summoned my nerve.

"Marek?" I whispered, knowing he'd hear despite the distance. No response. I dared to raise my voice. "Marek, can you hear me?"

"Sophie?" A brittle voice called from a completely different direction. "Is that you?"

Donna clicked over the tiles toward me, her flashlight making a dizzy streak on the floor. It moved like a firefly on espresso.

"My God. Donna?" I had to be hallucinating. "How did you get in here?"

"I followed you. When those two guys hustled you off, I followed. I figured you were in trouble." She lifted the flashlight and turned her light to shine on me full in the face. Didn't people know how much that sucked? Especially when you'd been, say, chained up in the dark for a good while. I shut my eyes and twisted my head away but she didn't notice my discomfort.

Then again, she usually didn't. Typical Donna.

"What have they done to you?" Donna used her snip-piest tone, reprimanding me as if this was my fault. Setting the flashlight down on its end so the light spilled upward, Donna examined the shackles where they hooked to the wall.

I told her about the dragging, about Marek in the alcove, about Still-Heart and his men. Well, vaguely about that last part. I left out the details so she wouldn't freak out at the vampire part. Most people wouldn't react well to that sort of revelation.

She started working out the locks with a piece of metal from God only knows where and freed one of my arms. Office manager efficient, right down to picking diabolical locks.

As it came loose and fell free, the weight of the chain still attached to my wrist nearly pulled my arm out of the socket. "Donna, we have to get out of here. Can we get Marek loose?"

"Where is he?"

I jerked my head toward the shadows hiding Marek from view.

"He's in there. Hurry before they come back." I shuddered. "The leader said he wants to keep me for himself."

She ceased fiddling with the shackle and whipped a sharp look at me. "What?"

"He was going to kill me but said he might keep me for himself." I remembered the pain, the touch of his mouth, the unspoken threat of more. I shuddered violently. "I'd rather die than let him touch me again."

Donna gave me a long look before she pursed her lips and yanked the chain free from anchor. I sagged against the wall, waiting for her to loosen my wrists. Instead of freeing me, she stood still, staring.

"Donna?" I hoped she wasn't losing it. Not now. "What's the matter?"

"What's the matter? What's the matter!"

I panicked. She'd blow our cover with her big mouth. I shushed her like crazy but apparently *crazy* was her department because she howled with rage.

"You are the matter. I cannot believe this!" She stomped away several paces, then whirled back. "Bad enough you're Golden Girl at *The Mag*. Barbara loves you. They all just love you. And why? I haven't a clue. I dress better, I have better friends... you don't even get your nails done." She spat the words like a condemnation.

"And now. This." She waved her arms around us, hands twisted into furious claws. Her eyes were crazed. "He is going to keep you? You? Oh, no."

She shook her head, grimacing. "You'll die first. You're not the Golden Girl here. I am!"

Holy crap. Donna's one of them. She wasn't just evil— she was *evil!*

Donna reached down and grabbed my chains. My arms had only started to reperfuse, the numbness giving way to useless tingling. I was too stiff to fight back. She turned in the direction of the alcove and stomped toward it, hauling me behind.

At the approaching racket, Marek lifted his head to watch. I felt his stare, the weight of his gaze both familiar and strange. The gleam of his left iris flashed like an emerald searchlight through the strands of his hair. I heard the growl of a caged beast.

Donna babbled, oblivious to the danger.

"I've done too much for my master to be pushed aside. He promised me. Me!" Pausing in her dragging she jabbed her perfectly-French-manicured finger into my chest. "Who is Still-Heart's favorite? Me. Who has the blood that sings of sweet seduction? Me. Who will receive his Dark

Bequest and share in his power forever? Me! Not you!"

"Listen to yourself, Donna! You're a moron. You're food. Nothing but food!"

"Well, now you are, too," she smirked. "The difference is: you'll be dead and I won't." She turned on her heels and started dragging again. "You know what? I cannot stand you, Galen. From the minute I met you, I despised you. When Chal told me to get your address from HR, I knew they had plans for you. When he told me to make sure you went to the parking garage alone, I could barely contain myself. I mean, how do you keep a straight face, knowing you get to screw over someone you absolutely hate?"

My legs finally obeyed and I put the brakes on, jerking her to a halt. I couldn't believe what I heard. "Chal? Chal put you up to this?"

There couldn't be two Chals, not even in a city this big. Too stupid a name.

"Chal was my meal ticket. He's the one who gave me to our master." Sparing me a look that said I must be even dumber than she originally thought, she took a fresh grip on my chains and yanked. "Finally, you'll get what's coming to you and I'll get what I deserve."

Closer to Marek now, close enough to see his chest rising and falling with each breath. Too close. I knew he watched every move we made, holding still, waiting for the moment to spring. Like Blind Horus, he'd be deadly to anyone who came near.

"Oh, yeah. He sees you. He smells you. How about it, Marek?" Donna pulled me, closer and closer. She'd feed me to him if she could get me close enough. I scrambled and tried to pull away but her grip was too strong. We were only a few feet away from him now. How far did his chains reach?

"I can't wait to see lover boy rip your head off." Donna dumped my chains in a heap and I staggered to a

stop. Grabbing me by the hair, she pulled my face close to
hers, twisting my neck painfully. Her minted breath hissed
onto my cheek. "Say 'goodbye,' sweetheart."

"Bella Donna."

That awful voice echoed from somewhere behind us.
Rabbit fur and tar and malevolence. Donna turned to it
eagerly, slave to the compulsion I fought to block out. Her
face wore a sick mix of blind love, wild joy, and vicious
desire.

Something inside me sank. I might have been able to
bum rush her on her stilettos but against him I could do
nothing. Hope evaporated like warm water on a hot sidewalk.

Cold hands of an unfightable force seized me, tearing
me from Donna's grasp, and I barely had time to register the
look on her face. Rapture. Triumph.

Then it faltered. Incomprehension. Fear.

I was shoved aside, away from Donna, away from
Marek. Landing hard on my knees and elbows, I rolled onto
my side in a crumpled lump. Fresh pain.

Still-Heart, nude except for clinging white leather
pants, stood like a panel of silk and marble. He gripped
Donna's upper arms, standing nose to nose, and his threat
gushed like heat from a burning building.

Babbling a stream of pleading devotion, she ran her
hands over his chest and through his hair, anything she could
reach, oblivious to the hatred pouring out of him. He
stroked her face with one hand, tenderly.

He leaned for a kiss, turning his cheek away from her
mouth and trailing his lips down her throat, eliciting a shud-
dering moan. When they parted, angry ribbons of bright red
dripped down their skin.

He licked his lips, an animal used to taking what he
wanted.

"Goodbye, sweetheart," he said smoothly, then tossed

her to Marek.

Marek sprang from the wall to the limit of his restraints and snatched her. With a roar he tore Donna open and devoured her, sucking greedily at her blood and draining her life.

I couldn't block out the sounds of what he did to her. I curled into a ball and plugged my ears but I still heard what he did to himself when he killed her. The Sophia wept with agony to feel what he did to his soul, shredding it like an unwanted curtain. I howled until my vocal cords ceased to issue sound.

Still-Heart tossed me against the wall and secured my chains. My throat raw, my body battered, I hung. Exhausted. Desolate. Hopeless.

Still-Heart stood a long time, watching Marek settle down, watching me as I slumped and waited. Donna's body lay cast aside like a broken toy, discarded and useless. A puddle of light from a lone torch pooled on the floor beside her body, flickering over her fingers, her perfect manicure.

This night would not end well.

Soft sounds of skittering against stone broke the drone of silence. In the archways blinked the white gleam of vampire eyes, and shadows slid around the edges of the room. The audience grew as the Master's vampires assembled.

Still-Heart entered through an alcove opposite to Marek and the crowd greeted him with a guttural roar. He'd donned a long jacket of pale silk, which he left unbuttoned over his bare chest. Streaks of blood stained his flesh. His vampires reached toward it as if the blood was a relic.

The Master seated himself with great flourish, gazing intently in my direction. I closed my eyes and swallowed hard, dreading the events to come. Where there was an audience, there was usually a show. My situation redefined the words *stage fright.*

Sounds of a struggle began faintly from somewhere outside the hall. I couldn't tell with the acoustics; noise seemed to come from everywhere all at once, like stereo speakers in a torture chamber. Still-Heart raised his head, expectantly, as if he'd heard the approach of a lover. His mouth parted and light gleamed upon his wicked teeth.

Heavy doors to my right swung open, hitting the wall with a massive bang. The shock reverberated through my abused muscles. The struggle spilled into the room and I watched two vamps subdue a black-clad man, grunting as they hauled him toward the front of the room.

Their captive put up an impressive struggle, managing to twist free and strike back several times. The vamps dumped him to the floor and one aimed a hard kick at the captive's side before backing off. The man stayed down, coughing.

Turning his face away, the vampire reached up to his face gingerly, jerking his hand away again. An angry cross-shaped burn marked his cheek and eye. The man must have used a crucifix on the vampire.

A cross! Why didn't I think of that? Damn me and my fashion choices again. What if I'd been wearing the one Jared gave me for my birthday last year? I knew it was blessed because Jared blessed just about everything he could wave his fingers at. Marek told me he didn't mind holy items because they only hurt the Fallen.

Marek did mind, however, who had given it to me. I'd left off the cross for his sake, wearing instead the Blood of Isis amulet he'd given me. I should have put my Crucifix back on when Frank was murdered.

I should never have let a man come between me and my God. *Oh, Jared, I'll never see you again.* As if nothing else this night had been a call for self-pity, I succumbed to useless tears.

The man on the floor groaned and tried to pull himself up, hunching over to favor his ribs. Still-Heart rose ceremoniously from his seat and flowed down the steps toward him, his long open shirt gently blown about by a nonexistent wind, looking like a cross between David Bowie and a Meatloaf video.

It might have been enthralling if I'd let the compulsions take root. Instead, the truth was ugly. Without the glamour, Still-Heart's intent showed plainly, and there was nothing theatrical about it. The monster was real. The threat was real. The ugly truth was real.

The vampire gestured, lifting the man from the ground and drawing him up straight with a cruel compulsion. The man balled his hands into tight fists as if he endured terrible pain, yet he uttered no sound.

Still-Heart circled him, assessing him like a sculpture in a museum. His voice came in layers, the sound of many mouths talking in unison, echoing in my head.

"You believe in sacrifice, don't you?" Still-Heart cocked his head, as if in sympathy. The man didn't answer. "How ironic. You have now become one."

Without looking away, Still-Heart raised a hand and turned his wrist. Silently, a group of his men moved forward, hauling an unresponsive Marek. His head hung between his shoulders like an empty sleeve, arms flagged and toneless. It took the strength of a half-dozen to move Marek and none of them seemed to enjoy the task.

They stopped a few feet away from Still-Heart and dropped him. I flinched, not wanting to see Marek hit the floor.

Marek snapped into sudden action and landed in a taut crouch, balancing on his toes and fingertips, holding himself mere inches above the stone floor, cataleptic no more.

Marek focused on the man who wiped blood from his

brow and looked around at the mocking church-like
fixtures, the watchful vampires lining the walls.

"You are so close, Thurzo," Still-Heart intoned. "Your
soul clings by mere threads. Drink down this life. Consume
the death and sever those threads! Join me, at last!"

The word hissed away into silence, a silence I could no
longer bear. I'd witnessed that man's courage and I would
not hang a silent victim any longer. I could not abide this
injustice.

"No!" My rage spilled up and out. "You will not hurt
that man. Let him go!"

"Sophie?"

A voice called to me, a voice I had so loved to hear, so
deep and sweet and soft in my ears. It didn't come from
Marek, who pulled himself up and reared, anger and aliena-
tion in his crazed eyes. The man in black whirled toward my
direction.

When I heard his voice—when I saw his face—my
courage and strength and resolve failed.

It was Jared.

40

"Sophie?" He turned to seek my voice and saw me bound to the wall behind him. "Sophie! Let her go!"

Still-Heart's expression changed subtly as a layer of exasperation coated his sinister satisfaction. "The human knows her. I should be surprised but, somehow, I am not. Tell me, how? Is she one of your flock, priest?"

"Let her go." Cords of muscle in his neck stood out as he fought against the vampire's invisible restraints. "Only a coward puts a helpless woman in chains."

"Wasted efforts, priest. I will not rise to your insults. Come."

Obedient to the compulsion, Jared shuffled closer, defiance blazing in his eyes.

"Again. What is she? Surely one such as yourself is entitled to divine revelation." Jared remained silent and Still-Heart sighed like a parent with an uncooperative child. "No matter. I shall see for myself."

Seizing Jared's head, Still-Heart looked at him, through him, his gaze unfocused. Jared gritted his teeth, trying not to cry out as the vampire sifted through his mind. With a push he released him. Jared's head flopped.

"Oh!" Still-Heart chuckled and leered at me. "I didn't expect that."

I wondered what truth he could have stolen from Jared's mind. I didn't wonder long.

"You wicked whore. You delicious, wonderfully wicked whore!" He laughed throatily and danced in place. Marek swiveled his head as well, wearing a murderous look. "You did all that? With a priest? Sweet Pain! I truly underestimated your worth!"

My face burned. I never hated anything before in my life the way I hated him.

Jared had closed down, not seeming to register anything the vampire said. What damage did he take, trying to keep our past from Still-Heart?

"I did not do anything with a priest." I seethed, enraged at the way he twisted past and present into scandalous sin. "I'm not depraved."

"We'll see, my newest desire. When your mind lies in tatters and your will is seared away, we'll see what you're capable of doing."

"Leave her alone," said Jared. He sounded sleepy, distracted. "Leave Sophie go, or else."

"Or else what? There's only one thing you're going to do, priest. You will die." Still-Heart backed away with a bow. "Horribly, painfully, agonizingly, at the hands of this beast, who, ironically, was also our dear Sophie's lover."

Still-Heart mounted the steps backwards as Marek advanced, rumbling deep in his throat, a lion warning its prey of its imminent end. "Jealous lover, it seems. Your soul will cleave the skies with the terror of your passing. Your god has forsaken you, priest. Marek will not grant you a peaceful death."

His words trailed off into gloating laughter. Frantically

I called Jared's name and he turned to me, calmly, his mouth silently forming one word.

Infinity.

Marek fell upon him. Bones cracked in Marek's savage grasp.

"No, Marek!" I screamed. This would be a slaughter in the truest sense of the word. My lover would kill my best friend. "Marek! Stop! Don't do this!"

The panic, the horror, the emotional overload ripped away whatever insulation I kept wrapped around the core where Sophia slept. No limits. No barriers. Sophia uncurled itself and drenched my mind in cold honey.

I could feel Jared as clear as crystal. He'd resigned himself to death.

Marek's mind was a tangle of blind rage. He knew blood was near and wanted it. He'd lost all sense of who he was, lost in the maelstrom of the deaths he'd endured at Still-Heart's hands.

I summoned all I'd ever felt for him—my love, my gratitude, my longing to save him, my need to bring him to spiritual safety. I crumpled it together, clumsily flinging it at him like a mental rock. "Marek! Resist him!"

The clumsy rock worked, stunning him. He withdrew from Jared, who fought to hold up his head. His knees buckled and only Marek's grip kept him from crumbling. I couldn't see Jared's face but I knew he still lived. The Sophia sensed his weakened presence, his emotions tangled with bewilderment.

Marek took a step back, shaking his head, holding Jared out at arm's length. "No. I... will... not." His voice was desperate and weary but I felt his iron-clad will behind the words. Marek fought the tide of evolution that threatened to crush him.

Enraged, Still-Heart glided from his dais, the movement much faster and more menacing than footsteps. It reinforced the fact that Still-Heart was a monster, no matter how ethereal he looked. The vampire seized both men and pushed his face close to Marek's, who bowed his head away. "You will. And you will turn, Thurzo. With this death, I command it!"

Jerking Jared's sagging frame toward him, the vampire closed on his wounded throat. The priest's arms jerked once, twice, before falling limp and still.

Sinking to his knees, spine bent and head thrown back, Marek echoed my screams. Jared's limp body hung from the vampire's arms before dropping to the ground. I stretched out with the Sophia and felt only Marek.

Jared was dead. I closed my eyes against hot tears. My fault.

Sudden silence made me wary but I didn't want to see anymore. I cracked my eyes and fought to focus on the slate ceiling.

I didn't want to see the body in black, crumpled on the floor like a used bath towel. I didn't want to see Still-Heart wiping his mouth with the back of his hand like a greedy kid. I didn't want to see Marek regarding me with a new strange interest in his eyes. He sobbed for breath and shook his head as he warred with himself and struggled to keep his soul.

Jared's soul was somewhere safe. Grief would have to wait. For Marek, there were no guarantees. I was the only salvation he had left. I had to focus.

I prayed Jared had died at peace with himself. The chance remained his death wouldn't have changed Marek, wouldn't have given him the energy he needed to evolve. Jared had never been afraid to die. He said *infinity,* whispered it like a protective spell the way he did as a teenager. He remembered. He wasn't afraid.

Please, God, I prayed desperately, spare Marek from his fate. Forgive him. He doesn't know what he's doing.

I'd become the new focus of attention. Everyone watched me, their dead eyes glinting in the uncertain light. The only sound was Still-Heart panting and laughing softly, awash with blood. His stare penetrated me, pushed past my resistance, probed my possibilities.

He watched me but spoke to Marek in a whisper, his voice fluid and hypnotic. "Yes, that's it. I feel it too, what you want. Take her. Finish this."

Marek's eyes flashed as he licked his lips.

"Infinity," I whispered and prayed I'd be brave enough, too.

41

Marek stalked toward me, coldly evaluating me as he approached. Nothing about his eyes looked familiar. There was no restraint in him. He'd plunged past reason. The torture of soul-ripping power buzzed in his head and drowned out thought. The Sophia was still bared, hypersensitive, and the menace of his intentions scourged me.

He didn't know me anymore, despite the nights we shared and the countless ways he'd discovered me. Marek had come to know me better than anyone else, had shared my own skin, had revealed the incredible secrets of my own spirit to me.

And now, he didn't know me.

A hundred memories flashed through my mind, all the times I had felt the danger he held back like a mighty dam. Now, the flood gates were thrown open. No more holding back. As he paced closer, closer, too close, I knew. Fear surged through me like the bite of an electric current, my desperate prayers forgotten.

He dropped onto me like an animal, devoid of reason

and recognition. His arms circled my ribs and crushed me against him. A terrified scream ripped from my throat and he drank it in, smiling, pinning me against the wall. Ragged gasps for air made his chest heave against mine and his heart pounded like a machine.

His face hovered over my body, smelling the blood coating innumerable small hurts. His other hand palmed my forehead, pushing it into the wall hard enough to dim my sight. Lips brushed my throat once and I swallowed his scent, leather and sandalwood, dirt and blood.

His jaws closed on me.

The pain—indescribable. I'd never been bitten before, not even by an animal. His teeth ripped into me, tearing skin and vein, and his mouth worked against the wound. His hair lay between my jaw and his, and he pulled my blood from me with a savage, hungry sound.

Marek used all of his body to hurt me. The pain that responded to the fire of his mouth unstrung my thoughts and pushed me all the way past sanity.

There is nothing seductive about a vampire's kiss. All the books and movies had lied. I fought to escape him, fought to be free of him. I kicked because my legs were the only things that could still move. I fought to get past the pain.

How can you get past so much pain all at once? He's dead, for Chrissakes. I could never get past that.

Marek's hand released my head and slipped up along my arm to my wrist, jerking it free from the manacle, stripping away the skin when the metal didn't yield. His mouth lifted and I cried, begging him for release, begging him to remember me. My other arm slid from its cuff as he used his power to free it, the impossible weight of my hand flopping it over his shoulder.

I struggled to remember my feet and tried to push away.

His eyes were green fire, so much greener now that his cheek and chin were slick with red. The return of his teeth, biting down into the damaged skin, stole my voice. He shook his head like a wolf and pain exploded as the muscles snapped. My head fell back against the wall.

My body sagged in his arms as my life bled into him, my heart beating faster, shallower. Cold. So cold. How could someone forget me after all we'd shared?

He shifted the arm that restrained me, holding me up to his mouth instead of holding me down. My feet left the ground. He used to kiss me like this. Now he killed me.

I'd tried to save him. I failed. Ironically, my death would be the one that turned him into the very thing he tried so hard not to become. I would be his undoing.

I tried to speak but it took several attempts before my voice worked. I reached a cold, tired hand up to cling to him, to the hair that lay across his shoulders, to the touch of tangles, the stiffness of matted blood. Such beauty and grace, ruined. All would end here at my ruined throat where he fed on my dying pulse.

"Marek," I whispered. "I'm sor... please... f'give..." And because I couldn't talk anymore, I put the last of my energy into a single thought of love and regret and pierced him with it.

His tongue slid over my throat before he drew back, a final taste of my essence.

"No." It was a whisper, clear and human-sounding. "Never."

There was a long space between heartbeats where I hung precariously before crashing back to Earth like a broken star. The Sophia fell silent and deaf and slipped away, abandoning me. I was alone in my mind. I struggled to breathe and waited for him to finish me. My consciousness slipped, my body becoming a distant sensation. No light at the end of my tunnel. *Please wait, Jared. I'm lost. Take me with you...*

Marek didn't seize my throat again. He pulled back further, his eyes searching my face. My vision had clouded and his green eyes became headlights in the fog. When he released me I dropped from his grasp, banging against the wall as I crumpled. He loomed high above me and I felt so small, gazing up at the giant who had forgotten me.

My head hit the wall as it drooped back but it didn't hurt. Nothing hurt. I slipped all the way down to the floor, my cheek slapping against the stone. My arms spilled down beside me and I hoped I wouldn't fall off, because I had nothing to hold onto now. The stone was cold and my cheek cooled against it.

Marek approached Still-Heart who sat on the carpeted steps, watching his ambitions bear bloody fruit. He started to applaud slowly, cruel slaps of sound, sliding to his feet to meet Marek at the center of the room.

Unblinkingly, I watched them both. Not that I could blink anyway. The little things I took for granted were slipping from me, one at a time. I saw Marek, washed in crimson. My crimson. My blood. My doing.

"I'm sorry." If I'd made sound, I didn't hear it.

Marek turned to give me a blank stare before disregarding me altogether. He turned to look around at each and every vampire in the room. They had all fallen still and silent as Marek had taken me. Now they watched and waited.

Marek roared. He let his power unfold like great leathery wings. I dimly felt him, silver and green and solid. His eyes flashed a gleam of icy blue and the air hummed with his presence.

Blue eyes. The Sophia's eyes. He had taken something from me and it had made him stronger. It would be my fault if he used it to hurt others.

He pulled it all back, leaving only a chill in its place. As he did so, his appearance changed, like movie magic. The dirt, the blood, his hair's bedraggled appearance all faded, leaving clean smooth perfection in its place. Smooth glossy hair spread out like a veil, perfect white skin on a clean-shaven face. Even his clothes changed, looking cleaner, undamaged. He assumed the same kind of perfection the Master had worn, a layer of illusion.

When he spoke, his voice was forged in steel and no ears could have blocked the sound. "All hail the Master."

As if on cue, everyone dropped to a knee in silent salute. Marek turned slowly, surveying the scene, noting each one with grim satisfaction before once more facing Still-Heart.

The vampire smiled, coldly and triumphantly, folding his arms across his chest and surveying Marek's command over his legions. As he turned back to Marek, however, an indecipherable look glinted across his cruel face.

"What are you waiting for?" Marek's voice was neutral, his tight smile giving the words an amiable disguise. "I said, all hail... me."

He struck like a viper, too fast to follow. One moment the vampire stood and the next he sank to his knees, holding Marek's arm to his chest in a parody of a salute. Marek pulled back violently, leaving Still-Heart on the ground. The Master stared at Marek, disbelief and rage blasting from him like a geyser. Lowering his hands from his chest, he looked down for a long moment at the stream of black sand pouring from a hole in his torso.

Still-Heart fell face forward with a muffled *umph*.

Marek held out the vampire's heart, displaying it to the legions. Disdainfully he tipped his hand to let the heart fall. It hit the ground with a meaty slap. He brushed his fingers together, condescendingly, before crossing his arms over his chest. Challenging. Daring.

The legions sprang to their feet and began stomping, gaining sound and force as they beat a cadence in tribute.

From the back a voice called, "All hail! Thurzo, Downfall of Masters!"

One of the vamps stepped forward, taking a knee before Marek. "What is your command, my Master?"

Marek smiled, triumphant and arrogant and gleaming with dangerous teeth.

"I have but one." Raising his arm, he swept his hand about the room in a gesture that included everyone, before glancing back down at the supplicant before him. "Die. Now."

He swung his arms together and clapped his hands once, sending out a smacking pulse of power that dazed every vamp in the room. They sank to their knees, many holding their heads.

Lucky for me, I was already on the ground. Being mostly dead seemed to have at least one advantage. It couldn't, however, block out the sudden shockwave. It felt much like being in a parking garage where someone had just detonated a bomb.

At the sound of his mighty clap all the doors banged wide open, hitting the walls simultaneously. The hells broke loose as swarms of DV poured in, attacking the still-dazed vampires.

Greco led the demivampire, his cries of vengeance scalding my ears. He was a butcher, driving what looked like hunting knives into every vampire neck within reach. I recognized several other faces from the security forces at Folletti's; even Caen, bloodied and laughing like a demon as he hurt whatever he could reach.

At once Rodrian took Marek's back and the two men, swords in hand, mercilessly cut down every vamp who rushed them. Rodrian, the younger but not lesser. They moved like reflections of each other, echoes dancing.

My eyes drifted closed in relief. Rodrian. He would take care of his brother. I didn't need to hold on anymore. A cold wetness crept along the edge of my cheek where it lay upon the stone floor and I bled away the last beats of my life.

The floor tilted and I cried out, panicked. Wait. The floor became soft and warm and not really floor at all. Someone had lifted me. I cracked my eyes enough to see the face of a strangely familiar stranger.

"Shh." The woman backed out the room carefully. "Nothing like a good diversion."

She moved without taking her eyes off the ones fighting closest to us and bolted to the door. I could feel her spirit as easily as I felt her body's warmth. Her power shone like a sun through copper gauze. She was strong and beautiful, with hazel eyes and hands yearning for a weapon. *Brianda?*

I tried to focus on her face as she sped down a corridor, away from the sounds of fighting and death. Her movements, though careful, rolled my head away so I couldn't see her. *Brianda. She needs to be in there with the fight and the dance and the blade with teeth. . .*

Her eyes were wide with surprise as she set me into another set of arms at the door. "Hurry," she commanded. "She's fading. Do not let her die!"

With a last look that seemed both puzzled and reverent, she sprinted back toward the great hall, drawing a sword from its sheath on her back.

"Unfortunately, this is going to hurt you. Close your eyes," the new stranger said. I couldn't turn my head toward the harsh voice. No matter. I was way ahead of him.

The pain that had been holding me aloft tore like a tissue paper floor. I careened down and out into the beckoning blackness. A few moments of falling, one last regret for the dead, and I finally, gratefully, knew nothing more.

42

I didn't know where I had been.

I remember it only in the vaguest, fuzziest of senses. When I had my wisdom teeth removed in high school, the dentist gave me a shot and told me to count backwards, and the next thing I knew I woke up in the recovery room as if nothing had happened.

This was nothing like that. Wherever I went, I was there forever. And it hurt, everything hurt, the entire time. I struggled to wake but I just kept waking up over and over into the same dream. I never realized I was dreaming but I felt flattened by desperation because I knew I had to get out. I was in Hell.

Then one time, I woke up and knew it was real. I was in bed. I felt boneless and hot and nauseous. Vaguely, I noticed several people in the room. Some I'd seen before, some I hadn't. None of them belonged in my bedroom.

I couldn't feel any of them and I thought I was dead, finally free of whatever made me so aware of these people who weren't people. They spoke in muted tones and water splashed.

Rodrian, keening softly, scooped me up against him.

A harsh voice scolded and he let me sink gently back into the pillow. Cold strange fingers touched my neck, unwrapping a cloth and prodding the flesh. I felt mentally and physically numb and the touch came at me from a distance.

"You're lucky you didn't tear out the stitches," said a harsh voice, vaguely familiar. "There's not enough intact skin to repair it again."

Although it took some effort, I eventually focused my eyesight. Rodrian sat next to me on the bed. His eyes seemed to be on fire and I zeroed in on them, the sharpest thing in sight. They were damp with tears that amplified the glow of his irises, making the flames within them appear to drip.

"Why are you crying?" It hurt to talk and I wondered if I'd been ill.

"Because I thought you left me," he whispered, and wiped his cheek with his sleeve.

His brother would have used a handkerchief. The half-thought confused me but my head hurt too much to think about why. I rolled my eyes toward one of the strangers, the owner of the harsh voice. "Who?"

Rodrian took a deep breath. "Sophie, relax for a moment. I need to remove the compulsion so you can remember."

"Don't do it too fast." The stranger's warning came from somewhere behind Rodrian. "I don't want emotional shock setting in. It can still kill her."

"Who?" My voice, weak but insistent, crackled.

"He's a healer. You'll remember why he's here in a minute."

Rodrian closed his eyes for a moment and held his breath. A curtain in my mind slowly slid back, reuniting me with my memory. All of it. At once.

I never took my eyes from his face as he unraveled the control he'd set on my memory. Maybe I blinked a few times. Rodrian gave me a look of marvel, perhaps thinking how brave and strong I must be. Truth was I felt pretty much dead and I simply didn't have the strength to react.

He smoothed back my hair and spoke softly, explaining that the people in the room were healers and that I'd lost a lot of blood.

"I remember," I said.

"Marek managed to close the... wounds on your..." He brushed unsure fingers at along the edge of the bandage as if he couldn't believe it was there. "If he hadn't..."

Rodrian bit his lower lip, unable to continue.

The harsh voice spoke up and the face of its owner came into view. An older, fair skinned man with short red and grey hair stepped closer to the bed. Dunkan?

He handed Rodrian a cloth, motioning he should place it on my head. "If he hadn't, you would have bled out completely. I've never brought back a human who was so close to death before. You're as close to a miracle as I've ever come and I do some pretty miraculous work."

"Indeed." Rodrian smiled up at him. "Your gifts are much appreciated, Pontian."

Appearing mollified, the older man gestured to the other people in the room and they left. Rodrian fixed the cloth upon my head, coolness against the heat burning from within.

"Rode." The dryness in my throat splintered my voice into a fit of coughing. He produced a cup of water and pressed the straw to my lips. I couldn't bear the pain past a few small swallows but the water helped. "What else happened?"

"What do you mean?"

My voice shrank. "Jared."

"Ah. You know he..."

"Yeah." I didn't want him to say the word. It would only make it true.

"We recovered him. Pontian... erased... some of the outward damage and set wards on his body to hide the cause of death. We returned him to his rooms, where someone 'discovered' he died in his sleep from a failed heart."

I pressed trembling lips together. Jared, whose heart had been strongest of all. His heart never would have failed.

He was in the ground before I'd even opened my eyes. "He was seen to, Sophie. I knew how much he meant to you. I took care of everything myself. Please, don't ever doubt that."

I tried to smile but it felt shallow. "Thanks, Rode. I needed to hear that."

He squeezed my hand and rearranged the cloth, powerless to do anything to help.

"Marek? Is he coming soon?"

"Oh..." Rodrian looked at the wall over my head and fresh tears welled in his eyes. He took three deep breaths before getting the words out. "His survival was as dubious as your own. He left instructions for your care and withdrew from us. He's gone."

His quiet voice held massive disbelief, betraying his confusion and pain. Even in my sorry state, my heart and will couldn't leave him to suffer alone. I closed my eyes and reached out for him with tired mental fingers, wanting to ease his pain.

I met cold resistance. My eyes flew open as I sought the source of the block.

Pontian stepped over to the bedside. "I'm sorry, Sophia. I can hear what you're thinking so I know what you're trying to do. You're weak and I cannot allow you access to your gift until I know it won't kill you. I've got your veins filled with volumizer to keep your heart pumping. The exertion of using your gift could cause your body to shut down."

"My gift? I don't understand."

"Your gift." He sounded a trifle annoyed he had to explain. "It's the ability to feel. Empathy. It's what makes you aware of us. It's what brings the Sophia. And it is tied to your blood, the same as our gifts."

I stared at him. "You knew? Why didn't someone explain this before?"

"Not everyone understands their own gifts, let alone the Sophia's."

"But you knew," I accused.

"Yes, because as a healer I get into people's bodies. I know how things work, which is why I can fix them when they break."

"Why couldn't you have told someone?"

"No one ever asked me. And I'm kept rather busy tending to this lot."

Nice bedside manner, I thought.

"Do you want manners or miracles?" He shrugged and left the room.

Rodrian had a pensive look on his face and seemed preoccupied with the way the blankets had been folded. "I didn't know."

I closed my eyes. "It doesn't matter. I don't want it back. Marek is gone."

"Sophie, you can't give up."

"I can't?" I cried but no tears came. My body couldn't spare them. "Why not?"

"Because I need you." He leaned over me, holding me again, careful this time not to disturb my head. His shoulders began to shake and I slid my hands around his neck, pressing him to me, utterly helpless to heal his pain.

We cried together before I slipped back under.

❦ ❦

When next I dreamed, I knew I dreamed.

I woke into the dream, sitting up. My neck hurt but it was merely a hint of pain, muted by the sleep that held my true consciousness down. Peering into the darkness I sought the cause of my abrupt alarm and found it. Standing at the foot of my bed was Marek.

Marek wore the darkness the way a portrait wore its paint. His loose hair fell over his shoulders and melted like a veil onto his black overcoat, giving him the appearance of a weeping monument, grey and bleak. His eyes, misty green energy, were the only flash of color in this room of shadow.

I leaned and reached for the light at my bedside, unable to take my eyes from him. Fumbling for the switch, I missed the lamp altogether and almost crashed onto the floor. He caught me and set me back gently against my pillow without turning on the light, lingering but a moment before retreating.

Although I couldn't feel him or his power, I remembered what had happened the last time he touched me. I cringed. If I cried for help, would someone wake me?

His voice was a deep whisper inside my head. *I cannot stay long. I will not have them know I was here, and I cannot abide seeing what I have done to you.*

Have you come to finish me?

I need your forgiveness.

I need you here with me, my heart and mind cried. *I need us back the way we were.*

I cannot be. He turned away and his long jacket whirled around him, as if a slow-motion breeze played with the fabric. *I am of this place no longer.*

He melted toward the open windows. The curtains swayed gently, reaching out to him with beckoning arms. *I was right about you all this while. You will always be with me. In my mind. In my heart. And, though it is to be my greatest grief, in my veins. Forever.*

Marek bowed his head, the glare of the streetlight making his outline a sharp contrast of light and dark.

I am sorry, Sophie. I loved you so much. Forget me, now. I will not taint you with mine own damnation.

The curtain billowed out, enveloping him and drawing him into the night. His voice faded into the sounds of wind. Tears, hot and wet and devoid of color, pushed me back onto the pillows. I surrendered to the shadows of sleep before I drowned.

43

I woke easily into the late morning sunlight and stretched, weary but awake. Reaching up, I rubbed my bare throat. No bandages.

Hmm. I must have overslept. Crazy dream.

Swinging my legs over the edge of the bed, I pushed to my feet and headed toward the bathroom, intending to heed nature's call. Instead, I flopped flat on my face onto the floor. I banged my knees and my elbows and the shock was almost as loud as the noise.

The bedroom door flew open and Dahlia rushed in, helping me to my feet, scolding me and coddling me at the same time. She helped me across the hall and onto the toilet, all the while talking, talking, talking.

All I heard was a voice in my head repeating itself. It was real. Not a dream. It was real.

She hovered over me, trying to avoid stepping on my feet or falling into my lap. Really, my bathroom was too small for more than one person. "You okay? You won't fall off the toilet?"

"I don't think so." My pride wouldn't allow for it. Bad enough she half-carried me while I was clad in a tee shirt and underwear. Self-esteem dropped another three percentage points because she even asked.

"Can you stand a bath?" Her voice held more tact than I'd have liked. "Because you really need one."

Okay, four points. I screwed my eyes up at her. "Thanks, Dally."

"No offense. I'll get the water started if you think you won't drown."

"I'm not ready to die yet."

"I didn't think so," she said with a grin. "But we'll skip the bubble bath just in case. It makes resuscitation a bitch."

Twenty minutes later, I soaked in the tub with the curtain half drawn. She insisted on being able to see my head from her watchful perch on the sink.

Dahlia filled me in on what had happened in my life while I'd slept through it. Posing as a cousin, she'd taken care of my affairs while I was ill. She called me off work, using the excuse I needed time off for a funeral.

"There's a load of flowers from your friends at work. Wait 'til you see the living room. You'll think it's a flower convention out there."

"How long have I been out of it?" I tried to talk around my toothbrush. The taste in my mouth had been overwhelming. Dahlia agreed it was too risky standing in front of the sink so she gave me a cup to spit in and let me brush my teeth in the tub.

Dahlia gave me a careful look as she replied. "Four days."

"Oh." I didn't know what to say. I never lost four days before. "Anything good come in the mail?"

Eventually I was dressed and propped up on the couch. She hadn't exaggerated; my living room had become a hot house. Fraidy curled on the table under a canopy of petals and leaves, peering out like the jungle cat he often pretended to be.

"I'll pour a dose of treatment," she said. Dahlia brought me something to drink and disappeared into my room.

I stared at the glass of ugly she'd left on the coffee table. She must have been mistaken. I mean, it was foul. Green and chunky. I doubted it was even liquid. If the muck had farted at me, I wouldn't have been the least bit surprised.

I still eyed the glass with suspicion when she emerged from my room, holding an armload of bedclothes. Her eyes lit with accusation. "You didn't drink it."

"Hell, no. That's not meant to be drunk." I pointed a finger at the offending glass. "That looks like it would take off paint."

"Doesn't matter. It's revitalizer. Pontian said you have to drink three glasses a day once you wake up. You stayed asleep longer than he expected."

I remembered Pontian. I didn't want him to show up and force it down my throat himself, as charming as he was. I sighed, defeated. "Can I have a cup of coffee, first?"

She winced, looking apologetic. "Nope. Sorry. No coffee. Pontian said it would chase out the stuff he filled your veins with. I mean, you don't even smell like real blood anymore."

I suppressed a big *ew.* "Didn't know I ever smelled like blood to begin with."

She smiled, almost wistfully. "Yeah, you did. It was nice. Sweet, like smoked apples. Now your blood is so thin, you smell like KY or something. Bland. Boring. Blah."

"Explains why I feel so blah."

She left the apartment with my bed sheets, taking them either to the laundry room or the dumpster. I chuckled weakly. Maybe it was the insane laughter of a broken woman but, hey, a laugh was a laugh. Beggars couldn't be choosers.

As the door slammed shut behind her, I reached determinedly for the glass of Mr. Yuck and almost took a sip. "Do it," I scolded myself. "Do it or you'll die and they'll send even more flowers and the cat will go feral."

I sat on the couch, alone for presumably the first time in four days, bewildered by the forest of flowers surrounding me. All I could think is, why? Why any of it? The flowers were meant to console me in the death of someone I loved. Which one? And why both?

"Damn it!" I punched the cushions next to me, desperate for something to throw. "Why both? Why does God do this? Why did He take my everything, again?"

I wept, my throat tight with the things I couldn't bear to remember. Now was the time when I needed answers and the Sophia was nowhere to be found. Exhaustion arrived promptly. I fell asleep where I sat before Dahlia returned, the glass of grime untouched. So much for trying to get better.

Truth was, I kind of felt like dying, anyway.

Dahlia was a true champ. She completely ran my business until I recovered enough to care for myself. I probably would have died if she wasn't there to make sure I drank the revitalizer she prepared. It was evil brew and must have had spinach in it for both color and flavor. Donna used to drink this slime at work, vamp slut that she was. No wonder she'd been such a bitch.

At any rate, my anemia rapidly improved. I got out of bed the day after I woke up, and felt back to rights within the week. Not bad, considering I had come through the fight with barely enough blood to register a measurable blood pressure.

I didn't see much of anyone except for Dahlia and,

occasionally, Shiloh. I got the impression she was being discouraged from coming over. In typical teenage fashion she rebelled and came over anyway. Seeing her flopped on the couch with take-out containers all over the coffee table gave a semblance to normalcy I desperately needed. It kept my mind off the salve on my neck and the itchy scab on my chest.

Dahlia made it clear from the beginning—she knew nothing about Marek. She wouldn't bring Rodrian over so I could pester him, either. The only thing she'd tell me was there was a tremendous upheaval in the business sector that was both vamp- and DV-managed. Rodrian had his hands full.

It was even harder to ask Shiloh about Marek. Her dad was going through hell. I couldn't help myself and I hounded her anyway. In retrospect, I know I acted like a selfish little shit because all I could think about was finding Marek. I didn't make room for anything else. It didn't matter what anyone else felt. Just me. The girls did what they could to redirect me toward productive things and honestly, I did try. I just sucked at it.

When I found I could climb up the stairs of the apartment building without rolling back down, I told Dahlia I'd be okay on my own. She protested, saying Rodrian would kill her, but I insisted I needed my space.

So did Euphrates. He didn't freak out at Dahlia the way he always had around Marek but his fur constantly stood on end, making him look about twenty pounds heavier. The cat would have a stroke if he didn't relax.

Reluctantly, she conceded after negotiating a once weekly visit to check on me and to bring more revitalizer. It was as good as I'd get and I didn't mind much, after all. Dahlia had become a good friend and I got the feeling she genuinely cared about me. I'd miss her if she left all together.

I needed time to put everything together. When

Dahlia was satisfied I could survive on my own and Shiloh decided the fun of rebellion wasn't worth listening to me whine anymore, I got my wish. I got my space.

Trouble was, once I was finally alone, I had no idea where to turn.

Except to trouble.

Pontian made a brief stop by my place the same day Dahlia packed her overnight bag. If I didn't know better, I'd swear he was stalking me. One minute I'm turning on Soap Net and the next he's standing next to the couch, leaning over me. He extended one hand to press the center of my forehead.

A fullness spread like thick fog through my skull, a familiarity, an opening of my senses.

"My Soph—" I started to ask but he cut me off.

"Of course. How else can you take care of yourself?"

Before I could formulate a proper retort he vanished. I sighed and rewound the forty seconds of *Days of Our Lives* that I'd missed.

With Dahlia gone, I called Barbara and asked permission to use the vacation time I'd accumulated. I kept a reserve of column letters so Barbara had more than enough material to cover my absence. It was only two weeks but it was two weeks longer. I could pretend. I could avoid. I could hide two weeks longer. And I could search for him.

Folletti's had been sold to a tycoon from New Mexico who wanted to establish a foothold in our city before the gambling vote. A little research determined the business was completely non-DV. I made one brief trip there. The wards, the bright eyes, the porcelain sugar bowl... all gone.

One night Dahlia raved about a new club down at the waterfront. *The Mag* had published a review on the place about two months earlier when it fell under new management. I had a pretty good idea who I'd find running the joint.

Dahlia wasn't good at keeping her feelings a secret from me. I felt guilty about not cluing Dalia in about my ability to read DV emotions. Apparently my gift wasn't widespread knowledge. Of course Rodrian knew, and Marek had known, and Pontian acted like he put it there in the first place. But outside my intimate circle, no one else knew.

I wouldn't show all my aces again, even if it meant not telling someone as close as Dahlia. I needed the extra information it allowed me to pick up from time to time, and when she mentioned the club, it was no exception. I gleaned what I could, deduced the rest, and made my plans.

I got dressed up and went out hunting.

The moment I walked in, every nose in the room caught a whiff of me. Each step was weighted by their eyes although I never caught anyone looking in my direction. There may as well have been a spotlight on me when I sat at the bar. Each second that ticked by meant greater danger. I was smart enough to realize it, yet too stupid to leave.

A familiar face appeared at the end of the bar and I gulped a large mouthful of Cosmopolitan. Rodrian leaned his head toward the bartender but locked eyes with me, nodding at whatever the barkeep told him before making a beeline to my stool.

I stirred my drink and met his gaze, dismayed to see his expression so far from hospitable.

Casually, he smiled around at the other patrons and subtly stroked his jaw before brushing the back of my neck. He turned to look down at me in an extremely patronizing way.

The signal to the demivamps was unmistakable. His mouth, my neck: he claimed me. The oppressive stares diminished and I exhaled with relief as the weight and the threat lifted.

Still smiling, he faced me but his eyes watched the crowd. His stern voice didn't match his expression. "You are leaving now, Sophia. You don't belong here."

"I belong with Marek." I said it with such force, I surprised myself.

It surprised him, as well, and he shifted his gaze to me. "You don't know him anymore."

"I'm the one who should decide."

"Sophie..." Rodrian's expression softened. "I won't embarrass you. I respect you too much. Finish your drink and leave. I've done what I can to protect you tonight but don't come back. Next time, you will be prey."

I took a deep breath and stood to face him. Thank God I wore heels; our faces were almost level. At least I didn't look like a seven-year-old staring up at her dad in defiance. "I am not prey. I am the Sophia. You will remember that."

My bluff worked. His gaze dropped in reverence but I wasn't sure it would last long. "I want to see Marek. If he tells me to leave, fine."

But he won't, I finished silently. I know he won't.

"Your efforts are in vain. Marek is not here." Rodrian blinked three or four times but I didn't need to see it. I was familiar with the taste of his power so I could tell when he lied. I'd spent plenty of time sitting in on his and Marek's debates. Knowing how each of them felt and hearing what they actually said was entertaining at times.

I reached up and grasped his arm, my sudden touch making him flinch. "Rodrian. I'm not stupid. You're full of shit and you never could lie to me."

"Gods, Soph, you just don't quit." He turn away from the crowd and slumped slightly as he rested his elbows on the bar. The veil of authority he'd been wearing slipped and my old friend, my Rode, shone through briefly. I slid back down onto the stool and for a moment we were friends, commiserating at a bar. "I don't want you to get hurt."

Could I be hurt any more than I'd already been? I held my tongue and sipped at my drink, waiting for him to give in.

Sighing, he straightened and shrugged his suit jacket back into place, another eloquent move that painfully reminded me of his brother. Resuming his mask, he made a quick jerk with his head. "Come with me. But I did warn you."

He turned and walked toward the end of the bar where I'd first seen him. I followed obediently, tugged along in his wake. I wanted to kick him. He didn't need to add a compulsion.

Bossy jerk, that Rodrian.

He led me through a door at the shadowed end of the bar and we entered the private management side of the building. As the door closed, the lights and the sounds of the club snapped off.

So did my bravery. The sudden loss of light and sound tossed me into a cold pool of alarm, and although his compulsion pulled me along, I stumbled.

"Stay with me," Rodrian said. "You don't want to get lost."

I made a pissy face at what I guessed was his back. I

couldn't scratch my ass if I wanted. His compulsion was too strong.

I couldn't kick him, either. Stupid compulsions. I followed him through the unlit area; Rodrian moved unerringly in the dark while I drifted dutifully behind like a good little Sophia.

If it weren't for the compulsion, I wouldn't have budged a step. I didn't like the dark, period, and the wards promised awful things would befall me should I wander off on my own. The effective security measure kept nosy humans from snooping. My breaths became shallow flutters, a mouse hiding from the kestrel. The palpable darkness pressed against the edges of my awareness like the filmy air current near a wall, hovering a constant inch from my face.

Claustrophobia to the nth degree.

I heard a door close behind us and dim lights revealed a small square antechamber. No wards. I breathed deep, the imaginary too-tight corset feeling gone. Rodrian paused before a large heavy-looking door but didn't open it.

"Are you sure you want to do this?" His voice was hushed but tinged with concern.

"Do I look unsure?"

"I don't want you to get hurt."

"Why? Does he beat up girls, now?"

He looked like he wanted to shake me. "Not that kind of hurt."

"Rodrian." I deliberately used his full name, swallowing the metallic taste that our traverse in the dark had left behind. I shouldn't have had that Cosmo. "Try me."

He lifted his fist and rapped twice. I discerned no sound or signal but after a moment he opened the door and motioned for me to enter. He closed his eyes as I passed.

I presumed it was Rodrian's office. First thing I noticed was a big black desk, tell-tale portfolios stacked on the edge. Second thing I noticed was Marek. He should have been the first.

He stood behind the desk, the chair against the backs of his legs as if he'd risen in a hurry. I almost ran to him but at a single glance from him I stopped. Something was wrong.

Marek looked exactly as I remembered. His hair, glossy and smooth in its silken tail. His stance, aggressive and imposing, arms crossed, chin lowered like a bull moments before the charge. His eyes, green cream rimmed with lush black lashes. Everything on the outside looked exactly the same.

On a deeper level, I knew he wasn't Marek. A stranger wore his shell.

Confused, I glanced back at Rodrian, whose eyes were trained firmly on the floor. Deference? Regret? Fear?

A chill radiated from Marek, a chill laced with threat and loaded with danger. Coldness seeped from him like a frosty command. I gaped, unable to connect what I saw and what I felt.

Marek stared back, his gaze running over me briefly, hungrily. His mouth twitched in an uncomfortable smile that never reached his eyes. He discarded the failed smile and his face lost all expression.

"Hello, Sophie." His voice had become so much more than mere sound. It carried on a discreet wave of power. It reminded me of something else. Something bad. The thought slipped away before I could think it down.

My voice stalled. I fanned my fingers in a tiny wave.

Marek titled his head. "Enjoying the club?"

I cleared my throat. "Not really."

"Then why did you come here?"

I didn't have an answer. Faced with a stranger, I wondered if coming here was a mistake.

Marek nodded. He'd heard my thought.

"Leave us." His eyes flicked toward his brother.

Rodrian slipped out, leaving me alone with a big desk and a man who felt as warm as the marble paperweight sitting upon it. Marek sealed himself behind his impenetrable wall of impersonal power. I couldn't feel him anymore and he was barely seven feet away from me.

"This is no place for you." He delivered the flat remark like a slap on the face.

My cheeks burned as if the blow had been physical. "Oh. I see. You're finished with me." I wouldn't cry, damn it. Angry was easier. "I outlived my usefulness. Is that it?"

"Sophie—"

"No, Marek. I'm a person. With feelings. I went through a hell of a lot with you. How could you just leave me? I would have given you my soul."

"Keep your soul. What need have I for it?" Chill became ice and his eyes glittered with hardness. I realized I'd said the wrong thing. He drew himself up, crossing his arms and assuming a stubborn stance. His eyes brimmed with challenge, leaving no room for kindness.

Ashamed, I lowered my eyes, feeling them sting.

But I'd heard something in his reproach, something that didn't fit. I pushed aside my humiliation and evaluated what lay behind those callous words. Now that I couldn't sense him, I could only listen and interpret. What was the heat behind the coldness?

Pain, my inner voice insisted. My compassion unfolded and the Sophia stretched, sending mental fingers to explore the sensation. He was in pain.

Marek turned his head, exhaling sharply through his nose.

His pain beckoned even though his demeanor pushed me away. I'd become a liability, a weakness to his new strength. The part of him that loved me was a chink in his armor. I knew it with my heart, even without the touch of his power to confirm it.

"Marek?" I whispered his name and dared to raise my eyes. Even so softly spoken, the sound of his name made him flinch as if stung by an insect.

I hadn't seen him since the night he overthrew the Master, half-crazed with blood lust and the pains of forced evolution. Not since the night he held me down, tore out my throat, and meant to ride the waves of my death toward some mistaken destiny.

I drew closer, hesitant half-steps, straining past the compulsions he slammed into me as if he sandbagged against a flood. A motionless Goliath, cast in marble, he threw his power at me in warning to stay away.

I'd never been afraid of him, not even the night he consumed me, destroyed me, nearly killed me. I was terrified now. I wasn't sure what this stranger might do. I didn't want to do this anymore but I still had to.

I wasn't sure he'd let me live if I did this but I couldn't live with myself if I didn't. I stopped short of pressing against him and reached up to cradle his face. The chill of his skin melted into warmth beneath my touch, a reluctant thawing, and suddenly the warnings ceased.

My touch opened a gate inside him and his anguish rushed toward me. A single tear welled and hung for the briefest moment upon his lashes, a suspended jewel, before it fell.

"Oh, Sophie," he whispered and drowned me in the depths of his gaze.

I swam through the despair that threatened to pull me under and I willed him to open up to me. I needed to heal his pain. The part of me that did such miraculous things awoke within me, ready to do whatever was necessary. Determined, I silently begged him to let me in. Nearly there. So close.

He pulled my hands away, and his walls sprang up again, locking me out. His voice sounded jagged and strained as if he forced himself to do something painful. "You must leave. Do not return. I'm not the man you knew. You cannot be near me."

His voice ceased but I heard his insistent mental whisper: *What we shared is over.*

I refused to accept it. I did not come this far, though more emotional and physical trial than a hundred women should have to bear, to be simply shut out by a stubborn man.

"Come back to me, Marek. Come back to the way you were." I would have begged on my knees were I not held fast by his hands, hands that once caressed me. "Find your true self. Let me find it with you."

"This is my true self, Sophia." Releasing my hands, he stepped back, increasing the distance between us. I felt the wordless threat he'd emitted countless times in the past. Now he directed it at me. I knew I wasn't safe from it anymore. "I have evolved past our life together. That Marek is dead."

"You gave up."

"I did not give up. I am obeying my nature."

My hope faded as his words struck home. The chill he radiated soaked into me, the killing frost of hope.

He must have evolved or gotten so close to the edge it didn't matter anymore. His nature had changed. The part that still loved me was a tiny voice against a cacophony of new power.

Marek was destined to fight. He'd been a warrior long before I'd been born, and would be long after I returned to dust. If loving me were a weakness, he'd fight that, too. All we had, all he helped me realize about myself, all he encouraged me to dream would one day be—all of it, gone.

It is over. He bored the thought into me like a drill, cracking my determined resolve to fix him. Fix us—

The realization staggered me, leaving my soul bare and

raw and wide-open. It hurt to swallow. It hurt to breathe. It hurt to exist.

Grief stole up beside me like a phantom, wrapped its suffocating arms around me. Grief, deep and warm and dark, swallowed me, took the world away, pulled me down and buried me. Grief poured into me like liquid, so much more than the vessel of my soul could hold. I struggled to breathe and every breath only brought more anguish. My head swam and I swayed.

I fought for control. I refused to look weak in front of him. Grief fell like rain, drenching me in torrents of pain.

I swallowed it down, pushed it into a place where it couldn't cripple me, packed it away. The anguish wouldn't all fit but enough did for now. The room came back into focus and I stared at the carpet, unsure where else to look. I couldn't bear to look at Marek, not now. Now I knew the source of his pain. He hated himself for loving me.

He strode past, the breeze of his passing rustling my skirt. I didn't hear him leave. My heart made too much noise as it shattered.

Rodrian reappeared, pressing hesitant fingers to my elbow. "Sophie, I..."

Him, I could feel. The pity of his affection made me angry and sick. I thrust the palm of my hand between his face and mine, cutting him off, not wanting to hear a single word. I didn't want a reason to blame him for what just happened.

He hitched his breath and bit his lip but didn't protest, only turned without a sound to lead me out. I submitted numbly to his silent compulsion. I wanted to scream but I couldn't draw enough air. It was all tangled up in my chest in a sob that fought to escape.

Rodrian led me to a private exit, sparing me the return trip through the club. At the door, he pushed it open, leaning to kiss me on the forehead before showing me out, lifting his compulsion as I passed him.

"Be careful, Sophie," he whispered. "Live long."

Without a word, I stumbled down the steps and hurried toward the main street. Cabs lined the street, waiting for fares, but I ignored them. My feet banged out an automatic pace, sidewalk after sidewalk, block after block, one foot in front of the other.

I walked home, wondering if the pieces of my life would still be lying where I'd left them. Wondering if they'd even fit me anymore.

45

I forced myself to survive.

It was like when I quit smoking. I'd quit and failed maybe a dozen times since my first cigarette. Trouble was I loved smoking. Loved it, loved it, loved it. Loved the taste, loved the drag, loved to chuff out the smoke in a big beautiful menthol-flavored cloud. Poison? Sure! Would it kill me? Sure! Loved it anyway.

I didn't want to quit. But it was something I had to do if I wanted to survive. At least that was what my doctor said. The last time I quit, I had an epiphany. I realized it was something I had to work at every day. Every morning I needed to wake up and quit all over again. Eventually the physical craving and dependency subsided, as I knew they would. It just took time.

The mental addiction, however, was always there. It always would be. One smoke would be the first of a boatload. Therefore, I'd learned to quit every day. It sucked, because I never stopped wanting a cigarette.

I did the same thing with Marek. That was how I

survived.

Eventually, I ceased to feel the ghost of his touch on my skin. I became accustomed to the feel of only my presence in the room, to walking under the blind stars alone, my jacket the only thing between the evening chill and my bare skin. However, the mental addiction to him was always there. It always would be.

I learned to quit Marek every day. It sucked, because I never stopped wanting him.

Time eventually ran out on me and it was time to go back to living. I didn't have a good enough excuse for hiding anymore. Best friends died. Lovers left. I needed to deal with it and move on. Everyone else did.

So, I did what every red-blooded, emotionally crippled, physically tortured, American woman did after she'd been abducted, forced to watch her best friend's death, and nearly eaten by her ex-lover. I went back to work.

Hey, the rent didn't pay itself.

When I returned to the office, my co-workers greeted me like a prodigal child and Barbara kept me in her office until lunch. She was never one to blatantly gossip so it took her all morning to subtly fill me in on the latest office dirt.

It only took me two seconds to announce I'd broken up with Marek. Weird, to be on the listening side of a conversation.

When she realized no more info was forthcoming, she switched to juicier topics. "And Donna—I just can't get over that mess with her."

I wagged my head and played clueless, rubbing at a nonexistent spot on my pants, and dreaded the sound of the truth. "Did you hear from her yet?"

"No. Just—nothing. She was such a professional. I expected more from her, more than quitting—no notice, no goodbye, nothing. When Amanda cleaned out her desk, she found this. I thought you should know."

She pushed an envelope toward me, a letter addressed to the column.

It was one of Patrick's. I chewed my lips, keeping back everything I wanted to say and offered a simple "Bitch."

Barbara's indignation was tinged with disappointment. "Just wait until she calls for a reference. No matter how they leave, they always call for a reference."

I headed back to my desk, intending to spend the next two hours reading mail in my cube. Still so strange to be at the office and not have to duck a single barb from Donna. Three letters into the pile, I felt a dull thud of shock.

Dear Sophia, it began.

Sophia. No one ever addressed a letter like that because the column was called "Sincerely Sophie." I dropped the letter on the desk in disbelief. One of the demivampire had used my column as a way to petition me.

I shuffled through the stack. Out of roughly forty letters, nearly a quarter of them began *Dear Sophia.* I checked the return addresses on the envelopes. All different. I logged on and Switchboarded the addresses—all businesses, no personal names.

I recognized a few of the business names from Rodrian's discussions and assumed the rest. The demivamps still thought I was the Sophia. I guessed they never got Marek's memo saying I'd been fired.

I penned a brief, polite letter citing my retirement, thanked them for their interest, and photocopied a thick stack. Although it consumed more time than I wanted to spend, I stuffed the envelopes myself, dropping them in the outbound mailbox on my way out the door. I ended up leaving around the same time as everyone else.

How about that? I'd actually put a full day in at the office.

I figured it would take a week for the letters to reach

their destinations and for the message to sink in. However, a month passed and still the Sophia letters arrived. I even received a formal invitation to a luncheon hosted by one of the Councilmen who'd been at my coming-out party, after which a serious discussion was planned.

The DV showed every intention of continuing to use me.

I was damned tired of being used.

I went out later than usual one night, my hair piled high and my neck shockingly exposed. Only the faintest of scars remained, a myriad of jagged lines streaking my throat like the moonscape. You could only see them if you got close and looked in the right light.

Personally, I could find them in the dark. They were the first thing I saw every time I passed a mirror.

I took a cab to the waterfront, where I knew of several DV businesses. Rodrian's new club was three blocks over, and one of the DV who'd written to the column used the address of a microbrewery on the corner. I marched determinedly up the street. My black pinstripe pantsuit was conservative enough for church but I felt like a whole new kind of whore. I wanted someone to look at me, lots of someones.

Lots of the right kind of someones.

I stopped the first pair of bright eyes I encountered with a look and told him to have Rodrian contact me.

The owner of those eyes barely acknowledged me at first. We were two people passing on a city street. He'd tried to slip me a compulsion at the sight of my slender throat; I supposed it was too tempting to pass up. When he saw the scars and their obvious implication, his inner light flared up, causing a cerulean bloom to spill into his irises.

At the mention of Rodrian's name he pulled back, locked down, and hurried past.

I smiled without humor, knowing my message would

travel quickly.

I gave my message to every pair of bright eyes I met, speaking to five or six people before catching another cab. I slumped in the seat for the entire ride home, exhausted in the wake of the adrenaline rush.

Overkill Sophie, that's me. It's not done if it's not done to death.

Sure enough, after midnight a few nights later, as I sat on the couch under the windows by the fire escape I heard a tap on the thin pane of glass. Of course, he wouldn't knock on the door like a normal person.

I knelt on the cushions and pushed up the stubborn sash, leaning my elbows on the sill. Rodrian crouched on the metal landing, his coat blending in with the cloak of night.

"Forgive me, Rode, if I don't invite you in for a drink."

"As tempting as it might be..." He eyed my pajamas, the corner of his mouth curling as he lifted his chin for a better view. "I would not come in for one."

I tugged my robe closed and took a deep breath. "I want my memory altered. Erased. I'm too screwed up to go on like this."

Rodrian said nothing. He simply shook his head.

I threw my pen at him and it clattered away to the ground. "Why not?"

Rodrian spoke with low gentle tones as if I were a child. "Sophie, you don't want your memory altered. You want your feelings to stop hurting."

Those simple words crushed me. I felt so tiny, so worthless. I spent months denying everything that happened.

Jared is dead. Marek is gone. I'm alone.

Despair opened its gaping jaws and swallowed me

whole. My hard-pressed veneer of control and strength dissolved and I burst into tears.

Rodrian grasped my hands and drew me out onto the landing. He pulled me under his coat, into his warmth. I huddled against him and his presence surrounded me. That special touch emphasized how alone I'd been. Encircling me with his arms, Rodrian rested his head upon mine and let me cry.

"Shh, little sister, shh." Rocking me gently, he whispered into my hair. He hurt because he knew I hurt, and he tried to comfort me as I'd once comforted him. "You were never meant for such pain, not when you ease it in so many. He doesn't wish for you to suffer."

I knuckled my eyes and hitched my breath. "Then take it away, Rode. Please."

"Not I, Sophie. I cannot do it. And he will not do it."

"But why? What have I done?"

"That's the irony, little love. You've done so much for him, even while you've been apart. You're a value to him. He cannot be with you, Sophie, but he watches. He stays away for fear he'll harm you, yet he protects you from uncounted and unseen dangers. He's been changed in terrible ways but you help him cling to all he can of his former self."

Rodrian cupped my face and peered deeply into my eyes. "A lesser person would have evolved. You make him fight, Sophie. You keep him from being damned. When you confronted him at the club, you were brave enough to risk pain and rejection, even death. And you did something amazing."

His eyes glowed with remembered joy and I delighted to see the hazel sparks, gleaming like molten bronze. I'd missed his bright eyes and seeing them made something ache inside, a fist around my heart.

"You siphoned away his pain, his grief," he whispered. "You removed something that corroded him. Just as you saved me the day I told you about my son. Pain and anger kill the soul, Sophie. You help to protect him... from himself."

He pressed a tender kiss upon my forehead and dark waves of hair fell loose from behind his ear, slipping past my cheek. "Can you understand, then? You must remember him, his name, even if you must remember the pain. If you are relieved of his memory, he loses you completely. He'd be lost without you to anchor him."

Rodrian pulled me to his chest for a tight embrace before releasing me.

"I'm sorry to ask you to pay such a terrible price, Sophie." He wiped the last of my tears away, blinking back a gleam of his own. "But I ask, nonetheless."

"I'm done," I whispered. "I don't think I can love again."

Chuckling ruefully, Rodrian turned to leave. "Just as well. Should any man dare come near you, Marek would eat him alive."

He raised his fingers to his lips, holding them out toward me in a noble farewell. In a flash of overcoat, Rodrian vanished into the darkness, leaving me to ponder my fate.

When the tax legislation had been passed (in the dead of night, attached to some three-paragraph piece of nonsense, and right before the House went on break, no less) several businesses began to change as if overnight.

My building went up for sale; I guessed the tax hike had already begun to hurt people. One afternoon I came home and saw men in suits touring the property. By the taste of their power, they knew exactly who I was. I hit Craigslist soon after.

The neighborhood had changed. The neighbors had changed. Too many new faces suddenly hanging around. Too many pulses of unfamiliar power. Too many things I was afraid to encounter after dark.

My new strengths emphasized my old fears and old weaknesses. Too many things for a Sophia to feel as she lay awake night after night after sleepless night.

Plus, I needed a change, right? I wasn't the same person anymore. I was still alone, true—but, like a flash in an otherwise starless night, I had known someone. I'd loved someone. I might be surrounded by empty darkness again but I wasn't lost. Maybe Marek didn't want me but he needed me. I'd find a way to save him. It was my destiny as Sophia.

I thought of the boxes and the flights of steps down which I'd be carrying them and sighed, wishing that being Sophia came with more practical powers. I hated moving but, like so many things, it was a necessary evil. At least I'd learned one thing over the last few months: when dealing with necessary evils, wear sensible shoes.

It's that sort of practical suggestion that made me such a popular advice columnist.

Acknowledgments

My deepest gratitude to my editors Rose and Stacy without whom this book would still be a diamond in the rough (or some other unedited cliché). Thank you for having faith in my work… Blood and souls for my Lord Editors!

About the Author

Ash Krafton's writing credits include stories published in *Absent Willow Review, Silver Blade,* and *Bête Noire.* Several of her poems have been published, as well, one of which was nominated for the Pushcart Prize. She is a member of Pennwriters and is also a contributor to the *Query Tracker* blog.

BLEEDING HEARTS won grand prize in the Maryland Writers' Association 2008 competition and has since won several other national novel writing contests, including achievement of finalist rankings in six Romance Writers of America competitions. A sequel, BLOOD RUSH, is nearing completion and a follow-up, WOLF'S BANE, is underway.

CPSIA information can be obtained at www.ICGtesting.com
Printed in the USA
BVOW020139160312

285183BV00003B/1/P